A FLAME FOR FATIMAH

BY:

TARIK CHATMAN

Table of Contents

The Day the Earth Cried

"Why the fuck do you keep tripping Renee? I told you, I ain't gonna be long." Product snapped into the receiver of his I5.

"You got a lot of nerve nigga. You ain't been home in two fucking days! You told these kids they were going to have fireworks for the 4th," Renee fired back.

Product cut in yelling. Clearly agitated beyond what frustration the call had brought.

"I know what the hell I said girl, and we're still gonna get the fireworks, damn!"

His protest seemed to go unheard as she continued to complain even after he cut in. Still very alert and aware of what he was saying.

"Well, dammit, the 4th is tomorrow, asshole!" Renee blew.

Product sat dumbfounded at the news. His days and nights had lately become a colleague of chaos and grinding.

Dates and holidays had begun to catch him off guard, except birthdays and reporting dates to the probation office. Had it not been for the mother of his children, these days would have been forgotten as well. From her bright eyes to the straight white teeth hidden behind a luscious set of lips, Renee was a beautifully built specimen. Her long wavy black hair reached just above the center of her back. Slightly below, the Spanish roots in her bellowed from her hips, mixing with her more dominant genes. Of course, the sister in her spoke loudest from the soft load of peachy ass she managed to carry. Product had been fucked up about her since the day they met years earlier in high school. Renee was a good girl who had been through turbulent times dealing with Product and his reckless lifestyle. Since this is often the case with a significant number of black males. As much as he loved her, the streets cast a wicked spell on him that seemed virtually impossible to break, even for her. He broke the lingering silence in a more humble tone, clearly disappointed in himself.

"Baby, I'll be there, ok?"

"I gotta go; I'm riding down Lucielle, and Brasco is up ahead, ok?"

Renee didn't respond, unmoved by his regret.

"Hello?"

"Renee?"

He pulled his face away from the screen to check if the call had ended. It hadn't. Renee was still on the line.

"Bye fool," Renee snarled.

"Aight bay," he started.

"I love you."

It was too late by then; she had already hung up. The message she was trying to convey hit its mark. Renee was pissed off, and Product knew it.

"Damn big Bro, Renee be going the fuck in on your ass blood!" Wet replied from the passenger seat.

Product looked over to his passenger, obviously not amused or in the mood to entertain his comments.

"Wet, be the fuck quiet lil nigga, ain't nobody asked you shit scrap!"

Product's stern look and harsh tone clearly suggested that Wet fall back, but not before he could let out a low giggling cough through his nose.

"I'm just saying thou!" Wet continued while letting out a thick cloud of smoke.

"You just saying what blood?" Product snapped.

Product didn't like the way he had barked at Wet. Catching himself, he changed the tone of his dialogue. After all, he couldn't be mad at Wet for his own personal issues showing. He smirked, trying not to be so hostile with the brother.

"You ain't talking bout shit scrap," Product said.

His smirk quickly faded away, looking at the remainder of the cigarillo, which Wet was taking pulls from.

"Pass my blunt bitch ass nigga," Pro demanded.

3

"God damn you little fuck, you just sucked all my lil gas up, huh?" Pro questioned. More like confirming the obvious. Pro could only shake his head.

Wet glanced at the butt, noticing how much he had smoked, then back into the cold eyes of his big homie. He hesitantly passed Pro the blunt replying,

"That shit smoking big bro."

Pro could only laugh at the monster he had helped create.

"Shut your lame ass up," Pro joked, snatching the blunt away.

"Smoking my fucking gas up and ain't put nothing on nothing. Roll another one before I get mad lil fucka."

Pro tossed a sack he pulled from his shirt pocket into Wet's lap.

Wet admired almost everything about Product. From his movement, style, and how he handled business. In Wet's eyes, the nigga was no joke. No need to mention he didn't play the radio. If you knew nothing else about him, you knew that. Wet often found himself doing and saying things Pro was known for. In actuality, Pro was pretty much his role model.

As the Tahoe ate up more miles of the Atlanta streets, Wet took in the scenery outside the S.U.V's passenger side window. It wasn't long before the blunt was twisted and lit. The tint on the truck did nothing to hide the activity outside of it. The urban arena that the Fulton County life gave its residents was unlike any other major black city. The "A" had a variety of perks one could take advantage of. If you wanted to blend in and out of the diverse communities within its perimeter, you could do so easily. Whatever you wanted to get yourself into could be found right around the corner.

"I be fucking up blood."

Pro admitted between two deep pulls of the kush. Shifting his eyes over to Wet, he checked the temperature on the subject.

"You feel me scrap?" Pro questioned.

"Yeah, big homie, I feel you right." Wet replied.

"It's like you live two lives, big homie. You got a family B, and then you bleed the streets unmercifully." Wet continued.

Had it been up to Wet, as much as he respected Pro's family obligations, he would much rather have his big homie committed totally to the streets. This was probably the one thing Wet didn't particularly admire about Pro and had made it clear before now the same way.

"On Brim dog, I ain't never gone settle down blood, that shits wack sauce. There are too many bad hoes on my flea-free collar." Wet started.

Pro started laughing. It turned quickly into coughs as the smoke almost choked him.

"No lil nigga, get the fuck off my dick stealing my shit pup," Pro said, still laughing.

He continued, "Fuck you mean your flea-free collar dog, all you fuck with be some flea ass hoes."

Wet frowned up, shifting his lips to the side at the statement.

"B, what you need to do is get you a sho nuff bad bitch scrap or better yet a real woman," Pro suggested with a serious face.

"Big dog, I got a main that shut shit down," Wet said, defending himself.

"Who nigga?" Pro asked, looking over to Wet, doubting his claim.

"You don't know this one yet, big bro." Wet replied.

"Get the fuck out of here." Pro laughed, still not believing Wet.

"On B's dog, look," Wet said, pulling his phone out. A few seconds passed, and a picture filled the screen.

"Damn Brim, what you got there?" Pro asked, impressed by the taste his lil homie had shown.

Wet replied in his best imitation of a Cali accent,

"This shit right here nigga, yeah this my little phat booty boo." He grinned.

"Her name is Kilani; she's Polynesian and black." Pro raised his eyebrows, nodding his head in approval.

"Oh yea dog, I remember her from the day that raggedy-ass Monte overheated on y'all coming from White Water," Pro admitted,

"I really didn't pay neither one of y'all any attention that day, fucking my play runs up wit y'all bullshit," Pro said. Remembering the irritation the ordeal had caused.

"Yea big bro, that's the same one. I tried to introduce you, but you weren't hearing that shit." Wet confirmed, laughing at how pissed off Pro was that day.

"Whaaat, so she fucking with your flame homie?" Pro asked as a real big brother would.

"Hell yeah, big dog. I mean shit, who wouldn't?" Wet replied, full of himself.

Pro smirked and put his hand out to shake up with the little homie. In one swift motion, they interlocked fingers and threw their hood up high.

"No doubt lil dog, you got a match size lil flame going on I guess. Hell, you learned from the best," Pro admitted.

Wet shook his head in agreement, smiling as he looked at the girl's picture.

Pro and Wet had a deep bond. The two had met back in 2005 at an apartment complex in the Duluth area of Gwinnett. Wet was only thirteen then with no understanding and no one to really give a fuck about his well-being. Wet's mother was an abused, forgotten-about smoker. The father had left early in Wet's childhood for whatever reason, leaving little Reantez "Wet" Miller to fend for himself against the harsh elements of an expanding and cruel metropolis.

Tez, or Wet as he preferred to be called, began with petty thefts out in Gwinnett, where he shacked up with his grandmother. After his mother could no longer take care of him or support herself for that matter, his Nana took him in. However, his grandmother's age gave him more freedom to do whatever he desired. Nana didn't have the energy to protest his behavior. He had been kicked out of several Gwinnett County schools. The last of which he only attended for two months before being expelled for numerous fights. He was given the option to finish his education at an alternative school, but he bucked and turned even more to the lure of the streets.

Meanwhile, Product had been moving work out of a complex called Saratoga Springs near Wet's neighborhood off Satellite Blvd. and Steve Reynolds. Product had been taking the extra precaution any dealer working a new area would do. Pro hadn't been moving packs in Gwinnett long before the bullshit reared its hideous face. In the midst of a transaction gone wrong, Pro and his right-hand man Teflon had lost two soldiers in a gunfight. They found themselves in a turf war with the S gang who migrated from California to that same area in Duluth.

The Oddest Turn of Events

A few weeks passed since the shootout had taken place with Pro, his partner Teflon, and the S gang. It was the summer of 2005; the heat had been agitating everyone. Causing the crime to rise at a rate the area had ever experienced. One night at Pro and Teflon's spot, the oddest turn of events would pull Wet and Product into each other's path. Teflon had been gone a few hours collecting payments from some of the other spots, which he would then take the money to the safe house in Dekalb. Pro stayed behind to work the lime and powder house. Traffic was unusually slow, and the whole vibe of the night felt offbeat. Pro was big on paying attention to vibes and taking heed to them. Pro and Teflon's motto had been, *A slipper is a house shoe, and nothing or no one would hold them underfoot.*

With an uneasy feeling growing in his stomach, Pro made his way across the plushly carpeted floor of the unit to the living room window. *Shit doesn't feel right*, he thought. Pro lifted one of the blinds and looked outside. He scanned the parking lot and then looked over to his 2004 Suburban. The scene was motionless aside from a man making his way through a manmade path. The brown paper bag in his hand contained a deuce bottle that he took a good hard swig from as Pro watched unnoticed. The man was simply following his routine after a long day's work. Nothing unusual. Pro had seen this same pattern for weeks now. Before leaving the window, Pro scrutinized the uniformed man as he wiped his mouth. Now standing under the parking lot light, the man took a moment to scratch the face of some game tickets he held. Obviously, not winners as they met the ground shortly after.

Pro shook his head, leaving the window. *Bum as nigga praying on a hit from that fuck ass scratch-off shit, need to get on his grind,* he thought. Pro walked back across the room to the kitchen, where a dish held a small amount of high-grade marijuana on the countertop. Next to the dish sat a bottle of Patron. Pro reached for it, clanking his pinky ring against the glass as he grabbed it. Taking the cork out, Pro took a shot before rolling up. The cold liquid burned a trail down his throat, causing him to squint his eyes.

"Ahhh."

Reaching for the Swishers, Pro glanced over to the T.V in the living room from the counter. The game system had been on pause for at least two and a half hours. Teflon had been spanking Pro's ass unmercifully on fight night.

Pro was snatched away from his thoughts as a loud clanging sound came from outside. Pro dashed back to the same window he looked through moments ago to check the lot. He didn't see anything out of the norm at first glance. He continued to probe the lot, still nothing. As he looked at his truck, he was sure there was some faint movement in the shadows behind it. Running back to the kitchen, he reached for the AK-47 behind the fridge. He slapped back the cock, readying the chamber with a round. Seconds later, Pro snatched the truck keys from the key rack stuck to the side of the freezer, putting them in the right pocket of his black polo shorts. After the keys had been secured, he took a second to kneel down to tie the red tube shoelaces in his black and red 95 Air Max just in case he had some live action outside.

Pro was now in motion towards the door of the apartment. Reaching it, he turned the knob smoothly enough not to make a sound. Pro peeked out of the door, almost crouching. The medallion on his necklace swung forward with his movement. He caught the encrusted diamond piece and quickly slung it inside his shirt. Scanning every inch of the area, he made sure that he was good on his exit. The crickets chirped loudly in the distance as Pro inhaled the summer night air. He made his way down the breezeway to the steps leading to the ground floor two levels down. A lone cricket chirped loudly from one of the steps below until Pro had gotten too close to it, causing it to jump away in silence. The steps ended on a flat concrete slab with units to the left and right of the stairway. Another set of five steps led out to the front parking lot where Pro's truck was parked. He almost decided to go to the parking lot that way but instead chose to take the back exit out of the breezeway. Going down yet another flight of steps leading to the rear parking lot, Pro emerged from the hall out into the open. A light breeze caught his short sleeve polo, causing it to dance on his back as he stooped low with his weapon. Rounding the building, Pro looked up to the light that had been broken, giving him cover from any nosey onlookers.

Taking the shoulder sling of the assault rifle, Pro slung the sap over his neck to make his climb up the bank towards the front of the building. This route, he figured, would give him more of an advantage to catch whoever may have been by his truck by surprise. Once on top of the bank, Pro pushed his back flat against the wall of the building for cover. Taking the shoulder strap back over his neck, he gave himself more freedom to maneuver with the yop stick.

It had been roughly two minutes and a few odd seconds since Pro heard the noise outside the window. He raised his wrist to look down at his red G. Shock while maintaining his grip on the handle of the A.K. The time showed 10:17 p.m. Pro made a habit of watching the time whenever he got into some shit. Five minutes was all he and Teflon had ever needed to get any dirt done. Pro got low to the ground and made his way to the nearest vehicle in the parking lot, eyes still fixed on his truck that sat about forty to forty-five feet away. Still tucked in the shadows, Pro inched closer to the truck like a well-trained Navy Seal. The palms of his left hand began to sweat as he clutched the stock tighter. Looking to the ground behind the truck, Pro recognized from a distance what had made the loud noise earlier, and his heart began to pound in excitement. The shiny four-way lug bar lay on the ground, shimmering and reflecting what little light caught its surface.

Pro crept from around a Kia Sportage, two cars away from the truck now, lifting his rifle up to take aim. Pro hadn't found a target yet, but his mind was already made up that the moment he did, he wouldn't hesitate to clap. Now, one car away, he noticed a minivan pulling into the parking lot with the lights already turned off. Pro stared at the Astro van intently, keeping himself cloaked by the darkness. Seconds later, three Mexicans exited the van with guns already drawn. Pro licked his lips, anxious to pop. Immediately, Pro recognized the blue flags and attire of the men. *Man, these fucking Migos got balls!* He thought that the S gang had apparently come to ambush Pro and Teflon's spot.

Unfortunately for them, Pro was already out of the apartment tucked away in the shadows across from the building with a growing thirst to pour some shit out. Pro laughed to himself. *These mafuckas tripping,* he thought. *Bitches trying to sneak me dog.* He concluded with a smile on his face that welcomed a good challenge. He could not make out the words the three men were whispering, but that shit didn't matter to Pro. If it were up to him, they would forever be silent after tonight. Pro glanced back to his truck quickly, then back to the men trying to connect the dots. Unable to make sense of it, he kept his focus on the men. He waited until the men had gotten directly under the building light so that he'd get the best shots available. Activating the green beam attached to his weapon. Pro put the dot on the back of the gang banger's head that exploded after two projectiles, one behind the other, came crashing into his skull. The body almost flipped forward from the impact, but instead, his footing caused him to twist slightly to the side as his face slammed head-on with the sidewalk.

One of the men yelled, startled and confused.

"Oh shit, man, what the fuck?"

Pro wasted no time sliding over to the other side of the Sportage, sending a hail of bullets at the other two men that had now become aware of where the fire had come from. They attempted to return fire, but just as the man holding the twelve-gauge took aim, seven shots tore away at his neck, chest, and torso knocking chunks away from his frame. The Mexican yanked at the trigger of the gauge on his way down, more so from reflex than purpose. The shot hit the Kia's headlights shattering broken glass and paint chips, barely missing Pro. Pro ducked away as the one man left standing clapped his Glock furiously in his direction. The shots bit away at the car's frame with five loud thumps.

The man bellowed to his friends on the ground.

"Levantar se levanter se, get up, get up Monster, get up fool."

Neither of the men responded, but one was still alive and the other lay grotesquely splattered on the sidewalk. The last man grew enraged looking at the condition of his friends.

"Donde estes Hijo de punta," he yelled, followed by four more shots at the Kia.

Pro considered running out into the open and dumping his A.K on the Mexican. Pro figured he had done so much damage from the shadows without an injury that he would give the Mexican no chance to get off a shot. Pro looked at his watch; the shootout had been going at least two minutes, and Pro had a quota to make with only three minutes remaining. Looking for a rock, Pro quickly found one and threw it across the lot towards some cars a few spaces away. The rock hit one of the cars, sounding the alarm.

The S gang took the bait and ran in the direction, firing the remainder of his clip. As soon as the clip emptied, Pro jumped out, running behind him firing his chopper. Four bullets tore into the building behind the Mexican, and the car in front of him missing him by inches. Almost simultaneously, the Mexican ducked and scrambled away into the breezeway. Pro fired more rounds at him as the man tried to make an escape. He was fast, and the bulk of the rifle was just enough of an advantage for him to put more space between him and Pro. By the time Pro got up the steps, the gangster had already made a dash down the steps toward the back lot. Pro looked down at the mess he'd made of the men that lay there; one of them clearly had no hope. Quickly, Pro moved his eyes to the other man making eye contact. Monster's eyes were as wide as saucers staring back up at Pro frantically. Monster's hands were clenched to his throat as he tried to stop the blood pouring from the large gaping wound in his neck. It was to no avail as blood gushed in large amounts between his fingers and down his forearm. Pro thought to throw one more round through his face but figured within the next couple of seconds, he'd be dead.

Pro wasted no time running to the suburban. He threw the chopper to the passenger side then swiftly jumped in. After fishing the keys from his pocket, he jammed the ignition key in and twisted the engine to live. The dual pipes blew smoke from the exhaust out into the night air. The breeze carried smoke towards the night sky. Pro knew exactly which way his fleeing Mexican had to go, and if he hurried, he would cut him off. The wide-body truck gained speed taking no breaks for the speed bumps ahead. "Klum Klum," the frame vibrated hard as the truck passed over one set of speed bumps. Approaching the intersection of the road in the complex, Pro took a hard right turn without slowing, headed towards the back of the apartments. Flying down the hill, Pro looked to the passenger's side window to the back lot and spotted the man fleeing towards the rear fences separating the complex from another complex behind it. Looking to his rearview, Pro noticed the truck's back door swinging open and shut. *What the fuck were they looking for in the truck?* He pondered. He brushed it off and focused on the task at hand; he had murder on his mind with no room to rationalize anything else.

Pro raced across the lot, gaining on the retreating banger every second. The lot was too much of a stretch for the man to make it to the fences. Finally, Pro had closed the gap. The man looked back into the headlights like a deer caught on the highway. The man tried weaving, but the wide grill caught him, "Blum," knocking him to the ground. Pro slammed the truck into park, almost snapping the gearshift in the process. Pro was on foot in no time, choppa in hand, standing over the broken and exhausted man. Pro was no stranger to the Spanish language from his ties with L.G.F. and Brownside homies, who he fucked with on the work. Although not yet fluent, he knows enough. Knowing that the man was injured, Pro spat out, "Senale donde le duele," which meant point to where you feel pain. With rage in his eyes and lip trembling, the man pointed to his hip. Pro took the barrel of the gun and lifted the Mexicans shirt exposing the area that had been broken from the hit. The truck's lights illuminated the area around the man, and Pro could see that his hip had already bruised black and purple. The Mexican squirmed in pain, looking back up at Pro, frowning angrily.

"Oue estas hacienda," he yelled at Pro.

"Shut the fuck up," Pro barked back.

"You thought you would jam on me tonight, didn't you mother fucka?" Pro taunted.

The Mexican snapped back, "Coju tu!"

Pro busted out laughing.

"Na fool, you're the one fucked tonight, you and them dead ass pussies you ran off and left."

Pro laid the barrel on the man's broken pelvic bone. Seconds later, a loud clap echoed through the quiet parking lot. Blood poured from under the Mexicans body at the exit wound. He screamed in agony, causing a light to come on in a nearby unit. Pro would have to finish him and get moving; surely, he had already passed his five-minute deadline.

The man looked back up at Pro, crying from the pain.

"Please let me live fool, I got a wife at home; she's pregnant!"

"Damn bro, you got a family?" Pro asked sarcastically.

"Hmmph me too dog," Pro said smiling.

Reaching down to the man's pocket, he snatched a flag away from it.

"Oh, fool, you got another family too huh?" Pro asked, then stepped over to the back of the truck, going for a full gas can he kept handy.

Pro finished opening the already unlatched cargo door. He almost shot the occupant from being startled.

"The fuck you doing back here lil nigga?" Pro questioned the boy.

18

Before he could answer, Pro had knocked him unconscious with the butt of the rifle. He grabbed the gas can then slammed the door lock trapping the boy in. Pro skipped back over to the Mexican and quickly began dousing him with gas.

"What are you doing man?" the gangster cried, spitting away the gas entering his mouth and nostrils.

"Shit homie, I'm just gonna bring a little light to your dark world! You feel me?" Pro proclaimed.

The man squirmed more, trying to crawl away as Pro sat the can down. Raising his rifle, Pro growled,

"Brim gang or don't bang fool!"

"Wait," the man yelled, putting his hands up.

Pro squeezed the trigger knocking his ring and middle finger off as a life-shattering round discharged through the man's hand then into his face. The impact spread blood and body fragments across the parking lot, at least four to five feet away as if someone had airbrushed it. Pro slung the strap over his shoulder then pulled a lighter from his pocket. Two strikes and Pro lit the man's flag and dropped it on top of him, quickly stepping back. "Whoosh." The body was instantly engulfed in flames.

Pro quickly jumped in the truck; after placing the can on the back floor, he headed out of the complex. Pro grabbed his cell phone and hit Tef's number on speed dial. While ringing, Pro found his Bluetooth in the console, activated it, and placed it in his ear. The phone was still dialing, then Tef picked up,

"Woop?"

"Aye, bro, don't come to the spot. Where you at anyway?" Pro asked.

Teflon noticed the vibe immediately and answered back,

"I'm at the gas station on Jimmy Carter making my way back that way. What's wrong, blood?"

"I'm gonna explain later dog, but ball Shamiya and tell her I need to park the truck in her garage," Pro explained.

"Bro, she's at the club on her set; just go ahead; you good, I'll meet you there," Teflon answered.

"Aight bet fool, get there b-sap dog, shit, it's 7:30 right now." Pro said, followed by, "Woop."

"Woop, Woop," Tef spit back.

Pro smashed down 85 South going towards Atlanta; he could see the police lights flying up Satellite Blvd to the crime scene. After passing a few exits, Pro crossed the Dekalb County line. Climbing the spaghetti junction and taking 285 East to Lavista Road, he made the exit a few moments later, then pulled into a quiet neighborhood. Pulling up to the house, Pro parked and got out of the truck to open the garage manually, then returned to the S.U.V. inside the garage. He could hear the loud thump of bass banging from the speakers in Teflon's Camaro as he turned onto the block. Just as Pro turned the truck off, Teflon was parking on the street in front of the house.

Tef jumped out of the truck and walked around to the driveway making his way to the garage. As Tef entered, they shook up with a smooth motion of their hands then closed the garage door.

"What's brimming fool?" Tef asked.

Happy to see his homie alright, mean-mugging, knowing something was wrong.

"Shit bro, everything we do," Pro answered, walking around to the passenger's door of the truck to get his banger out. The Kalashnikov had served its purpose and had done a damn good job as far as Pro was concerned.

Tef watched Pro's movement.

"What the fuck happened Bro?" Tef asked, still lost.

"Wild shit dog," Pro admitted.

He continued to explain.

"So I'm sitting in the spig waiting on you to get back, twisting one, right? Shit is dumb dry, I'm talking bout not one play hit the door, bro."

Teflon jerked his neck back in disbelief, frowning.

"Damn bro," Tef said, listening intently.

Pro continued,

"So I heard some shit outside; I got to the window to look out and see some movement by the whip bro. So you know I grabbed the Yop and got out there," Pro explained.

"Fo sho," Tef responded, giving Pro his full attention.

"So anyway, I'm moving on the truck from the shadow's blood. I be goddamn if the S gang ain't pulling up on some creep shit dog, you smell me?" Pro hunched his shoulders; like what were they thinking to try that shit.

Teflon's eyes widened to the news.

"Whaaat," Tef said, surprised at the courage of the S gang.

Pro continued.

"Yeah Brim," he answered with a chuckle.

"So I get to rocking at these mafuckas, you know. Yeah, so when I go get the gas can to light this swalla ass up with his flag dog."

Tef interrupted, confused.

"Woe woe woe wait a minute, hold up mu, pardon my Brim. You set them on fire dog?" Tef asked, looking almost sympathetic.

Pro inhaled hard then let it out as he spoke,

"Dog, this bitch had the nerve to say let him live and that he had a pregnant wife and shit with this S.O.S ass flag hanging out his pocket, bro," Pro explained like he was on the defensive.

"I had to dog," he continued.

Teflon burst into a hard and painful sounding laughter. Pro looked on at Tef's amusement with a serious face.

"My bad, my dog but you brazy as fuck mu!" Teflon admitted.

"Look blood, so anyway," Pro said as he stepped to the rear of the truck.

"While I was getting the can," he said, opening the door

"I find this little fuck nigga."

Teflon looked confused,

"What the fuck," then back at Pro.

Pro hunching his shoulders, replied,

"I have no fucking idea dog."

The boy stared back at the two of them with a nice bump on his head, scared to death after all he had seen. The boy's frown did nothing to hide the fear overwhelming him.

Teflon stepped closer,

"What the fuck you doing back here?" Tef asked.

"I'm sorry," the boy spoke softly, breaking the shell of the mask he had tried to disguise himself in.

Teflon snapped, backhanding the boy in the mouth.

"I ain't ask you were you sorry, I said what the fuck you doing back there?" Teflon continued reaching in the truck, slapping him again.

"Fuck you mean you sorry lil nigga, you help set my boy up to get killed, and now you sorry?" The boy's mouth, now bloody from the blows.

"I didn't have nothing to do with that, I swear to God," the boy cried out.

Pro looked on grimly as Teflon interrogated the little dude reliving the events that occurred earlier.

"Fuck you mean you ain't have nothing to do with it, boy? Why you in the truck then?" Tef continued, now holding the boy by the collar of his shit, ready to strike him again.

Whimpering and in pain, the boy replied, now sure he would die.

"I was just trying to get the speakers so I could get some money man. I swear that's all, man, please don't kill me. I'm sorry man, for real."

Pro and Teflon looked at each other then back to the boy. Tef snatched the boy out of the truck to the garage floor. Slapping him again, Tef yelled,

"You mean to tell me you out here bout to get murk bout some fucking speakers fool?"

A wet spot puddled the floor under the boy's legs as tears rolled down his cheeks. Teflon looked up to Pros eyes, wide in disbelief.

"Yoooo, this fool pissing dog," Teflon announced.

Teflon and Pro burst out laughing at the kid. At that moment, a burst of heart came from the boy hearing them laughing at him. He swung, punching Teflon in the jaw.

"Man fuck y'all kill me then; I don't give a fuck. I ain't got nothing to live for anyway," the boy yelled out with his pride hurt.

Teflon shook the little blow off, smiling at the boy.

"Ooooh," Tef taunted.

"So now you hard nigga, you was just pissing tho."

Pro looked on, watching the boy closely, trying to get a feel if he was sincere or not.

"Get the fuck off me!" the boy yelled, kicking his legs at Teflon.

Tef punched him hard in the stomach, curling the boy up. The teen coughed after a deep grunt. Pro broke it up.

"That's enough Tef, let him up dog."

Pro looked at the boy,

"If you telling the truth, that means you kinda kept me from getting caught slipping tonight, so I owe you. Now my bro Teflon don't discriminate; he wacks mama's, kids, pets, and all. So seeing that I just stopped him from wacking your ass, you owe me too." Pro continued.

"So I figured if you can keep your mouth closed about all that happened tonight, we could call it even. What do you think?" Pro asked while helping the boy up.

"Yeah, we even; I won't say shit," the boy replied, holding his stomach.

Pro roughed the lil dude's mohawk. "Let's get you cleaned up, Wet."

"Who's Wet?" the boy asked.

"Oh, I forgot to tell you, that's part of our deal. That's your new name for pissing all on yourself," Pro answered.

The boy shook his head in refusal as Teflon pushed him into the house laughing.

A Poisonous Dog Bite

Eight years and plenty of action had passed since that night. Wet was now twenty-one and well known for living up to his name. The irony is that his name no longer had anything to do with wetting his clothes, at least not his own.

Pro glanced over at Wet, realizing how much he had grown since they met. He now sat texting on his phone, bobbing his head to the homie Rocko as Pro drove down Lucille Ave, heading to the Shed. The Shed was a name given to the park by the locals in the West End. This part of the city was primarily a Muslim community once controlled by Alimin, formally known as H. Rap Brown from the panther era. Pulling into the park, Pro turned the music down to speak to Wet; the song could faintly be heard in the background.

"Aye, every day we live the wild life."

Wet was still singing, caught off guard as the music went low.

"Look, bro," Pro said.

"Be on your shit today dog. For some reason, I feel this brack might try some slick shit, especially by me telling him this the last time. Copy?"

Pro looked at Wet to make sure his words had sunk in.

"No doubt, big bro," Wet replied.

"What, you think he gonna try to lock us bro?" Wet asked, knowing that he wouldn't allow that to happen.

"I don't know lil bro, it just feels weird, and you know how I am bout them vibes dog!"

Pro turned and looked around as he spoke.

"It may be nothing; just keep your eyes open."

"Fa sho, you know you always be knowing shit Brim. Like a slick psychic or some shit." Wet said while laughing and passed the blunt to Pro.

As Pro inhaled, he noticed a green Durango turning in.

"I think that's them bro," Pro pointed.

The Durango pulled in slowly a few feet away.

Wet's phone vibrated, and he sent another quick text out before sliding the phone inside the pockets of his camo cargo pants.

"Let's do it,"

Pro said, reaching for the door handle to exit. As Pro's hands grabbed the latch, a thought flashed across his mind and slowed him from opening the door. Pro sat back in his seat, then reached inside of his Louis Vuitton button-up, drawing a Heckler and Koch 9mm from his concealed shoulder holster. He readied his sleek-looking firearm, slapping one round into the chamber, then slid it back into the holster. He then proceeded to exit the Tahoe.

Parked in front of him, Sergeant Hemlock of the Atlanta Red Dog Unit exited the driver's side of the Durango. The two men approached each other, and Pro paid attention to every detail of the sergeant's body language. Pro instantly knew that Hemlock was wearing a vest, which was suspicious, especially after the comments Hemlock had made in the past about not needing one. The men extended hands to shake and greet.

"What's good, Hemlock, taking extra precaution these days, huh?" Pro asked sarcastically.

"Don't flatter yourself asshole, you're not a threat. We got a big drug raid on White Oak in a bit."

Hemlock explained, trying to throw Pro off.

"We need to make this quick!" the sergeant continued.

"Not a problem," Pro agreed.

"You know how I feel about this shit anyway."

"Yeah yeah yeah, about that," Hemlock started.

"What's the big deal? I mean this pansy shit about not wanting to continue our business and all?" Hemlock asked, looking over the rim of his Oakley sunglasses.

Pro replied with hostility in his tone.

"I mean what I said, this shit is it. Shit, I've been hiding from my people too long; it's only a matter of time before someone finds out. Fuck that, cause if it does come to light, I'm gone get violated, man, and I told you that."

"Violate huh?" Hemlock asked, grinning like a real-life evil villain.

He continued after a short pause, and the grin evaporated.

"Listen, my man, let's not forget who needs who here! Remember, you're mine, you son of a bitch!" Hemlock scolded.

"Damn mafucka, how long you been holding that shit over my head man?" Pro asked, in complaint.

"Hmmmm, good question," Hemlock admitted.

"Let's just say until I'm well off with no need for this fucking headache of a job I have to clock into. See, I have to do that while you fucking monkeys eat sweet pieces of pie in our faces that you barely lift a finger to get."

Hemlock had damn near turned red in the face and was practically foaming at the mouth.

"Look at you standing here like some fucking celebrity," Hemlock spat, looking Pro up and down.

"And what are these hideous-looking shoes you wearing any fucking way?" Hemlock asked, frowning down at Pros footwear.

Pro looked down to his feet, smiling at the man's hate. The lime green Felix, Italian gator gym shoes, in all actuality, were quite attractive, and he knew it. They were a perfect contrast with the white linen short set Pro donned.

"Does it really matter man," Pro hissed back?

Hemlock stepped closer to Pro's face.

"Yeah, it fucking matters," he growled through clenched teeth.

"These god ugly shoes probably could pay my fucking mortgage, and that's exactly what the hell I'm talking about," Hemlock explained.

"Now we will continue to do business, or I'll bust your ass so wide you will be able to fit a landing strip at Hartsfield in it."

"Do you understand me? Do I make myself clear, you son of a bitch?"

"Hmmph, man, whatever; let's get this shit over with," Pro demanded.

Hemlock gave a hand signal to the other officer. Pro was suspicious of the signal but carried on with the motions.

"The money is in the truck with Wet for the last package; let me go grab it so we can count it," Pro suggested.

"Naa, don't worry about counting it; I'm in a rush, I told you. Just grab the bags from Tally, and I'll swing over and get the money myself." Hemlock instructed.

31

"Aight fuck it, I'll go grab the package from Tally now." Pro agreed.

"You goddamn right! You will boy and stop pressing my fucking buttons, capeesh?" Hemlock insisted.

Pro almost snapped from the sergeant's remarks but bit his lip, suppressing his anger, knowing he'd get his turn in the long run. Hemlock and Pro locked eyes for a moment as Hemlock spat a wad of chewing tobacco to the side. After a short stare down, the two went about their business. Hemlock headed toward the Tahoe, and Pro took towards the Durango. Pro examined the scenery around him, looking for anything suspicious. His six-and-a-half-foot frame gracefully flowed through the summer sun rays as he maintained an almost too confident stride.

Wet had been watching both Pro and Hemlock the whole time from inside the Tahoe, his baby nine clenched tight in hand, waiting for any sign of fuckery. Before Hemlock could make it to the truck, Wet slid his firearm behind some papers under the seat, figuring that everything was cool. Officer Tally jumped out of the Durango to meet Pro; the two nodded without any exchange of words and made their way around to the back of the Dodge. Tally opened the trunk door. Pro crossed his arms, one inside his shirt, waiting to see the packages. He stood just enough to keep an eye on Hemlock, who had made it to the Tahoe.

Tally noticed from his peripheral that Pro was paying too much attention to his sergeant and attempted to take his attention away. The two had never spoken during any of the prior transactions. However, Pro cunningly played the game, aware that something was definitely up. He just couldn't place his finger on what exactly.

"So, what do you think about that whole Treyvon case?" Tally asked.

"You know man, I haven't really been following it, but I'm willing to bet that peckerwood beats the charges," Pro answered, deliberately using the racial insult.

Pro glanced over his Cartier glasses back in Hemlock's direction. Pro noticed that Wet was now reaching inside the back seat of the Tahoe.

"Yeah, man, I'm sort of in a rush, so me and your bro agreed to do it like this," Hemlock insisted.

"Just show me half counted out, and I'll take you guys' word that the rest is all there," Hemlock continued.

Wet began pulling stacks wrapped in bank bands indicating the denomination and placing them on the seat. Pro was curious as to what was taking them so long at the Tahoe. Hemlock sat behind Wet, looking around with his hands on his hip, trying to look casual.

"Yeah, man, you're probably right, but they should fry his ass," Tally reasoned, hardly convincing enough for Pro to believe.

As Tally reached for a box at the edge of the truck's floor, Pro thought to himself, *what the fuck is Wet doing?* Tally opened the box and took a box cutter from the floorboard. He slit one of the packages open, then handed the blade to Pro with a dump of cocaine on the tip. Pro took his finger and swiped a taste to his tongue, never withdrawing his left hand from inside his shirt. Satisfied, he stepped back and crossed his arms as before.

"Good?" Tally asked.

"Yeah, it's straight; how many tho," Pro questioned.

"It's just fifteen," Tally confirmed.

"Aight wrap it back up and let's go," Pro requested, glancing back at Sergeant Hemlock and Wet.

Hemlock was fidgeting around with his belt, a move Pro had seen repeatedly with undercover narcs before they upped a hammer. Pro clenched his Heckler tight under his shirt, quietly sliding the safety off.

"Sure, no problem," Tally said, smiling.

"Just pass me that tape on the floor over there up under the seat."

Tally's smile was even faker than the bullshit conversation he had started.

Pro had no intention of going to jail today, and if that was Hemlock's idea, then he could forget it; that's not happening. Pro reached in with his right hand lining up the hammer to get a shot off if need be when the worst circumstances he could imagine transpired. Pro was rattled to the core as he heard a thunderous round fired followed by another.

"Bloom bloom."

Pro followed his instincts, aware that they were alone at the park, and there was no doubt, either Hemlock or Wet had fired those shots. Without wasting a second to look, Pro sent a double-up of four shots spiraling through the fabric of his own shirt at Tally.

"Blum Bla Blum Blum."

The officer stumbled back, falling from the heat lodging in his upper ribs and chest, close to his heart. Pro looked over the seat inside the Durango through the windshield towards his truck, where Wet laid sprawled halfway in and out of the Tahoe. Wet's body was limp; all Pro could see of him were his Jordan's and his camos. The sergeant had fired two fatal shots from a snub nose seven into Wet's dreads. Hemlock grabbed the bag of money, leaving what was on the seat for story props. Hemlock started running toward the Durango, clueless of his partner's condition.

Pro looked where Tally lay wheezing on the pavement with four holes so close together they almost made one. Tally panicked, gasping for air that refused to fill his lungs. Pro upholstered his gun and mercilessly smacked one more sizzling projectile through Tally's skull. The force seemed to make the officer's head almost bounce up from the concrete as the fragments of his thoughts splattered onto Pro's linen shorts. Pro wiped at his mouth and cheeks, feeling wetness there, at the same time noticing a tiny chunk of pink fleshy meat stuck to the lens of his designer frames. Clearing it away, Pro noticed that the officer's gun had fallen from his grip. *Damn*. Pro thought. That could have been him if Tally had been a second faster. Pro felt relieved; Tally had no idea that Pro's pistol had been aimed at him the whole while.

Hemlock, finally in view to see what had occurred, dropped the bag yelling at Pro firing, "Son of a bitch."

Pro hurled two bullets back in Hemlock's path. Both men missed and took cover, hiding on opposite sides of the Durango. Hemlock ducked low by the driver's side front tire, taking a moment to slide the 357 back into the hidden waist holster. Hemlock pulled a radio.

"I got a 280 delta," Hemlock announced, drawing his 40 Cal service pistol, cocking the firearm quickly as he peeked up to get a visual on Pro.

As Pro hunched low by the rear end on the passenger's side, he weighed his options. He heard the code and knew that it must be close. Pro concluded that whatever their distance was, it wouldn't be long before the park would be swarming with police. Pro wanted nothing worse than to kill Hemlock, jump in his Tahoe, take Wet's body, and get the fuck out of dodge. Realizing it wouldn't be easy, Pro opted for an alternative route. Quickly looking back behind him, he saw a route for escape on foot. Turning back to do a spot-check on Hemlock, the two men made eye contact through the glass. Pro took the opportunity to achieve his initial goal busting Hemlock's ass. He quickly aimed his firearm, shattering the windows between him and Hemlock with a single shot. Hemlock ducked it, motivating Pro even more, to proceed with the alternative.

Taking a deep breath, trying not to visualize getting shot in the back as he ran, Pro built the nerve and tore out. No sooner than Pro started to run did shots take off behind him, missing him only by centimeters. Three bullets plucked up patches of grass at his heels as he hit a sharp B line toward some fences. As he ran, Pro turned his body just enough to clap two more reckless shots at Hemlock. The sergeant ducked the close call again, watching the fragments of the car tear away near his head. Collecting himself, Hemlock took a few seconds, then charged behind Pro, pistol aimed high. Pro just made it to the fences; taking a leap halfway up, he pulled himself over the rest of the way with his arms. Hemlock moved swiftly through the grass at a full sprint. The sergeant knew if he'd taken time to aim and missed the target, too much ground would be between them. Pro dropped to the ground on the other side of the tall fence. Turning to look back at the pursuer, he noticed how much the sergeant had gained on him. Pro then took off through the backyard of the residence he landed in. Before Pro could make it to the front yard, Hemlock was already halfway up the fence. Pro didn't want any unnecessary attention from the neighborhood occupants, so instead of firing at Hemlock, he took off quietly, sprinting across the street and down the sidewalk. His athletic build split through the fresh morning breeze at a track runner's speed.

The neighborhood was so quiet and serene; Pro could hear his feet as they tapped the pavement. Seconds later, Hemlock popped out between the houses hot on Pro's trail. Hemlock, closing more of the gap, ran almost equally as fast as Pro. The two men were both worthy of competing as Olympic medalists. A few more houses and Pro would have reached the end of the block at the intersection. A teenage girl still in her pajamas watched from her porch as Pro shot past. Pro hadn't noticed her really until hearing her say in the phone she was holding.

"Baybeee, why this man just,"

The rest was a blur as he barely got a glimpse of her. Pro deviated from the route at the next house, seeing an A.P.D. cruiser shoot past at the intersection. Cutting through the grass to the driveway of the residence. Pro assumed that the passing police cruiser hadn't noticed him; too busy racing to the call about shots fired at the park. Maneuvering down the driveway, Pro's hand swiped across the front end of a white 1992 Thunderbird. Droplets of condensation rolled away from the streaking handprint he'd left. Pro glanced back towards Hemlock. It was discouraging to see how close Sergeant Hemlock had gotten. Sergeant Hemlock was a well-built brute of a man. He moved his 210-pound frame through the chase like a defensive end, hunting a quarterback.

Pro, however, wasn't the prey any officer would prefer. He was alert, methodically viscous, and in all reality, didn't give two fucks about anything outside of his family. The floating seeds of the dandelions traveled in the gust, met Pro's feet. The grip of his gator gym shoes squeaked faintly in the moisture of the morning dew as he crushed the damp blades of grass underfoot.

"Bloom bloom," two close loud shots disturbed the short-lived silence. The shots caused splinters of wood to tear away from the house near Pro's head. Nearly falling, Pro turned from a half-crouch and slung four hot, unbraced, angry pieces of lead at the sergeant, then rounded the corner behind the house. Hemlock had eluded the bullets rolling to the passenger side of the Thunderbird. Shortly after, Hemlock popped back up as Pro made a dash for the garage. Hemlock clapped three more rapid shots at Pro, the last of which knocked a nice-sized piece of tissue away from Product's left shoulder.

"Fuck!" Pro winced through clenched teeth. With his back flush against the garage wall, Pro reached the Heckler around the side, letting one off. "Bloom." A lone shot exploded into the Thunderbird's back window, throwing shimmering pieces of glass everywhere. Hemlock ducked low and made his way to the back end of the car.

Pro had already sprinted away from the garage wall heading for the fences. The fence squeaked from its raggedy condition as Pro hopped it. Running perilously through the high grass and weeds of the unkempt yard, Pro began to get weary. Sweat dripped from Pro's well-kept waves, saturating his brows and continuing a course to his eyes. Using his forearm, Pro took a quick wipe at the stinging perspiration.

Afterward, he noticed an out-of-place makeshift wooden door, completely ajar leading into a house in front of him. He scrambled up the concrete steps snagging his shoe on a broken hollow spot of the slab but kept his footing.

Sergeant Hemlock rounded the garage, now able to see Pro in the next yard at the door. Aiming his weapon with both hands firmly in place, Hemlock took two crisp shots at Pro. The slower-moving version of Pro was still able to dodge any further damage as he caught a glimpse of Hemlock before the shots got off. Pro followed the hallway he was now in, passing an indescribably filthy kitchen to his right. The stench of the house could make even the strongest of stomachs retreat, cringing. Pro ran into a dead-end in the hallway after deciding not to take the steps apparently leading to the basement. *The front door in front of him had been restricted by some flimsy pieces of plywood, and there was not enough time to remove it,* he concluded. Before Pro could process another thought, Hemlock came crashing through the door behind him. Catching sight of Pro, Hemlock immediately yanked at his trigger, discharging a round at Pro. Product weaved, falling back, letting the remainder of his clip loose from where he lay on the floor. Three powerful shots thumped hard into Hemlock's chest, knocking him off his feet onto the floor.

Pro tried to get control of his breathing, looking on in relief. Pro's weariness had obviously altered his memory. Pro sat exhaling from relief that he had finally put the wild corrupt man on his back. Hemlock lay there still regrouping from the shots stuck in his Kevlar. Pro stood up from the pile of mildewing clothes he had fallen on, turned, and kicked a hole through the flimsy wood blocking the exit.

Meanwhile, Hemlock slowly slipped his right hand to the hidden waist holster to retrieve the snub nose. Another kick and most of the door was cleared, hanging to the side of the threshold. As Pro stepped out into the cool of the July morning, his short-lived victory came to an abrupt end.

"Don't move another muscle, goddammit," the sergeant demanded. Hemlock didn't have an aim on Pro yet as he tried sitting up to focus. Pro stood still, slowly turning his head to look back over his shoulder at Hemlock. As Hemlock pointed his weapon, Pro played two options through his mind: make a move or give up; the latter wasn't at all logical. Although he was tired and hurt, laying down would not be how he ended this.

The decrepit porch was weak enough to give in at any minute, it seemed. In the midst of his thoughts, Pro darted to the right like some unseen force had taken over. Almost as soon as Pro made a move, Hemlock fired twice, barely focused, still blurry from the wind being knocked out of him. Pro's dart took him over the porch rail, right of the door, and onto the ground. He ignored the pain, got up, and scrambled toward the street, running as fast as his worn body would carry him.

Sergeant Hemlock was slowly getting up, now feeling a tender spot on the back of his head. Apparently, he had bumped it as he fell, which would explain the dizziness he presumed. As Hemlock made it to the door, he shook his head to rid the starry effect from his eyes. Looking to the right, he saw Pro already in full stride, although distinctly slower than before. Hemlock's rage burned so deep that Pro had managed to get out of the shot's path.

"Motherfucker!" Hemlock growled.

A woman across the street screamed an eardrum-piercing wail snatching Hemlock's attention away as Pro fled up the street. Hemlock looked at the woman as he stepped off the porch. Through one nostril, Hemlock took a hard sniff in and spit the phlegm to the side, uncaring for the woman's dilemma. Pro only had a good five-house lead on Hemlock as he continued his pursuit. An A.P.D. cruiser flying down the street in Pro's direction noticed Pro running bleeding with his gun still in hand and clipped him. The front end of the cruiser knocked him to the pavement. In the fall, Pro's head collided hard with the concrete making a hollow-sounding thud inside his head. The impact burst the caramel-colored skin over his brow, leaving a large gash.

Watching from a slight distance, Hemlock slid between two houses and placed the 357 under the fender of a broken down Skylark until he could come back for it. Shortly after, he raced to the cruiser like a Hollywood super cop. The officer had cuffed Pro already, with him leaning over the hood. They unarmed him and continued the path down. Pro's consciousness was blinking. Hearing Hemlock's voice inform the other officers of his credentials. Pro's thoughts twirled.

"He's poison," Pro tried to reason, but his words slurred and failed him.

As the officers put Pro in the car, he could vaguely make out Hemlock speaking before the door closed.

"Officer Tally of the Red Dog Unit," boom, and the door was closed, cutting Pro off from the rest of the conversation.

Red Dog rang in and out of his mind in reprise as he slurred more unheard words. "They poison man, poisoncus dogs bite." He tried to keep his focus on the officers, but his body had been through a lot. With his face against the glass, Pro slipped out of consciousness. Across the street not far from the crying woman, a boy took in the movie-like scene from his scooter, heart pounding from the activity he had seen.

Drenched in Blood
Rice St. July 4th, 2013

Pro woke up to a throbbing headache as the inmates in the day room screamed and yelled obscenities to each other and the C.O.'s. Product's whole world had spun entirely out of control in a matter of minutes. He laid across the bunk, making shapes in the ceiling above as his eyes came into focus. Trying to bring together where he was and why it became today's endeavor. Pro had plenty to be upset about with all that had played out in the last twenty-four hours of his last reality show. However, what stood out the most in his mind was the sound of Renee's voice, it was the freshest memory he had at that moment, and it was on repeat. "When dammit? The 4th is tomorrow!" Pro tried placing when he had heard that. *That had to be yesterday*, he thought. The feeling that he was letting his children down started to develop in the recesses of his heart. "Damn," he sighed as he turned his head toward the cell's door. Wet's murder hadn't sunk in yet; it was only a blur and too surreal to fathom at the moment.

The barcoded wristband snatched Pro back to reality, noticing it as he rubbed his face. The picture on the bracelet was of an almost unrecognizable broken man. The eyes of the photo peered back like nothing in life mattered. It clearly showed how much hate and fury could be seen in Pro's eyes. Surely, whoever snapped the picture sensed it as well. Pro frowned back at the photo of himself charged by its energy as a sense of rationale began creeping back into his thought process. A sharp pain tore through the nerves of his shoulder, further reminding him that the shit was real.

Flashes of Wet's legs hanging limp from the passenger's side of the Tahoe jumped out at Pro, causing him to slam his eyes shut and grit his teeth. *Damn Wet*, Pro thought. He put his hand up to his bandage over his left brow, mashing its saturated center. The pain kicked in like it was just seconds ago since the injury occurred. Shaking it off wouldn't be easy for Pro. Product had been through countless life and death situations with plenty of scares. However, this scare had a sting to it that penetrated his soul; although the flesh would heal, the memory wouldn't.

The intake routine was long and drawn out, most of which had only been experienced through a sedated state. He remembered vaguely being cuffed to a bed at Grady Memorial Hospital. In addition, the stench of a holding cell packed with more occupants than should be allowed was still fresh in Pro's nasal passage. The cell was most likely built to hold thirty odd people, but it had been crammed past capacity with no less than sixty. Most of which desperately needed a place to eat and shower for free. As Pro contemplated how fast the few hours passed, the bunk vibrated from below. The smell of its aftermath instantly pissed Pro off.

"Da fuck dog? Aye man, what you got going on?" Pro asked, already getting down from the top bunk. Pro slid the Bob Barker shower shoes on, rushing toward the door holding his nose.

"Aye man, don't nobody want to smell yo ass dog," Pro barked, frowning back in the sleeping man's direction. He grew more irritated.

"Aye man, get yo ass up!" Pro yelled louder.

"Mmmmmmm," the man just mumbled and rolled over.

"Damn," Pro complained.

He took a look at himself in the mirror by the sink he stood near. The gauze on his forehead would need changing soon. The blood had begun to take over the white thread of the bandage. Pro could feel the dampness of it on the tip of his fingers as he mashed at it. The arm sling he wore held his left arm close to his body. Product had never been the type to let wounds heal under wraps. As a kid, he would pick his scabs and pull the dry skin around the sore until it bled again. Not that he intended to make it bleed; more than that, it was an irresistible habit. His adult life hadn't been much different; he just developed a better sense of when to quit.

Pro slipped the oversized blue shirt over his head and maneuvered his injured arm out using his right hand.

"Fuck," Pro gripped as the pain flared deep inside his shoulder. Regardless of how much pain it would cause to look at the wound, he was going to examine it. After freeing his arm and getting past the wraps, Pro finally had to assess his damage. He pushed at the surrounding area with his finger,

"Shiiiit," he whispered.

It was a pretty nice wound, one that will remain for the rest of his existence. Pro thought how Renee would rub his scars; her soft hands had always had some kind of magical healing effect wherever she touched him. As he visualized her, he thought back to when he had come home with a bullet still in his leg. Coming inside the house, he got a quick snack, then climbed in bed next to Renee as she lay sleeping like nothing had happened. The following day he woke up to Renee going bananas in profanity.

"Why the hell is all this blood in this bed boy?" she asked, screaming.

"Get yo ass up; what's wrong with you?" she continued.

Pro looked down to the foot of the bed as Renee snatched the blankets and sheets away. The bed was a deep crimson, burgundy color, and the fabric of the mattress spread was drenched in blood. His daughter Fioni stood in the doorway, checking on the commotion.

"What's wrong with daddy?" she asked.

Innocence radiated from the little girl's face as she waited patiently for her answer. Pro looked at his daughter, taking a long inhale, and then dropped his head back to the pillow to avoid Renee's eyes.

"I got shot last night," he exhaled.

Bion, his second oldest daughter, popped up in the doorway next to her sister.

"What? You got shot last night?" she asked, sounding like Pro's mother, who Renee was already on the receiver within seconds.

"His ass laying right here bleeding like crazy."

Pro didn't even realize that she had made the call. *Sheeesh*, he thought, *this won't be good.*

Renee pushed the phone at Pro. "It's yo mama," she informed him, looking like some little brat tattle tale sister.

"Yeah, what up ma?" Pro said like he knew what was next. Just as he expected, the speaker of the phone erupted into a flurry of profanities.

"Bitch, get yo ass up out that damn bed, da fuck wrong with you nigga and them kids in there seeing that shit. You bout a stupid mafucka," she spat.

Pro had heard enough. "Ok, ma, I'm up, I'm up!" he protested.

Renee had already packed the needed items to get the kids and Pro to the truck and to the emergency room as she rushed through the various rooms, getting them together.

All that seemed like yesterday, Pro thought. Here he was again fucking up as usual somehow.

"Cunningham, you got visitation," the speaker in the room informed. "Cunningham, you got visitation," the officer on the M.C said even louder than before.

Pro took a few minutes getting himself ready.

Damn, she bout to trip, Pro thought, knowing it had to be Renee. His thoughts continued as the nasty taste of the cheap toothpaste hit his mouth. *She didn't waste any time finding me.* When he finished all he needed to do, Pro hit the button next to the door.

A loud pop sounded and disengaged the latch. Pro pushed the door open and stepped out into the dorm. It took Pro's eyes a second to adjust to the light of the dorm.

"Yeaaa fuck nigga, I want my money, or we gone hit puss ass nigga," one man yelled from the top range to another man out of Pro's view down below.

Pro walked between seas of unfamiliar faces making eye contact with the ones he felt were paying too much attention to him as he passed. He was injured but still a threat as far as he was concerned. Some continued their conversations and games; others kept their eyes locked in on Pro.

"Nigga fuck you and that money, Holmes," the voice from below said, now visible to Pro. He looked up at Pro and shook his head in disappointment.

Pro continued walking toward the steps leading to the bottom tier and the exit.

"Aye man, that's that nigga from the news, y'all," a voice slowly muttered from the table to the right of Pro.

"Damn, they about to roast that nigga," another man said.

Pro heard the men but didn't key in on them, not knowing or even caring who they were talking about. Finally making it to the red zone by the door, Pro swung his good arm overhead, waving to the officer in the booth to let out. Seconds later, a buzzing noise sounded from the mechanisms controlling the door as the gears came to life inside the wall rolling the door back. Pro walked out, taking in the scene as he passed another dorm. A few rods and signs went up, none of which were family. Pro made it to the corner and noticed a floor officer sitting in the seven hundred pod. He walked in, eyeing her as he inquired where to go. The officer sat there occupied with nothing looking back at Pro. She offered no direction, just a wide-eyed stare scrutinizing Pro, smacking and chewing gum behind heavily glossed lips. Pro didn't know what to make of her demeanor at first until she stopped chewing and responded.

"You gone go to hell," she said, fully convinced that he would.

Pro looked at the officer square in her eyes, trying to understand her hate. There was nothing there. The coldness in her stare was clearly some kind of relationship gone wrong, male-bashing type, shit Pro concluded. He had no idea that all of what she had felt was for him and him only. Pro looked up after hearing voices on the top tier, where a few detainees were having their visits, and determined he'd go up the steps. Walking past the unfamiliar faces behind the glass, Pro made it halfway when a tap on the booth's window caught his attention. The inmate's side was unoccupied, and the man motioned with his hands for Pro to approach. Pro stood a few seconds analyzing the man from under the bandaged brow.

Who is this grease ball, mafucka? Pro thought to himself.

The man stood about 5 feet tall, lean with a cocky posture. The silken Armani suit made him look more Italian than was necessary.

Pro thought *this slick mafucka look like he done spent hours preening, putting every single hair in place.*

Pro's instincts had established that this man was money. The cufflinks, watch, and tie pin clearly suggested this was no one from the D.A's office. Pro picked up the receiver and pulled the chair out. The taller, younger version of Danny Devito took his seat and spoke into the receiver.

"Ouch, buddy, you don't look so hot. How are they treating you back there?" The man asked.

Pro spoke back dryly, never being the one for small talk. "Who are you first, my man, and two, how da fuck you think I'm doing?" Pro was already aggravated that it wasn't who he expected. Renee was the only one he wanted to see or begin with. The dumb questions were also a pet peeve for Pro.

"Take it easy, tiger, I'm doing your people a favor," the man stated, dripping with arrogance. He continued, "I'm Giano Deatheri, Deatheri, and Associates; you've probably seen the commercials.

Pro had, hell everybody had, the firm was well-known amongst the underworld circles.

"I'm here to pull you out of this mess you've gotten yourself into." The man pulled his briefcase closer, hitting the latches while holding the phone with his shoulder. "The big guy sent me in case you're wondering, and I cost a pretty penny," he said, nodding his head, still stroking his own ego. Pro just stared back blankly, waiting for whatever. "Sweet Mary, mother of Jesus, fella, what the hell happened? I mean, you got a lot going on here and still early but this heavy shit."

Pro still without sentiment, replied, "You tell me," Deatheri looked on in disbelief.

"Ok, you've gotta be kidding me," he stated.

Pro's code of silence overall was for any and everybody. Something his mother had taught him since birth; never volunteer information. Giano didn't have the patience to entertain Pro.

"Look, I'm going to make this simple for you," Giano continued. "I am your attorney; maybe I didn't make that clear during our introduction. In my field of practice, I defend people such as yourself and others in higher financial brackets. That being the case, we normally communicate. The advantage to that is," he continued. "I get a better understanding of how I'm going to defend you and what angles I'll attack from; that's if you're interested, of course. If not, oh well, I mean not to throw it in your face or anything, but when I leave here, I'm going to go outside to the parking lot and get in my Aston Martin, the coolest thing ever. I'm going to drive over to Roswell, where I'll meet with the hottest blonde on this side of the hemisphere who just so happens to be the daughter of a very, very wealthy investor. After we go over a few things, lunch a little bit, cocktails of course. I'm going to drive her over to my estate, have her swallow my cock, and fuck her brains out, all before rush hour traffic starts. Long story short, I'm pretty comfy with things right now. You, on the other hand, my friend, from the looks of it, will need a miracle to beat the death penalty they are going to throw you as it is."

"The fuck you mean death penalty?" Pro erupted, standing up from his chair. "You got me fucked up," Pro snapped, moving his body angrily. "Death penalty for what, I defended myself. What was I supposed to do? Let the mafucka kill me? Hell naw man be for real," Pro explained, answering his own question.

"Listen, pal," Deatheri said, looking as if the meeting was wearing him out. "I know you're tired, you've had a long twenty-four hours, you lost a lot of blood, suffered a severe head injury and all, but the fact is, this isn't just going to go away," Deatheri explained. "Now we can do this whole little song and dance and try to escape the reality of what we're dealing with here and the magnitude of it. Ultimately, my friend, it will only make it all the easier to land your ass on death row, point blank period, Deatheri explained. I mean, don't you get it? The system is designed to work against you especially. You're black, a known gang banger, and your records are longer than my stock portfolio. Bottom line, you're guilty in the public's eye from that alone," Deatheri had Pro's attention. "Now, I'm not going to sugar coat this nor blow smoke up your ass as to how fucked your chances of beating this one. Let's look at this for a minute," Deatheri suggested, pulling a few papers from the Armani briefcase." We're looking at a triple homicide."

"What!" Pro exclaimed. "The fuck you mean triple homicide dog, I shot one motherfucka in defense." Pro pushed the issue defending himself.

Deatheri swiftly took control of the conversation. "They have a gun with your fingerprints all on it that just so happens to be the murder weapon used on an officer of the Atlanta Police Red Dog Unit. That officer's name was Christopher Tally, who was shot four times in the upper portion of his body, and one point-blank to the head." Pro sucked his teeth, staring coldly back to Deatheri as the man continued. "They have the vehicle registered to your fiancé, where they found the body of an associate of yours shot dead in execution-style with two bullets in the back of his head. He was lying on top of thirty-five thousand dollars with his cocked handgun in reach. Clearly implying he wasn't comfortable with his surroundings. They found powdered cocaine and a few more thousand leading away from the truck, which suggested a drug-related robbery."

Pro took a deep breath, confused as to what the hell was going on, and he had heard enough. Pro wouldn't tell on anyone even if they were police; all would be handled in the streets that was his courtroom. Needless to say, he made no mention as to who killed Wet, but the rage of being blamed for it on top of the fact it was Wet that blew a fuse inside of Pro. Taking the phone, Pro bit down hard, clenching his jaws, and took a hard swing striking the glass. Unsatisfied with the damage, he got back on the phone in need of taking some frustration out on something or someone.

"Listen, mafucka, don't ever let that come out of your mouth again, that I killed Wet," he yelled. "I don't give a fuck how it looks; I didn't do it. I shot that hoe-ass pork skin to keep that bitch from killing me, and I would do it again and again and again if it came to it. Fuck that cracker's life, my lil nigga gone man," Pro said, almost in tears about Wet's death. The reality was starting to settle in, and Pro's head pounded with every beat of his heart, intensifying the emotion.

Deatheri flicked his toothpick around his open mouth, looking back at Pro. "It gets worse, my friend," Deatheri informed him. Pro lifted his head to make eye contact with the attorney. "Not only are they saying your friend's blood is on your hands, but the same gun that killed him was also the one from which the little girl was killed across the street from the vacant house you were in."

Pro cut him off, screaming in rage, "What little girl, man? Don't fuck with me, motherfucka!" Pro's face contorted in confusion and anger as his chest rose up and down rapidly.

"Listen, man, you're making this harder than it has to be. What do you think I'm making this up?" Deatheri asked. "They have samples of your blood where you left a trail from the house behind the path leading into the vacancy, which is right across the street from where six-year-old Fatimah Johnson was killed. You were there, you shot the pursuing officer, Sergeant Hemlock in the chest with one of the guns they found on you, so if you want to keep playing this game and act like you don't know what the frick is going on, be my guest, go right ahead. Just find yourself someone who will entertain it; I'm done. Tell your big homie the consultation is on the house, and good luck, asshole," Deatheri snapped as he collected his belongings.

Pro threw the phone hard at the glass. "Fuck you man!" Pro spit in a rage. Pro needed to let off some steam in a hurry; he was on the verge of blinking out. Just as Pro yelled to the attorney, a man in the next booth could be heard.

"Man goddamn, keep that shit down over there; we trying to have our visit, bro."

Pro bit the invitation and ran around to the booth the man had hollered from.

"What nigga?" Pro snatched the phone as the man's girlfriend watched in amazement. "Nigga shut the fuck up," Pro started slapping him with blows to the mouth with the phone. Caught off guard, the man had no chance to defend himself from the swing. "Twack." Two teeth fell to the floor as blood ran over the lips of the dread head.

"Stop! What are you doing?" The man's girlfriend hollered. She continued, "Oh my God, somebody stop him!"

Pro kept swinging as more blood flew from the man's face. The floor officers ran up the steps to the altercation. By now, the other visitors had begun to peek in at all the commotion. One of the officers reached out to grab Pro after making it close enough. Without faltering, Pro rolled out of his grip and shoved him off with his good arm. The dread head slid to the floor, holding his mouth. As the other officers cornered Pro, they pulled tasers ordering him to lay down. Pro wasn't trying to hear it; he was gone.

The ranking officer spoke up. "You better calm yo ass down, boy, before we hit your ass with this Georgia Power, now!"

Pro was out-numbered and in no condition to keep it up. He looked back to the officer who had made the threat. "Suck my dick hoe ass nigga," Pro's word's came to an abrupt end as Mr. Shaw, head of the black team, shot the prongs from the taser into Pro's chest, cranking its wattage up. Pro went into a flurry of convulsions and spasms down to the floor. The officers quickly aided Mr. Shaw and got the restraints. Turned the taser off, and almost in the same instant, knees came dropping down into Pro's back. The officer first put the leg shackles on Pro, then began throwing blows into his back and ribs. Pro was in enough pain as it was.

"Get the fuck off me," Pro demanded.

The on-lookers in visitation watched wide-eyed at the disturbance bringing Shaw to interrupt. "Not here guys," Shaw continued.

The officers picked Pro up and dragged him to the steps and down to the main floor. Some of the detainees spoke up in his defense. "Aye man, y'all done did enough, nigga ain't gone let y'all keep getting away with that shit man."

Officer Shaw looked up to the inmate talking from the visitation booth. "Aye, man, enjoy your visit now before you find yourself fucked up, you hear?"

The man sat back in his booth after flipping him a bird.

Pro was out of the visitor's sight now. The officers took advantage of the situation to deliver several more body blows, and Pro began to cough up blood. As he slumped from the pain. The crisp white letters reading Fulton County Jail in Pro's uniform pant leg had now been stained with his blood and saliva.

"That's enough, y'all," Shaw insisted. "Now, do I need to put your ass in the hole?" Shaw continued.

Pro looked up to the man unrelenting, "Do what you do, black ass cracka," Pro was a die-hard. Still wincing from the pain, but nevertheless, he would never fold; his pride was too large.

"Take this mental health ass nigga back to the dorm, and lock him down in his room until further notice," Shaw commanded the other officers. "We got something for your ass," Mr.Shaw promised, grinning viciously. "Make sure he don't get no trays until he gets his shit together," Shaw demanded.

The officers nodded and dragged Pro back to his dorm. The sergeant had already arranged for Product's roommate to be taken to another room.

"Don't lose weight mafucka," the officer said, slamming the door behind Pro as they pushed him into the cell.

The beds were stripped to the bone, leaving Pro with no pillow, mattress, or sheets. The officers went to great lengths to make sure that Pro would be uncomfortable. Left to rest his body on the cold steel that furnished the room. Pro stopped by the toilet to spit, then tried to rest on the hard surface of the bed. Somewhat happy to be without a roommate. Pro was as tough as they came, but his body could speak for itself; surely this shit was getting old already. Through the pain and discomfort, Pro attempted to gather his thoughts, repeating those often used words of a man behind the wall.

"Damn," he sighed.

Pro's mind began to twirl around the severity of his troubles.

"What the hell are they trying to do to me?" he pondered. "Hmmmmph," Pro sighed. "Sergeant Hemlock, goddamn this mafucka poison. This cracka framing me for Wet. What the fuck?" he said through clenched teeth to the bunk overhead. Closing his eyes, Pro tried to find a little girl somewhere in the log of his cluttered memory. She was nowhere to be found. Pro could barely recapture himself back at the abandoned house. Had it not been for the polluted smell still fresh in his mind, the house would've entirely faded from his recollection.

The menial words of the officer in seven hundred made more sense, "You gone burn in hell," Pro reflected back to the hate in the floor officer's eyes.

Pro's head was pounding with pain, and the confusion offered little refuge. Pro opened his eyes, looking back up at the bunk over him. The names of several hoods burnt into the steel represented the detainees who once came and went.

"This shit crazy," Pro admitted, "I need to holla at da fool Theory. This shit is just way out of control; he probably snatched a nigga stain and everything, hmmph. This shit is fucked up; I done got the lil bro killed by my negligence." Pros thoughts began to close in on him. *How the fuck can I make this shit right?* Pro began to beat himself up the more he weighed his burden.

My Baby
July 4, 2013, 1:45 a.m.

T he phone laid buzzing hard under the breeze of the air-conditioned room. The smell of an exotic strain of marijuana filled its expanse.

"Buzz buzz buzz." The cell vibrated even harder, it seemed. The moan of a female fit itself right in between the silent moments after.

"Mmmmmh," she whined. "Shut up," Theory said in a playful but dry, demanding voice. Reaching over her well-curved chocolate body to retrieve the device, Theory roused the animal laying there next to him untying. The phone vibrated once more and then stopped. Just as Theory's hand had counted its way to the nightstand, the soft body of the female snuggled up closer. Clearly, her goal was to take Theory's attention from whoever was interrupting.

Theory laughed, knowing her all too well." Don't be so selfish, Nessa."

Nessa sucked her teeth at his words. She poked her lips out as her thigh smoothly found its way under his sack. The screen on the phone lit up as Theory pressed at the buttons, and a glow radiated over both of their faces. Theory could feel Nessa's lips kissing at his chest as her fingertips traced the center of his abdomen. Maintaining his face, Theory scrolled through the text messages. One text message from Fuli Fitted was highlighted on the screen, as well as a missed call.

Damn, I wonder what the homie got going on, he called and text, Theory thought.

Reading the text, there was no question that something was wrong.

"West all day homie, Brim shit no brakes."

"Aye, big bro, it's some bullshit going on up here. Pro is all over the news, and calls are coming in from the fam like crazy. Bark at my line S.A.P., mashing on um 1st."

Theory deleted the text to move on to the call option; he let out a stretching yawn as Nessa disappeared under the silk sheets.

"Fuuuck!" he said, exhaling.

Never using her hands, Nessa wrapped her warm mouth around Theory's soft and unsuspecting manhood.

"Get up, Nessa!" Theory protested.

She paid no attention to his request and continued flickering her tongue around the head of his nature. The call Theory was placing sounded from the speaker as he punched the numbers in, shortly after it began to ring. Three and a half rings later, a voice confirmed the connection.

"Big Fool, wet up homie?" Fulio answered.

"Every day!" Theory replied, then continued.

"Da fuck going on that way, bro?" Theory asked, already agitated from what news he had already received.

Nessa took in more of Theories dick as it grew in her mouth, motioning her head in a smooth pull.

"Bitch you ain't heard nothing I said; I'm on the goddamn phone, man," Theory snapped at Nessa.

Startled, Nessa came to a quick halt, just letting his meat lay calmly in her mouth without releasing it. Theory continued the conversation, taking the phone off speaker as Fulio proceeded to explain.

After a brief giving of the details, Theory erupted into the phone.

"Na, that's some bullshit; he wouldn't do that, bro. You know that! They lying dog, facts!" Theory contested, shaking the king-size bed as he spoke. "What you mean there's more dog? What is it, what the fuck is it?" Theory's patience had worn thin already as a long pause came over the phone. "Fulio?" Theory yelled.

"Yeah, big bro, I'm here," Fulio answered.

"Man, what da fu," before Theory could finish, Fulio spit it out.

"They saying the bro killed the lil homie Wet um Brim."

Theory stopped short, speechless. "What," Theory said, shaking his head.

"Yeah, they said on the news he shot him twice in the back of the head execution-style bro," Fulio explained.

"Alright, homie," Theory spoke calmly into the receiver. "Put all the homies on point and let the extended families know we got it under control," Theory instructed. "Get a lawyer for the homie first thing, and all y'all lay low," Theory continued. "I want y'all to clear, just in case the spots get hit, and I'll be on my way in the morning. Big one's homie."

"Bigger ones," Fulio replied back.

Theory pushed the end button, killing the call as he laid his head back on the pillow. Nessa slowly started to apply suction on the shaft she had yet to let go of. Theory nonchalantly reached up to the ashtray sitting in a cut-out cubby shelf of the headboard and collected what was left of a blunt wrap from an earlier and transparent red torch lighter. Striking the lighter, a blue flame with an orange tip appeared. Theory rolled the end of the half-smoked wrap in the flame until it caught. The glow at the wrap's tip shone brightly as Theory took in a long pull. Theory held the smoke in for a few moments after trail flowed from between his lips into his nostrils. Between puffs, he could feel the saliva being slurped away from his erection, then drenched with more in its replacement. Theory rubbed at his temple with the same hand he held the wrap in. After a few seconds, Theory let out a painful-sounding cough as the smoke overpowered his lungs. Nessa reached up and rubbed his chest, lightly scratching his skin with her nicely manicured fingertips.

Nessa had been riding with Theory for a few years; she knew how to calm him from just about anything when no one else could. Theory was a mellow dude for the most part, but when he did finally get upset, he was a raging bull, which Nessa couldn't even calm the storm. Theory grabbed the remote from where it lay next to the ashtray. Taking in yet another pull of the weed, it sizzled as he pointed the controller towards the 91-inch flat-screen mounted on the wall. The screen came to life, throwing its light all over the room, causing Nessa to go into a frenzy under the sheets.

Nessa was Pulling and sucking in fluent motion. Theory couldn't control the reflexes of his body jerking from the enjoyment, yet his face never allowed it to show. Theory snatched the sheets back to look at Nessa, jerking his stiffness with an unamused look. He blew smoke down in her direction. Nessa positioned her body to give him a better view of her ravishing build. Squatting flush back on her legs, her bent thighs looked like someone had poured melted chocolate over them as they glistened in the light. Theory took in every soft contour her body offered. She stood a thick 5'9 slightly bow leg with vicious curves leading to her hips.

Her waist was tiny and highlighted her ass needlessly. The crease in her back flowed into her wide bubble, creating a sinful spread. Her flat stomach dripped seductively down into her midsection, forming a V line that continued into her meaty camel toe. While she flaunted a set of rounded 32 c's. To make it plain, Nessa was tight work; the way she was put together reminded Theory of a volleyball player mixed with a stripper. Cold combination, as he would call it.

She opened Theory's legs and got between them, never letting his dick free from her mouth. With one hand rubbing Theory's thigh, Nessa took her free hand to pull the hair hanging delicately over her breast out of the way. She managed to move most of it except for a piece that fell from the rest, almost hiding a hard nipple peeking through the stands. As she took Theory into the back of her throat, she softly caressed his sack, looking back up into his eyes. Her enchanting state had torn many men's will to shreds, and the slight slant went well with her deep chestnut brown gaze. Theory took in a deep breath as his heart began to pound the rush of his high along with the madness of Pro and Wet sat pulsing in his griming demeanor. The mix of pleasure and pain was something Theory was all too familiar with. Nessa squinted; looking through her, she had been there times like this before and sympathized with the torment deep within him. She knew it a way no one else did; she knew it a way no one else was allowed to know; penetrating his armor came with a price that ran others away.

For the first time in what seemed like hours, Nessa popped his dick from the grip of her jaws and began stroking it as she straddled his left leg and hunched her wetness on it. The slippery substance secreted from between her thick vaginal lips onto Theory's leg. Raising her massive ass up in the air behind her as she reached down to wipe her juices. She collected some of the wetness and gently rubbed it onto Theories penis, like lotion. Theory pulled from his wrap for more smoke as she jerked him. Taking his eyes away to look back to the T.V., he changed the channels flicking through several new stations. Nothing out of the ordinary. Weather, Treyvon updates, and the regular news. Nessa kept to her duties as he surfed. She massaged the silky-smooth lubricant all over his shaft, giving it a luster in the light of the TV. She stroked it slowly, then slid her hands flat behind the back of it and pulled it forward more to flick her tongue underneath it. His spot under the head where the shaft began was her point of focus. Its ultra-sensitive tingle would get Theory where she wanted him to be. She waited patiently for Theory's eyes to meet hers as she handled his dick with a sense of ownership. The moment he looked, she knew she would make him bust. Theory knew how much she appreciated him; he could feel it in her proficiency as she demanded his eruption. Theory began breathing fast, flowing hard caught in her gaze as she smiled in victory, still working her tongue. Nessa wasted no time giving his head a few fist pumps with her hand, then taking him deep into her throat, working his dick into a hard orgasm, sucking and pulling it simultaneously. The wad blasted into her throat, almost choking her, but she recovered as if it was something unacceptable.

Theory palmed her fat ass as she sat up from the eruption. Knowing that it would entertain, she made the cheek in his grasp jump seductively to some unheard rhythm. After consuming all of his release, she gave the head of his dick a parting smooch with a slip of the tongue at the end to see her allegiance to his satisfaction. Theory sucked at his teeth in a cocky unmoved demeanor, then nodded his head in approval. His coolness had always amazed Nessa. He was smooth and a man of few words. Theory was a captivating sight, and when he spoke. It was passionate, and Nessa was under his spell, entranced with how he combined composure and fierceness into one manner. Although this was always his methodical routine, she knew something else was going on inside of Theory. She didn't know the extent of what was unfolding but knew that Theory would want some time and space to process.

Her voluptuous frame slid enticingly to the foot end of the bed, where she slipped her feet into a pair of hot red stilettos. She stood up and observed Theory, then she laid back sideways, perching her elbow on the pillow facing the TV. The heels put her at an easy 6'2. She began turning, trying to find her things on the floor as the silhouette of her arched back and rotund ass rocked to one side, jiggling from the movement. Locating them, she bent over and picked up a lime green pair of thongs and a pair of red and white pinstriped polo boxers from the floor. Throwing the boxers on the bed to Theory, she walked her way around to his side of the bed. She towered over him, pulling her hair into a ponytail then tied it with her thong. Looking down at Theory, she took the rest of the sill burning blunt from between Theory's fingertips. Theory looked up at Nessa with one eyebrow raised, blushed, then turned to find his boxers. The chocolate stallion stood there watching her as she pulled smoke into her lungs. Theory reached for his boxers, then grabbed them, only to have them snatched away by Nessa seconds later. After snatching the boxers, Nessa slung them over her shoulder, sliding her arm through the leg opening. Theory turned toward her now eye level with her thick meaty cameltoe with the landing strip.

"So what can I have, Nessa?" Theory asked, full of playful sarcasm.

Nessa was good at what she did. She was able to lighten up Theory's mood when needed, and though he may not smile as much on the outside, he was happy around her, and she knew it. Looking down at Theory and batting her long eyelashes mischievously, she attempted to answer, blunt in between her lip's sill.

"This puss," before she could finish the words, the blunt dropped from her mouth, unable to talk with the wrap in her mouth.

Theory gave a half-smirk and breathy laugh. "Yo stupid ass know you need to quit it," he taunted.

She grinned sideways, pursing her lips, then picked the wrap up from the floor.

"Now, what were you trying to pu pu say, Nessa?" Theory jokes.

Nessa wasn't really a smoker. Whenever she took a toke, it was only to have her opportunity to imitate Theory. He could talk with a blunt hanging from his lips as he smoked, and it was Nessa's desire to mock him by doing it. She just couldn't capture the feat.

"You know what I said. I did it that time," Nessa said, rolling her eyes.

"Baby, you almost got it," Theory encouraged. "Clearly, I can have that pussy boo, but what about my drawers, or do you plan on wearing both of our underwear as hair ribbons?" Theory asked, running his finger down the landing strip.

"See, I was going to give them back to you, but since you want to tease a bitch, I changed my mind," she explained, still demonstrating an untamable seductiveness.

"You changed your mind?" Theory asked.

"Mmmmmm," she quickly answered, throwing her head to the side, confident in how fine she was. "And what?" she said, placing her hands on her hip as her neck rolled.

"So is this my punishment?" he asked as he stared, amazed and amused at her ruby piece.

She turned away slowly, cutting her eyes back at him then she began walking toward the bathroom. Theorie's eyes followed her as the rocking and bouncing of her chunky ass cheeks lifted with each step. Knowing that he would still be watching, she let it shake a little extra, then smacked the dog paw tattooed on her right cheek, answering, "Nah, it's not to punish you, it's just so I'll know when this pussy is on your mind," she laughed in a sexy way and disappeared into the bathroom leaving Theory to his thoughts and a smile.

He shook his head and turned back to the T.V as the proceeding moments dissipated. Still nothing on a triple homicide. Theory looked on in disappointment. Still nothing on the news he surfed, then there it was, highlighted like a top story on CNN.

"Shhhhit," he grieved, not wanting it to be true.

Theory slid to the foot of the bed and turned the volume up on the set.

"Back to today's story, a member of the notorious gang known as the Bloods was arrested earlier this morning in a triple homicide involving one narcotic agent, another gang member, and a six-year-old girl who was struck during the shootout. Several protests around the city have begun to form anti-gang rallies led by the N.A.A.C.P, and others have begun to put pressure on the A.P.D. saying that their neighborhoods aren't offered the same protection as the upscale areas of Atlanta. The family of six-year-old Fatimah Johnson is gathering this evening for a candlelight vigil at the home where the girl was fatally struck by that bullet today. Nicole Smith is live on location covering the story."

The scenery changed on the screen showing the reporter standing off from a house where people had begun to gather in the background holding candles. A memorial with pictures, candles, and sorted teddy bears decorated the porch steps of the house behind the reporter.

"You're live, Nicole," the station journalist indicated.

"Thank you, Pat," she began.

"Well, as you can see here, Pat, such a sad event for the family and friends of little Fatimah Johnson, who was struck earlier today by a stray bullet here in Atlanta. So far, what we've gathered from witnesses and other sources is that the child was playing at her home here in Western Atlanta today," the reporter pointed behind her as the camera zoomed into the porch. She continued as the passing camera followed two children accompanied by a teen placing bears on the steps of the house. "The mother who watched this whole horrific ordeal from just a few feet away was too shaken to speak with us this evening. I'm sure the parents out there can understand the grief the family must be feeling tonight," the reporter expressed as the clips of crying family members and upset residents began to appear.

The first clip and sound bite was of a heavyset woman in her mid-twenties looking very familiar to Theory, who stood with tears in her eyes wailing in pain.

"Oh my God, my niece, she's gone. Why? Why?" she cried, her eyes almost closed from swelling.

A man standing next to her pulled her close and tried to console her with tears in his eyes also. She weakly pounded his chest as her make-up ran a course with tears down her cheeks. The clip quickly changed to another female more composed yet clearly saddened by the incident.

"I was walking my dog when I heard the shots, then I heard screaming down there by Nita's house. When I turned the corner," she pointed to the corner she had been walking from. She continued, "When I got down there, Nita was on the ground," the woman paused, covering her mouth with her hands as her eyelids started to blink rapidly, trying to hold back the emotion. "She was on the ground, saying God, please don't take my baby, and rocking Fatimah in her arms, but she was gone." The woman wiped at her eyes as tears began to stream down her face.

Nicole Smith's voice was heard as the clip changed again. "Here's a word from an eyewitness who actually saw the chase this morning first hand, still rather shaken; she shared with us not long ago what she had to say.

The teen stood with her arms folded, smiling in a pair of pajamas with a scarf wrapped around her head.

"It was crazy; I was on my porch, talking on the phone, the guy ran through my neighbor's yard, and the officer was running behind him. It happened so fast. It's like when I looked up, they just came out of nowhere," the girl pointed while she spoke. "The boy ran around into my neighbor's driveway, then the officer shot at him. I just went in the house hoping no bullets came through my window and stuff. It's like as soon as I got in the door, it was a whole bunch of shots. I just laid on the floor until it was over," she continued, smiling as if she was trying to be cute for whatever friends might be watching. "After a few minutes, there were more shots, then it stopped."

Nessa came out of the bathroom toward the kitchen when she noticed Theory glued to the TV. She didn't interrupt; instead, she just stood behind him, watching as well.

"It's just been a horrific experience for the members of this community today Pat," Nicole explained. "Our prayers go out to the family of little Fatimah as well as Officer Christopher Tally, who died today in the line of duty, leaving behind a wife and a newborn. We did have a chance to speak with her, here's what she had to say."

The clip changed to show a white female with a baby in her arms. The redhead continued crying out, and she was bouncing the baby, more to have something occupying herself than calming the baby.

"I just can't believe Chris is gone; I mean, we just started our life together. We got our baby, and he loved us, and now he is gone. It just isn't fair," she said with a very strong country accent, sniffling as she spoke. "We're gonna miss em," she managed to get out before breaking down.

The screen went back to the studio with Nicole in a small box still reporting.

"Pat, that was the wife of Officer Tally. Mary Diane Tally and their newborn. It's just hard to imagine what she must be feeling right now." Pat nodded, looking sympathetic as Nicole continued to speak. "We tried to speak with the Miller family, but they didn't have anything to say, still a very intense and emotional moment for everyone involved." Apparently, Reantez Miller, A man known as Wet, looking like a stone-cold killer, took up the screen as the reporter continued. "Was killed in his involvement in a drug-related robbery. The gang member has an extensive record from juvenile on. Detectives are still putting the pieces together of what happened here," Nicole continued as clips of the crime scene and the Tahoe were shown with officers surrounding the trucks. "We did get a chance to speak with detective Nassi, the lead detective who had this to say."

Nicole is shown standing next to a muscular young man wearing a dress shirt and tie. "So detective, thank you for speaking with us. We know how busy you must be with the crime scene, but what can you tell us this hour?" Nicole asked as she pushed the microphone close to Nassi.

The dark-skinned man's eyes looked twice his age. The serious demeanor and tone gave a tacit declaration of his skills." Ugh, there's not much I can say; we're still tying some loose ends together, Nicole. We have one suspect in custody."

Pros face showed up on the screen as the detective continued. Theory sat shaking his head as Nessa stood in the bathroom, quiet and attentive.

"He's awaiting questioning, and the investigation is still going on. We're looking to make sure that everything is consistent and we cover all our bases. Umm, we may possibly be looking at the involvement of other individuals, who, if that's the case, are still at large. To say the least, we just want to make sure that justice gets served for all the families involved in the tragic loss today, Nicole."

The camera showed Nassi and Nicole again.

"Thanks, detective," she said as they exchanged neds. "Thank you, Pat; we'll keep you updated on this story as it develops from Atlanta; I'm Nicole Smith CNN World News." Nicole's screen disappeared from the TV set.

"Thank you, Nicole," Pat said, looking back at the camera. "Such a heart-wrenching story out of Atlanta."

Theory has had enough, turning the set off as Pat began to go into his spill. Theory sat, trying to place where he had seen the heavyset woman before.

Damn, who was that? I know I've seen her before, Theory thought and couldn't remember, but he was sure he knew that face, and somehow it was close.

"Damn Pro, I know you ain't did this brazy ass shit dog," Theory said aloud, looking at the chandelier above.

Nessa closed her eyes, shaking her head in grief. She wanted to approach but then took off to the kitchen as she was never seen, feeling Theory's frustration.

Things Just Don't Add Up
The previous day July 3, 2013,
Detective Intakes Angle

The crime scene was full of activity as the onlooker's snapped pictures from beyond the yellow tape. The informed officers pushed the lingering stragglers away from the restricted area, roping it off after. The heat of the early July day had begun to rise as the sun moved towards its pinnacle. The A.P.D. Forensics team had placed bullet markers around casings from the shells littered the parking lot and grassy area. A body slumped halfway in and out of the Tahoe truck was under heavy examination along with the body identified as Officer Christopher Tally as it lay a few feet away from the other.

It was a gruesome and ugly backdrop for such a lovely day. Detective Nassi was called in to lead the investigation. However, he was considerably young to have made lead detective, his record of accomplishment was impeccable. He received many accolades in his short career for his role in some of the most high-profile cases Atlanta had ever seen. Nassi was a street-savvy brainiac, which gave him an advantage over even most veterans in his field. Although he had plenty of reasons with all he had going for himself at such a young age to be cocky. Nassi was a pretty humble, down-to-earth guy. He handled most of the cases tied to gang affiliation and other organized crime rings, which in the scope of all that came with it were probably considered the most dangerous. It was his passion though, and his way of giving back.

As Detective Ilakin pulled into the parking lot, he scanned the landscape before exiting his Cadillac sedan. Sergeant Reynolds made the call, barely giving Nassi any information beforehand, other than get your ass over there pronto and find out what the fuck is going on, followed by an offset, please. Nassi was tastefully dressed in brown slacks with a white shirt pinstriped in brown squares and coordinated with a brown tie. Nassi also wore a matching pair of brown Stacey Adams with a perforated design on them. His well-tapered, small fro was curly at the top then blended into a temp fade on the sides flowing smoothly into his sideburns, giving his baby face a more distinguished appearance. Most people assumed he was of Dominican descent. Still, his ethnic lineage was a mix of African and Native American with a dab of Mexican, giving him a variety of characteristics.

Nassi's upbringing was that of an average black youth in between two major cities. Detroit and Atlanta had been a significant influence on his attitude and street sense. His father's family line consisted of heavy criminal and gang activity, which caused a lot of pain within their once united family. Nassi wanted badly to break the cycle of murder and incarceration that plagued his people.

"Detective," a familiar voice called to Nassi as he exited. "Could you come here and take a look at this?" It was Inez Santos from the forensics team.

"Sure, I'll be right there," he replied as his eyes ran over a few sheets of a file he was handed by an approaching officer.

"So who was the first to respond on location, and do we have a report yet?" Nassi asked as they continued to walk together.

Officer McKenzie was a timed nerdy type with liver-spotted skin and self-esteem issues. Nonetheless, he meant well.

"Not yet, Detective, as far as a report, Sergeant Hemlock of the Red Dog Unit and Officer Tally were the first to get here," the wiry framed man informed.

"So, where are they now?" Nassi asked, looking down at the shorter man.

"Ugh, well, Sergeant Hemlock is being looked at by the medical unit, and as for Officer Tally, he's laying over there," McKenzie explained as he pointed in the direction of the

Durango, continuing. "Unfortunately, he won't be able to tell us much."

Nassi had no idea yet, but officer Tally would have a lot to tell in the hours to come, and this case would be far from open and closed. Nassi looked over to the Durango from where Inez had been calling for him moments ago. Shoving the file back into the officer's chest, he started in her direction, piqued from the mess that was already beginning to unfold.

Officer Santos greeted him as the two men approached, eyeing Nassi with an interested glare in her eyes. "Hello detective, long time no see."

"I agree it has been a while; we have to start meeting under different circumstances," Nassi replied with a charming tone.

Officer Santos gave a cute grin handing him a pair of black latex gloves. Taking the gloves, Nassi's face shifted from the warmness that had just been there to a more stern and serious countenance. When it came to his work, he was meticulous and attentive. Officer Santos found his veneering extremely attractive. She snapped out of the muse she was in, following suit alongside Nassi as he squatted down to examine the officer under the sheet. Taking a pen from his shirt pocket, Nassi pulled the sheet back with its tip. Officer McKenzie almost lost his breakfast, looking down at Officer Tally's busted face. The bullet had done some devastating damage at such close range. Nassi turned, looking up to the squeamish officer in disdain.

"Aye, McKenzie, would you mind? We're trying to work here. How about helping the uniforms get some of these noisy people from around here or anything? Just go, please," Nassi suggested.

McKenzie fixed his glasses on his face, still holding a hankie in his hand, covering his nose and mouth. He waved Nassi off, shaking his head. "Oh, I'm fine, just felt a sneeze coming on, these damn allergies," he lied, trying to save face in front of Officer Santos. She was aware but played it off like she hadn't noticed while trying hard not to laugh. His whole charade was transparent, but she spared him from the shame. She had been around worse scenarios in comparison anyway. McKenzie continued, "I'll go and see if Hemlock is still with the medical unit and find out when he'll have a moment to start on the report. I don't want to be sneezing all over the crime scene, possibly disturbing evidence," he explained, barely humoring himself with an exaggerated laugh.

"Yeah, do that," Nassi demanded, annoyed more with the condition of the officer than McKenzie.

McKenzie hurried away before the disguise he thought had worked crashed him.

"Tough guy, huh?" Santos joked, trying to make the mood less tense.

"About as tough as an eighty-year-old man's anus when he's defecating," Nassi answered.

"Yuuuck, you're disgusting," Santos replied as the two shared a laugh.

They both had grown to enjoy each other's company. They had worked together on numerous occasions but never socialized outside of work. It wasn't a lack of interest there; it was more of the professional attitude they assumed of the other that kept either of them from crossing the line.

"If I'm disgusting, what do you call this guy?" Nassi asked, studying the hole in the man's face.

Santos replied after a deep breath, "I know, right." She looked up to the Durango, then back to the Tahoe. "It's all pretty odd, in my opinion," she said, shaking her head like she was occurring to accept something.

"What are you talking about?" Nassi asked, observing her body language.

"I mean, between you and me so far from how it looks, things just don't add up," she continued. "I don't know how the report will read, but I overheard Hemlock talking to the uniforms before he went to be examined, making himself sound like some superhero," she said, rolling her eyes then continued. "So it's like they pull up and catch some gang members in the middle of a transaction turned robbery, get in a shootout. I don't know, maybe I'm getting ahead of myself," she said, shutting down, feeling like she was rambling.

"What is it," Nassi urged her on.

"I'm just saying this crime scene looks sort of awkward from how he was explaining. It's nothing; I just overheard fragments from a distance trying to piece it together; that's all. Don't mind me," Inez explained, brushing it off.

"Inez, you're one of the best in our business," Nassi admitted, locking eyes with the mesmerizing beauty stooped next to him. "You have an eye for this stuff, and it would be naive for me not to give merit to any opinions you may have, so if you have any suggestions, I'm all ears," Nassi revealed. He reached for the smartphone on his hip to take pictures. "Inez, if you don't mind and you're not busy when I get the report and we wrap up here, would you mind going over a few things with me. I mean, like in a quieter setting like over dinner or something?" Nassi asked hesitantly, never looking away from the phone as he snapped pictures.

Inez let out a smile that had been bubbling inside of her, then regained her composure before he noticed, or so she thought at least. Nassi looked back to Inez after flicking a few more pictures and offered a knowing grin catching the redness still flush in her cheeks.

"Whatever," she said, trying to contend with his swagger.

"It's all good. I'm the same way when someone shoots me kudos about my talent, hell you're good; who can lie?" Nassi admitted. "So, will you help me?" he asked.

"Sure, what time?" she asked, still red in the face.

"Sometime after nine tonight," he suggested.

"It's almost a date," she said, smiling.

"Almost," he replied.

The detective took several more snaps of the body from different angles, standing up.

"Has anything been moved," he asked, looking around the immediate area surrounding the body.

"No, the medical examiners are really strict about us moving the bodies or anything like that. Gets their panties in a bunch when we do, so to save ourselves the headache, we left it just like it was," she informed, eyeballing the entry wounds to Tally's upper rib and chest area.

Meanwhile, detective Nassi scanned the ground, coming across a few white threads with singed edges. Nassi squatted down near the tiny fibers of the cloth.

"Inez, can you collect these and put them in a sample bag for me?" the detective asked, directing her attention to the threads.

"Not a problem, sir," she answered.

Nassi took more pictures from the scene inside the Durango and, from that point of view, facing the other vehicle.

"Inez?" Nassi called out to the Latin beauty.

"Yes, Detective," she answered, almost enticing him to make an unprofessional comment.

Maintaining his demure, he disclosed his plan of action. "Look, I'm going to go over here to the other truck and check some things out. We both have a lot of ground to cover, so I'll catch up with you in a bit, okay?"

"That's fine, Detective," she answered, looking over to him with passion in her expression.

"Run a check to see if there's gunpowder on Tally's hand and if that 40. Cal lying next to him ever got a shot off," he asked.

Although she would typically do all of that anyway, she continued on like it was something of a special request. She quickly took the clip from out of the pistol smelling the inner mold.

"Nope," she said, looking back at the clip, "It's full to the last dot."

Nassi grinned as he pondered, *damn, she's a sexy something!*

Inez gave a wink as if she could hear his thoughts, then agreed to his petition.

"I'll still check for powder, and the number is 770-238-1983," she informed him.

Nassi punched the numbers in, then saved them in his contacts. "Okay, I got you, later then," he then began to walk towards the Tahoe.

Equally Concerned

Detective Nassi stood over the young man's body, taking pictures of the money and the fatal gunshot wounds. The body was more in the truck than out, Nassi noticed. The floorboard had caught Reantez's body, holding him stiffly in place.

"Not long before that lifestyle catches up with you, huh?" Hemlock asked, standing behind Detective Nassi.

Nassi turned to look at the voice behind him, meeting eyes with the cocky statured man.

"How are you, detective?" Hemlock asked, really not caring.

"I'm fine, Hemlock," Nassi answered. "And you?" Nassi returned the question equally concerned.

Hemlock shrugged as the two men reached out to shake hands more for show than anything else.

"You got yourself quite a mess here, Hemlock," the detective admitted.

Hemlock's eyes looked awkward after hearing the comment before shifting his gaze away then back to Reantez. "Eh well, it could have been worse," Hemlock admitted, not sure how to take Nassi.

Nassi sensed some sort of arrogance on the man from his response. Nassi searched for any emotion in the man; he was numb, it seemed to the detective. Hemlock took center stage before the detective could finish his thought well.

"That son of a bitch killed Tally," Hemlock explained, looking over to the Durango where his partner lay with a distant stare in his eyes. "You know it's part of the job; it happened before; you just never get used to it, you know?" Hemlock continued.

The detective studied Hemlock as he spoke. "So, what happened here?" Nassi asked, taking a small tablet from his pants pocket.

"I'm so exhausted right now, detective, and I'm just a little out of it, so bear with me. "I'll do my report in a few for a full account of the details. In a nutshell: Me and Tally see these guys in what looked like a transaction from the main street. We pulled in slowly as a black Monte Carlo pulled off, who we assume had dropped this guy off," Hemlock explained, fanning his hand in the body's direction. "They call him Wet." Hemlock continued, "He's one of yours," the detective listened intently. "I've had a few run-ins with him around the area, a real fucking tyrant," Hemlock spat, stating his opinion. "Just as we circled around to pull in, Kadarai Cunningham, also known as Product or Pro, shot him twice in the head. I sped into the parking lot to apprehend the assailant. When he noticed us, he took off, fleeing on foot. Tally got shot after exiting the truck to take up pursuit. I took cover shooting back, then ran behind the perp as he headed for the fences," Hemlock explained, pointing it all out with his hands. I chased the perp back that way for a block or two, where I cornered him off in an abandoned house. We got into a tussle after he ambushed me, shooting me center mass, and emptied his firearm; thank God for my Kevlar. A little girl was struck by one or two rounds across the street from the second firearm he produced, which is the one that we wrestled over."

Nassi scribbled in the pocket-size spiral notebook looking back up at Hemlock as the lies dripped from his tongue. Nassi had never really got to know Hemlock from their occasional meetings. Still, he had been wary of him since catching him beating up on another officer he claimed had failed to pay a gambling debt. The fight was after hours at a downtown mini bar that many of the guys frequented. Nassi had been the one to break it up. No one went to jail; they just swept it under the rug. The broken nose of the officer Hemlock had been punching on never allowed him to look like the same man afterward. Hemlock often cracked on how disfigured the poor guy was now. Since all that, Nassi had no cordial feelings towards Hemlock.

"You're pretty lucky to be alive," Nassi admitted, still able to relate to the man's ordeal.

"Yeah, I guess. Just wish it was a different way, you know, that kid. Tally shhh," Hemlock sighed, shaking his head.

"Yeah, it's a shame it had to be this way," Nassi agreed, then paused. "Sorry about your partner too, man," Nassi sympathized. "Look, take it easy or try anyway. I know you still have those post-shoot-out traumas probably raging in our muscles," Nassi said, continuing. "Just when you get around, try to finish your report, I'll take a look at it, and we can get this all over with."

"Yeah, this shit is pretty much an open and closed case, that little fucker Kadarai Cunningham is going to fry," Hemlock growled.

Nassi could see the anger in Hemlock's eyes. Nassi could understand; he had been there, his own pain was still fresh, some days were just better than others, as well as coping with it. At any rate, the detective had an idea how the tiny ripples of this new current would grow into catastrophic waves, causing a flood of deceit, death, and double-crosses to float up some of his old injuries.

"Well, Hemlock, I need to get back to it, pal, thank you, and once again, man, I'm really sorry," the detective consoled him.

Hemlock seemed almost reluctant to leave but took off anyway without saying anything else, no handshake, nor anything. The detective thought he knew what it was, that feeling Hemlock had, Nassi was wrong, oblivious of the man's corruption. Nassi turned and focused back to where the young man lay lifeless, snatched away from the vibrant and energetic body he once wore.

It was too real for the detective to see himself lying in that truck dead. He had walked a thin line in his youth, bordering the fences that separated what public opinion called the good guys and the bad guys. However, for Nassi and his opinion, the guilty guys aren't really the bad guys in some cases and vice versa. Nassi took more snaps, then moved around to the driver's side back door. Grasping the latch and gaining entry, the detective snapped pictures of Reantez lying there. Nassi frowned at the monstrosity, full of indignation and disappointment.

This shit just goes on and on, he thought.

The splattered mess layered over a portion of the interior of the back seat in a gruesome unevenness. The exits that the slugs had burrowed left a huge leaking aperture in the Miller kid's forehead just above his left brow. He lay on top of some bills neatly banned and stacked under his left arm, except for a few that were pushed away from his forward thrust. There was a stack still in the clutches of his stiffened grip. Nassi looked closer, then noticed the barrel of a handgun barely peeking from under the passenger's seat. Nassi tried playing the scene out in his mind's eye, unsure of how accurate it may have been, regardless it had become a habit of second nature. It didn't make sense to Nassi that the barrel would be at reach as opposed to the handle. Nassi zoomed his camera's focus close in on the gun, took four to five snaps then saved them to the album. After a few more photos of the entire back seat and Reantez, Nassi stood back up about to make his way around to the passenger's side front. Then he heard a buzzing noise coming off the Miller boy's body. It sounded again as the detective stooped back inside. Nassi quickly concluded, there must be a phone on him. He wouldn't be able to reach from this side without staining his shirt, so he stepped back out from the truck. Making it around to Reantez's side, standing behind the body, the detective took a moment before reaching for the device to see who would notice. It looked clear until he caught the peering eyes of Hemlock across the lot staring back at him. It was a strange look, almost adversarial, Nassi thought, but whatever his deal was, the detective wouldn't miss the chance to get his hands on that phone. That would've been like having superman's strength and opting not to use it.

Nassi stooped down with his back to Hemlock and patted the pockets down on the body; no phone, but it was still buzzing.

He thought, where the fuck is it, trying to hurry when the most likely stash spots popped into his head. The detective was familiar with the extra convenient pocket space gym shorts offered and was not surprised when he found the phone there. The battery life was at two bars, meaning that it wouldn't be long before it would be powering down. Nassi turned the phone on silent, then slid it into his pocket in one smooth motion. He stood back up to meet the approaching footsteps coming from behind him.

"Detective, what you got?" Hemlock asked in an insolent tone.

It was all over Nassi's face that the question had rubbed him the wrong way, more so the fact that Hemlock was in a sense over his shoulder, and Nassi hated that. Hemlock tried to mask his interest, not knowing what to make of the detective's expression.

"Anything we can use to find the men that dropped him off?" Hemlock asked.

"I'm not sure," Nassi began, "I was going to jot some records in my notebook when I noticed the gun there on the floorboard," Nassi said, pointing. "Strange." He continued, "That is, of course, if it belongs to the Miller boy."

"Why is that?" Hemlock pried. Not wanting to give away too much of his own thoughts.

The detective threw a spin in the mix to put Hemlock at bay. Nassi was a swift thinker, and his inspiration was as if some sixth sense from God knows where.

"I think he was expecting trouble to have that gun at such close proximity," Nassi explained.

"These fuckers live on the edge, always aware that death is right around the corner," Hemlock replied coldly.

"Yeah, I guess," the detective responded, eyeing Hemlock closely.

Trying to get some alone time, Nassi urged.

"I really need to examine your report; what kind of progress have you made?" aware that Hemlock hadn't made any.

Hemlock could take a hint but offered some sarcasm of his own that gave rise to some suspicion in Nassi's thoughts.

"Detective, be careful with tampering and whatnot. You might bite off more than you can chew," Hemlock suggested as he continued. "These guys behind this don't play fair, it seems."

"Are you referring to the Bloods?" Nassi asked clearly and to the point.

Hemlock hunched like he didn't care to give the detective a good answer. Nassi looked at Hemlock, not knowing what to make of his body language, and simply responded.

"It's all in a day's work. I'm not worried."

Hemlock let out a "Hmmph" then spit to the ground in front of Nassi before turning to walk off, leaving Nassi staring at his back.

"I'll be sure to watch my step," the detective said, referring to the glob of tobacco.

"That sounds safe," Hemlock replied, never turning to look back.

Nassi thought, *what an asshole*, and got back on task. After shaking Hemlock off, the detective began examining under the seat through the passenger's front side and noticed how the gun had made a path through some cigarillo wrappers and other debris like it had been pushed. The grain of the carpet behind the weapon made it more evident, being that it was going in the opposite direction, tailing from the gun. The first thing that came to mind was that it made more sense as to why the gun was in that position; Nassi took more pictures as his brain began firing just as rapidly as the snaps froze those images.

Reantez didn't get dropped off if this was his gun, the detective thought. Shortly after, he stood up with the gun in his hand, then walked it over to officer Santos.

"Inez, get this fingerprinted for me immediately, please," Nassi asked, holding the pistol between his latex-covered fingers.

Officer Santos grabbed an evidence bag, opened it, and allowed Nassi to place the weapon inside. Picking up on Nassi's intensity, Inez questioned.

"Is everything alright?"

His weariness was sticking out like a sore thumb, and his face was stone, hardened, and serious.

"You were right," he admitted, "Something's not right," he informed.

"I'll have this fingerprinted by the time we meet up, ok?" she said.

"Yeah," Nassi replied from somewhere distant.

"Are you alright, though?" Officer Santos asked, concerned.

Nassi snapped out of his brainstorming from where he had been in previous moments, like it was a painful feat, "Yeah, yeah, yeah I'm fine, I'm sorry. We'll meet later, ok?" he replied then he was gone.

Bending a Few Corners

It was just about nightfall when detective Nassi finished going over the crime scene and its two-block radius. Did a news interview and made it to his loft overlooking the Atlanta skyline. The detective was preparing to meet Officer Santos at The Oceanaire, a restaurant right off of Peachtree, for a date or almost a date anyway. The little girl's mutilated face left from the shoot-out was fresh in his mind and fueling anger deep inside of him. The family deserved justice, and Nassi was determined to bring them just that. So far, Kadarai and his gang were on the detective's shit list, and he would bring everyone responsible down if it was the last thing he did.

After washing and grooming himself into a neatly shaved novelty, Nassi scented himself with a splash of Issi and slid into a pair of khaki-colored Ferragamo pants with a matching V-neck. He thought about wearing a chunky wrist ornament but decided not to, so he wouldn't give the wrong impression. *This was business, not show and tell*, he reminded himself. Nassi had somewhat of a lavish lifestyle, arising from the check pulled in from the department. He had done pretty well playing stocks, as well as the profitable business he invested in with an elder cousin of his. Chatam & Ilakin Construction Company was doing so well that Nassi really didn't have to work at the department. Still, it was more than a job to him, and the Miller boy and the precious Johnson girl were the type of fuel that kept him involved.

Nassi made it to the parking deck and was pulling out onto Cheshire Bridge in no time. After bending a few corners, Nassi hit Inez's number on his phone.

"Hola," a sweet voice chimed in.

"Hey! How close are you, Ms. Santos?" Nassi asked, trying to sound professional while smiling at her charm.

"I'm turning off of Ponce De Leon now, so about ten to fifteen minutes if traffic stays at a good flow," she informed, using some military jargon.

"Kool," Nassi answered back.

The music in the background gave the call some kind of mood as Total's "Kissing You" played softly in the speakers. As smooth as Nassi was, that part hadn't been planned. The music was random and just so happened to be going like a soundtrack to Nassi's movie.

"Is that the plan?" Inez asked, giggling.

"What?" Nassi asked, confused.

"Whatever, see you soon," she said, killing the call and his question with one stone.

Nassi, now hearing the song from a different perspective, wondered if she had been hinting at the words. He chose not to entertain the thought to save himself from the embarrassment. Unfortunately, the thought persisted and did just that.

"Damn, she clearly thinks I'm being fresh," he laughed.

Nassi hit a button on the ceiling giving the breeze outside access into the vehicle through the sunroof. The city was thriving as usual for a typical Wednesday evening in July. A thick gloom was hanging in the atmosphere bringing Nassi's thoughts back to the more relevant issues at hand.

Shit's Getting Weirder by the Minute

It wasn't long before Detective Ilakin and Officer Santos met inside the restaurant's waiting area. Nassi made a quick pit stop at a random flower bed to grab Ms. Santos a bright red rose. After a brief greeting, hugs, and smiles, the two pushed deeper into the establishment, led by their host. Nassi walking behind Inez, couldn't help but notice her shapely body as she gracefully sauntered down towards their reserved seats. The long wife beater she wore covered just enough of her plump ass that only the bottom of her meaty cuffs gyrated as she walked could be seen. The black liquid tights with yellow prints and yellow high heels made her look a lot different than what Nassi was familiar with. The bracelets and accessories gave her a model type of look. Inez now stood a staggering five foot seven and a half inches with the three-inch heels on. The tattoo on the back of her right shoulder gave her some additional flavor. Nassi tried to make it out, but it was too late, they made it to their seats, and she turned her body to slide into the quiet booth.

" Would you like to start with any drinks?" the host asked.

The two looked at each other as Nassi took his seat across from Ms. Santos. The two tried to feel each other out, whether alcohol would come into play when Nassi spoke up.

" Yes, I'll have a coke," he said, waiting for Inez's choice.

" Yeah, that sounds good, make it two," she said, smiling with her bone-white teeth showing.

She looked happy to be out with Nassi. The host took off to get drinks as Nassi began with some small talk.

"Ms. Inez Santos! Jesus Christos! So this is you off of the clock?" She blushed." You look great," he admitted.

"Thanks," she said, giving Nassi a playful side view of her gorgeous face." You're looking handsome as usual," she replied, catching Nassi by surprise.

Flattered, he was still able to swing a confident smirk and "Thank you" back at the vixen. "So, what branch of service were you in?" Nassi asked, convinced she had from some earlier identifiers.

" Oh, I get that a lot. Technically I've never been in the service, not registered anyway," she continued joking her explanation out. "I am your almost ordinary military brat, who might as well have been enlisted."

Nassi laughed, warming up to the vivacious and picturesque cover girl across from him.

" My father, the late great Colonel Miguel Santos of the United States Marine Corps, is to blame," she said, making her voice stern and deep, accompanied with a salute.

" I'm sorry," Nassi offered his condolences.

"Nah, it's okay, it's been a while now. We still miss him, though," she said, waving Nassi off with her hand. "He was a great guy," she continued, looking back at Nassi with a sense of gratitude in her tone. "Ugh, enough about that," she suggested.

The waiter's timing was perfect, as the man placed two tall glasses of coke on the table along with some dinner rolls in front of the couple. "Good evening, my name is Terrance," the waiter informed.

The heavy-set black man gave off a feminine persona as he complimented Inez on her whole get-together by designer and style. Nassi recognized a few names mentioned before the waiter lost him rambling on. Nassi was not entertained, more like disgusted, to say the least. Still, Inez was clearly enjoying every minute of it urging the man on.

"Honey, I got a bright orange pair just like them," Inez said, fingering her big yellow earrings, which Terrance had been talking about so enthused. Nassi has had more than he could stand of the man as he waited patiently for the two to end it. Not sure if his face gave it away how uncomfortable the man's presence was, Nassi wondered why the husky gay dude had rolled his eyes as he continued.

"Anyway, what can I get you guys?" Terrance asked, looking at Nassi with a fake smile, then to Inez with a more genuine one.

"Just give us a few minutes, miss thang," Inez suggested.

"Okay, sweetie, take your time," Terrance said, smiling big at Inez as if he had eaten the whole 'Miss Thang' thing up.

Nassi shook his head as Terrance took off. Nassi was all over Inez as soon as the waiter left. "Miss Thang?" Nassi asked, looking terribly confused.

"Come on, Nassi," she laughed. It's 2013; it's not as much of an oddity in this day and age," she defended.

"Okay, but that doesn't mean we should condone it," he protested.

"They are humans too, and they just want to be identified as the gender of their choice," she explained.

"They don't have a choice; they were made to be who they are," he countered.

"Exactly," she agreed, smiling.

"No, that's not what I mean. I mean, well, you know what I'm saying."

"Yeah, but just let um be," she said calmly.

"What are you, some kind of gay pride activist?" Nassi asked.

"No," she laughed. "I'm just one of those people who accept people for who they are and who they want to be without prejudice," she continued. "My roommate is gay," she revealed as she picked her menu up. "Mmmm," she hummed way too fast to fool Nassi. He went with it, not wanting to pry too much into her private life; besides, the topic was off track from what needed to be discussed anyway.

"What do you see?" he asked.

"This rainbow trout sounds awesome," she admitted.

"Yeah, it does," he agreed.

"Whoa," He said, looking at a picture on the menu. "This lobster tail and scallop platter look too tasty; that's what I'm having."

"Mmm," she hummed again. "It does," she agreed. "I think I'll have the calamari and a salad."

A few moments passed, their orders were placed, and the plates arrived maybe 15-20 minutes later. Dinner was served, and talk about the case started. The prints on the gun belonged to Reantez, and there were quite a few other tidbits that would be more useful coursing it in another direction. The detective had been brought up to speak on some different angles and key things that had gone overlooked. Inez had informed him of the hair samples found on a broken kitchen drawer on the floor in the vacant house that was undergoing D.N.A and other testing. All the details coming to light gave birth to Nassi's suspicions, which were now growing like some mutant creature inside of him. After scrolling through the pics Nassi had taken with his phone, the couple had already washed their hands and were now preparing to eat. Before Nassi could smash into his plate, Inez snatched his hand away in hers to offer quick prayer. She pulled a necklace from inside her wife-beater with a pendant of a small cross hanging on it. Kissing it after an amen, her almost silent offerings of gratitude were now complete, and the two went at it. Nassi wasn't religious, but he respected the belief of others in their spirituality.

"So if Reantez was actually a passenger in Kadarai's truck, why did Hemlock see him getting dropped off?" Inez asked.

"Well, he only said he may have like he wasn't completely sure," Nassi confirmed.

"Still, it makes no sense," she admitted. "Everything is consistent with him being in the Tahoe's front seat at some point," she continued. "There is footage to coincide with Reantez being at the BP gas station buying cigars, then getting inside the truck with Kadarai. We linked that from a receipt found in the truck, which rules anything else out," she explained.

"I found a phone on the Miller kid and pocketed it," he said reluctantly as he chewed more of his meat. "I have it charging now, but I'm kind of locked out of it. It died before I could find a plug to fit," he revealed.

Inez laughed, "Give me a break! You mean to tell me the super sexy wiz-kid detective being restricted from something. Now who or what could resist you," she said, twirling a glass of wine she ordered with the meal, which he assumed had started to do the talking. It was like she had heard his thoughts and answered them out loud. "No, I'm not drunk, and you know you're sexy; now go get the phone, so I can get you in it," she suggested. Nassi's cheeks would have been red had his complexion allowed. He hurried a few more bites from his plate then excused himself to go and get the phone from his car. Inez admired him, studying his frame as he walked away. She took a scallop from Nassi's plate followed by another as eight scallops quickly turned into four before she thought to stop.

"Damn, that's good," she murmured to herself. She took another sip of the aged wine. She noticed an intruding pair of eyes evaluating her from a table a few feet away. The man was sitting alone and looking very out of place. Inez tried not to stare back, occupying herself with a compact she pulled from her small pocketbook. The small 2.5 caliber pearl handle next to it gave her a boost of confidence and reassurance that the meaner they looked, the uglier they cried. It wasn't an original quote of her own, just something her father had instilled in her during her personal combat training under his strict tutelage. Inez looked back up, and he was gone; the man had disappeared. She scanned the entire room even as she stood, but there was no sign of him anywhere. Inez took her seat and blew it off after her puzzled look retreated into her brow.

Meanwhile, Nassi was unplugging the phone outside, letting the comment Inez made about him being sexy run away with him. He looked in the rearview mirror smoothing his facial hairs in place, getting the big head. As Nassi looked, he noticed a dark figure pass slowly behind his reflection. The eerie pace the man had made him attempt to get a better visual as he turned to catch the back of the man's frame through the back window. All he could make out was the black t-shirt with a small glowing white check on the back just below the collar. The man kept pushing, never turning back as Nassi exited the car to go back inside the restaurant. Passing a family leaving, Nassi was subject to the ridicule of an obnoxious teen making jokes for his family at Nassi's expense.

"Hey y'all, it's Will Smith from Bad Boys. What you gonna do, what you gonna do when they," the boy's song was cut short as his father popped him in the head.

"Shut up, David," the father demanded, nodding at the detective.

Nassi thought to himself what age was too young for someone to be labeled an asshole, concluding the boy to be at least fourteen. Nassi decided that he had made the cut. The truth was; Nassi actually got that a lot when he wore his shoulder holster in plain clothes. Other than that, the comparison to Mr. Smith was only in race, almost anyway. Shortly after, the multiracial Nassi was back, taking his seat closer to Inez in the booth, flustered but okay. He quickly noticed more than half of his scallops gone looking at his plate. Noticing Inez justified her actions.

"Regardless of how pretty she is, never leave your food unattended. People do all kinds of craziness," she explained.

"Like what? Cast a spell on them so they can kidnap your mollusks," he joked.

She laughed clearly in comfort with Nassi. "They were so delicious, I couldn't just eat one," she admitted.

"It's cool ma," he said, smirking as he forked one to feed it to her.

She took it in her mouth and slid it off the fork slower than necessary, looking back into Nassi's eyes. Finally, after getting the muscle down, Nassi handed the phone over. Twenty to thirty seconds later, they had access. Nassi looked at Inez, impressed.

"Not exactly by the book, huh?" she asked, referring to the evidence being moved from the scene.

"Yeah, well, it's just a means to an end," he defended.

Hell, it's obvious she doesn't mind as willing as she was to break the code, he thought to himself before second-guessing his trust. In his head again, she responded in a timely fashion.

"I don't condone it, but after all, I am female, and we're naturally noisy," she admitted.

Nassi burst into laughter, "How the hell do you keep doing that," he asked.

"What?" she smiled, excited by his cheer.

Inez was more grounded than he had imagined her to be. She was easy flowing, opinionated and gorgeous. Still, after all that, she had the wit of a rocket scientist, mixing it all into a thick enticing gumbo.

Nassi started looking through the pictures in the phone's photo album. The first image he noticed was of Reantez alive and well, along with some mixed island-looking girl; they were drenched and hugged up near some water ride. It was a screensaver and had been edited to add a frame and text; it read, "Wet and Kilani on some wavey shit '13' Brimming like a MaFucka," in red italics. The girl's body covered most of Wet up as he hugged her from behind. The two of them were holding up signs with their hands, and the red two-piece and bandana around Kilani's head of long hair made it clear what they enlisted in. *The duo made a nice looking couple*, Nassi thought, then spoke out loud.

"Beautiful children with so much potential."

Inez agreed with a sigh, "Hmmm," as she looked on next to Nassi.

She took another sip from her wine glass and inched closer to Nassi as he scrolled through more slides. The following images were of Reantez and Kilani in front of the amusement park sign cheesing. It was the White-Water Park, a summertime favorite for the Georgia residents, bringing people from far and wide to enjoy it's refreshing refuge from the heat. The following seven or eight images were more of the two stripping down at the trunk of a black Monte Carlo. The pictures Kilani had obviously snapped gave less of the ride than when Reantez had taken them. His snaps gave a better description of the rims and the red pinstripe on the side of the frame.

"Hemlock said that the car that may have dropped Reantez off was a black Monte Carlo with Rims," Nassi said in a tone just audible enough for Inez to hear.

Inez thought they had been able to rule out the drop-off and chalked it as maybe; just a bad perception on Hemlock's behalf, but *did it have merit,* she thought confused.

"Shit is getting weirder by the minute," Inez replied close in Nassi's ear, keeping their discussion to a private pitch.

The two continued to study a few more pictures and video clips. One with Reantez at a studio rapping as he rolled blunt caught Nassi's attention, knowing that a lot of information was often disclosed in music from experience. Nassi shook his head in disappointment at Reantez.

"That boy could've easily made it big, do you hear him? That shit is hard," Nassi admitted feeling Reantez flow.

Inez just pursed her lips, shaking her head. "It's a shame," she replied.

The verse wasn't what either of them had expected. Reantez was rapping about what kind of role he would play in his child's life and how he would raise him, predicting it would be a boy. Pretty commercial had he just gone a tad bit lighter on the profanity he chose.

Texts and tons of them started taking over the phone's display. Queen B... Queen B..., Queen B... for as far as the screen would allow. The most recent read, "Okay, I'm worried!!!" with a sad emoji face. The sad emoticon said a mouthful taking up its small space on the screen. The time sent was 8:24 p.m., less than fifteen minutes ago. Clearly, Queen B had no idea what had happened to Reantez, and Nassi loathed the fact that if he wanted some information, he would have to be the first to bear the bad news to the Queen, whoever she was.

Inez looked at Nassi as he pinched the bridge of his nose, mindful of all he had on his plate. She rubbed some tension out of his shoulders and suggested the quicker, the better. The only family member the department had been able to contact was Reantez's grandmother. She took it pretty bad from how family services had described. She may have been too distraught to have spread the news, the detective assumed of the grandmother.

"Or maybe she doesn't know Queen B," Inez said, hunching.

After taking a moment, Nassi built his nerve, then proceeded to send the call through. The ring-back tone played Future and Rihanna' Love and Affection' halfway through the bridge, then an excited voice picked up.

"Boy, I'm gone kill you," the girl said, clearly happy to be receiving a call back from the number. The playful threat she had just made would probably reverberate from this day on.

Tezzi Bear

Detective Nassi was, in a sense, caught off guard with the choice of words the Queen had chosen to use.

Beginning anyway, Nassi replied, "Hello. Is this Queen B?"

"Who the hell is this and why you got my nigga's phone?" She snapped.

For some reason, the way she talked seemed unnatural, Nassi thought. It was like she wasn't used to talking this way, Nassi surmised.

"My name is Detective Ilakin of the Atlanta Police Department," he started.

"What?" She interrupted. "I don't want to talk to no fucking police. Where is my man?" She continued. "Is he in trouble or what?" she asked in a tone almost unbearable to Nassi.

"Look, ma'am, I don't want to discuss this over the phone. It would be better if we could discuss this in person,"

Nassi suggested. "This is a very serious matter," he continued. "If you want to help, we need to meet if that is at all possible," Nassi explained as calmly as he could manage.

"I don't know you. You could be anybody, and where is Tez?" she asked, sounding believably irritated, still in her rant.

Inez could see the frustration on Nassi's face as he tried getting through to the quarrel with some young lady on the line, and as loud as she had been, Inez heard every word. In these types of situations, it's critical how you disclose information. You don't want to move too fast, letting it be known that you're working a homicide. It's just easier to make that transition gradually. The problem lies in the simplicity of getting that done, and Queen B wasn't helping.

"Ma'am, please hear me ou…" Nassi started before Inez reached over and took the phone from his hand. He looked at her, mouth still opened in mid-sentence as she mouthed.

"I got this."

Nassi allowed the intrusion to see how it might play out, letting Ms. Santos do whatever it was she planned to do but kept his eyes locked in on her as she began.

"Good evening, ma'am. My name is Officer Inez Santos with A.P.D. I don't want to startle you, but something is terribly wrong, and we need help. Reantez Miller had an accident today, and we're trying to get some information from someone he trusts, someone who could help. We don't want to waste our time or yours because every minute at this point counts. We only assumed you to be someone important to him, who might want to help from your text on his phone. We don't mean to inconvenience you, and if you can't help, then all thanks for your time," Inez explained, barely taking a breath but giving the first time to respond.

The short pause of silence was filled by a more humble voice. "Is he okay?" the now tolerable voice asked softly.

"Ma'am, it would be best if we could talk in person," she began looking at Nassi for encouragement.

Nassi nodded, pushing Inez to continue.

"You're not in any kind of trouble, I promise you. If you need to check my credentials, please call the department and give them my name and badge number. They will tell you who I am. The number is," before Inez could start, Queen B had begun giving her the information. Inez formed her lips to say, "Pen, I need a pen." Before Nassi could track one down, Inez stopped Terrance as he passed carrying drinks to someone's table.

Taking one from his apron, she began to write on a large napkin folded on the table. Terrance kept walking after whispering.

"Just hold on to it, honey."

After a few seconds, Inez had written down an address to the location where they could meet up with the Queen Bee. Detective Nassi eyed Ms. Santos, surprised at how unstrained she had made the phone call seem. He took the napkin to look at the address as Inez wrapped up with the

Queen. Looking down to her watch, Inez decided they could be at the residence in the next twenty-five to thirty minutes. After getting Queen B to agree, Inez ended the call, letting out a deep breath.

"That went well," Nassi confessed.

"Yeah, well, sometimes you have to be a female to get the best results," Inez said, smiling.

"Oh my god, you have to be the first female chauvinist I've ever encountered," the detective jokes.

"Shut up and let's go. We got thirty minutes to get to Roswell," Inez said, pulling Nassi out of the booth by his hand.

On their way out, the couple approached Terrance, giving him a hundred-dollar bill to pay for the tab.

"Keep the change," Inez said, patting him on the shoulder.

"Thanks, and come again," the partly framed man insisted.

The two pushed out to the parking lot walking swifter than usual.

"What are you going to do about your car?" Nassi asked curiously. Now realizing the dilemma.

"Can't I park it somewhere close by?"

"Let's drop it off in the parking deck of my loft," Nassi suggested. "It's not far from here, it's safer for your Beamer, and it's on the way," he continued.

Fifteen minutes later, Inez pushed the button on the clicker to secure the doors to her BMW I class. She made a quick stop at her trunk to grab a small gym tote and slung the trunk down, causing a mechanical thud. Making her way to the passenger's side of Nassi's ride, Ms. Santos sat down to a comfortable temperature seat and some smooth R&B playing low from Nassi's sound system. Nassi punched the coordinates into his GPS and began to cruise, waiting for it to lock in the directions. Seconds later, they were en route as the sedan smoothly shifted lanes passing slower moving traffic. Inez continued to examine the contents of Reantez's cell phone on the way. Finding the outgoing texts, she pinpointed what was plainly Reantez's last few messages. They had been to Queen B. The time of the message ranged from 9:45 a.m. until 9:51 a.m. She was able to make out the majority of the back and forth texts, with the exception of a few words that seemed a little coded.

"Nassi, do you have any idea what a K9 is?" Santos asked, looking over to the detective as the lights of the highway they were on rolled up his shirt and off his head.

"Inez, what are you talking about?" he questioned, taking a glance. "I mean, I know what it is to us, but this is some type of coded gang terminology for someone, I think. I've never heard them refer to each other as K9's" Nassi said.

"Look, I'll just read the texts or the last few anyway before the incident and just tell me what you can make of it," Inez suggested.

"Okay, that will work, run it down to me," Nassi said, entertained.

"July 3, 2013, 9:45 a.m. Bay wyd?

July 3, 2013, 9:46 a.m. Was the response from Queen B. Nothing laying in the bed waiting on you to come," Inez cleared her throat, a little ashamed.

"What?" Nassi asked, noticing the shift.

"Beat this pussy up," she continued.

Nassi looked over, shocked like he had heard an invitation.

"NO, the text says waiting on you to come beat this pussy up," she explained.

They both looked to be in some way moved by the wordplay.

"Anyway," Inez continued trying to stay cool, "9:47 a.m. Queen B' wyd and y didn't you call me back last night with a sad emoji face.

9:47 a.m. Reantez "Just smoking a blunt riding down Lucille with big homie on the way to meet up wit the K9's. Sorry, I was tired as hell from White Water, weren't you?'

9:48a.m. Queen B 'yeah, I was, but I still wanted to talk to you, IMU <3. I showed my sister our pics. She's jealous lol.'

9:48 a.m. Reantez' IMU2, after I smoked that blunt, it was over with lol. Tell yo sista quit hating wit her big ass head.'

"Wait," Nassi said. "So apparently Queen B is Kilani from the White-Water screensaver," he began.

Inez agreed with a nod.

"That text was at 9:47 a.m., and he's riding down Lucille with the big homie," Nassi continued.

"Which is probably Kadarai Cunningham," Inez said it with him.

"What time did you have for the transaction at the B.P? Do you recall?" Nassi asked.

"I believe 9:28 a.m., if I'm not mistaken," she answered.

"Okay, roughly seventeen minutes prior to the first text he sent out," Nassi explained.

"It was the B.P. on the Lee Street exit at West End in that same area," he finished.

"So what about the Monte Carlo?" Inez asked.

Aware of what she was getting at, Nassi started. "You can't rule it out or anything yet for that matter," Nassi suggested. "Take, for instance, they are going to meet with the K9's which could probably be the occupants of the Monte," Nassi explained.

"Since we're at it, I thought to do this earlier, but we rushed out before I could mention it," Nassi began. "Go to the pictures again and see if you can get an I.D. on the plate for that car in the background at the park; if so, let's call it in," Nassi suggested, adjusting himself in his seat.

"Oh wow! I can't believe that we haven't done that yet," Inez laughed. "No more drinking for you, buddy," she recommended.

Nassi smiled, happy to have the light-spirited assistance of Ms. Santos on this one, even if she was slightly buzzed.

"That's why we're going to do it now," Nassi said, bringing her to focus.

Inez found a picture showing the plate and zoomed in on it, "Okay, I got it," she began. "Delta, alpha, bravo 483," she said in a more serious tone, evidently able to juggle business and amiableness in one hand.

Nassi called in to dispatch from his car's radio, waiting for a response. Seconds later, dispatch came back over the radio. The vehicle was registered to a Shimiya Edwards of Dekalb County. Detective Nassi was also able to get an address for that name. Ms. Santos jotted the information down on the back of the napkin that she had written Kilani's address down on.

"Well, it's a start," she said, looking out of the window at a passing Honda blacked out by the tint. Inez looked back to the phone and continued reading the text off to Nassi.

After she was done, Nassi concluded that if Kilani was willing to talk, she'd definitely know who this K9 person was because of how uncomfortable she was with Reantez dealing with whoever it was.

"Yeah, you're right," Inez agreed. "And surely it's not someone Reantez or this Big Homie trusts, cause he's saying here he's going along so he can watch the big homie's back," Inez explained.

"I know I shouldn't jump to conclusions, but let's say, Kadarai Cunningham, supposedly this Big Homie, thinks that Reantez is setting him up, gets the jump on him and kills him," Inez said, trying to find a fitting scenario.

'It's possible but unlikely," Nassi explained. "Reread the text," he suggested. "Make sure you didn't omit anything," he continued.

She continued reading them over slower. "To work forensics, you do have a detective train of thoughts, you know," Nassi admired.

"Mmmph," she laughed. "Whaaat! I wanted to be a detective. I just ended up taking a different angle of it in a sense," she explained." Forensics to me is just that, so I still get the outlet of expressing my hidden passion. It's just a little less danger this way; sort of a milder thrill so to speak," she revealed.

The detective glanced up to his rearview mirror then back to Inez. Ms. Santos finished reading the messages, and the two compiled a roster of questions to ask Kilani. It was plain to see she held a good variety of information that would be useful. The more challenging part would be getting her to understand the tragedy that had taken her Teezy bear.

The Laments of Kilani

During the ride, Inez retrieved a pair of Nike running shoes to go along with a matching windbreaker and a well-oiled, immaculately kept baby Glock 9. The earrings had been removed, and the ponytail gave Inez the look of someone in for the ride. The two pulled into a high-end secured community. After checking in, the sedan made its way to a luxurious estate surrounded by a tall gate complete with cameras and a call box. The gate was already open, giving access to a beautiful cobblestone driveway. The yard was plushy green, lit by yard lamps and a majestic light pole.

"Jesus, this is fancy," Inez commented.

"I mean, it's not as big as my place, but hey," Nassi joked, admiring the manicured landscape.

A young-looking female stood from an oversized porch chair on the columned enclosed slab. The driveway did a 360 around a garden of floral arrangements in its center. The big floppy panda bear house shoes bobbed as the girl stepped down from the porch steps. Nassi could tell that her eyes were puffy from his view in the car as she approached, wearing a thick black housecoat.

"Great," Nassi sighed, now able to see plainly that she had been crying.

The girl stopped and wrapped her arms around herself in the yard, waiting for Nassi and Inez to get out. The two exited the vehicle and slowly approached.

"Are you Kilani?" the detective asked, compassionately reaching a hand out to shake.

The girl took hold of his hand and replied, "Yes," in a trembling voice full of fear.

The girl looked terrified. "Where is he?" she asked, hardly able to get the words out unchecked.

Nassi pulled her in for a hug. Inez looked away to keep her emotions in check. Nassi had suffered an insurmountable loss in his family and saw the look in Kilani's eyes that reminded him of that pain, making the big brother in him replace the detective momentarily. It was the embrace he gave that answered Kilani's question. She nearly fell to the ground, weak to the knees from comprehending the message the detective had silently relayed. Inez's head was still turned as she choked back tears of her own, hearing the laments of Kilani growing stronger. Detective Nassi held the girl up, placing his chin on the top of her head, holding tighter in a closed-eyed silence. Inez came over, realizing that the comfort needed to be shifted from herself towards Kilani.

Placing her hand on the girl's back, she rubbed where Nassi's arms had left space. After a while, Kilani lifted her head from Nassi's tear-drenched shirt and asked.

"What happened?" as she took her sleeve to wipe across her face.

Nassi suggested they take a seat, pointing toward the porch. Realizing the gesture, Kilani led the way as Inez followed close behind. Now seated across from one another at a handsomely made outdoor dining set, Nassi began with the details. A few more times during the story, Kilani broke down and hid her head in the folds around the wrist part of her bulky cotton housecoat. She agreed to answer some questions and offered the two refreshments, which they respectfully declined. She informed the detective that the black Monte Carlo belonged to Reantez, and it was in one of the big sisters of the hood's name. Nassi now understood why Kilani's dialect had sounded so artificial earlier. The girl's background was unquestionably, from a wealthy stock, which was also indicated in her use of proper and articulated English; now that they were communicating, it was easy to distinguish.

The 'Big Homie' was, as they guessed, none other than Kadarai Cunningham, who under no circumstances would have done the killing according to Kilani's impression of him. Kilani explained that there was no way that the Monte Carlo had been there since the motor had overheated coming back from the water park yesterday. As far as Kilani knew, the car was still parked at Reantez's grandmother's house, where Kadarai had picked them both up before dropping Kilani home.

"Kilani, can you tell us who K9 is and who they were getting these packs from?" Nassi asked.

"I don't know their names. Just that it's some dudes tied in with the police who get the work from evidence or drug raids or something like that, but they are dangerous because they threatened Kadarai, and he didn't want to deal with them anymore. So Reantez was watching his back when they met," she explained.

Nassi fired another question; looking at Inez, he asked, "Have you ever seen them or heard Reantez describe them?"

"No, but Tezz always calls them some crooked ass crackers," she informed.

Detective Nassi asked a few more questions of the girl before deciding she had been enough help. Preparing to leave, Nassi handed his card over.

"Call me if you hear anything else that may help us '

The girl nodded and took the card, sniffling with tears still coursing her cheeks. Ms. Santos rubbed Kilani's hand, then they departed. Before they could get in the car, Kilani stood there watching, then called to Ms. Santos, needing to tell someone of her news since Tez would never hear of it.

"Ms. Santos," she yelled.

"Yes, sweetheart?" Inez answered.

"I'm pregnant with his baby," she said, placing her hand on her stomach as more tears began to stream.

Inez put a hand up to her mouth as tears puddled in her eyes. Inez walked back to Kilani, giving her another long embrace.

"You'll be a great mother, and he'll be a beautiful child," she predicted.

"Thank you," Kilani replied. "I'm three months, but I know it's a boy."

"I think Reantez knew it too," Inez claimed.

"No, he never," Kilani stopped mid-sentence and balled.

"Yes, sweetie, he knows," Inez claimed. Taking the phone that belonged to Reantez, Ms. Santos sent the clip of a video they had watched earlier about his unborn child to Kilani's phone. The phone in Kilani's housecoat pocket rang as the ring back played. Kilani looked at it, tears glowing in the light of the screen.

"Don't open it until we're gone, Ok?" Inez asked Kilani.

Kilani agreed and took off towards the house. Inez watched, still in sympathy for her until she had been secured behind her door.

Nassi blew the horn, "Let's get out of here."

Inez shook it off and walked to the car, getting in as tears distorted her view of the house from behind the passenger's glass. Nassi brought the car to life, but before putting the Lac in gear, he looked over to Inez, who couldn't seem to pull her eyes away from the house.

"You ok?" the detective asked gently.

Inez took a deep inhale, nodding her head yes in a rapid motion, with a newfound respect for what it took to be a homicide detective. Inez looked over to Nassi, wiping her eyelid with her index finger.

"I'm sorry, it's just," she started.

Nassi cut her off before she could finish. "Shhh," he said, placing a finger on her lips.

"Just use it," he suggested.

Inez blinked a couple of more tears out, nodding in agreement. "Yeah," she whispered, and the two pulled out slowly, allowing a moment of silence to calibrate their agenda.

According to Plan

"It's certain they're still together," the man said into the receiver.

"Good, you know what to do," the raspy voice replied from the other end of the line.

The call ended, and the men who had received their instructions readied themselves to follow through according to plan. The car in their rearview made its pass slowly by the parked Honda, with the occupants trying to look in but to no avail; the tint wouldn't allow it. The men leaned back in their seats so that they wouldn't be seen through the windshield as the unsuspecting motorist drove by. Once the passing car made it out of the neighborhood, the men made their move.

Mah Mah

"Nita, here you go now, please try to eat something," the elderly woman pleaded.

Nita sat in a daze looking off into some other place as the grief closed in on her. Aunt Janice placed the plate on the wooden coffee table next to the sofa. Aunt Janice looked at Nita feeling the anguish of all the sorrow the day had brought. Nita wasn't in any shape to do the household task that her aunt had taken on for her. The other two children, Hakiel and Tara, had been fed and were in for the TV. Tara, the older of the two, had her arms wrapped around Hakiel. At eleven, Tara was sharp and a beneficial resource to her mother, Nita. Hakiel, her eight-year-old half-brother, who would typically be entirely too wild and active to sit still, allowed the comforting of his big sister to soothe his dejected thoughts of what had happened to his little sister Fatimah. Hakiel and Fatimah shared the same father, and had it not been for their age difference would easily go for twins.

Tara's father had taken off not long after she was born. Rather than step up and take on his responsibilities, Tara's father chose, like so many black males in our society, to chase loose women and the next blunt. Nita had been strong in her independence, and she dedicated herself to raising a productive child against all odds. Nita made up her mind that she could do without the help of Tara's father if necessary, and it was obviously necessary. To put it plainly, Ray had done absolutely nothing to contribute to Tara's benefit, while Hakiel and Fatimah's father had been the complete opposite. Besides straddling the fence of legitimacy, Zilla was a good dude. He filled that void in Tara's life like she was his own. Which, as far as she was concerned, was the reality of it. She was his, and he was the only father she knew and needed, for that matter. After a few years, Nita bore Zilla's own biological children, which in turn altered nothing of the relationship he had with Tara. In fact, if anything, it brought them even closer as a family unit.

Tara now sat on the floor rocking with Hakiel, the little brother Zilla had given her, looking back to her mother cemented to the couch paralyzed from the wound in her heart. Tara's feelings were everywhere between anger, fear, and hurt as she thought about the calamity that had torn into their world. Tara also tried to imagine how her father would take the news once he heard it, which was a troubling thought, especially in his predicament.

Zilla had been gone five and half years after becoming state property and now serving a life sentence for a club fight that ended with one man being shot to death in the parking lot. Zilla had actually been the one trying to resolve the conflict between his friend Divine and an old running mate. After blows had been thrown in the club, the chaos spiraled into the parking lot. Divine made it to the car, grabbing his pistol and hurrying back towards where he had seen the man fleeing. Divine chased after him, and Zilla followed, trying to get Divine to fall back. Apparently, one of the guys from the other crew had been prepared for drama too. While Divine chased the fleeing man through the lot, an associate of the other guy stepped from around a jeep knocking Divine's legs from underneath him with a pump. A deep "bloom" rang out, vibrating throughout the lot, causing Divine to fall, dropping his gun. People started screaming and running all over the place, pulling out of the lot in a frenzy as one car almost ran the shooter over. Zilla, by that time, had picked up the gun, and before the man could adjust to finish Divine off, Zilla let three bullets rip at the man's face, "Blam, blam, balm." All three hit the man, dropping him to the side of the jeep. Divine survived, but in the attempt to get him away from the scene, Zilla was detained and charged with the shooting, never making it out of the parking lot. The way the cameras showed it in court, Divine and Zilla looked to be the aggressors, which didn't sit well with the jury. After it was all said and done, Zilla ended up with life without parole, and Divine has a matching sentence with ten tacked on the end of it for good measure.

Since then, Nita and the kids visited every other weekend, supporting Zilla through the whole trial and after. It was only their support that gave Zilla the strength to endure the last five and half years. During that time, Zilla had lost his father, one of his little cousins had been raped, several friends had been killed, and on top of all, his appeals to the courts were denied. Even as bad as all that had been, it could in no way compare to what he would feel now. Fatimah would certainly take the cake, and no one would be anxious to tell him.

Aunt Janice continued to stay at the house after the family mourned. Zilla's sister Shuntiva stayed also. Tiva sat at the dining room table in front of an ashtray with more butts in it than made sense. Tiva started smoking yet another Newport, taking strong pulls like a veteran. Lipstick decorated the filters of most of the butts, which was testimony to how many of them belonged to Shuntiva. A half drank glass of Cognac also occupied a place on the table in front of her as aunt Janice placed a hand across her shoulder, passing on her way to the kitchen.

"Tiva, you sure you don't want a plate either?" she asked, hoping the girls would try to put at least a little bit down.

Tiva got up from the table carrying her glass and followed aunt Janice into the kitchen, blowing smoke into the air.

"No, ma'am," Tiva started. "I can't eat, but I'll help you clean this mess up." Tiva offered.

"That's Ok. Tiva, I got it, sugar. I just wish y'all would try to eat something," aunt Janice pleaded.

Tiva pulled at the cigarette shaking her head. "I can't believe this is actually happening."

Aunt Janice turned from the sink with a coffee cup in her hand to look at Tiva as she expressed her feelings.

"When my brother finds out, he's gonna do something crazy, and I know it," Tiva continued, starting to let her emotions surface again. "I don't want to tell him," she said with her voice beginning to crack.

"I know, baby," aunt Janice consoled as she put the coffee cup back into the dishwater. Aunt Janice rinsed her hands, then dried them on a white and yellow towel hanging from her apron. After drying her hands, aunt Janice took Tiva's free hand and held it. "This is terrible, but right now, you're going to have to be strong for your brother," aunt Janice explained with a stern look as her saggy neck and cheeks shook from the motion her body took as she spoke. "He is going to need someone to give him positive support through this, to remind him how important it is not to make the situation worse," she suggested.

Tiva's shaking hand brought the glass to her lips, and she threw the remainder of the drink back into her throat, wincing afterward at the burn. Aunt Janice took the glass from her, stooping to make eye contact.

"You heard me, child, you must be strong, Nita needs you and Hakiel, and your brother does too."

Tiva lifted her head to meet the elderly lady's eyes, then, before speaking, licked her lips, holding them in a few extra seconds. "Yes, Ma'am."

The two turned, hearing Hakiel as he came to the kitchen door.

"Tee Tiva, can you pour me some more Kool-Aid?" the boy asked, with what looked like a tired expression on his face.

Both women knew better what his demeanor was. The boy was stressed and trying to wrap his mind around what had happened to Fatimah.

"Sure, baby, I'll pour you some, but run and get your bike from outside and bring it in. When you get back, I'll have your drink on the table. Don't forget to wash your hands when you're done," Tiva explained.

"Ok," the boy replied, then was off to do as he was told.

Aunt Janice tightened her grip, nodding to Tiva, then went back to washing dishes after handing Tiva a clean, dry glass for Hakiel's drink.

Hakiel opened the door, getting ready to go and get his bike like Tiva had asked him when Tara stopped him.

"Boy, where you going?" she asked in a demanding tone.

Hakiel looked back like he had done something wrong. Tara's style of speech was motherly, and her stare was intimidating, but he regained his composure.

"To get my bike, Tee Tiva told me to bring it in."

Tara stood up to follow him out, and the two of them exited the door to the porch. Hakiel normally would've jumped straight off the porch into the yard, but his mood only gave him the energy to walk down the four steps around the shrine that had been placed on them for Fatimah. Hakiel looked down to the still burning candles and teddy bears, already missing the sound of his sister's voice.

"Hakiel, can you play with me instead of Jamal today?" a request she had often made sounded in Hakiel's memory.

Tara rubbed Hakiel's back, urging him to move into the yard. Hakiel went towards his bike to pick it up from the sidewalk when he heard Jamal call to him from his yard four houses down.

"Hakiel," Jamal yelled.

Hakiel turned and looked towards Jamal as he approached to see what was going on with his little buddy. Hakiel was only three months older, but he was the more outgoing and aggressive of the two.

"What's up, Jamal?" Hakiel yelled back.

"Are you ok?" Jamal asked, concerned about his partner, as he made his way down to the yard walking funny from his shorts almost falling off him.

135

"Boy, pull your pants up," Tara demanded, being firmer than usual, trying to keep her wet eyes in check.

Jamal struggled to keep from showing whatever was in his pocket, weighing them down, as Hakiel replied.

"Nah, man," he said, almost sounding grown from the sincerity in his voice. "I miss my sister already, and I've been hearing her talking in my head," Hakiel explained.

Tara looked at Hakiel, sympathizing, then decided to give the boys some alone time taking the bike inside herself for Hakiel.

"Don't be out here long, Hakiel," Tara said, sounding like a younger version of Nita.

Hakiel threw his head up at Tara, implying that he understood.

"I'm sorry bout Mah Mah," Jamal said, caringly referring to Fatimah; it was the nickname Jamal had actually come up with that had stuck with her throughout the neighborhood. Jamal came up with it from how Fatimah would always try to boss him around like someone's mother in her own little cute way, and he would miss her too, they all would.

"What's in your pocket?" Hakiel asked, curious as to why Jamal's shorts wouldn't stay up.

"Yeah, about that, I wanted to tell you, but Tara was out here, but I gotta show you something, but not here," Jamal explained.

"What shawty, what is it?" Hakiel pressed.

"We gone have to go in the backyard so nobody can see us," Jamal explained, still trying to get control of his shorts.

"Come on," Hakiel said, leading the way.

The boys quickly went to the backyard and, in the grass behind some stacked-up equipment next to a beat-up station wagon, broken down in the backyard. Jamal couldn't wait. It was already in his hand, shining like a piece of jewelry.

"What the hell you doing with that boy," Hakiel asked as soon as he laid eyes on it. His eyebrows were damn near to his hairline in disbelief.

Jamal looked at Hakiel with a sense of pride, "We gone kill that man that shot Mah Mah when we see him," Jamal promised.

"Give me this damn gun for you hurt somebocy," Hakiel snapped, taking the gun away from Jamal.

"They already locked him up anyway, so quit being stupid," Hakiel continued.

"No, they didn't," Jamal said, frowning in disagreement.

"Yes, they did," Hakiel insisted, getting louder as he grew agitated from the topic alone.

Tiva had heard Hakiel through the window in the kitchen and called out to him.

"Hakiel, boy, what you gone do with this Kool-Aid. do want me to put it in the back of the icebox?" she asked.

137

Caught off guard, Hakiel ducked lower, feeling like he could be seen. He couldn't, but it was instinct, plus the fact that he was in possession of something that would cause him to get the ass whooping of his life should the wrong people find out was plenty good reason to play it safe.

"Yes, Ma'am, you can leave it out. I'm coming," he yelled.

Tiva left the window to fire up another port, taking a seat back in the dining room. Tara, hearing the fuss, decided that Hakiel had been out long enough and took off to go get him.

Meanwhile, Jamal whispered to Hakiel, "Listen, the man who shot Mah Mah hid this gun. Where do you think I got it from?"

Hakiel looked at Jamal, considering the good question he had asked.

"I was in front of Ms. Tammy's house, and I saw everything that happened," Jamal explained, still whispering.

"Hakiel," Tara yelled from the front yard, interrupting. Jamal and Hakiel began to move frantically to hide the gun before Tara found them.

She didn't play, and there was no room for chance-dealing with her. They put the gun in a stash that already held their porn collection and some other miscellaneous contraband inside the station wagon before Hakiel responded.

"Yes, I'm coming."

The boys took off to get as far as they could get away from the gun before Tara closed in on them on the side of the house.

"What y'all doing back there?" Tara interrogated intuitively as a parent.

"Just talking," Hakiel replied, continuing towards the front yard. Tara looked back in the yard, investigating, then followed the boys back to the front.

Tara headed straight for the steps. "Come on, Hakiel," she insisted.

"Alright," he replied, dapping Jamal.

"Hakiel, I know you don't believe me, but I bet he's going to come back looking for it while we're asleep," Jamal predicted. "It was in that car bumper at Mr. Tones' house."

"I'll talk to you tomorrow," Hakiel committed.

"Bet," Jamal agreed, taking off back to his house.

Hakiel looked back over to the skylark across the street from Jamal, squinting his eyes and pondering the truth of what Jamal was suggesting.

"Boy get your butt in this house," Tara demanded after her patience had expired.

Hakiel walked back up the steps taking another look at the shrine as he passed. "I love you, Mah Mah," the boy whispered, patting his hand over his heart.

Trying to Connect Something

The silence had become eerie, and Nassi didn't want Inez to become caught up in her emotions. He needed her alert and detached from those feelings, aware of how they could consume a person should you dwell in them too long. The detective grabbed the remote from the console and changed the low playing R&B to something more energized. Nassi cranked the volume to a blaring as Kendrick Lamar's Faded blasted through the speakers. They were out of the neighborhood and picking up speed headed towards the ramp back to the highway. Inez looked at Nassi with an almost disturbing stare, turning the volume back down. Nassi made eye contact then hunched his shoulders as if he was asking what the hell. Inez shook her head, no, like she was debating something internally.

"What's the matter?" Nassi asked through wanting eyes, eager to jam.

"Nothing, I don't mind the music or anything, I was just thinking," she explained like she was still in thought.

"What is it?" Nassi asked. "Look, I hope you're not getting caught up with emotion about this whole thing. It will only complicate issues," Nassi clarified, assuming he knew what was troubling her.

"No, no, no, it's not that," she began. "Did you pay any attention to that car we passed?" she asked, looking in her side mirror.

"What car?" Nassi asked, turning the music even lower.

"The Honda, the black one right outside Kilani's neighborhood, with the tint we were looking at," she explained.

"Yeah, I remember. What about it?" Nassi asked, hunching his shoulders, wondering what the big deal was.

"It had a raised hood on it made from carbon fiber like the racer type, right?" she questioned, apparently trying to connect something in her mind.

"Yeah, I believe so," Nassi answered. "What about it?" he pressed.

Inez's eyes were glued to the mirrors. Nassi noticed and took a more investigative look for himself as he turned to the ramp.

"I believe I saw that same car earlier," she claimed. "We were on our way to Kilani's, and it pulled up on the side of us, then dropped back casually. It wasn't too odd then, but now that I know it was that same car outside Kilani's neighborhood, it seems a bit fishy, and I believe it's a few cars back."

"What, like right now?" Nassi inquired, sparked by Inez's accusations. Nassi began to search his rearview to catch a visual of the car, but as they merged into traffic on the highway, the big rig behind them blocked his view. Nassi jumped over a lane, then another, trying to be positioned to where he could pinpoint the car she was talking about. There was nothing; either he was too late, or Inez was tripping. Whatever the case, Nassi didn't want to make a fuss and just went with the flow.

"So, what do you think?" Nassi asked, eager to find out why she assumed the Honda was popping up here and there.

"I don't know," she said, sounding irritated.

Nassi didn't want her to feel unsettled, so he attempted to mellow the mood as well as express something he had been contemplating anyway.

"Inez," he started.

"Yeah," she replied in a breathy response, feeling a bit embarrassed.

"I just want you to know that I really enjoyed your company, and I'm glad and thankful you met up with me tonight," he revealed.

"Well, it would be a bit understated for me to say, I enjoyed you too," she admitted smiling beautifully.

"This won't be the last time, will it?" Nassi asked, looking passionately over at the Spanish diva.

"I should hope not," she said enthused.

"Maybe we can do it on a more frequent basis with less distraction," she suggested.

Nassi couldn't help but laugh. Inez was just as interested in him as he was in her, and she didn't try hiding it at all.

"Well, the date that we're almost having has been sort of an emotional rollercoaster. I'm pleased with who I chose to get on the ride with, even if it didn't take your heels to make you tall enough to get on," Nassi joked. "Nah, seriously though, I don't believe there is a distraction strong enough that would cause me to lose sight of how attracted I am to you," Nassi admitted.

Inez rolled her eyes, blushing. "You are so adorable," she complimented, reaching over to rub Nassi's ear lobe.

The chemistry between the two was strong, but how far they were willing to go for each other would be tested by the future in due time.

I Saw It All

Hakiel made it into the house, locking the door behind him. Looking at his mother, he noticed that she hadn't moved a muscle. Tara was heading over in Nita's direction, coming from the kitchen, then found a spot to lay next to her on the couch. Nita's hand found its way into Tara's freshly braided hair as she began caressing the strips of scalp underneath. Nita waved her hand, motioning for Hakiel to come close; naturally, he did while looking into the saddened eyes of the woman who had given him life. Hakiel's heart throbbed as the sentiment set in. Hakiel wrapped his arms around Nita's neck, kissing her on the cheek as he came to stand on the side of the sofa. Nita's eyes slammed shut as a tear crept down the crease of her nose.

"I love y'all," Nita said. It was the first time she had spoken in hours.

The two almost spoke at the same time in reply.

"I love you too, Mama." Nita threw her free arm around Hakiel, and the three held on tight, letting the energy of the moment generate through their bodies, as Tiva and aunt Janice watched from the dining room table.

Tiva's eyes filled instantly as she sat there quietly bearing witness to the bond Nita and her children shared. Nita's aunt looked on, praying that all their pain be eased as well as for Fatimah's peace. Realizing there would definitely be many more nights to come when the lord would have to provide that much-needed comfort. After a few hours, mostly everyone had made it to bed. Tara tossed and turned in her sleep having vivid flashes of her little sister as her consciousness danced from a dream state and back. Aunt Janice had retired too, lying peacefully in the guest room, giving her worn body a well-deserved break from the day's activity.

Meanwhile, Tiva drank herself into a deep and heavy slumber, laying her large frame on the couch in the basement as the quiet storm played low from the radio next to her. As for Nita, she still hadn't managed to bring herself to rest. She sat in the living room, watching the last of the larger candles flicker outside in the twilight breeze from the living room window. Hakiel couldn't sleep either; he sat perched in his window upstairs above the living room in the quiet, dark area while his thoughts reflected on Jamal's accusations. Hakiel visualized the shiny gun he held earlier while thinking he needed to find out what Jamal had seen.

If, in fact, they did arrest the wrong man, it meant the killer was still out there and was going unpunished. Although Hakiel was young, he knew to some degree the code of the hood, and in his mind, he thought; *maybe it would be better that the killer be sentenced by the judges who held court in the streets. If anyone could get it done, his father would with no question, or maybe even he would,* he thought.

Outside, a few cars passed at intervals, some letting their music pound and tick up the block when Hakiel noticed a car's headlights slowly making their way down the street. The driver killed the lights a few houses before making it in front of Mr. Tones, which piqued Hakiel's interest.

"I bet he'll come back looking for the gun while we're sleeping," Jamal's voice said in Hakiel's memory. Hakiel positioned himself to get a better look, staring intently at what was playing out outside his window. A few seconds later, a white man in dark clothing emerged from the still-running vehicle, moving swiftly towards the same Skylark Jamal had pointed out. Hakiel knocked a game controller off the small shelf just below the window, trying to inch closer by accident. The controller clapped loudly on the hard floor, just missing the Atlanta Falcon rug that stretched toward his bed.

"Shit!" Hakiel whispered, hoping he hadn't disturbed anyone in the quiet house.

Meanwhile, the man outside the window was in a panic, moving as if something was terribly wrong and missing.

146

Hakiel concluded what the man's trouble must have been and that Jamal had been right all along. Hakiel's anger blazed inside, thinking since Jamal had been right this far, then he knew what he was talking about. That meant Fatimah's killer wasn't behind bars but right outside now in plain sight. Hakiel's mind raced a thousand miles per second cluttered with ideas, consequences, and revenge. With his heart pounding in a fury, Hakiel made up his mind and knew exactly what he would do regardless of what kind of repercussions would ensue. Hakiel turned from the window in a hurry, ready and willing to go and handle his business to avenge his sister when he was met by a starting deterrent.

Nita stood in his doorway looking like a guardian angel that had been crying for humanity since mankind's fall from grace. Her eyes were deep and penetrating yet full of compassion and love. Her dark shoulder-length hair draped down the sides of her hollow face. At the same time, her high yellow complexion was slightly illuminated from the dim light of the bathroom in the hall.

"You ok, sweetheart?" she asked in a tone so caring. Hakiel looked up.

However, the rage was still pumping through his veins.

"Mamaa," Hakiel said, struggling, not knowing how or if to tell his mother what was going on. The thought of upsetting her weighed heavy on his faculties, but he couldn't let the man get away, he thought.

"What is it, baby?" Nita asked, walking close to Hakiel, noticing his heavy breathing. Nita reached out to touch Hakiel's face. The suspicions of his temperament she felt his chest to find his heart on the verge of jumping out, it seemed. She rushed to the light switch, flickered it on, then back to Hakiel.

"Baby, it's ok," she said. "I know, baby," she continued, sure that he was missing Fatimah and upset about it.

True indeed, she was exactly right, but the magnitude of what was going on inside of her son eluded her. Hakiel forced himself to say something before the man slid away unpunished.

"Mama," Hakiel said, grabbing her hands from his body. "Come look," he said, pulling her to the window just as he was getting in the car. "That's the man that shot Mah Mah," Hakiel explained with urgency in his tone as he pointed.

Nita had missed his face, but the way the car sped off did strike her as odd. However, the pain of what she was hearing took more of her attention studying the speeding vehicle.

"Baby no," she cried, sobbing over Hakiel with both hands now on his face, thinking that Hakiel's agony was taking a toll on his thought process.

Hakiel was furious. The man was getting away, and he didn't know how to get his mother to believe him but showing her the gun was definitely out of the question at this point. Nita misinterpreting his expressions, continued.

"We gone make it through this baby, I promise, I know you miss her, I do too Kiel, lord knows I do," she continued. "Let it out, baby. I'm here. Go ahead and let it out," she said while giving him a comforting embrace," so she thought anyway. The truth was; the affection was much needed and a soothing sentiment, but Hakiel's feelings wouldn't allow that comfort to form. He was too angry, and revenge was clouding his thoughts. Nita sat him on the bed, taking a seat next to him. Nita pushed Hakiel's head down into her lap. As he gave in to his emotions, unable to do anything else about what he knew. There was nothing left, no way to pull off his plan, so he did the only thing that he could. Full of all those feelings mixed into confusion, agony, and hate trying to pull his mind from the perplexing dilemma at hand got the best of him, and so he cried hard. Nita began rocking, humming a song that had always eased him, which was his dad's favorite. Nita's tears rolled down her cheeks as the melody of Mary J. Blige, "My Life," filled the room.

Hakiel laid there listening to the tone until the world surrounding him drifted away into darkness.

Trail of Blood

A fter some stimulating conversations, Detective Nassi and Officer Santos pulled past the guard station and into the parking deck of Nassi's place. There wasn't much action at that hour, except for a group that Nassi immediately recognized. The four people were getting out of a white Infiniti truck with rose gold accessories and thirty-inch rose gold rims. Fat Louie V. Nassi's neighbor and his nephew were joined tonight like most nights by Fat Louie's group Young and Flashy, the girl duo. Fat Louie was about thirty, and his nephew was in his early twenties. The two girls were at least twenty, dressed scantily but at least covered to some degree. The two men both wore t-shirts promoting the record label with hats to match. Fat Louie donned a humongous charm on a belly-length bangle link with the same logo as the shirt. The younger male, his nephew, wore a smaller chain encrusted with ice. The group was now at the back of their truck, removing some small boxes containing flyers, talking and laughing. At the same time, the nephew moved about in a drunken stupor. He was apparently the reason behind the group's laughter, carrying on with his jesting. Nassi pulled in, slowly parking in his space, as Inez collected her things. It was agreed that she'd spend the next few hours sobering up. Nassi turned the car off as the sunroof slid into the grooves allowing it to close securely, as the laughter outside faded away almost into a mute.

"Are you sure it's ok, Nassi?" Inez started. "I wouldn't want to get you in any trouble with anybody." She asked, explaining her question.

Nassi just looked at her in silence, unable to resist, reached over, giving Ms. Santos a soft kiss on her cheek. Her hands grabbed at the side of his face pulling him into a deep french as he pursued her succulent bottom lip. The two went in deeper, savoring the long-awaited moment while caressing each other. Just as things began to flow, all hell broke loose. A speeding car slammed on its brakes right behind Nassi's Cadillac as two assailants jumped out holding sub machines, already letting loose. Nassi and Inez had just enough time when they noticed to get to the floorboard as the men exited the Honda. Inez had been right; it was the same Honda she claimed was following them. Nassi felt ridiculous for doubting her, as he looked under himself to make sure she was alright. Bullets tore through the back window and into the seats they had occupied seconds ago. Fragments of the seats leather and glass ripped away with bullets inching closer to the couple. Nassi drew his weapon, hardly able to move from the awkward position he had been forced into. Inez's tiny frame could tuck down into the space under the dash.

However, Nassi could only lay across, shielding her as more fire thumped away right above him into the vents and lower windshield. A different ring of shots clapped from some other direction as one of the men yelped in pain.

"The fuck man?"

Nassi couldn't make out what was going on, but he had armed himself by that point, ready to capitalize on the distraction. Nassi returned fire holding his gun above, licking shots toward the rear left and right between the seats. Inez's ears rang from the thunderous boom of Nassi's cannon. Shells bounced from his firearm against the surface of different objects of the car's interior. Nassi took a quick peek, noticing the shooters had taken cover. The detective took advantage of the moment by popping Inez's door to make an exit. Sticking his pistol out, Nassi clapped two blind shots out of the door, then took a look; there was nothing. Just as Nassi began to exit, he ducked back in as a drum roll of shots pounded out of someone's gun. Nassi could hear the girls screaming as the shots continued. Nassi got out, staying low to the ground. He placed a hand on Inez's shoulder.

"You ok?" he asked quietly.

She shook her head yes, nodding quickly and nervously.

Satisfied, Nassi laid on the ground looking under the car for feet, he didn't see anybody, but he did notice a trail of blood leading away from the back of his car. Nassi stood up in a half crunch when another shot tore through the once quiet parking lot "Bloom" That shot silenced one of the girls who had been making a fuss as the other yelled.

"Meesha," in a high-pitched panic.

Nassi stood all the way up, rounded the car swiftly, making his way to the Honda. The vehicle was unoccupied. The detective looked over to the Infiniti truck where the younger male who had been humoring the rest of his party lay twisted to the side with his gun still in hand. The boy looked like he was still in pain, torn down by the hail of bullets. Nassi went back to get Inez when she met him halfway with her gun drawn. Nassi took two fingers pointing to his eyes without saying a word then, with his index finger, made a circular motion in the air. Inez understood, nodding with a militants glare in her eyes, gripping her weapon tight.

The two tactically moved through the parking lot, securing each other and their surroundings. They made it over to the Infiniti truck, where Nassi checked the pulse on Fat Louie's nephew. He was already gone; Nassi closed the young man's eyelids then moved on. Inez, close behind to where Young sat, holding Flashy in her arms, trying to keep her conscious. Flashy had a hole through her half-exposed breast, which was spilling out onto her partner, Young, and onto the concrete. Young tried stopping the pour with her hand, but it was seeping through the cracks.

"Bloom Bloom." More shots rang out from the lower deck in the exit direction.

"Stay here," Nassi instructed Inez as he swapped clips.

The detective took off running toward the lower deck hopping over the concrete divider, shortening his travel, before picking back up on the trail of blood. A burst of rounds sprayed through the glass a few feet away as Nassi caught a glimpse of his neighbor before he slid down the side of a car, clutching his stomach. Nassi saw the two assailants scrambling towards a dark-colored Impala, with one of them moving like he had been injured. Nassi fired on them, thumping the uninjured man in the back twice, and he fell against the Impala.

The driver got out with an assault rifle running around to cover for his friends. The magazine dumped round after round in Nassi's direction as he fell to the ground taking cover, still able to see his neighbor. Nassi crawled over to his neighbor big Louie to check on him. He was hit up pretty bad, but he would make it. Once the opportunity presented itself, Nassi raised back up to get some shots off when a rain of bullets continued to drum, breaking the cars between Nassi and the shooter down to the axel.

When the fire finally stopped, it was followed by the squealing of rubber burning as the car sped away. Nassi popped up running on foot, dumping the remainder of his clip at the fleeing vehicle as an explosion of glass fell to the ground like confetti from where Nassi hit the window. The Impala turned off fishtailing, leaving Nassi in the dust. Nassi waved at the smoke and dust in a futile attempt to clear it away from his face walking back to the lot.

Sirens in the distance, not so far away, could be heard approaching. Nassi helped Fat Louie up and began walking him towards the exit to meet the ambulance when he noticed that the lot's guard had been shot in the face and laid slumped over the control panel. Nassi concluded that he had been hit with a silencer; otherwise, they would have heard. Nassi apologized to Fat Louie about his nephew and explained that he would run back to their deck to check on Flashy and Inez.

Once Nassi made it to where Inez and the two girls were, it was apparent what Flashy's condition was. Nassi dropped his head after seeing the girl's head leaned to one side as Young held her, drenched in her best friend's blood. Inez got up and held her hands out, one still holding her pistol.

"What the hell was that?" she asked, obviously pissed and rattled.

Ms. Santos had fired her weapon in training, but this was a completely new ball game, the side of the job she didn't want to experience. Nassi shook his head.

"I don't know," he answered, kneeling close to Flashy checking her vials.

Young's head pressed against Flashy's, crying and sniffling at her girl's condition. Sirens were bellowing on the lower deck with more on the way.

Meanwhile, Nassi imagined how the captain would jump down his throat at the mess, three dead, one injured, and no leads as if he didn't have enough to deal with already. Nassi looked over to Young, feeling for her but needing some kind of catalyst to help him understand what had just happened.

"Young, can you tell me what you saw?" Nassi asked, being patient and understanding of how she must feel.

Nothing could have prepared him for what happened next.

"I seen the same fucking thang you seen shawty, them niggas pulled up trying to kill yo police ass, and Louie and his nephew tried saving you," she spat with saliva connecting the roof of her mouth to the bottom. "Now look," she yelled, crying a steady flow from her tear ducts. "You got my girl killed and Louie's nephew, cause whatever the fuck you got going on with the Bloods," she continued with hate in her eyes, blaming Nassi. "This shit is your damn fault. I wish Louie would've just let them burn yo pig ass," Young cried.

Inez felt terrible hearing how the girl went off on Nassi but let her have her feelings. Nassi ate every word respecting where Young was coming from and familiar with being the reason as she reflected on a time before. Oddly enough, similar, yet a little more personal.

Nassi allowed the blame to attach itself to him like an alien looking for a host. After a couple of hours passed, Nassi had undergone the harshest ass chewing of his career. Saw Fat Louie off to the hospital and reviewed some footage from what the parking lot cameras revealed to him; a familiar black shirt with a Nike check under the collar. Nassi was also convinced that the men had shown the guard some kind of credentials, making him comfortable enough to open the gate; shortly after, they shot him. Inez had been paged to come into work until, of course, it was found out that she had actually been a victim in the shooting as well. Captin Brendaunt found plenty to say about that and gave Nassi twenty-four hours to get a full detailed report on his desk, including a good enough reason of, "Why the fuck evidence was being removed from the crime scenes," which were his exact words.

The short captain had a way with words, which Nassi thought of him as a black version of Tony Soprano on crank. Nassi revealed that the phone had given some helpful leads and that he had asked Officer Santos for some assistance. Captain blew a head gasket threatening Nassi's job, and I quote, "One more hair on his ass was raised from the wind off some more bullshit Nassi had stirred up he could turn in his badge and gun" end quote. The captain explained that he wanted this shift brought to a silence so that he could hear a rat pissing on cotton in this town. Nassi knew that would be just as complicated as it sounded but agreed anyway to get things under control.

Nassi was now sitting in his man cave of a living room, planning his next move, already tired of the domino effect causing such unrest in his would-be stress-free life. After all, things were just now starting to heal, he thought as Young's words continued stabbing at his heart. The truth is, the job sometimes pulled a lot out of him, but never to this extent. Shit was completely out of control, and weird wasn't the right word to describe it at this point. *This was some far-out shit, or somewhere along those lines*, Nassi thought, exhaling. It was getting thick, and bodies were being sent to the morgue same day delivery like company mail. At the same time, Nassi sat trying to find the address to return to the sender. Things were pointing at the gangs, but then again, this wasn't their norm, and Nassi would know that best. When they viewed the footage from the cameras in the parking lot, Nassi noticed that the men were not like average bangers.

The stance when they shot and their posture when moving with their weapons wasn't how Nassi had seen bangers in action. True enough, except for some who were ex-military or trained from some other involvement, you'd get that. Still, as Nassi saw it, it was rare to get three moving in unison like these guys did. Whoever they were and whatever their goal was, Nassi looked to put a stop to it and quickly.

First, on the agenda, Nassi decided that he would pay Kadarai a visit down at Rice Street, then back to the crime scene of the active affiliates he was familiar with. Inez came into the living room quietly drying her hair wearing a Chattam and Ilakin T-shirt promoting Nassi's construction company, along with long socks from his sock drawer that only fit so snugly because they were new. Nassi looked at a poster on his wall that read:

"*The future as I see it by Marcus Garvey; It comes to the individual, the race, the nation. Once into a lifetime to decide upon the course to be pursued as a career. The hour has now struck for the individual Negro as well as the entire race to decide the course that will be pursued in the interest of our liberty. We who make up the Universal Negro Improvement Association have decided that we shall go forward, upward, and onward toward the great goal of human liberty. We have determined among ourselves that all barriers placed in the way of our progress must be removed, must be cleared away, for we desire to see the light of a brighter day. The Philosophy of Marcus Garvey.*"

While reading many times before, Nassi felt the drive in him come alive. He desired better for his people, and he was fed up with the loss of lives in the black community, sincerely wanting in some way to make a difference. Nassi's eyes shifted to another poster in the room. The poster was of black leaders past and present with everyone from Nat Turner to Barack Obama. Nassi thought of how far they have come as a people, but yet it all seemed to be nothing. The roles had been reversed; they had become their own oppressors to some degree and were carrying out a systematic plan devised by something far greater than any celestial human being could've developed. The rim and wreckage were putting a rift between the people causing their defense to weaken. Most were too intoxicated or high to be a factor, while others found reason to celebrate the fact that they had made a few dollars inducing their minds to blow it on more of the products and merchandise that would never benefit them. Yet their only honest thought would be that they would ball out. Malcolm X's eyes stared back at Nassi with a finger up to his temple like he was asking Nassi telepathically what he would do to bring forth change.

Nassi's brain raced through flashes of the deaths that had come over the last twenty-four hours, submerging him in an ill mood. Inez stood admiring Nassi from the doorway of his room.

"Are you going to get some sleep or what?" she asked, coming around to flop down on the sofa next to him.

She sat Indian style as a fresh scent flared from her body, taking Nassi away from his musing. She was gorgeous in her natural look to the point that anything she added was complimented by her and not the other way around.

Nassi's eyes followed the contour of her visible shape, intrigued by how much woman she was.

"Yeah, I'll go get a shower, then get a few hours, I guess," Nassi answered.

"Yeah, you need one bad," she joked.

"So why do you think the Bloods are trying to kill you?" Inez asked, keeping the situation relevant.

"I'm not so sure it's them," he explained.

After explaining his reasoning, Nassi revealed his agenda, then got up to get a move on. Nassi grabbed his V-neck from the arm of the couch to throw it in the laundry hamper. Inez examined his upper body or what was left exposed from what the tank top hadn't covered. Nassi walked toward the laundry room off the kitchen, still under heavy observation as Inez found herself turned on by his muscular tone.

"You know I wouldn't have minded," she said, letting her thoughts escape her lips.

"Minded what?" Nassi asked before gulping some juice out of a carton he'd found in the fridge.

"Us taking a shower together," she revealed as her finger lightly stroked across her exposed thigh.

Nassi hadn't noticed due to his back still being turned to her.

"Really," he said, now turning. "That would've been nice. Fine time to tell me," he said sarcastically, too late to catch his body language. "Well, maybe next time," he continued placing the carton back on the fridge shelf.

"Maybe," she asked, full of attitude. "There's no maybe to it," she demanded, clear of what she wanted.

Nassi pulled his tank off as she spoke, putting it in the hamper along with his socks. Inez stopped short of whatever she had planned to say, watching him strip down to a pair of boxers, laying his pants in a bag that would make it to the cleaners at some point.

"Ummph," she moaned a little louder than secretly; Nassi picked up on it, asking.

"Is that a good ummph or a bad one?"

Inez sucked at her teeth before answering, "Let's see how good of a detective you are and figure it out," she said, working her charm.

"I have such a demanding caseload I'm working on right now. I don't know if I have the strength," Nassi explained more honestly than playing.

Watching the muscles tone in his back as he closed the laundry room door, Inez pushed.

"Yes, you do, boy," in an overly convincing tone.

Nassi walked back towards the bathroom with a fresh towel he'd grabbed while in the laundry room, giving Inez another eye full before the walls blocked her view. Nassi disappeared into the shower, still talking.

"How can you be so sure?" he asked loud enough for Inez to hear before turning the water on.

Inez got up from the couch, feeling the clump spot saturating the grey boy shorts she wore as her labial area produced wetness, bringing a caving to her vaginal muscles that were becoming a little hard to ignore. Inez stalked towards the bathroom, thinking how they say sharing a traumatic experience with someone strengthens the attraction. Debating this truth, Inez watched, wondering what was coming over her. She wasn't exactly sure if that was what it was or not, but she was positive about one thing; she wanted Nassi, and she wanted him now.

As she stood in the doorway to the bathroom, Inez put two fingers flush against her vaginal lips and pressed at it while her thighs enclosed her hand, squeezing it in tightly. Nassi's silhouette was easily seen through the steamy shower door giving Inez more fuel to act on her impulses. Nassi had left the door to the bathroom open; like an invitation, she justified, as she slipped off the socks and t-shirt.

"So, are you gonna answer or what?" Nassi asked, still yelling, thinking that Inez had stayed put in the living room. He had no idea she was in the bathroom because the first thing he did upon entry was soap his face and hair, which was so full of suds.

Inez's perky nipples became hard as her mind took off, playing out what would be happening in the near future, taking her still wet hair down from the ponytail. Inez grew goosebumps as the excitement tingled her insides. Inez rubbed the circumference of her fully exposed breast, then down her hips slipping the wet boy shorts out of the folds of lip she had mashed them into.

"Let's just call it an educated guess," she answered, sliding the shower door back.

Nassi began to stiffen slightly just from the sound of Inez's voice being that close to his nude body. Inez noticed it quickly and reached down, assisting its rise as Nassi washed the soap from his face. Before he could get his face completely clear, a pair of lips captured him, sucking away at his bottom lip as a warm, smooth moving tongue softly entered his mouth, bringing his heart to a wild beat. Nassi's hands gripped the bottom cuff of Inez's voluptuous ass cheeks, lifting her with ease, then slid her slowly back down on his manhood, reaching for something deep inside her. Something far beyond the physical.

Just Do It

"Listen, you retarded fuck, I don't care what you have to do, just get it done!" the raspy-voiced man growled through the phone.

"It doesn't make sense to me how some finger-licking, greasy-faced hip hop detective was able to put the slip on your so-called rained professional jarhead sons of bitches. Can you explain that cause I'm having a hard fucking time understanding?" he asked, furious about the failed attempt on the detective's life.

"Firebird sir, we...," Puma started.

"We what?" Firebird interrupted.

"Well, we," Puma attempted to explain again before being cut off.

"Well, what? Well, nothing, you fucking idiot, there is no explanation," Firebird snapped. "A well is where they are going to end up finding your pathetic ass chopped in tiny pieces floating around if you don't get this shit under control and now. I want that fucking porch monkey Kadarai's ass dead too before his arraignment. No excuses, just do it!" He continued growling. "Do you have any idea what I have to deal with while you fucks are wrestling with these simple tasks? Huh, do you? The gun is gone, by the way, in case I forgot to mention." Firebird explained, revving himself. Do you understand how fucked that makes my predicament?" He asked, sounding like he was turning red.

Puma couldn't get a word out as his boss continued to blast obscenities and degrading comments through the line.

"Do you? No, you don't, because you dim wits are too busy fucking up to realize what can happen if this shit is not handled. Now get your shit together or prepare yourself to be on leave of duty permanently, and that goes for Coyote too. Do you fucks understand?" Firebird asked, sounding calmer now than he had the whole call.

"Sir, yes sir," the men answered. Coyote had been listening over the speakerphone, sucking a cigarette down to the fiberglass.

Coyote's wounds had been stitched after the bullets were dislodged from his leg and arm. The vest he had worn did nothing to cover those regions of his body, leaving his vulnerable spots open to gunplay. Puma only had a few bruises on his back where the detective struck him in the back of his vest, making him upset that he hadn't killed him at the restaurant. A buzzing noise sounded. Puma got up, walking past a row of crates and the green Durango. The warehouse was dark except where the workstation was lit by a halogen lamp hanging directly behind it. Puma looked at the cameras to see who was flinging. Noticing his colleagues standing side-by-side awaiting entry. Puma quickly stepped over to the garage door and unlocked the latch, rolling it up halfway, allowing the two men to enter.

Puma shook both of their hands, then closed the door back down, securing it. The team walked back towards the workstation, where a few folding chairs occupied the space near Coyote.

"Firebird is pissed," Puma explained. "So we can't get any more mishaps," he continued. "He wants Kadarai dead before arraignment, whenever that is. Assuming it's soon, we need to get moving and get our contacts in the county jail in position. As for the detective, our plan has to be foolproof because we can't get another shot, plus it still has to look like the red team. Puma pulled some papers out from a tote bag, placing them on the workstation's surface.

"Let's get down to business."

From His Bleeding Heart

"A FATHER'S GRIEF" by Kendale Mahone

"Today I awoke, all was on my mind was regret, I risked it all and lost the bet. Please forgive me. My selfish acts affected far & close; Lord knows I've never intended to hurt. I love y'all the most; please believe me. I'm sorry for not being there; I'm guilty of leaving you. There's nothing I wouldn't do to earn you again. There's plenty that I would do. There are no excuses, I know I shall suffer for my sins, but God knows I made a mistake, and mistakes are made among men. Every prayer, I ask not my sins be a burden upon anyone else because it was only selfish of me to think of myself. A life is gone, hearts are broken. Children un-fathered because of me and my stupidity. There is so much sorrow. I know the feeling I have the same it questions my heart. I caused the pain."

Hakiel woke up still in his mother's arms; she had finally given in to exhaustion, allowing her fatigued body to get some much-needed rest. Hakiel slipped out of her grasp, smelling the aroma of sausage and eggs coming from downstairs. Getting out of bed, he tripped over a few scattered toys yet maintained his balance as he continued on to the bathroom, eyes half-opened. He took a swipe at his face before lifting the toilet seat, then relieved himself. After finishing, he flushed then turned to the sink, twisting the knob for the cold water. Looking for the soap, he noticed it had been moved. Sure of where it would be, he moved over to the tub pulling the shower curtains back, then saw several of Fatimah's toys lying in the bottom. Others were also scattered about the sides and hanging from the soap shelf staring back at Hakiel as if they were conscious of Fatimah's absence. Hakiel grabbed the soap taking a deep breath to gain some calm, touched by the saddening reminders lying unanimated yet colorful against the cold porcelain. Hakiel snatched the curtains back closed as a shiver ran through his body. He walked back to the sink to wash his hands, then brushed his teeth after looking at himself in the mirror. Seeing Fatimah staring back at him, Hakiel blinked forcefully.

They resembled each other so much it seemed to him that his eyes were hers making him no longer want to look at himself. Their features were identical and would be a constant reminder throughout the rest of Hakiel's days. He quickly finished his business and decided to pick up his toys, saving his mother from the hassle. Afterward, he walked over to the window to look over at Mr. Tone's car. It was abnormally quiet outside for a summer morning. There weren't any kids out playing or doing the usual. It was like life had been sucked out of the neighborhood.

Hakiel looked back over to his mother, noticing how she looked to be grieving even in her sleep. Hakiel's mental wheels started turning again as the vengeance seeped back into his heart from its overnight resting place. With his mood shifted back to where he'd been last night. His face became serious and determined as he left his mother to rest, quietly leaving the room.

The guest room was tidy, and back like no one had ever slept there. Aunt Janice was up and about, causing those savory fumes that gave the whole house that mouthwatering smell, Hakiel concluded. Making it downstairs, Hakiel followed his nose to find Tara helping aunt Janice in the kitchen. Tara was buttering some biscuits fresh out of the oven singing with aunt Janice.

"Good morning, handsome," aunt Janice said, greeting Hakiel with a smile.

Hakiel wasn't convinced as to whether or not this morning was good but replied anyway to avoid being rude.

"Mornin auntie," he said, not sounding excited.

Tara looked at him understanding his tone, and tried to lighten his mood some.

"Hakiel, come taste my biscuits," Tara said, taking one off the pan and placing it on a saucer.

Hakiel came close, watching as Tara took a butter knife, opening the smoking layers of dough through the middle.

Once opened, she sliced a square of butter from a stick already out and soft, then topped it with a spoon of Welch's grape jam closing the top piece of the biscuit back on. Tara handed the saucer to Hakiel. He took it, then bit into the fluffy golden bread, dropping jelly on his chin as the melted butter mixed with a smile, knowing it was good as Hakiel devoured the soft piece of dough.

"Dang, slow down, boy," Tara said, amused by how much he was enjoying it.

"Go sit down. I'm gone fix you a plate," Tara said, feeling proud.

Aunt Janice smiled at the two of them as Hakiel sat at the table waiting patiently. A knock sounded at the door shortly after. Hakiel turned his head to look out the window in the dining room to see if a car had pulled up but didn't see one. By the time the doorbell rang, Hakiel was already up and on his feet.

"Sit down, Kiel. I got it," Tara demanded. She skipped past Hakiel with him deciding to follow anyway.

"Who is it?" Tara asked in an aggravated tone.

"It's me, Mal, Tara," Jamal said from the other side of the door.

"He is eating!" she snapped, leaving the door closed as she walked away.

Hakiel watched as Tara went back to the kitchen, tripping on her nerves. Hakiel opened the door himself.

"What's up Mal?" Hakiel asked his partner.

Mal gave Hakiel that look as I told you so, then asked, "Did you see him?"

Hakiel looked over his shoulder, then back to Jamal, nodding, knowing precisely what Jamal was talking about. Hakiel opened the door wider for Mal to come in, holding his finger to his mouth not to say anything about what they knew.

"Hey y'all," Jamal said, speaking to aunt Janice and Tara.

Aunt Janice was the only one to speak back. "Good morning Jamal," she said, sounding sweet as always. "Would you like something to eat?" she asked.

"No, ma'am. I'm ok, thank you," Jamal said politely, taking a seat at the table with Hakiel.

Just as the boys settled in their seats, Nita came down the steps wearing a robe, still looking tired, and cried out.

"Hey Mrs. Johnson," Jamal greeted, noticing her first from his seat.

"How you doing, Jamal?" she asked, sounding hoarse but pleased to see him.

"Fine," he replied respectfully to the one who had been like a second mother to him.

"Hey, mama," Hakiel spoke, turning to look back at his mother as she approached.

Once she made it close enough, she bent slightly to kiss his forehead. "Hey, baby."

Hakiel made it easier for her by lifting his head into the kiss, just as Tara came out of the kitchen holding his plate. Noticing Nita, she spoke.

"Hey Ma," while placing the plate on the table in front of Hakiel.

"Hey pooh," Nita replied, touching Tara's cheeks.

"We made breakfast, mama. You want some?" Tara asked, hugging her mother around the midsection.

"You made breakfast? That was so nice of y'all," Nita admitted. "Sure, baby. I'll have some," Nita said, walking into the kitchen to make coffee.

Aunt Janice put a kiss on Nita's cheek. "Well, how are you, my favorite niece?" she asked before grabbing Nita a mug.

Nita shook her head, saying what words couldn't. "Hurting, auntie, but they keep me going," Nita said, looking down at Tara pouring some already brewed Folgers into the mug she had taken from her mother's grip.

"Momma, try to relax. I'll bring the coffee to the table ok,"

Aunt Janice nodded, understanding Nita's comment.

Tara hurried about the kitchen, gathering creamer and sugar to take to the table. Nita didn't protest; instead, she found a seat at the table with the boys; then, the phone rang.

Before Nita could get up, Tara was already on her way to grab it, dropping Nita's smoking mug of coffee off on her way. By the third ring, Tara made it to the glass lamp that stood on the far side of the sofa, snatching the cordless from the base. Tara pressed the talk button and answered to hear a familiar yet disheartening voice.

"Hello," she answered into the receiver.

Her eyes grew large in fear as remorse took hold of her body.

"Hey Lil mama, how you doing?" Zilla asked, sounding excited on the other end.

Tara was quiet for a second, reluctant and nervous before pushing herself to speak; with a noticeable quiver in her tone, she answered. "Hey, daddy," while looking over to Nita.

Nita's eyes slammed shut as her mouth opened, raising her tongue to the roof of her mouth as the moment she had been dreading fell upon her. Within seconds, that face contorted into yet another painful-looking expression.

"Happy fourth of July, sweetie. What y'all gonna do today?" Zilla asked, still sounding happy.

Nita took a teary glance up to the ceiling blinking hard, trying to control her tears.

"Ummm, nothing, sir," Tara answered, overwhelmed, not knowing what to say.

Nita gathered enough strength to get up and go to the phone as Tara struggled on through the conversation.

"Nothing? What, no fireworks?" Zilla asked, sounding shocked but still unaware. "Where's your brother and sister? I can't believe I don't hear them fighting in the background." Zilla asked, curious as to why it was so quiet.

Just then, Nita made it to the phone, taking it from Tara, who was now in tears as well as Nita.

"Aziel," Nita spoke into the phone, reluctant to continue with what had to be done.

"Hey, beautiful, what's good with my earth?" Zilla asked, sensing something but still clueless.

"Aziel, I got some terrible news, and there is no easy way to say it," Nita explained, forcing the words to unchoke from her vocal cords.

"What's wrong, love?" Zilla asked, in the blind as to how devastating the blow would be.

"Aziel, Fatimah's gone," she revealed, breaking down after barely being able to get it out.

"Gone where ma?" Aziel questioned loudly, trying to wrap his mind around what was being said. Knowing it couldn't be good from how Nita sounded, Zilla still couldn't grasp what she meant precisely and became instantly frustrated. "Yo, Nita, what the fuck you talking about ma gone where?" Zilla pressed.

Nita was still breaking down, crying all over the phone, still trying to explain through her hoarse and cracking voice. "Aziel, Fatimah was shot yesterday morning; hit by a stray bullet while we were outside cleaning the porch. Our baby's gone," she wailed, sounding unexplainably hurt, full of sorrow and heartache.

"No, no, no, you bugging Nita," Zilla contested in disbelief. "Put Timah on the phone, yo," Zilla demanded, denouncing Nita's words. Zilla used all his might internally to make the situation into something else, bringing his mind to a blur, unable to accept Nita's accusations.

Nita balled, using her hand to lower herself while holding on to the back of the couch. The muscles in Nita's stomach clenched and contracted tighter as her cries escaped her diaphragm. Hakiel left his seat, now standing in the living room watching his mother. By the time she made it to the floor, he was by her side, hugging her tight with Tara attached to her other side, whimpering from the hurt inside.

"Aziel, I'm sorry, I'm sorry," Nita cried like it was her own fault.

The line from the other end was silent. Aziel comprehended the reality of what Nita was explaining. Startling Nita into a more emotional whine, the phone slapped against the box it was connected to three or four hard, loud times, which apparently broke it as the line went dead.

Tiva woke up downstairs with a splitting headache from a terrible dream that held hands with the factual circumstances of this realm. She had dreamt that her brother knew about Fatimah and was in a bloodthirsty rage. On the verge of accumulating more time to his already lengthy sentence, which would make his appeal process even harder. Tiva got herself together in the bathroom downstairs in the basement, washing her face and brushing her teeth. The mirror showed a puffier than usual face and some swollen eyelids with the imprints of uneven sheets going in strips across her plump cheeks. After cleaning herself up, Tiva followed her regular routine. Firing up a Newport, noticing she only had one more left in the pack; she would have to get more soon. The basement steps cracked as Tiva's heavy frame made it up to the kitchen when the sounds of crying became audible. Tiva didn't want to start her day out the way it had ended, but there was no way around it.

After making it up the steps and through the kitchen, Tiva saw where the crying was coming from. Hakiel had a frown on his face, now storming out of the front door with Jamal tailing behind. Tiva assumed him to be going to blow some steam and decided it best to let him be. Aunt Janice was helping Nita up from the floor amid her fit, still wailing pitifully. Tiva came over to help when aunt Janice filled her in on what had just happened.

"Your brother called," she said softly with a firm stare. Aunt Janice's lip tightened as her chin lifted, implying to Tiva this was that time she would need to be strong.

177

"How did he," Tiva started.

Aunt Janice cut her off, knowing what her question would be, shaking her head no to say it, but it didn't go well at all. Tiva looked off in several directions before a flood of tears she'd tried to prevent broke through, causing her to sink back into the depths of her nightmare from this side of the parallel.

Hakiel's anger had gone past his breaking point. He swiftly followed the route on the side of the house back to where they had stashed the pistol. Hakiel went straight to it, pulling it out with tears streaming down his face.

"What are you going to do, Kiel?" Jamal asked indifferently, scared for his friend.

"Kill that mafucka," Hakiel declared from his bleeding heart.

"Kill who? Boy, you done lost your damn mind," Tara snapped, seeing the gun in Hakiel's hand.

The boys had no idea that she had followed them. Worried about her little brother doing something stupid, which now appeared to be the case. Tara slapped the gun to the ground and was now taking swings at Hakiel's backside. He tried to overpower her, but she was too much to handle, even with her more diminutive stature.

Jamal yelled, "Y'all stop fighting," which was safer than trying to help Hakiel.

Tara continued swinging while she interrogated Hakiel. "Where you get a damn gun from?"

The boy scrambled, trying to duck the blows as they came crashing into his backside.

'Let me go, Tara," Hakiel demanded, trying his hardest to buck out of her clutches.

"It's not his Tara," Jamal protested.

She still swung until she got tired, pushing Hakiel to the ground when she had finished.

"Then who's is it, and what is it doing at my house?" she questioned with her braids thrown wildly all over her head. Tara pulled her hair back from her face and the disarray it was in.

She reached down to pick up the gun with the apron she had untied from her waist, then folded it up inside, never putting her hands on it.

"It's the mans who shot Mah Mah," Jamal said.

Hakiel sat on the ground near the station wagon, frowning and breathing hard, looking at Tara from under his lowered brows.

"What are you talking about, Jamal?" Tara asked, confused and panting from the commotion.

"They locked the wrong man up. I saw the whole thing, Tara. I swear I did even to God," Jamal pleaded. "He even came back last night to look for it," Jamal continued.

Hakiel's eyes shifted from Tara over to Jamal, knowing himself that his words were true. Hakiel knew Jamal had stayed up and seen the man from his question when he first came over. But hearing how Jamal described exactly what happened last night, he became more convinced at the merit of his initial story. Tara looked at Hakiel with his chest still moving rapidly up and down, trying to get a feel from him.

"He's telling the truth," Hakiel said, with a more pleading expression than moments ago.

"How do you know," Tara asked, still in between and not entirely swayed.

"I saw him with my own eyes last night, mama did too, but she only saw him speeding off," he continued. "She was too sad and stuff to believe me, but I saw him looking for the gun just where Jamal said he found it."

"Yeah, he was here. I got a picture of him in my mama's phone and everything." Hakiel looked at Jamal, surprised that he had got all of that. Jamal was on point, and Hakiel appreciated their friendship even more at that moment. "I can get it when my mama gets back from the store."

Hakiel wondered how upset his mother would be with him once she found out about him and the gun. Tara and Hakiel looked at one another, searching each other's eyes for clarity that neither of them could offer, then back to Jamal.

The Essence of a Woman

'Essence of a Woman'

I'm sitting here reminiscing, getting drunk off our love

In my own world, getting lost in my own thoughts

Finding for just one taste or just one touch

Either God was with me on this one

Or it was of luck

You're symbolical of what a real woman is really supposed to be

You're sexy as hell, with a touch of class

You turn me on effortlessly

The essence of a woman lies within you

And every morning God wakes you, I see living proof

You're a certified, dignified, and bonafide lady

And ever since I've been in this jam, you've been down to ride, baby

Always know and understand that you got me in the palm of your hand

And no matter how others may see you
I am and will always be your number one fan
I thank you for the good times
And I appreciate the bad
For without the bad, the good would be unnoticed
So with that being said
If you didn't know, then
Then you should know now
That I'm focused
I'm focused on you
I'm focused on me
I'm focused on what all our possibilities could be.
Written by Adarrell Marshall

Nassi's towel still hung on the shower door unused as drips of water rolled from the shower's head to the bottom of the tub then down the drain in a steady stream. The once neatly maintained bedroom was now in shambles as if a tornado had torn a path through it. The blankets, pillows, and sheets lay on the floor, including a broken lamp and an alarm clock. Several miscellaneous items had also been swept away from the dresser during the commotion. A few hours had passed, Nassi and Inez sweated through the majority of that time, going at it like teens getting their first dose.

The ceiling fan spun, set on a low speed, with the couple laying directly under its light breeze. Inez had her leg thrown over Nassi's, holding him captive under her curvy tan leg. Hearing her phone, Inez was pulled slightly from the depth of her sleep, yet still not fully awake. It took another ten minutes and a second chime before she could free herself from it. Her eyes opened, slowly penetrating through the blur, acquiring her focus. Nassi's armpit being the first in her line of sight brought her awareness that she could now feel between his lips. Inez stretched, letting out a quiet yawn rolling away from Nassi softly to the edge of the bed. She paused at the end of the bed once her feet touched the floor, blinking through squinted eyes. Turning to look back at Nassi, still caught in the astral web, she frowned in *a what the hell kind of way,* shocked at how destructive they had been. Turning back, Inez shook her head in disbelief. Looking down, she noticed deep purple bruises on her thighs. Inez attempted to stand, but if the dresser across from the bed hadn't been there to reinforce her, she would've met the floor face first. Her knees and legs were weak, failing to give her the support she needed to walk. Inez giggled, finding it funny now that she had safely avoided injury. She took a few moments getting her legs in working condition, stretching them and whatnot. While trying to rub the soreness out, she noticed more bruises on her arms.

"Damn," she mouthed.

Continuing to examine herself, she found a few more and was humored at the thought of; whether she had her ass whooped? Whatever the cause, she enjoyed every minute, and if up to her, there would be plenty more where that came from. Inez scanned herself in the mirror, finding yet another bruise on her forehead; however, she wouldn't be able to blame Nassi for this one. It happened during the shootout, as she ducked under the dash trying to escape the hail of bullets. Luckily, that was the extent of her damage, she thought, knowing it could've been worse. Inez noticed a chain and locket hanging from a sticky hook attached to the mirror. It was shaped like a heart and very attractive looking. Inez reached for it studying its design and elegance without any special doing of hers. Opening it completely, she immediately recognized a younger version of a familiar man. He was dressed in a tuxedo, holding a lovely looking young lady dressed in a violet prom dress with a white and violet corsage. Inez was in awe at how adorable the couple looked. Nassi hadn't changed much aside from his size and facial hair. Inez's thoughts raced to where this attractive girl was now.

Her feminine traits of nosiness, which she had spoken of the day prior, emerged, pushing her to snoop through Nassi's things. She pulled a drawer open and stumbled across some more recent pictures of the same woman and Nassi as adults. Inez began to wonder if she would end up being some fling in Nassi's collection, fucked and forgotten about. Growing embarrassed, her thoughts of building something with Nassi began to regress.

"I'm such an idiot," she thought. "I've waited all this time to get this asshole to notice me trying to get through this damn shield and all of that polite gentleman crap only to find out he's got a girl." Inez's emotions began to flare, feeling cheap for sleeping with Nassi knowing that he had someone.

Her intentions at first were to clean up and help him get the day started; now, all she wanted to do was get the hell out of there. Inez closed the drawer and began collecting her belongings in a fit, making more noise than necessary. After a few over-exaggerated grunts, Nassi found Inez moving angrily about the room.

"What's wrong?" Nassi asked, caught in the blind as to what her problem was.

Inez mumbled a few unrecognizable words to herself, finally finding her grey boy shorts in the bathroom. Knowing they were dirty, she was reluctant to put them on but decided she would rather put on dirty panties than allow Nassi to continue looking at her bare ass.

"What the hell is wrong with you?" Nassi pressed, finally noticing her attitude.

Nassi stood up from the bed, still nude from their escapade. As a pillow came flying in his direction, Nassi ducked it, keeping his eyes open for what might be coming next.

Inez reached to pick up the company t-shirt she had borrowed from the floor to cover her breast.

"Uggh," she grunted, resenting the fact that it had anything to do with Nassi; she took the shirt and threw it to the side like it was a detestable thing.

"Okay, I take it you're mad about something," Nassi stated, looking at her confused.

Her phone sounded off again, giving her an indication of where the rest of her things should be. The sound was coming from under the bed bringing Inez to her knees, crawling in that direction. Nassi became ever more irritated that balls and shaft were hanging above her.

"Would you please move and get your dick out of my face," she asked in a splenetic tone.

"Not until you explain what the hell is wrong with you?" Nassi replied, looking down at her.

"I don't have to explain anything to you. I'm not your girl," she confirmed with a sassy sarcasm.

Nassi looked to the side, shaking his head, confused at where he's gone wrong. Meanwhile, Inez moved around Nassi's legs reaching for her tote bag under the bed, finally getting a grip on its straps. Before looking back down at Inez, Nassi did a double-take at the mirror, now sure of what caused the issue. Nassi moved slowly to the mirror, noticing the poem locket.

"Uh, thank you," Inez said, still in her sarcastic mood.

Nassi had finally moved out of her way. Not that it mattered anymore; Nassi didn't respond, grabbing the locket from off the hook then sitting back to the bed staring at the picture. Inez gave a disgusted look at the sight of him dazed off into the picture.

"Don't worry, you can call her over as soon as I'm gone. I'm sure she won't mind," Inez spat.

Nassi refrained from commenting, just comfortable enough to let out a sigh, shaking his head in an honoring smile.

Growing more irritated, Inez snapped, speaking fast as if she would begin speaking Spanish at any moment. "Why didn't you just tell me when I asked you on the ride over if you had a girl, man?"

Nassi closed the locket then looked over to Inez with a look she hadn't seen in him before.

"I don't," he said, pursing his lips to the side.

"Come on, man, I saw the pictures in your drawer. She's wearing your fucking ring showing it off, so don't lie and say it was high school love," Inez snapped.

"You're right. It was more than a high school love, and yes, in the picture you're talking about, that was the day I proposed to her," Nassi replied, looking as if hurt for some reason she hadn't figured out yet. "She was killed, Inez, about seven years ago," he explained.

Inez's heart instantly dropped, "Oh my G. I Nassi! I'm sorry please forgive me, I didn't mean," Inez began.

Nassi cut her off, not wanting to get into it. "It's okay; you couldn't have known it's on me this time," Nassi said, looking down to the locket again.

Inez rubbed Nassi's knee from where she sat on the floor, trying to relieve the tension she had caused.

"If you want to, you can tell me, I'll listen," Inez offered now in a more relaxed yet sympathetic tone.

Nassi really didn't want to go through it but felt it was probably a good start to confide in Inez. She was, after all, his only candidate for something steady, which Nassi had been considering before the date. The problem was; he never knew how to approach her, plus he was still skeptical about letting anyone else enter his life.

"This shit's your damn fault," Young's voice screamed through Nassi's mind causing him to bite down, clenching his jaws.

"This shit would've never happened to my sister if it wasn't for you nigga. It's your fault my sister's dead nigga, you dog," Another voice echoed from somewhere in the files of Nassi's memory.

Nassi knew that if they were ever to have anything, he would have to open up to Inez. During the ride from Kilani's, they had discussed quite a few things, and being intimate acquaintances was the backdrop to it all. After some convincing heart-to-heart and some charm, Nassi came out of the defensive position, meeting Inez halfway with the idea. Now was the time to bring her closer to his world, sharing a part of his dark past in hopes of the sun emerging once more. It would be challenging, but if they would have any foundation, it would start upon the building blocks of communication.

Inez got up from the floor to sit next to Nassi on the bed, pushing the mute button on the phone that was now ringing again. Giving Nassi her full attention, she got behind him, massaging his shoulders and neck. If he decided to tell her, it would be a great start; if it wasn't a good time, she would understand and be there for him regardless, she concluded. Nassi took a deep breath as his mind drifted back to the night of the incident.

"Well, like I was saying earlier, it happened about seven years ago. I had just gotten hired at the department, and things were finally looking up for me. Bria and I made plans to get married that fall. We were renting a place out in Clayton County at the time. I was twenty-two years old, and she just made twenty that year. I was able to save a nice bit of money from my side by subcontracting some minor construction gigs. Bria was working part-time at her aunt's salon while taking classes online in accounting. We pretty much had our whole future planned out. We would buy a house and have one or two kids after she graduated. I would get my construction company off the ground and live the family life happily ever after," Nassi's face was dissolute as he explained. The whole subject was laborious from the beginning, but he continued suppressing the pain it induced. "So that weekend after I got the job on the force, we agreed to celebrate. We went shopping earlier that day, and she found this amazing dress at a boutique near Phipps Plaza. I remember her coming out of the dressing room with it on, doing the Tina Turner dance when she performed Rolling because the dress reminded her of the one she wore in the movie. We laughed all the way to the cash register, where she was able to continue long after I had stopped from hearing how much the dress would cost me." Nassi laughed, finding a smile-worthy moment within the memory.

Inez rubbed his arms smoothly and affectionately. "So after shopping and preparations for our celebration night, we left our place to go to an upscale nightclub downtown," Nassi frowned before speaking his next words. "We never made it," he explained as his thoughts drifted to that tragic moment.

"Baby, that was my song," Bria said, turning the radio down looking at Nassi smiling.

Nassi smiled back, already enjoying the night with Bria. The two pulled into a B.P gas station to fill up before jumping on the highway. Nassi ran in to pay for the gas catching a few stares on his way back out. He was clean, and he knew it. He wore a pair of Gucci loafers to match his all-black Gucci slacks and button-up. Although his money was legitimate, he could easily pass for a dope boy from the outside looking in. He was leasing the 2005 Dodge Challenger they were riding in. The 23-inch rims came at a super low price from a police auction a few weeks prior. Pulling off from the gas station, they made it a few lights down when it happened. A truck pulled up on the side of

Nassi at the red light. As four masked dudes jumped out with guns.

Nassi continued, "It was too late for me to make any kind of move."

"Get yo ass out this car nigga," one masked man said, pointing the pistol through the window on the side of my head. Bria screamed as one of the hijackers came to her side, pulling the door open on Bria's side.

"Wait, man, wait, we getting out, take it easy," Nassi pleaded.

"Shut the fuck up nigga, and put this bitch in park fo I rock yo hoe ass nigga," the masked man said on Nassi's side.

"Bria started crying at that point. The dude snatched me out, went through my pockets, and then made me lay face down on the pavement. The other two guys jumped back in the truck. The jacker on Bria's side had already slung her to the ground." Nassi remembered her crying.

"Why y'all doing this?" she asked in complete terror.

"Shut up bitch," the robber said.

The truck sped off once the two accomplices got inside the challenger. Nassi made the mistake of trying to intimidate the man from where he lay face down on the pavement. He assumed it would persuade them to reconsider what they were doing.

"I'm the police, don't do this, you won't make it far, just give me my car, and this never happened. Keep the money, man it's cool." The man behind the wheel stomped the accelerator, darting a few feet away before burning a 360 in the middle of the street, coming back towards Nassi and Bria. Pulling back up beside them, the man in the passenger's side stuck his upper body out of the window to talk to Nassi, who still lay belly down on the ground. The car came to a slow roll.

"Aye, did you say you the police?" the masked man asked, having the convenience of only a few motorists passing yet minding their business.

"Yeah, I'm a police officer. You know it's a minimum of fifteen years for carjacking, man?" Nassi said, confident he's got through to the man's logic.

"Fifteen years that's it shiiiiit throw this in too,"

"Bloom, Bloom, Bloom, Bloom," three out of the four shots hit Bria dropping her to the pavement as she'd tried to get up and run when the gun was raised.

Nassi took one to the chest as he jumped, running towards her seeing the same thing. The car peeled off. The approaching traffic mostly passed at first, too scared and suspecting some kind of a setup.

"I yelled for help like I never screamed before," Nassi reflected. "My phone was in the console, so I couldn't call anybody. Finally, a guy stopped to help, then a few more people, but she stopped breathing in my arms. The last words she told me were that she would always love me. I tried to get her to hush and save her breath, but she knew it was over and chose to give her last. While at the hospital, her brother showed up, storming in, looking possessed. He went off on me, cursing and blaming me for what happened. Deep inside, I know he was right. If I had kept my mouth shut, they probably would've just left us alone. Playboy was on the warpath, ready to kill everyone about his baby sister, including me. Within a two or three-day period, he and some of his Bloods find out who the men were that had jacked Bria and me. Their resources were a lot more helpful than ours had been with the investigation. Instead of the men being brought to justice, Playboy and his comrades had gone on a killing spree. They killed nine people in total. They would've beat the rap too, but the civilian that Playboy used for all kinds of running and whatever knew too much and was already scared of Playboy figured he would get from under his feet by turning state. Needless to say, they got some outrageous times. Then two years after, I was going on with everyone involved. Then Playboy's cousin, Divine from New York, attempted to kill the snitch at a nightclub one night after bumping into him. That night Divine ended up getting shot; he lost one of his legs, but he lived. Some guy with Divine named Aziel ended up shooting back and killed the gunman, but the snitch got away. Divine and his friend both were sent down the road with long sentences. Since then, I've never been able to forgive myself, and I've just been holding on to Bria." Nassi looked away as the pain clenched his heart. He continued through it, "I would send her brother money often until he got involved in gang wars. He got stabbed by some other group like seventeen times, nine of which were between the neck and head." Nassi shook his head, resenting how things turned out for Playboy. "As long ago as all that's been, it seems like yesterday," Nassi explained, fidgeting with the locket in his hand causelessly.

Inez's heart poured for Nassi, wrapping her arms around his body as much as she could. In a hushed tone, she offered her condolences. "I'm sorry, baby."

Nassi got up from the bed to hang the locket back in its former place. Inez watched with a newfound respect for Nassi and the cherished piece of jewelry he stood to hang. Inez felt strongly the desire to be the one who would fill that yard. She sat back on the bed and caressed him; this made Nassi let out a breath like he had performed quite a job. He stared up at the ceiling, trying to get past it as Inez merged into his line of sight, leaning over him from where she was sitting next to him. Inez found the bullet wound on his chest and ran her finger around the rim of the keloid skin.

"Nassi, I know I can't replace what you and Bria had, but I want to be the one who brings your heart back to life," she explained with passionate and sincere eyes looking down at him.

Making eye contact, Nassi looked back up to her, "I don't need you to replace anyone, Inez. I need you to be you so that I can move on and stop letting my past contaminate my present, causing me to reject all the possibilities for my future."

Inez's heart beat harder from Nassi's words as she sat silently for a few moments before speaking. She leaned over to kiss his wound, causing him to close his eyes as if something inside of him unlocked. Inez whispered as she held on to him, "I got you."

Rousing The Dogs

Theory woke up around 8:20 a.m. to find that Nessa had already left to run some errands before their 11:30 a.m. departure. According to the note she'd left, she took the initiative to purchase two one-way passes online for the flight leaving Arizona for Atlanta. Theory spent the last two hours since waking, eating breakfast, and taking a hot relaxing shower. After drying and lubricating his body, Theory threw on a pair of shorts and slipped his feet into a pair of corduroy house shoes. Theory grabbed his cell phone from the cut-out shelf on his bed's headboard, walking over to the bed. Theory began scrolling through the contacts until he found the number he was looking for. Pushing the send button, Theory walked toward the doorway leading to the hall. Before exiting, he snatched a Versace housecoat from the arm of the love seat in his oversized bedroom. Theory wrapped himself in the silk fabric bringing his arms through the sleeves of his robe. On his way downstairs, the phone rang two times before a voice came over the line answering.

"Shawty, what's up?" the voice said, recognizing the number.

"Wiley, what's up, fool? How you doing bro?" Theory asked, smiling, knowing Wiley would reply with some super cool ass response.

"Shit shawty over here kissing on Mary loud ass, riding down Redan on my way to check on a property," Wiley said between pulls.

"Whaaaaat, that strong pack?" Theory asked, knowing the answer.

"You gotta know it," Wiley laughed, coughing his reply out. "What you doing up so early?" Wiley asked after catching his breath. "Aint it bout 6:00 a.m. over there?" Wiley questioned.

"Na bro, it's like 10:20 a.m. over here. We're only three hours behind you," Theory explained. "Aye look doe Wiley, I'm bout to catch a flight that way in a little bit, man," Theory began. "I got some business in the town, so I'm gone need you fam," Theory explained.

"What you gone need potna, you know it, I can help, I got you shawty," Wiley said, choking from the smoke.

Theory stood in his kitchen, pouring himself a glass of strawberry lemonade. "Really, bro, I'm gone need one of them m-building corner cuts, plus I'm trying to whip one dog," Theory explained.

Wiley laughed, "Man, that's it, I thought you was bout to get me for some hellacious shit," Wiley admitted.

Theory and Wiley went back from doing time back in the day. These days, Wiley was fucking with some heavy shit on a federal level, so code language was always necessary when it pertained to his line of work.

"Oh yeah," Wiley asked, not really needing further confirmation. "I got you, bro when you T.O. hit my line, and I'll have you ready," Wiley confirmed.

Theory walked back upstairs from the kitchen, stealing a sip from his glass before responding. "Hell yeah, bro, that'll work," Theory said after taking another swallow.

"Aye, when the last time you hollered at T bro?" Theory asked, questioning about a mutual friend the two ran with.

"Man, shawty out there in yayo with a Heat jersey on and some South Beach sandals, kicking up sand." Theory and Wiley shared a laugh at the statement.

"Yeah, that sounds like him too," Theory admitted.

"I talked to um a few days ago. I'll text you the number when we get off. He is doing really good, though," Wiley confirmed.

After a little more small talk, the call ended with things already in motion for Theory's arrival. The text with L's number came through as Theory began to get dressed for the day. Getting suited, Theory placed another call. The ringtone banged through loudspeakers as Kool Kutta's "Only IF" played.

"Yeeeoh," a recognizable voice said from the other end. "What's up, fool?" Theory asked.

"Nikas like us dog, West banging?" Kutta said, sounding piped as usual.

"Us family, "Theory replied

"Aye dog, I'm bout to be that way in a lil bit, bro," Theory explained.

"Yeah, dog, I figured that. I know what happened with da lil bro's too, sorry to hear that dog." Kutta said, offering his condolences for Theory's younger brother.

"Yeah, man, shit is all out of control," Theory admitted.

"So we all are supposed to get together later on this evening to address these issues with Wet and Pro," Theory continued.

"What's your agenda looking like, bro?" Theory asked.

"Shit, bro, just hit me when you land. I'll pull up. I just got my guys in there recording these tracks, and we've been in here since 2:30 a.m.," Kutta explained, calling shots to the staff in his background between time.

"Aye, man, y'all go ahead and do them add libs." Theory heard him say to the group.

"Yeah, that's the shit, bro, work dog," Theory supported.

"Who you got over there, Potnaz Only?" Theory asked already familiar with various artists on Lorenzo Ent.

"Hell yeah, bro, these niggas don't get no breaks, shawty?" Kutta said, sounding like a new-age guy. His hard work was paying off. He had literally turned the group from a local buzz to something on the verge of international stardom. The work ethic Kutta Karleone had instilled in the group was the cornerstone to their mounting success, and Theory was proud to see the homie doing his thing.

"Fucking right bro, dats west up," Theory saluted.

"Well, look, dog, as soon as I get my shit together, I'm gone hit your line and let you know, bro. Westside." Theory confirmed

"Yeah, bro, make sho you do that. West WEST, "Kutta replied before the call ended.

After pocketing the phone, Theory started placing some items in the luggage that Nessa had already pulled from the closet. Looking over to where her bags lay packed already, Theory shook his head, evaluating how much shit she'd planned to bring."

"Goddamn Nessa," He said to himself. Theory had one bag to pack, which would be plenty deciding that anything else he may need could be purchased in Atlanta. *No sense in being weighed down*, he thought. Theory's mind sprinted back to Pro and Wet. The situation was a mess and would undoubtedly cause some tension within the family, Theory predicted. Tossing a few more things in the luggage, Theory zipped his bag and set it on the floor near Nessa's. Theory scratched at his goatee feeling the pressures of his responsibilities pounding on his mental. Dogs broke the silence, barking loudly outside. Theory walked over to the bedroom window to take a look at what was rousing the dogs. Nessa was pulling up in the pink cotton candy painted A8 Audi he bought for her on Valentine's Day. The pink and white ostrich interior highlighted her skin tone as she opened the door, exposing her juicy thighs. Theory watched from the window upstairs, admiring his jewel, as the white sundress flowed over the sultry curves of her body. Her hair and nails had been done, Theory noticed as she made it to the trunk to grab even more bags of god knows what. Theory followed her beautiful legs down to the white high heels she wore, catching the light flashing from her diamond-studded anklet. Theory could tell her toes were done as well as she stepped past the white 22-inch flats with pink accents mounted on her ride. Theory left the window to meet her downstairs so he could grab the dog food she'd left in the trunk. By the time Nessa made it in, Theory was on his way past her.

"Ugh, excuse you," Nessa said, looking Theory up and down, taking up the doorway with her leg kicked out. Theory beat her to the punch before she could get started.

"Damn girl, look at you looking all sexy and shit," Theory complimented, bringing a blush to Nessa's face.

"Shit, you make a nigga wanna fuck that hairdo right on up before anybody get to see it, boo." Theory continued.

That was all Nessa needed. "Aint it cute?" She agreed, smiling, enjoying his praise.

In all honesty, it did look good apart from the flattering, Theory thought to himself.

"How did you get all that done on such short notice though, baby?" Theory asked, curious to know.

"Boy, stop, you know I'm a valued customer, a bitch get out the bed when I call," she explained, laughing.

Theory laughed too.

"Shit, you just ought to be as much as you get your shit done," he said before kissing her.

Her scent filled his nose as she began to get deeper into their kiss.

"Umm umm," Theory protested, pulling away.

"You gone have us stuck here," He explained playfully between pecks of sugar.

Nessa smacked her teeth, always eager to get it on with Theory.

"I know, baby, but we can have a quickie." She said, almost whining.

Theory laughed. "Girl get yo fine ass in the house and finish getting everything together," Theory said, smacking her on the ass.

"Quit smacking my ass if you ain't gone give me none." She said, forcing an ultimatum.

Theory smacked it again, then dodged the swing he knew would follow, dashing out of the door.

"Punk," Nessa huffed. The dogs were still barking happily, hearing their master approaching with the big bag of food he'd gotten from the trunk of Nessa's car. Theory sat the two bags down to open the tall wooden fence. The Presa Canario backed up, wagging their numbed tails in excitement, letting Theory through. Walking toward the back of the house, Pacino and Egypt fought playfully behind Theory, following him to their feeding area. Theory put the bags of food in the shed, grabbing one that was open already.

"Y'all gone be good while I'm gone, "Theory spoke to the dogs, causing them to bark like they understood. Theory filled both bowls as the two continued to roughhouse.

"I don't know why mama got y'all some more food all this food y'all got back here," Theory said to Egypt.

The female looked at him cocking her head sideways making a noise that sounded like a human "hmmm." Theory patted both of their heads, then walked over to the water hose and turned the spicket on. Theory shot a spray at the two playing with his prized dogs as they dodged the water, barking at Theory in objection. Theory's laughter was interrupted by the sound of Nessa's voice calling to him from the patio door.

"Bookey, Pro on the phone collect," Nessa yelled.

Theory dropped the hose leaving the dogs barking in complaint behind him. Theory stepped up to the patio, grabbing the cordless from Nessa.

"Bro, what the fuck, dog?" Theory asked with mixed feelings of confusion and disappointment.

"Big bro, listen, they trying to frame me dog," Pro started.

"You know I wouldn't kill Wet big dog; that's my heart right there, bro," Pro explained with pain in his voice.

"I know dog, I've been telling the homies that same shit, Brim." Theory confirmed

"Yeah, dog and this fucking lawyer came down here a few hours ago talking bout you sent him, but I ain't know to trust um or not. You know I was on the bullshit cause his vibe was just too damn cocky for me dog with all I had going on." Pro continued, "Big bro, believe me, it ain't what they saying, dog. Then they claim I killed some little girl on top of all that other shit; I'm bent on that big fool," Pro explained with disbelief in his blaring tone.

"I know, bro, I heard," Theory said in a heartfelt reply.

"Shit, bro, I don't know what to do, but I need to get out, dog, and I don't know if it's safe on this phone cause the skins are behind this shit, bro," Pro informed him.

"Whaaaaat?" Theory said already aware that there had to have been more to it.

"Yeah, big dog, I ain't gone lie, I fucked up bad bro with this cracka named Hemlock on the force man,"

"Yooo, say no more, Brim," Theory interrupted, wanting Pro to take it easy on the line.

"I'm bout to jump on the plane in the next hour, dog. We have already booked our flights. I'm gone talk to the lawyer to see if I can talk him back into working your case Pro. My man is the best in the business down there; listen to me when I tell you," Theory explained.

"I'll rap with you in visso, so you can put me on point, but just maintain Brim we gone get you out of this shit homie, just know that." Theory instructed.

"That's what it is, big bro, west, west," Pro said, confident in Theory's words.

"West west," Theory replied, ending the call.

Hanging up the phone, Theory's face looked as if it could kill, and Nessa stood observing, knowing that it would happen somewhere down the line.

The Spot

"Yoooo, man, one of y'all mafuckas pick the goddamn phone up! I know y'all hear that shit!" Brack Pronto yelled from the back room. There was no answer, no one replied, as the phone continued to ring. After another two rings, Brack Pronto, angered from having to cut his recreation short, pulled his dick from the entertainment's mouth. She sighed "Uggh" in frustration as Pronto pulled his shorts up to his waist, pushing her out of the way. Pronto grabbed his Rugger from the nightstand and slid it in his belt before exiting the room. Looking back to the thick caramel cutie, Pronto instructed

"I'm gone be right back, ma. Don't move, stay just like that," he insisted with a smirk.

"What? Nigga please," The girl said, already moving to lay on the bed Pronto had been sitting on.

"You a stubborn mafucka," Pronto said before moving through the doorway. Walking through the kitchen on his way to the front room, Pronto grabbed the still ringing phone from the table. Unplugging it from the charger, he pushed the talk button and caught the call. Still making his way to the front, Pronto answered.

"Yeeeoh"

"Brack, why the fuck y'all ain't picking up this goddamn phone dog?" Low Fitted asked, sounding a little more than upset.

"Ain't no excuses, bro. I'm squatting with two of the most delinquent, game-playing ass mafuckas on the planet." Brack replied before going into a fit on Baby Pop Off and Vita DeKaprio.

Pronto snatched the game plug from the socket.

"Excuse my Brim, "Brack said into the phone, showing respect to the homie.

"So this shit more important than picking up the damn phone?" Brack snapped.

"Damn, big dog, you done broke it, "The young gun protested."

"Shut the fuck up," Brack snapped again with a penetrating stare.

"Anything could've been going on with the homie, Low Fitted calling and can't get through," Brack Pronto continued.

"We ain't know it was the homie calling." Baby Pop Off defended.

"Exactly, I know goddamn well you ain't know cause y'all mafuckas on this punk ass game instead of getting the phone," Brack lashed in a high-pitched tone.

"Aye Brack, pardon my Brim foo," Low Fitted interrupted.

"Take care of that later bro, right now, I need y'all to get everything out of the spot. We hot." Low fitted explained.

"Say no more, Whoop," Brack replied

Low Fitted whooped back then ended the call.

"Oh, y'all know y'all getting dipped," Brack confirmed, snatching the blunt from Baby Pop Off's lips to take a pull.

"Yo, get everything dirty out of the house, B Sap," Pronto said, rushing to the stash of duffle bags in the living room closet. The boys jumped up, sensing the urgency rushing to the various hiding spots collecting the paraphernalia. Brack Pronto went about gathering up the firearms as Baby Pop Off, and Vita DeKaprio rounded up the scales, baggies, and weed.

"Yooo, Tanji get up here," Brack called to the girl in the back.

Baby Pop Off went to the door up front and opened it looking out. "Ayeee, Lil Hot, tell Tinka to bring the whip down here ASAP." Baby Pop Off instructed the brunette outside.

Lil Hot looked back at Pop Off through her green eyes, instantly agitated by his tone, unaware of what was going on. Lil Hot rolled her eyes on then stood up from where she sat on the porch with Tinka in sight up the sidewalk.

"Oooooooweeee," Lil Hot called to Tinka in a high pitch coo.

Tinka looked back to where the call had come from. After getting her attention, Lil Hot held up four fingers with her right hand waving it, signaling what was needed. Tinka Bell exchanged a quarter sack with a guy she was standing next to after taking his money, wrapping up the transaction she was in the middle of.

"Damn Shawty, when you gone, let me take you out?" The guy asked, looking her up and down." I don't do that. I just do money, baby," Tinka said, counting the cash he'd handed her." Then you short $5.00 nigga, talking about a date when a bitch can't even get her whole ticket on a pack." She said, laughing. "I'm good pay," Tinka said, turning away to go to the car. "Buy one of those dusty foot hoes, MacD's on me with my $5.00 fool." She insulted as she walked off. The guy just watched as Tinka's wobbly ass rocked from side to side in her tight denim shorts. The 5'4 inch Baby Face Hustler was strict about her chore, with no room to entertain pawns in the game. "You gone want me one-day shawty." The dude said, feeling chumped off. He opened the sack he had just purchased, smelling it. "Damn," he huffed. Tinka had satisfied yet another customer. After a few minutes passed, the Malibu rental pulled in front of the apartment building. Tinka Bell jumped out, pulling her shorts from her deep creasing curves, separating her dinky and chunky thighs. Hot, where are we going, ma?"

Tinka asked Lil Hot, passing her on the sidewalk on her way to the unit door. "Ion know what bra and them got going on." Lil Hot answered.

"Pop Off came to the door trying to sound like somebody damn daddy tho, bout to piss me off," she continued.

"I was gon go and check, but you know I gotta watch yo back bitch, I ain't gon walk in while you out here," Lil Hot explained.

Before the girls could get to the door, Vita DeKaprio was damn near falling out of the apartment with two bags.

"Lil Hot move yo high yellow ass out the way, fool," Vita said, stumbling past.

Already on point, Tinka skipped behind him then passed him to open the passenger's side door. Once open, she went inside the glove compartment to pop the trunk. Vita dropped the bags in, then surveyed his surroundings. Everything was normal as far as he could tell. "Uhh Nigga don't call me over here no fucking mo, I'm so sick of you," Tanji fussed, being pushed out of the house with Brack Pronto close behind.

"Man, look, it's just a bad time. Ima fuck with you later," Pronto explained.

"Nigga fuck you, give me some money for something to eat," Tanji snapped.

Lil Hot bit the attitude.

"Bitch get yo broke ass on and watch who the fuck you talking to hoe before you get that ass tapped," Lil Hot spat.

Tinka Bell started laughing hysterically, looking at Tanji's expression through chinked eyes. Tinka was high as hell tripping from the commotion but still on her shit and ready for whatever. Lil Hot was the type to catch a mafucka off guard. Hot was pretty enough to model but to put it plainly, the girl was as vicious as a rattlesnake earning her the name Lil Hot Head Brim. She followed in the footsteps of her older brother Hot Head Brim. Their traits, characteristics, and demeanor were frighteningly similar in comparison. Hot Head was away serving time in V.A. on a body. With the temper, his baby sister Lil Hot Head had, it wouldn't be long before she'd caught one of her own.

"Bitch, why you standing there with yo face all screwed up like you bout that life? You need to beat yo feet and get the fuck from in front of this building," Lil Hot snapped, walking up closer to the girl.

Tanji rolled her eyes with a "spssh" sound rolling from her lips, trying to put the last of her clothes completely on. Before Tanji could slip the t-shirt on over her halter top, Lil Hot cocked back and smacked the daylight out of Tanji.

"Thwack," the loud clap connected flat onside of Tanji's face turning her sideways from the impact.

"Woe woe woe Lil Hot, bool out blood," Pronto said, grabbing Lil Hot before she could crank up how she wanted to.

Pronto knew her well enough to discern that the slap was just an appetizer for hunger inside of her that never seemed to get full.

"Bitch, who da fuck you rolling yo eyes at hoe" Lil Hot yelled, pumping her neck back and forth as she spoke.

Pronto had a tight hold on her, trying to calm her.

"Tanji, just go, ima get at you ma," Pronto instructed.

"Un uh, I'm straight on you, man, Tanji said, picking up the bag she'd dropped from the ground. Lil Hot bucked, trying to get loose from Pronto's grip causing Tanji to take off, walking fast with one shoe half on.

"Damn dumb ass hoe put ya fucking shoes on at least," Tinka said, laughing.

"Damn y'all, trippin man, we already hot." Pronto scolded, shaking Lil Hot as he spoke.

She just looked back at him from where she stood as he held her from behind with an attentive look over her shoulder. She stared in his mouth as he fussed, then back into his eyes. "Come on, Brim, damn," he complained.

"Come help us get this shit up outta here," Brack demanded, trying not to get caught in her enticing eyes. Brack pushed Lil Hot away from his body as she attempted to close the space between them, and she fell towards Tinka from the push. Lil Hot gave Tinka a devious smirk of satisfaction. Tinka, still high and tripping, caught all of it laughing.

"Bitch get on," Tinka said, helping her homie gain her balance. Lil Hot turned to look at Pronto as he walked into the building, still fussing and catching his tattooed back as he disappeared through the doorway.

"You are terrible," Tinka admitted.

"Fuck that hoe," Lil Hot said, referring to Tanji.

Just then, Baby Pop came off through the doorway with a duffle bag full of guns headed towards the car.

"Damn, why don't y'all go grab something so we can smash around here taking pictures and shit." Baby Pop snapped off using an analogy.

"Please just be quiet," Lil Hot Head said in a disgusted tone, taking off to help inside.

Tinka Bell stayed outside to watch the car, rolling one to smoke before the ride, while she waited for the rest of the gang to finish. Tinka took a quick glance around what she could see of the apartment complex, wondering what the big deal was. A few regulars passed by, blowing at Tinka as she waved the deuces to some and threw up the B's to others. Tinka noticed the rest of the group scrambling out of the house with more bags and Vita carrying the game system under arm. She was aware of the incident with Pro and Wet but didn't know what that had to do with the spot. Neither Pro nor Wet had ever spent much time there, so she was dumbfounded as to why they would be hot. Pronto was the last to come out of the house, locking the door behind him with his button-up short sleeve wide open, barely hiding his pistol.

"Tinka y'all drive the Malibu to the 5th and drop, we gone meet y'all at 1st," Pronto instructed.

"I ain't driving, Lil Hot gone drive, she's the grown looking one," Tinka suggested.

Lil Hot grabbed the keys from Tinka as Baby Pop Off and Tinka climbed in. B.P.O., the abbreviated name Baby Pop Off chose for himself, ducked low in the back seat. Pronto and Vita DeKaprio walked down to the other car parked in the lot down four units away as Lil Hot pulled off slowly.

"What da fuck going on, big bro?" Vita asked, looking around as the two walked.

Pronto was in full stride, pulling his Newport with a face as cold as stone. He answered as he exhaled.

"Shit homie, the bro Folio told Low Fitted to clear all the spiggs dog," Pronto explained, pulling the keys from his pocket.

Vita was a scrawny lil dude, but anytime Pronto made the call to eat, the lil homie got it done, no questions asked.

"Dog, why you think Pro killed Wet?" Vita asked as they approached the donk.

Pronto hit the automatic start bringing the old school classic to life. The doors unlocked, and the trunk began to warm with bass.

"Bro, don't get caught up in that media shit, you know the homie ain't do no shit like that on purpose dog," Pronto explained, unsure himself of what really happened. Pronto looked over the top of the car at Vita before getting in. Vita opened his door, following suit. The two jumped in as the top slid back towards the trunk. Pronto pulled his Newport hard, cranking the beat-up louder in the Chevy. The 26 inches red and chrome floaters flickered glares of light onto the pavement, reflecting the sun as the tires crawled back slowly. The candy red paint appeared to be dripping wet under the Atlanta, Georgia sun rays as the big body dinosaur reversed from the space it had been parked in.

"Yo Vita, text Low Fitted and tell um we all clear," Pronto instructed.

Vita grabbed the phone punching the text as the homie Pronto beat through the complex playing Rick Ross's "I'm the biggest boss."

Shot At Freedom

"Listen, I understand the risk, but you owe us if you want to ever see the light of the day again, so make it happen. The boss wants it done by arraignment, but I want to make an impression since my face isn't looking so good. I'm pushing to get it done before the first appearance, which is tomorrow, so that means you need to do it today." Cunningham has 72 hours to appear before a judge; he's not to make it. Are we clear?" Puma asked his man working on the inside.

"Yeah, man, I guess I don't have much of a choice, but you promise this gets me back on the street, right?" The man asked nervously.

"Yeah, sure, this will take care of everything," Puma claimed.

The man stared at Puma intently through the glass.

"Remember you gotta make it look like the Muslims did it," Puma informed.

"How am I gonna do that?" The man asked.

"I don't fucking know you wear a fucking kufi, for god's sake, just figure it out. Listen close; if you get caught up on this, it's on you." Puma explained. "So you're going to have to be smart about it, don't just run in headfirst; give it some thought for your sake."

The man took a deep breath, trying to collect the strength to pull the job off. Puma stared at him, knowing the man was trapped between a rock and a hard place. Laughing, Puma finally spoke. "Look, man, it's not like you have much of a future with the time you're facing. Hell, the way I look at it, this is your break. You know how many people would jump at this opportunity. Society could give two fucks about some gang banger killed in jail. Hell, if they did happen to know who'd done it, he'd be a fucking hero after all the shit this asshole done. Now on the flip side of that, society couldn't care less about some habitual felon with a history of armed robberies and drug dealing going down the road on recidivism for the rest of his life. You do the math cause right now it's you or Cunningham," Puma suggested.

It didn't take the man long to come up with the figures.

"So, how do I get close to him?" The guy asked, moving his hands with emotion. He was now convinced this was his only shot at freedom.

"Ata boy," Puma encouraged.

"I'm going to get you guys moved into the same dorm over at the pretrial building later today. In fact, Kadarai will have already been moved by the time they come for you. Someone will bring you the steel once you're over there, and it's home free after that, as long as you get it done," Puma continued with a firm and cold gaze in his eyes. "Now, if there are any more Bloods in the dorm, it's going to be difficult, but it still must be done. You'll just have to be craftier." Puma explained.

The man twisted his mouth and nodded in agreement. Puma wasted no time leaving the booth without another word exchanged and left the guy sitting there half scared to death.

Do Your Job

etective Nassi had gotten off to a later start than planned. Inez's phone had been going off the meter during the talk she and Nassi had. Once she got around to returning those calls, she received information from the lab in reference to some evidence she'd asked a colleague to examine. It turned out that the pieces of fabric that Nassi found between the truck and officer Tally's body matched the fabric of Kadarai's shirt. This explained the singed holes in his shirt without injury. Obviously, Kadarai had fired his gun from under his shirt. The gunpowder on his shoulder holster also suggested it had been fired while still inside the holster, which seemed a bit strange. Finally, Inez and Detective Nassi concluded that Hemlock's story was blatantly inconsistent with where this tiny, almost overlooked piece of evidence placed Kadarai during the shootout.

Aside from that, a powdery substance also found behind the Durango tested positive for cocaine. This meant that drugs were in close proximity to officer Tally at some point yet never introduced to evidence for some odd reason. After going over more specific details, Nassi and Inez concluded that Hemlock was trying to cover something up. The detective had seen it before, where an officer wants a guy so badly that he starts to harass him until he almost has him red-handed, but jumps the gun and ends up not having enough to pin him like he wants. Then he's forced to trump up some bogus charges only to later try to cover his own tracks of foul play. The line between law enforcement and criminal activity seems to be getting thinner and thinner these days. Inez and Nassi agreed to meet up later and check up on the cameras at the restaurant. They'd realized that the suspicious man from the parking lot with the Nike shirt had been there and was probably the man eyeing Inez at the table. Things were definitely becoming more complicated, as Nassi reflected on Hemlock's words. "This is an open and closed case."

Yeah, right, Nassi thought, determined to get to the base of what was going on. Already in the process of taking care of his first point of business. Nassi pulled into the Fulton County Jail parking area, ready to pay Kadarai Cunningham a visit. Once inside, the detective was informed that Kadarai had been moved to the pre-trial building off of Memorial Drive. After fighting the ridiculous traffic, Nassi finally made it to the location and checked in. The detective was told that he would have to wait for a while and that the inmates were still going through the process of being placed in a unit.

Apparently, detective Nassi had been only a few minutes behind Cunningham's own arrival to the pre-trial building. It took about 45 minutes for clearance to visit. At that time, a floor officer instructed the detective on where to find Kadarai. Detective Nassi took the southwest side up to the 7TH floor. A floor guard who accompanied him to the dorm where Kadarai was said to be housed met him. The officer placed a card up to a scanner to the side of the door, and the mechanical gates buzzed, allowing Nassi's entry. As the detective walked into the brightly lit dorm, he heard someone yell "12 with a suit on goddammit," bringing all attention in his direction. The dorm was full of people as smoke billowed into the air from several places. There were two floors with groups of men scattered about everywhere. Nassi continued to the activity room designated for the visit. The officer occupying the desk near the room smiled at Nassi.

"He'll be right down," she informed.

One inmate left her desk with some forms he'd just taken from a bin sitting on the desktop. Another inmate stood to the side of the desk with one arm hidden inside his uniform, looking googly-eyed at the attractive young officer.

"Boy, get on before I get yo ass lockdown," she threatened in a southern twang.

"Come on with da bullshit shawty you always flexing on a nigga and shit, wit yo cap ass," The inmate spat as he continued to pull on himself.

Nassi entered the room, closing the door behind him. The yelling and shit-talking weren't completely muted out as Nassi heard someone yell "Throw it" in the background, whatever that meant. Nassi turned to look and assumed they must have been talking about the officer who was now walking toward the yard with her ass damn near to bust the seam of her too-small uniform pants. After waiting about three to five minutes, Kadarai finally showed up. Detective Nassi stood to shake hands with Kadarai, but Kadarai passed the opportunity up, scrutinizing the detective through cold and pain-filled eyes.

"Kadarai Cunningham, I assume; how are you doing? I'm detective Nassi Ilakin from the Atlanta Police Homicide Division. "

Kadarai took a seat leaving Nassi standing unacknowledged

"Yea, alright?" Kadarai said, clearly not in the mood.

Nassi noticed he looked pretty hurt, seeing the bandages and arm sling. The matters at hand were too serious, and Nassi didn't want to insult Kadarai with any jokes or small talk. The detective pulled a small recorder from his jacket pocket and placed it on the table. The detective then removed the suit jacket and placed it on the table as well. Nassi stared into Kadarai's eyes, trying to formulate a comfortable method of communicating with him, to get what he needed to know and what needed to be done from this point. Kadarai looked as if he was already frustrated, making Nassi edgy on how well this interview would turn out.

"Look, Mr. Cunningham, I'm going to be upfront with you; this case is a mess," Nassi started.

"Dog, if my lawyer ain't on the way here, I don't wanna talk to you, and I ain't signing shit, y'all can suck my dick," Kadarai said straight to the point. The detective humbled himself, knowing that feeding into Kadarai's attitude would get him nowhere. Kadarai stood up about to leave, aware that he had rights.

"Wait a minute Kadarai, just hear me out." The detective pleaded.

Look, you don't have to sign anything, and I'm not recording," The detective said, pushing the recorder close to Kadarai. Kadarai looked down at the device, sucking his teeth.

"So what," Kadarai said, still standing looking eye to eye with the detective.

"I'm not gone lie to you and tell you I'm on your side." the detective started.

"No shit," Kadarai cut in.

Nassi shook his head to the side. "Look, I'm only concerned with the families getting closure which they can only achieve if justice is served. The detective explained, poking at the table with a finger.

"That can only be done if I get the guilty person behind all of this." The detective said, frowning with a harsh tone.

"So what the fuck, man, what? You came to remind me what the fuck y'all detaining me for? I know my fucking charges dog." Kadarai questioned, running out of patience.

"Kadarai, I'm here because I don't think the police involved are able to give us an accurate account of what transpired in some areas. I'm not saying they are lying; there are just a few inconsistencies you may be able to shed light on." The detective explained, locking his fingers.

Kadarai bit his lips at the detective's words, studying his face for sincerity.

"It's not adding up, and if there's anybody who can see that there's some sort of covering going on here, it's me." The detective explained. Kadarai's heart started to pound as he took a seat, letting the detective's words register.

"Listen, I know the code automatically puts us at odds; I've worked with some of your brothers, and I know what you are." The detective continued.

At the end of the day, we are one and the same, the same people, and we are losing at an alarming rate. If it's not the prison system, it's senseless violence leaving our youth stuck in some hole in the ground before they've even had a chance to live." Nassi continued, becoming more passionate as he spoke.

"You're supposed to be about the people as well. Although I don't agree with everything you do, there's a lot that you've done as an organization that I have been proud of, I'll admit that. The fact of the matter is that we can't continue to allow ourselves to be taken advantage of and victimized by some machine exploiting our greater purpose."

Kadarai watched attentively as the detective spoke.

"Brother, I'm not trying to preach to you. I just want you to know and understand where I stand on the issues facing our community. My line of work is how I give back, for people like Fatimah and Reantez." Nassi explained, reaching inside of his shirt pocket.

"Have you seen the girl they claim you shot and killed?" Nassi asked with a caring demeanor on his face.

Kadarai shook his head no slowly. Detective Nassi placed the photo of Fatimah on the table and slid it across to Kadarai. Kadarai picked the photo up, looking at the little girl. His heart sank to the pit of his stomach, staring at the precious face of the beautiful black child while thinking of the seeds he himself had planted.

"Can you imagine how her mother is feeling at this very moment, or better yet, put yourself in her father's shoes?" The detective said with emotion pouring from his soul. Kadarai took a deep inhale and then released. Detective Nassi watched, giving him a moment to gain clarity before speaking again.

"You didn't do this," the detective claimed, looking at Kadarai. Kadarai knew that but didn't really know what angle the detective was playing. He had been through the whole good cop bad cop routine before and didn't trust anyone with a badge.

"So what makes you so sure? I mean, it can't be that. They got me locked up for it," Kadarai said, making it clear he needed more persuasion as to what the detective's intentions were.

"What's strange among many oddities I'm finding, in this case, is that the caliber gun that killed Fatimah is the same that killed your friend Reantez or Wet. Who we at one point suspected was meeting you at the park for some kind of drug transaction. However, tracing the receipts we found in his girlfriend's truck back to a B.P gas station, we discovered he had actually ridden with you. This brought us to conclude that it wouldn't have made sense for you to go through the trouble of bringing Reantez to the park just to kill him." The detective explained, rolling his sleeves up as he reached for some papers in a manila envelope.

"On top of that, according to Sergeant Hemlock of the A.P.D Red Dog Unit, who was the officer pursuing you, by the way...." Nassi informed Kadarai, unaware that Kadarai knew exactly who Hemlock was.

"His statement was that he pulled up to apprehend you after seeing the commotion in the park, jumped out, guns drawn to be fired in your attempt to get away. Supposedly, this is when officer Tally got struck." The detective stopped and looked up from the paperback to Kadarai, forcing a fake smile.

"Bullshit." The detective said, slamming the papers down on the table. Kadarai frowned at his body language but still listened close to the account and silently wondered where the detective was headed.

"At some point, you were standing next to officer Tally with him, totally oblivious to you having your weapon pointed at him under your shirt. In fact, it was still in the holster. This is consistent with the entry wounds on the left side of officer Tally's body. Now from the angle they allegedly pulled in from, it would've been virtually impossible for you to have done. If you were running and shooting from where the report describes," Nassi revealed. Kadarai's heart was now beating wildly, hearing how on target the detective was with what had actually played out.

"If you had a gun in hand, there would have been no need to try some movie script ass shot from under your shirt sending several magical curving bullets into officer Tally's thoracic cavity. That's just above the diaphragm left pleural cavity where you punctured his left lung, shattering his pectorals minor by the 4th rib teres major in the process. In layman's terms, you couldn't have fucked him up like that from where they're saying you were standing, let alone stand over him for the close-range headshot." The detective explained.

"So my question amongst many is where was Hemlock during this seemingly one-on-one confrontation, and two, where is the gun that killed Fatimah and Reantez?"

Kadarai was enthusiastic about speaking after all he'd heard.

"That's a damn good question," Pro reasoned, looking concerned. "Man, I ain't no rat even to catch a rat, but I can tell you this, I only shot that cracker in self-defense, man," Kadarai pleaded.

"I believe that, but if I'm going to be of any help to you, I need to know what really happened." The detective pushed.

Kadarai shook his head, letting out a sigh.

"Man cut the bullshit," Nassi yelled, growing impatient. "Listen, man. I had some guys at my place last night trying to kill me, meaning they went through the trouble of finding out where I live, man. On top of that, for whatever reason, they wanted it to seem like it was a hit done by your family, so don't.... "

Kadarai interrupted, "My family? How you figure that?" Kadarai asked angrily, taking offense

"They were wearing red bandanas around their face; all three of them," Nassi explained.

"Man, my people, ain't did that homie," Kadarai defended.

"I don't think so either, but something is definitely going on. We are apparently dealing with something a lot bigger than either of us are giving credit." Nassi suggested, sounding more like an ally. Kadarai felt the urge to get to a phone and question the homies about the detective's accusations.

"Look, man, I'm sorry, but you're going to have to do your job, dog, and it sounds like you're pretty good at it so far. Like I said, homie, I don't rat. Call me stupid, dumb or whatever, but you won't call me a rat ever dog." Streets will handle whatever you can't blood," Kadarai said as he stood up and handed the picture of Fatimah back.

"Nah, man," Nassi laughed in disgust, "You keep it as a reminder," Nassi said, handing Pro a card with his contact information on it. The detective looked at Kadarai, disappointed, shaking his head as Kadarai took the card. Seconds later, he was gone leaving Product standing in the activity room with his thoughts.

Listen To Me Close

Leaving the activity room, Pro glanced over to the exit watching as the detective stood in the sallyport, waiting for the second door to pop. The detective looked back, locking eyes with Pro with that kind of intensity only a passionate detective could produce. Pro felt in his gut that the detective would stop at nothing to get all parties responsible for yesterday's deaths. As much as Pro wanted to punish Hemlock, he knew that he would have to face the music for his role in all that had taken place. The court would place a heavy penalty on him, but his brothers would also once everything came to light. Pro wouldn't shy away from any of it. He was a diehard and ready for whatever came his way. The doors opened, allowing the detective to make an exit. Pro's attention was drawn back to his environment. The dorm smelled of cleaning chemicals mixed with weed and cigarette smoke. Pro walked across the heavily waxed floor toward a man who stood talking loudly to himself in front of the TV.

"Deesh negush tupidish hell, hmmph. How mafuck go let me wutch shum the fuuuuuck." The bald-mouthed man said, sounding funny. "Hell nawl I'm gone wutch it goddamnit cawsh I wancha wutch it hell not cawsh you done let me, what kinda shit dat eyuh." The man continued, turning back as if someone he had been talking to was still in range to hear. Product didn't notice anybody in the immediate area and figured the man was just crazy. The man's left eye was cocked awkwardly in his left eye socket, and his skin had a leathery shine to it. Pro noticed how the man looked like he actually needed a break from the street. It was easy to tell that some extremely hard drugs had torn the man down from a once capable stature to a now more feeble condition. Pro walked past, sure his fate would be different; whether that would mean he'd be better off was entirely up to opinion. So far, Pro's fate wasn't looking to be as prominent as he had planned it to be. Pro took a plastic chair from a table close to where the man stood, over to a column between the floor, at the top of where a phone had been mounted to the beam. Pro didn't have the resolve to call Renee yet, knowing that she would be upset. In the recesses of his mind, he could envisage how their conversation would go, bringing him to postpone that course of action. However, Pro needed to reach out to the homies to determine if they knew anything about what the detective had claimed. Pro punched his inmate number into the phone, waiting for the prompts to allow him to continue. Dialing the numbers, he looked around, checking to see who would be able to hear him once he began his conversation. Satisfied, Pro spoke his name as the recording instructed. The phone rang and was then answered by a hardened female's voice. Pro instantly knew who it was.

"Wush good?" The girl asked, unsure who was calling. The recorded voice came on giving instructions for call acceptance.

"If you will accept a collect call from "Da Pro," Kadarai's voice boomed. The girl, already knowing the routine, punched the number one, connecting the call.

"Damn homie you alright? We've been worried bout you. They have been saying all kind of shit, dog, we ain't know what the fuck." She spilled over the line, happy to hear it was Pro. "Nah, sis, I'm blown at this shit," Pro said, letting out a breathy exhale. "It's a bunch of fuck shit," Pro complained. Hannah Bandana held the phone listening to her big homie as she ceased to tap the buttons of her computer's keyboard.

"Yeah, they trying to frame me and shit, talking bout I killed Wet um Brim and some lil girl," Pro explained.

"Damn love, I knew you ain't do that shit, big bro. The other hoods are making all kinds of static like you got us hot, and this anti-gang movement is beefing up. The bros had us clear all the spots, just in case the gang task force decided to raid. Bro, it's been crazy around the whole city; the police presence has doubled." Hannah said, talking fast.

"Yeah, I figured that. So who there with you, homie?" Pro asked.

"Just me 1st 48, Ace, AK and S. O. Proof right now. Buck 50 and Krew Ella just went over to the lil homie Blip spot to pick up Park B," Hannah responded back. She took a moment and notified the house in the background, who she had on the phone.

"Aye y'all big homie Product on the phone," She yelled.

Pro could hear the barks in the back.

"Whoop, Whoop, put my mafuckin big bro on the loudspeaker, Bandana," 1st 48 yelled, coming into the room with Hannah. Hannah smiled, pushing the button to activate the loudspeaker. Ace K and S. O. Proof followed behind talking shit as Ace K used one of Pros catchphrases.

"Whaaaat da fuuuuuck" Ace yelled.

"West banging big fool, you good?" S. O. Proof asked, yelling.

"Yeah, dog, I'm alive, you know, shit brazy doe cause if I could trade places with Wet right now, I would dog," Pro said, grieving his lil homie.

"Yeah, big bro, we be knowing, that was a little version of you all over again. We gone miss um man." 1st 48 said.

Hannah Bandana stood up from the computer handing the phone over to 1st while she looked outside the window.

"Man, they framing me, but Hannah gone fill y'all in. I already explained to her what's going on, but y'all know what's going on with me. That shit they saying some bullshit fam." Pro explained.

"I be knowing big bro, "1st began.

"I just got to arguing with one of the homies from another hood last night talking bout you. He gone have the balls to say, "Pro got us all hot, now they putting pressure on all the families from him doing that dubbed out shit," 1st 48 explained.

"Tell the truth nigga, y'all hitting is not considered arguing." Hannah interrupted, coming back from the window.

Pro sat quietly listening as 1st continued.

"It really wasn't no hit like that, big bro." 1st 48 said, looking at Hannah with a mug.

"We just shot the fade because after I told um keep my big bro name out the mud, he kept talking shit, some shit I assume his big homie telling him. So I told him whoever told him that bullshit should get smacked in da mouth, but since you the one repeating it, you gone get smacked in the mouth. So S. O. Proof took the clock and watched us. I popped that baby then slapped him in the mouth like I said I was before the time ran out." 1st 48 admitted. 1st was only 18, but he was serious about his issues.

"Aye, man," Pro spit obviously overwhelmed with everything.

"Y'all just chill, dog, look I appreciate you defending my honor and all that but fuck that shit right now, bro; shit is bigger than that right now, dog."

1st 48 sat taking in the big homies words knowing he was upset.

"Fuck what the rest of these niggas saying, dog y'all know what's up with me, and we don't need shit escalating between us and the other hoods while this is going on bro!"

"True." Hannah Bandana said somewhere in the background.

"When can we put some money on ya books, bro?" S. O. Proof asked, sounding concerned.

"Shit, Brim, don't even worry bout dat right now homie, I need y'all looking into some other shit," Pro replied. Ace pulled hard on the blunt he was smoking, looking in 1st 48's eyes, knowing from Pro's words some work had to be put in, which was his area of expertise.

"What's Poppin bro?" S.O. Proof asked, eager to get to it too.

"Any of y'all heard anything about some detective getting rocked it late last night?"

Pro questioned the group. They all searched each other's eyes before responding 1st 48 answered for the rest, "Nan, bro, what's good on that?" He asked, curious to find out what Pro's question was about.

"Yeah, dog, this detective just left asking me all kinds of shit bout the case, so the dude was from homicide." Pro started.

"So he speaking all kind of facts, knowing I ain't rock Wet and all that. Pro continued.

"Damn, bro, so he gone get you off?" 1ST 48 asked excitedly.

"Dog, listen!" Pro demanded

"Dude saying some homies tried to flat um last night like they trying to shake him from the investigation."

"Naaaah bro, we ain't," 1ST 48 started but was cut short by Pro's lash.

"Shut da fuck up and listen, dog, I'm trying to tell you!" Pro spat.

1st 48 piped down, knowing from Pro's tone he was understandably in his short-fused mode, but he couldn't be blamed for his fucked up mood.

"This mafucka saying he don't believe they were homie, because they moved too tactically and professionally dog. Listen to me close, bro, they fronting like the family, but they know that I know." Pro informed, speaking into the phone harshly. The group eyed each other looking confused, as the blunt passed from Ace K's hand to Hannahs.

"If it's who I'm knowing it is," Pro stressed with emphasis.

"They gone flat the detective point-blank," Pro said in a convincing tone before taking a pause.

"So we need to done these mafuckas," Hannah yelled on point.

Her emotion and love for her big bro charged the whole group. Ace K bit his lip passionately, wanting to bang beside his big bro on whoever. S.O. Proof looking at Ace K began to rock his upper half, turning his fingers into guns by his side. "Pom Pom" Proof sounded his gun noise.

"Exactly," Pro started.

"Check with da homies and the rest of the family, make sure it ain't none of us. If it is, put um on point to fall back, we don't need no fucking heroes or retaliation on the detective for working the case. He may be the only hope to get me back to the world." Pro stated, firmly believing the reality of his words.

"We on it, bro," 1st 48 said.

"Yeah, y'all locate him, keep an eye on um, so y'all can make sure whoever is trying to flat um is shut down," Pro explained.

"Enough said, big bro!" Ace K stressed.

Pro gave them the information on the card between glances at Fatimah's picture also in his hand. Pro gave a few more instructions before the recording informed them of the 60 seconds remaining.

"Aye, do not let anything happen to dude," Pro demanded

"Hannah, take my babies some fireworks over to the house, don't tell Renee where I'm at or what's going on yet. As a matter of fact, don't even go in; just put the fireworks on the side step and bounce. Leave a note from daddy," Pro insisted.

"Done, big bro!" Hannah responded as her feminine emotions almost surfaced. She knew how Pro felt about his kids and the things he had done to ensure their safety.

"Big ones, y'all," Pro said firmly from the core of his soul.

"Bigger ones, big bro, love you, stay up, a collaboration of voices merged into harmony through the phone.

"Love back whoop," Pro said before hanging up.

Pro's hand held on to the receiver as it hung from the hook. He looked down to Fatimah's picture laying on his lap, now stuck in her gaze. Closing his eyes for a brief second as the pain in his body and heart continued to wreak havoc. It was time for more pain pills. Pro felt the burning sensations throbbed at the edges of his torn flesh.

"Yo, my man can I get that phone when you're done," a voice asked respectively from Pro's blindside.

"I'm through, go ahead," Pro said, taking a painful stand. He grabbed Fatimah's picture all in one motion. The man watched as Pro moved away, observing his afflictions.

Pro made it to the top, managing the climb up of the steps where his room was located.

Pro heard a man advertising.

"I got sticks of it, Biggerettes, two for threes, 3 ways and fuck flicks get at my movement."

Pro had almost walked past the man's room as he made eye contact with the occupant, smoking a joint on his bed.

"You homie?" Pro asked, already pretty sure.

"Fucking right, Damu," The stocky dark-skinned man answered, recognizing one of his own. Pro and Smoke greeted each other as he stood, welcoming Pro into the room.

"Damn dog, what the fuck happened to you?" The man asked, blowing smoke from his nostrils. Pro thought to himself how the homies name Smokey Ru seemed to fit perfectly from the first impression.

"Dog, it's a long story, but I got shot and hit by the police car dog," Pro said as his injuries seemed to pulsate more from the mention of them.

"Damn fool, look like you need this more than I do," Smokey Ru said, passing the joint. Pro declined the offer with a hand gesture.

"Shit bro with 40 after life I got nun, but time, I feel you though," Smokey Ru said, taking a long drag of his joint.

"Damn fool," Pro sympathized.

"Yeah, I know right, fuck it doe, it is what it is," Smokey Ru stated.

"Yeah, man, maybe some other time. I'm burnt out right now, homie, and when I go take these pain pills, I'll be out of it for a while." Pro explained

"Shit, that's what's good, fool. Get at me when you get up. You know where I'm at," Smokey Ru said, reaching his hand out to shake up with Pro.

"Alright my dog. Aye, you the only one in the dorm bra?" Pro asked before leaving.

"Hell yeah, dog, 3 homies just went down the road from here within the past weeks and a half." Smokey Ru informed while trying to keep the smoke in his lungs from escaping.

"Fo sho then, I'm at your flame in a minute, bro, whoop," Pro said as he moved on through the door. Once in his cell, Pro finished making his bed, then followed his pain pills with some vile tasting water from the sink. Swallowing it all in one gulp, Pro tilted his head back, making the passage easier for the drugs to go down. Pro glanced over to the chips the old head had given him at the Fulton County Jail over at Rice Street. Pro tried to give them back along with the rest of the items, but the man refused. The old man said it was the way he received his blessings; giving to others. After the officer notified Pro to pack it up, his door popped open. At that time, Pro made a quick call to the big homie Theory, who should be arriving shortly, Pro imagined. Grabbing the bag of shebang, Pro laid down on his bed, munching until the dizziness came on. Pro occupied the room by himself; however, it would only be temporary at the rate people got locked up in Fulton County. A few more chews and Pro went out like a light, with the bag of shebang still on his lap. After about 15 minutes into Pro's nap, Smokey Ru walked past on his way to a transaction. Noticing the door wide open, Smokey Ru quietly locked Pro in, securing him from the wickedness roaming about unchained in their unpredictable surroundings.

"Damn homie," Smokey Ru said to himself, clearly upset with Pro being off guard. Smokey went about his business, tucked away in captivity from the world he once knew outside. Still a hustler and optimistic, he took nothing for granted.

Dreadful Nightmares

It was the 4th of July, and the year's fireworks had begun early. The shootout yesterday threw the whole city into an uneasy temperament. The phone sitting on the wooden nightstand rang angrily on its base, punching disturbance into McKenzie's sleep. Head under the pillow, McKenzie's hand swiped blindly back and forth, feeling for the old-fashioned phone seeking to dry his dream. The walls of the one-bedroom apartment bounced the ringing from corner to corner before he finally grabbed hold of the object. McKenzie pulled the phone from the hook to meet his half-covered chest. McKenzie's parched throat began in a dry rumble "Heeelooo," he said, allowing his eyes to remain shut. "Officer McKenzie, it might be in your best interest to get up and pay attention." The Darth Vader sounding voice came across like it had been a part of the dream. McKenzie attempted to stay submerged in the depth of his astral journey, but it all quickly dissipated. "Davi, in about ten seconds, if I don't get the response I so desire, I am going to turn your every waking moment into a continuous collage of

242

dreadful nightmares." McKenzie's eyes popped open like he'd heard the voice of someone he'd hid in the archives of forbidden skeletons. After blinking a few hard blinks, McKenzie's body perched up on the supports of his forearm." Who is this?" McKenzie asked, sounding paranoid. McKenzie looked over to the nightstand then a spider crawled onto his hands around his wire-framed glasses. Noticing the blurred time brightly standing out from the Marlboro digital clock on the wall. McKenzie slid on his lenses, bringing the red glowing 5:30 am into focus. "Now that I have your attention, I'm sure you gather by now that this call is of great importance to your wellbeing."

Firebird began. "In regards to your question, I will allow you to know who I am." The voice explained. "I am known as Firebird." He admitted. McKenzie, listen closely because this will be the last question you will have the privilege of asking." Firebird informed as his coldness traveled audibly undisguised. McKenzie's eyebrows rose into a confused and intimidated expression. "Should you decide to continue with the questions, the men I have staking the 4514 Brunswick Lane residence will gladly slay the two occupants before they can even begin their 7:30 am breakfast." McKenzie's heart froze still as the man continued." Then Abe, the collie, and the sack of wrinkles you call your parents and adore even more than yourself will be stuffed and placed in your pathetic apartment as a reminder. McKenzie could think of a slew of questions to ask. Still, the threats Firebird had made were accurately aimed at McKenzie's logic. "Okay, don't hurt them. I am listening," McKenzie stuttered in reply. "McKenzie, my intentions aren't to bring harm upon your family or yourself." Firebird explained. You're simply a means to an end, but the moment you defer from my humble request, you'll become collateral damage." Firebird promised through an unmerciful growl. "I under... I understand." McKenzie submitted. "Good, very good, Davi," Firebird smirked to himself.

Kill Our Romance

After taking a relaxing bath spiked with scented oils and beads, officer Santos stared at herself in the mirror, wondering where she was headed. She was never the one to be disoriented; she felt puzzled as to why her compass needle was on the fritz. Independence was the core of Inez's strength. Still, somehow over the course of one adventurous yet romantic night, she'd already begun to feel dependent on Detective Nassi. Combing her hair into place, she had a few flashbacks of how intimate and hot the raw sex she and Ilakin shared in the shower had been. Vivid images of how delicate it had all started, followed by the savagery of two wild beasts colliding throughout Nassi's condo, played in her mind's eye. It began with a passionate kiss once Inez found herself lured into the steamy shower, unable to resist Nassi's coolness.

Inez crept in behind Nassi's naked and wet body, letting her fingers caress the contours of his back. She was wet long before she entered the bathroom and could no longer allow

245

Nassi's gentleman-like attitude to shun her desires. Nassi turned to meet her seductive gaze as she pushed closer to let her lips connect with his. Without any extra effort of Inez's, Nassi's love stick became a concrete obelisk between her thighs. Feeling him rise, she kissed him deeper, sucking and pulling his lips away from the phone. Inez's pussy muscles began to throb and pulsate as her heart rate increased. Nassi's hand gently slid behind Inez's head.

Using her hair to pull her head back, exposing her neck as his wet tongue tickled her esophagus. Nassi's other hand cuffed Inez's breast bringing a wanting moan from the depths of her diaphragm, making her weak as Nassi began to take control. Initially, Inez seemed to be the aggressor. However, with each passing moment, Nassi's hormones began forcing her into submission. Within seconds, Inez found her back pressed firmly against the shower's wall as Nassi's tongue teased her hardened nipples. Taking as much of Inez's breast as his mouth could handle. Nassi's fingers worked into the swollen cameltoe gaping her legs apart. The softness of her lips aroused him even more as his fingers pushed into her vagina, parting them to find her clitoris. Inez sucked in, panting with short hard breaths lusting for the moment when Nassi would enter her. Nassi's game was only beginning, and although he could sense from her body language what she wanted, he had plans of his own. Nassi's hand pressed firmly against Inez's stomach like he was using the force of his push to make her pussy push outward. Licking down under the cup of her breast, his tongue took a course past her navel and onto her pelvic bone as he came to his knees in front of her. Inez's body shook from the sensations as the tingle electrified her body in a way she'd never felt before. Grabbing the back of Nassi's head, the natural reaction of her body hunched out towards Nassi's mouth. Nassi caught her in the suction of his lips, applying a strong yet gentle pull on her succulent pussy causing it to change colors as the blood behind her skin rushed to that area. Motivated by her grip on his hair, he pushed into her lips harder with his face as the warmth of his mouth took her to another place beyond ecstasy. Nassi flicked his tongue in a rapid motion, then slowed to suck at her clitoris like fruit on a summer's day. The passion overwhelmed Inez's faculties, and her mind filled with dazzling stars and electricity dancing between her brain cells.

"Mmmh." She moaned louder as the feeling took hold of her like she had become possessed.

Nassi had a firm grip on Inez's meaty ass cheeks, pulling her into him as if there was still too much room between them. The fact was that they were so close that even air would have a hard time finding a crack of space to escape. Inez's nails dug into Nassi's scalp as she hunched faster and harder into his tongue. Lifting her head, she let out a whine while trying to bring her legs to close. Nassi wasn't having it; he would not allow her to escape his grip as he sucked deeper into her wetness. Inez screamed herself into a powerful orgasm as the water of the shower streamed down her beautiful shape. Nassi's mouth loped at the mix of water and her feminine liquid until her shakes turned from strong jerks to slowed squirms. Nassi's tongue had escorted her from one sensation to the next without ceasing, slowing when the time was right. When his mouth finally detached from her crevice, it sounded off with a smack like he'd taken a bottle from a baby's mouth. Inez looked down into his eyes, peering up into her soul like an angelic being created for her pleasure. Nassi stood, lifting her up, then on to his hardness as she gasped for air. He eased into her slowly inch after inch with passion in his eyes while the remains of her orgasm were still inside her and lubricated his stiffness. She made an attempt to say his name, but before she could get it out, he took her mouth with his own, capturing the breadth of her words inside his lungs as he inhaled her into another deep kiss. Their tongues played wildly inside each other's mouths as Nassi stretched into her walls. Nassi's heart was pounding like an Indian drum. Inez's eyes rolled back into her head, scratching blood from Nassi's back. The sting of her nails took Nassi into hyperdrive as he increased the speed of his thrust, now pounding away at her pussy. Inez moaned, meeting Nassi halfway as she bounced her ass up and down on Nassi's dick using her thigh muscles. Nassi carried her out of the shower bumping into everything close, not wanting to break his stride. Inez was locked in for the ride letting her guts wrap around everything he threw inside of her, taking the bumps and bruises along the way. The couple passed the nightstand twirling as Inez's foot caught the lamp, knocking it to the floor bringing the digital clock down with it. Nassi went for the dresser, using his hand to clear a place to sit Inez's juicy ass up as he kept his pounding going on. The sight of Inez's jiggling cheeks in the mirror amplified Nassi up, making him go in harder. A figurine on a shelf above the mirror tumbled down, catching Inez on the side of her forehead then onto the floor. She never felt the pain of it to catch up with the pleasure of Nassi's rock-hard dick. Nassi picked her up off the dresser, not wanting to cause her any more unintentional injury throwing her onto the bed. Once in the bed, Nassi flipped Inez over to enter her from behind. The sound of her ass clapping into his lower abdomen as he rotated into her depth turned her on, causing her to bring another powerful nut down her juice box. Nassi splashed into her wetness like a mad man slapping her cheeks as she threw her ass violently down on his shaft. Juices rolled from her insides onto Nassi's balls as he began to growl, releasing a massive load of cum into her warmness.

Inez smiled back at her reflection, using makeup to cover the bruises her hair wouldn't hide. She thought of how she had been scared of being rejected by Nassi only to find out that he was just as interested in her as she was in him. Before long, Inez found herself wet, allowing her thoughts of Nassi to run wild, bringing her to need some sexual ease. Clearly, Nassi had awakened the animal in her. She laughed to herself, locating her vibrator prepared to stimulate the urge, hell she had time to kill, she reasoned. After pleasing herself, officer Santos left her place with a newfound passion for her detective and his work. Several untied issues left her to debate what order she would tackle her agenda. Inez wouldn't have to clock in for at least another hour and a half. Thinking back to the restaurant and the mysterious, out-of-place man she'd seen, she thought of paying Terrance, the more than feminine waiter who served them, a visit. Rationalizing it, it is better to call ahead, she spoke into her phone.

"The Oceanaire Seafood Room," the number dialed out, and after two rings, a woman answered.

"Hello, thank you for calling The Oceanaire Seafood Room. May I help you," The receptionist said warmly.

"Yes, I'm Officer Santos with the Atlanta Police Department. You have a waiter there by the name of Terrance. Would he happen to be in?" Inez asked politely with a firmness in her tone.

"I'm sorry, ma'am, wait." She stopped mid-sentence. "He's not in any trouble, is he?" the receptionist asked, being nosey.

"No, no, of course not," Inez replied. "Okay, well, he's not in right now," the girl replied.

"Do you have a number I can reach him at," Inez asked?

"Oh no, I'm sorry, ma'am, our policy prohibits us from giving our employees' personal information out. However, if you like, I can take yours and have him contact you," the receptionist offered.

"Okay, sure, that would be great. Would you please notify Terrance that it's urgent" Inez requested after giving her number.

"Yes, ma'am, not a problem, and have a great day, the girl said before ending the call. After about ten minutes, Inez' phone rang,

"Hello, Officer Santos speaking," Santos answered.

"Hello, this is Terrance, my co-worker from the Oceanaire said you were trying to reach me," Terrance said in a huff.

"Terrance, hi, how are you? This is Inez. I was dining with a gentleman last night, and you were our waiter, Inez stated plainly. Terrance replied dryly,

"Okay, and?" His attitude was hardly hidden.

"Do you remember me with the huge yellow earrings?" Inez asked.

Terrance cut in, "Oh yes, girl, how are you?" Terrance began, "How did you end your night, you wild hot thang you?" Terrance kicked into gear like an old girlfriend prying for the juicy details.

Inez laughed. "Let's just say we got it in," Inez said, smiling.

"Umm hum," Terrance hummed, "Well, what can I do for you, Ms. Get It in?" Terrance asked with a grin.

"Look, I need your help. I'm not exactly a detective. I work in forensics; what I need is a still shot, but in order for me to get that, I would have to go through the legalities of getting a subpoena from the courts to view the restaurant's camera footage" Inez claimed.

"What, from last night?" Terrance asked, sounding suspicious.

"Yes," Inez admitted, eager for Terrance's help.

"Did that bastard meet another woman in the parking lot?" Terrance interrogated, sounding like some male bashing hood rat.

"No, nothing like that," Inez cut in, stopping Terrance in his rant before it went any further.

"There was a guy who came in last night, he didn't place an order, and after the detective went outside, he followed.

"How did I miss him, I wonder?" Terrance questioned himself aloud.

"I don't know, but I didn't," Inez began. "For some reason, my gut is telling me that the man had a role in the shootout leaving a woman dead last night," Inez stated, not wanting to go into detail.

"Oh my God, for real, okay, okay, let me think," Terrance sounded nervous.

"Terrance, listen, is there any way you can access the camera footage from last night and send the image to my phone? I need to run it through the face recognition program at the lab?" Inez asked, almost pleading with Terrance.

"Yeah, yeah, it shouldn't be a problem," Terrance agreed. Inez gave a description and the seating placement so that Terrance could narrow it down after finding the correct timestamp. The two ended the call with arrangements to link back in when Terrance arrived for his shift at four o'clock that evening. Inez, en route to the lab, pulled through the Chick-fil-A drive-thru for a quick chicken salad and a shake before her hunger got out of control. Inez got to the lab a little early with a satisfied appetite with her stomach and heart feeling like life couldn't be better. It had been a while since she felt wanted and desired, and it gave her a high that she didn't want to come down from. Inez floated into the lab as if she rode in on a cloud, humming with contentment. Arriving at her desk, she punched in her password on the keyboard to her CPU. When her screensaver popped up showing a lioness crouching in a field on a hunt, it brought to mind the role Inez was seeking to play in Nassi's life. The thought of him took over, and without even realizing it, she pulled the phone from her hip dialing his number. Catching herself, she quickly hung up before it could start ringing, thinking she should just text.

"Hey you," was not the newest message in her sent box. Nassi responded almost instantly as if he was waiting on her text. "What's up gorgeous?" he replied. Inez sends a smiley face back, followed by a heart emoticon. "I was just thinking about you," Nassi admitted. Inez looked around to make sure no one could see the effects her inbox was having on her. Fortunately for her, everyone around was too busy to notice her blushing. "Same here!" She stated the obvious. Before Inez could get her next text out, Nassi was calling. The phone did a half-a-ring, and Inez was on the other end, full of excitement. "Hey," Inez answered, sounding happier than her usual self.

"Hey, mommy, what you up to?" Nassi asked, trying to lay a sexy tone down.

"Nothing, at work thinking about last night," Inez replied, her smile evident in her words.

"Oh yeah?" He quested as he exited onto Lee St. from I-20.

"Yeah," she blushed. "I'm in the lab now. I wanted to get an early start looking at these samples from the crime scene," Inez said, pulling locator slips for the items she needed. "Oh, don't get mad at me, but I tracked Terrance down," Inez explained.

"Who the hell is Terrance?" Nassi asked, sounding territorial.

"The waitress from last night," Inez joked.

"Who?" "Wait a minute, the gay guy from the Oceanair?" He asked. "Inez, why do you insist on making him a female? He's a dude sweetheart," Nassi said, still driving up Lee St. "So what, you guys planning on hanging out now?" He continued without an ounce of humor in his voice.

"Eventually, maybe if my new man is willing to refrain from being an extreme homophobic," Inez laughed, still picking at Nassi.

"Uggh," Nassi sighed before getting quiet, letting her words register. *Did she call me her new man*, Nassi thought to himself, still hearing her words ringing through his mind? They both tried to speak simultaneously, calling each other's name, then there was silence again. Inez broke the moment from quietness. "Nassi look, it's like I told you; no pressure, you don't have to commit to me," Inez began. "I'm feeling you, it's true, but we're just getting acquainted."

"Inez," Nassi interrupted.

"Yes," she answered, caught off guard by the interruption.

"I can't wait to see you again," he started, "Everything about you feels right, and I haven't been able to get my mind off you," Nassi informed her. Inez almost came to tears, knowing how deep the gash in Nassi's heart was, yet he was warming up to her being able to express these feelings. She smiled as a sigh of relief overtook her body with a slight tremor. "So what's the deal with Terrance, love?" Nassi asked, putting the conversation back on route.

"Well, like I said, don't get upset, but I have him pulling the footage from last night at the restaurant. I really want to run that guy's face through recognition," she explained.

"Oh yeah, that mystery man you were talking about last night," Nassi replied, remembering her reasoning.

"Yeah, I just can't brush him off. My senses are screaming and pointing," Inez stated, moving away from her desk with some papers in hand.

"Well, hey, I don't have any objections. After all, you were the one on point last night," Nassi admitted.

"Well, I'll take some credit for the earlier part of the night, but you were stiffly on point in the latter portion of the night," she joked. "Hell, you still had me weak this morning," Inez teased, letting her inner freak flirt. Nassi burst into a hard laugh, feeling Inez's bluntness.

"Aye, man," he said, still smiling and laughing. "There is more where that came from," he teased back.

"I bet," Inez said, letting her lower lips clinch.

"Damn," he said, reminiscing. "Okay, well, look, I'm headed over to the Johnson's residence now to check on the family and retrace some of the scene," Nassi explained. "I got a few things done today already," he continued. "I saw Kadarai earlier, and he assured me his people had nothing to do with what happened at my condo," Nassi explained. "He knows without a doubt the whole rundown; he just won't break from that code of the street bullshit," Nassi vented. "I mean, I respect and all, but goddamn, it makes my job hard," Nassi said, sounding frustrated.

"Don't worry, honey, we will get to the bottom of this," Inez encouraged

"Dynamic duo huh?" Nassi said with a superhero kind of chant.

"Absolutely," Inez affirmed proudly.

"Oh yeah, one of Pro's people called me as well and said we needed to talk, so we met over by the Varsity," Nassi informed Inez.

"Well, what happened?" she asked, giving him her undivided attention.

"Nothing; just confirmed that they weren't involved with us getting shot at last night and that if we had any more issues to contact her." He finished.

"What! It was a female?" Inez asked, almost sounding jealous.

"Yeah, they have females enlisted," he laughed.

"Was she pretty?" Inez asked, already regretting it. *What the hell is wrong with me,* she thought, figuring she sounded foolish.

"Well, she's definitely not Inez Santos, but she wasn't just butt ugly," he said, making her aware that his eyes were for her only.

"Umm Hmm," she hummed, feeling better that Nassi hadn't crushed her for sounding so insecure. "So she confirmed pretty much what we knew already?" Inez asked.

"What the hell?" Nassi blurted out, "Okay, look, babe, I'm on the Johnson's street now. I'll call you back in a little bit, love," Nassi said, sounding disturbed.

"Okay, be safe. Don't we have people trying to kill our romance?" Inez said, understating the reality of their situation.

"No doubt, mommy later," Nassi said, sounding rushed before he killed the call. The call ended, and Inez tuned into the reports in front of her. She figured Nassi was likely irritated pulling up to the Johnsons house because it was still crawling with news cameras.

The fabric samples that she and Nassi found on the ground matched the shirt Kadarai was wearing. This being the case, it automatically threw shade on the position the officer's account placed them in. Inez's mind began to storm, playing the scene in her head. Instantly she realized that Officer Talley's body was found to the right of the fabric samples, which made no sense if Kadarai had been gunning from the right of Talley. Amazing how a piece of cloth could tell a story of its own, she thought. The singed edges also showed traces of gunpowder, connecting the entry wound to Tally's left side. Inez cross-tested the gunpowder with the traces found on Kadarai's pistol, and within minutes, she knew she had a match. Inez's senses flared as the heat seared into the back of her neck, feeling like she was being watched. She turned to look behind her but found nothing out of the ordinary. Though that did nothing to stop the goosebumps from rising on her flesh. Bringing her focus back, Inez flipped through the file, highlighting paragraphs and jotting notes. Looking at a page describing the degree and angle of the first bullet entry into Talley's side, she paused and thought. It appeared to her to have entered in more of an upward angle. That made sense if Hemlock's account was accurate. Inez was convinced that there was definitely some foul play with the scene, but why, she pondered? Inez went back to her desk on edge as her thoughts raced like Indy cars on a superspeedway.

Why would Hemlock paint this story inaccurately? Inez kept asking herself. She knew the Red Dog Unit had some sketchy tactics. Still, he *just complicated the case, which would ultimately compromise a just conviction. Why jeopardize that?* She thought. *He's hiding something, but what and why?* Inez continued flipping through more paperwork she had compiled yesterday. She looked back at her notes and all the inconsistencies she had only spoken to Nassi about. There were traces of cocaine on the scene, but none admitted into evidence worth causing a fuss about. "So they say?" she huffed. It was found in close proximity to Tally and where she now knew Kadarai had been. There were a few chards of glass found on Talley's clothing but none in the vehicle, yet more glass littered the area close to Talley's body. Shaking her head in disbelief, Inez was beginning to suspect crooked cops gone wild. To top the cake, track marks were showing that at some point, there was some sort of vehicle parked in that same area which undoubtedly had housed the glass found on the scene. "What the fuck is this" Inez exhaled, overwhelmed with what was becoming more evident by the second. Breaking Inez from her intense investigation was a loud yet familiar voice, "Santos," her superior, Victoria

Scoutt, yelled. Inez looked up like she had been caught stealing or something, startled by the woman's voice. "My office now!" Victoria demanded, enunciating each word. Inez closed her files and left her cubicle, headed to Victoria's office.

"Yes," Inez said calmly, entering the office. Victoria wasted no time getting to the point of their meeting.

"I need you to take a few days off, we are kinda done in on hours, and I have to let a few of you go for three or four days," Victoria stated firmly.

"What? I'm in the middle of something here; why me?" Inez complained, sounding too much like a spoiled kid for Victoria's liking.

"Listen, it's nothing personal, just do it; leave whatever you're working on and what you haven't completed. We'll have someone cover for you," Victoria instructed. "Try to relax for a few days. Hell, I'd love a break like this with pay," Victoria explained, sounding like she was doing Inez a favor.

"Fuck that! This is some bullshit!" Inez snapped, letting her emotions for the case get the best of her. Nassi warned her about this type of emotion, but it was too late, and the cat was out of the bag.

"Excuse me!" Victoria spat back as she stood from behind her desk, turning as red as a cranberry. "If you don't want a few days to turn into a permanent vacation, I suggest you get your pathetic bratty ass out of my office and follow orders like a good little Nina," Victoria demanded, flexing her authority. Inez stormed out of Victoria's office, slamming the door so hard behind her that the wall shock. Making it to her desk, Inez sat at her cubicle, fuming. She logged out of her CPU while simultaneously snapping pictures of the documents she had highlighted just in case. There was no flash, so Victoria was clueless about what Inez was doing behind the low wall of her cubicle as she watched intently from her office. Inez looked back in Victoria's direction, and even through the blinds, she could tell Victoria's head was pressed to a phone. Now knowing why she eyed her closely earlier. Inez still wanted to take the files with her, convinced now that this was obviously bigger than what she and Nassi imagined. Inez made an attempt to hide the files in a newspaper lying on her desk. No sooner than she had started for the exit did Victoria come out of her office

"Officer Santos," she called to Inez. *The fuck is this lady being a pain in my ass.*

"The files, please," Victoria demanded, tearing an entrance under Inez's skin. Inez, already aware this was coming, lifted her head to the lights above. "Jesus Cristos," she sighed before turning to take the files to Victoria. Inez walks over to Victoria. She could have torn holes into the floor as she pushed the files into Victoria's waiting hand. "Thank you, dear," Victoria smirked. Inez returned an agitated fake smile and gave Victoria her back as she walked away furious. Before Inez made it to her car outside in the parking lot, she sent a slew of rapid texts to Nassi's phone.

Inez punched buttons fast enough to start a fire as her heels clicked against the concrete. Just as Inez made it to her car, she heard a voice calling to her." Officer Santos," the timing startled her as she looked around to find officer McKenzie damn near on her ankles.

"What!" she barked, then finished her text.

"I don't mean to bother you, but I really need to talk to you," McKenzie said, placing his glasses back in place from the strut over.

"I don't have time now, McKenzie, and I am completely pissed off," she admitted. Figuring McKenzie making another lame attempt at her phone number. McKenzie moved in closer.

"Listen, Inez, you're in trouble; I want to help," McKenzie stated matter of fact with a knowing look in his eyes. The statement froze Inez in paranoia for a few moments, already aware that there was plenty of reason to believe him.

"We can't talk here, so I'll pull around so you can follow me," McKenzie instructed. Inez didn't speak, but her nod, accompanied by some serious blinking, gave him the go-ahead. Inez got in her car nervously and readied her firearm with a chambered bullet. Before pulling out of her parking space, she waited a few minutes as she texted Nassi. Meanwhile wondering why he hadn't replied yet. McKenzie pulled up beside her and waved her to follow. She followed McKenzie while keeping a close eye on her mirrors as she dialed Nassi's phone. The phone rang until voicemail kicked in, "Goddammit, what is he doing?" Inez yelled out loud while pounding on the steering wheel. McKenzie hit a hard left down a side street like he'd almost forgotten his turn.

Inez followed a little more cautiously than he'd made his turn but still kept up. She was anxious to know what McKenzie knew and, even more, how he could help. McKenzie sped up as the cars moved down a two-lane street. *This dude drives like a maniac,* Inez thought to herself, wondering why McKenzie was in such a rush. She had never thought of McKenzie being of any use to her but concluded how help could come from the most unexpected places sometimes. McKenzie's driving was just ridiculous, though, she thought as he shot through another intersection like a madman still picking up speed. "Okay, asshole. I'm not going to kill myself racing behind" Inez's words were cut short, stuck within the air that had been knocked from her lungs as a large black blur, t-boned into the passenger side of her compact car. She never saw it coming. Inez knew she had the right of way through the green light. Glass shattered from the passenger's side windows as the impact caused Inez's head to whip sideways into the driver's side window. Blood streaked across the side of her head like a bear's claw had ripped the tissue away, splashing against the cracked window that formed a dripping red spider web in the glass. Inez fought to remain conscious, but the pain made her wish she could just sleep it away. The car's cracked glass, along with the blood in her eyes, obscured the images moving around outside. Anticipating that someone was coming to help her, she tried calming herself not to panic, but what she heard next killed any thoughts of rescue. "Good job McKenzie, get her in the van, guys," a raspy voice instructed. She tried feeling around for her gun, but the door tore open just as she got her hands on it. Lacking the strength to move any faster, the two strong hands pulled her away before she could act. Once out in the open air, she attempted to scream for help, but somehow her yell was caught in her mouth suppressed into a hardly audible muffle. As soon as she realized it was due to a very large, gloved hand, everything went black. Inez heard a door slam and more men talking while her feet were being bound and her hands cuffed. She fought to the best of her ability. Still, the prick in her arm, followed by a fiery sting, silenced her murmuring, and brought her into a darkness beyond the sack over her head.

Blood for my Blood

"Count time, count time, gentleman, everybody out, backs against your doors, please." The officer yelled over the intercom, preparing the inmates in his housing unit for headcount. The sound of the officer's voice snatched Kadarai from a halfway decent place, spewing him back into a deluge of pain that was now the fabric of his reality. "Shlluuur," Product slurped in as he inhaled.

Working his body to sit up reminded him of just how painful his life had become. A sound came from the floor as Pro lifted up, followed by a crackling noise. Looking down to where the noise had come from, he noticed the chip bag he'd been snacking on before passing out underneath his foot. Pro licked his lips, followed by a dry smack of his mouth as he reached to retrieve what remained of the bag's contents.

"Count time, count time, 104, 107, 112, 215, 211, 225 were waiting on you." The faster you come out, the quicker you can get back to whatever it is you do," the officer yelled, sounding more irritated.

"Shut yo puss ass up with that loud ass dick sucker you running nigga," someone barked from a room downstairs. Pro laughed to himself at the comment as he made his way to his door, smacking on a Dorito. After exiting the room, Pro glanced to the right as he stood just out of the threshold. He noticed some unfamiliar face he hadn't seen earlier, as well as Smokey a few doors down. Smokey caught Pro's glance "West West brim, how are you?" Smokey asked, looking concerned. "West banging Ru, I'm booling famo, how you?" Pro responded then questioned the homie. "Goddamnit, quiet please," the officer said, disappointed that he lost his count. It didn't matter that anyone was talking; he would have fucked up the count anyway. He was known for it. "Please, guys, let me get my count," the oversized officer requested. After catching a firm nod of approval of Smokey's wellbeing, Pro's attention followed the husky voice of the officer on the floor below, starting his count over. "Bring your slow ass on," a man laughed from Pro's left, two doors down. Pro took in more faces trying to see if he recognized any as he scanned through the ones visible. With the lifestyle, Pro lived, being aware of his surroundings was vital. With his background and status, something that simple could be the determining factor of survival. Not recognizing anyone of significance, Pro lifted his head back, looking toward the ceiling, still not accepting how he ended up in this predicament. After a few minutes passed, the officer passed by Pro as his shoes protested against the weight they were carrying. Pro caught a glimpse of his nametag on the lapel of his uniform, reading officer R. Holtz. Holtz walked by, whispering numbers to himself while pointing a pen toward each inmate he passed in a sort of rhythm. Pro watched the heavy brown-skinned man, thinking that although the other inmates found things to degrade about that when it was all said and done, the man would at least be going home. Unfortunately, their fate would be a little different, which made Pro's stomach turn. "Alright, count clear, count clear," the unit officer informed. The inmates broke away from the positions they had been in and went about their various routines and businesses. "Aye Aye Aye, let me get that line after you," someone yelled downstairs, making reservations for one of the phones someone had obviously made it to first. Smokey Ru made his way over to Pro with probably one of the most hardcore strides Pro had ever seen aside from TV. "Whoop, Whoop," Smokey barked in a deep bass tone.

"Whoopty whoop," Pro replied, making his hand available to shake paws with Smokey.

"Aye, Brim, no disrespect to your gangster," Smokey started while taking Pro's hand to shake.

"The next time you feel like passing out dog," Smokey's head nodded with each word.

"Lock yourself in the room, homie," Smokey finished, frowning like he was in some sort of pain.

"Damn Ru, the meds they giving me got me all off my square, bro," Pro admitted, shaking his head in shame.

Pro had passed out on some house shoe shit, and he knew best of all slipping was a no-no.

"I'm gone hold you down, homie," Smokey vowed with a committed glare in his eyes. "But stay on point," Smokey demanded.

"B to the L homie, thanks, bro," Pro replied, grateful to have someone around.

"Piru love baaaby," a computerized chime sounded as the remake of Zapp and Roger's, Computer Love blared from Smokey's pants.

"What the fuck," Pro asked with an unbelieving grin on his face.

Pro recognized the song from an old Blood and Crip album titled Banging on Wax. "Pardon me, homie, that's the big bro," Smokey informed Pro, as he did a half duck and rolled back into his room. At the same time, in one motion, Smokey reached into his orange uniform bottoms and into the pocket of his drawers. Pro followed behind Smokey into the room, pulling the door up behind him. Once in the room, Smokey came out of his pants holding a Verizon flip phone to Pro's amazement. Pro stood laughing and shaking his head as Smokey flipped the phone open to answer the call.

"West mobbing big homie?" Smokey asked into the device.

"Us and only us fool," The voice said proudly through the loudspeaker.

Pro looked on like Smokey had lost his mind, then took a paranoid glance out of the room's window to locate the officer. Relieved that the officer was slumped lazily at his desk. Pro turned to look back over to Smokey, who was now smiling from ear to ear, shooting the shit with his big homie over the line. Smokey paced in a small area of the room then walked over to where Pro stood as the voice over the line kicked more wordplay.

"Yeah, homie, I ran through that pack in 4 hours flat no bull," The voice bragged, laughing.

Pro thought that the voice sounded familiar, especially how the person went to great lengths not to use profanity. Pro shook it off, not being able to place it. Smokey tapped Pro's good arm to get him to slide over from something on the wall. Pro looked confused but followed the body language and shifted out of Smokey's way. Smokey sat the phone on the sink then hooked his fingers around the corners of a speaker attached to the wall as he spoke back to the caller.

"Whaaaaat! You moving it like that big bruh?" Smokey asked, sounding excited about the caller's apparent accomplishments.

Smokey never needed much cause to celebrate with a fat joint. Just about anything would put him in the mood to fire up. After a few tugs on both sides of the speaker placed on the wall, its seal of paint gave out as Smokey slowly pulled its square shape from its place. Smokey gently let the speaker down to hang from a single yellow wire that held it stable while allowing him to access the hollow space behind it in the wall. At this point, Pro realized that Smokey had pretty much made the best of a bad situation, enjoying a few luxuries that couldn't be easily attained.

"Aye, homie any other way, and I wouldn't be Banger Ru," The caller laughed, still flaunting.

"I know that fool's voice blood," Pro laughed, grabbing the phone from the sink.

Smokey felt relieved that Pro had brought the phone closer allowing him to hear and do what he was busy doing meanwhile.

"Banger Ru west up homie," Pro said with a smirk hooking through the side of his face.

"Awwww junk," Banger Ru said, knowing only one person who hit that west up with such a smooth drawl.

"Yeah, that fasho, my G west brinacking," Pro replied, happy to hear Banger Ru's voice. The two had history and grew pretty close over the years. The two had stayed in contact, keeping in touch through letters and phone calls since Banger Ru had caught state time for clapping a nigga out in Milledgeville, Georgia.

"Damn homie, I was hoping it wasn't true, but one of your drops told me you had got locked up. Pro, what happened, homie?" Banger Ru asked, suddenly sounding hurt from the realization.

As Pro explained in the background, Smokey had finally got his hands on the stash hidden inside the wall and was placing the speaker back in place. After Smokey fixed the speaker back in its former condition, he proceeded to roll a picture-perfect joint, using two rolling papers. Licking and sticking them together, he was now ready to roll one the long way. "Yeah, homie, shits heavy, but I'll pull through it, you know me. I just can't believe my pup flat-lined on me, you know," Pro grieved to Banger Ru.

"I know homie, Wet was that nigga dog. I'm gone miss him, bro," Banger Ru expressed, taking a calming breath.

The two reflected on how they had all kicked it when Banger Ru was free. Banger Ru and Wet were the reason why Pro hadn't completely given up on the 90 babies. They had given him hope that at least some of them thought before acting and were capable of taking him into the future holding the torch. After a few more minutes of catching up, Pro and Smokey let the homie Banger Ru go tend to what business he had to take care of. They knew his situation was a little more complex with the new phone scramblers they had out at the prison. The joint was still burning, and Pro was already feeling the effects creeping into his thought process. Pro looked at Smokey through slanted eyes as his lids became heavy.

"Why you pass me that Bali bro, that shit got me feeling brazy?" Pro asked, rubbing his throbbing shoulder. Smokey leaned against the wall on the backside of his bed, playing with the jagged shank he had pulled from the stash.

"Dog, I'm high as hell too," Smokey admitted, as the joint hung from his bottom lip. A loud boom from the day room caught Smokey's attention as he sprung to his feet, recognizing the sound of the main door into the dorm. Smokey peeked out of his window to make sure it wasn't a shakedown. Satisfied, he took a seat getting back comfortable in his spot, digging under his nail with the gruesomely made knife.

"What was that?" Pro asked, barely able to lift his eyes.

"Some new dude just came in the dorm," Smokey hissed

"Why you say it like that?" Pro questioned, sensing something.

"This nigga is, of course, with the Khufi team like the majority of these cats." Smokey spat, sounding like he was fed up.

"You don't like the ocks, huh, homie?" Pro asked, trying to gain an understanding of why Smokey made the comment.

"It ain't that homie. I mean, we got big homies that have been Muslim born and raised. Only in Georgia's penal system do they act and function like a gang organization. What I'm saying is, it's just amazing that niggas want to find Allah, Jesus too for that matter, once they ass get jammed up. Them niggas don't be thinking bout none of that when they out there doing whatever the fuck shit they are doing out there in the world blood." Smokey said, showing his emotion through his hand movements, pointing and waving in one fluid motion. Pro's expression showed that Smokey had made a valid point. The door to the main entrance slammed again, but before Smokey could get up, he heard the nurse yelling.

"Medication! Medication!" Knowing that the nurse had arrived on the floor, Smokey reminded Pro that he was due for his dosage.

"Go get your meds, homie. That fine-ass nurse Woods is out there dog," Pro got up to make his way to the day room as Smokey collected a few packaged sacks that were on the market for whoever might need a fix of the meds he had to offer. Exiting the room, Pro noticed the light-skinned woman passing out the meds on the main floor.

"Damn dog, she is bad as hell." Pro agreed

"I told you, homie," Smokey grinned.

"I'll be out in a second. Let me spray the room down with this blunt spray and tighten up right quick," Smokey said as he tucked his shank under the mattress. Pro figured he probably just had taken it out of the stash for the evening but not really needing it. Pro laughed at the homie's movement.

"Where you get all this shit Ru, blunt spray, phones, shanks, pacs, what else you got?" Pro asked, not really looking for an answer.

"Hey blood, it's a dog's world, smell me?" Smokey smiled, knowing Pro was digging his flow.

Pro attempted to pull himself together, not wanting to give a wrong first impression looking too high in front of the nurse as he made his way toward the steps. Before Pro could get going, he was delayed by a slim, brown-skinned man wearing a kufi, a costume the male Muslims wore for headdress. The man was carrying a net full of his belongings and a sheet that he had turned into another form of a sack by tying the corners together. Pro assumed it held more of the man's items. As the man reached the top step, he and Kadarai made eye contact. They held each other's gaze a little longer, which made Pro uncomfortable. Something was strange in the man's eye, and Pro wasn't the one to leave anything to the imagination, so he broke the moment.

"You know me or something?" Pro asked with venom dripping from his cold eyes, never oozing his stare.

Caught off guard, the man wearing the kufi almost panicked as his heart began to pound, knowing that his target Kadarai Pro Cunningham was standing right before him. He had heard what Product or Kadarai was capable of, but seeing him in person made the man a little more than timid. Not knowing what to say, the man grew enough heart to let his shaky voice sound off.

"Oh nawl man, umm, I just thought you looked familiar." He answered nervously.

"From where my nigga?" Pro asked with his aggression showing.

The man just shook his head, lost for words, not knowing what to say.

"What, you saw me on the news or something?" Pro continued to drill him.

Pro had no idea, but he had just given the man a way out.

"Yeah yeah yeah" The man jumped at the opportunity.

"That's where man, the news, damn they got you all over the TV." He said, offering a weak smile. Pro studied the man's demeanor, turned off by his snake-like smile.

"I'm Saduj" The man tried introducing himself. Pro didn't entertain any more talk with the man and rudely pushed on to go handle his business.

"Motherfucker." The man whispered to himself from the mix of fear, hatred, and anxiety of being that close to Kadarai. He started working himself up now that Pro was gone. Pro's rudeness was a good push for Saduj to do what he had come to do for the officer who'd come to visit him. Puma had suggested a favor, and Saduj could definitely use one to get off the time he was facing. From what Saduj could tell, it would be a pretty easy kill with Kadarai confined to an arm sling, plus he looked rather fragile with all the injuries. Saduj would still be cautious, his target was no

275

pushover whatever the physical condition he'd been caught in, and heart was a hard animal to conquer. Saduj made it out of his brainstorm and headed to the room that officer Holtz had directed him to, passing Smokey on the way. Smokey mean-mugged the man as he passed, but Saduj never looked his way; he was caught in his thoughts. Smokey watched as the new guy got to room 225. Saduj stopped to put his bags down so that he could open the door.

"Ain't that a bitch?" Smokey sighed, irritated that the new guy in the kufi would be Pro's roommate.

Smokey went about his business visiting his regular customers and soliciting others after getting a location on Pro who was standing in the pill line trying to catch nurse Woods. Meanwhile, Pro listened to the soft voice of the nurse that stood on the other side of the skinny white man between them.

"You're welcome sir, have a nice day, okay, and try not to put too much pressure on that ankle," the nurse instructed the man in front of Pro.

The skinny white man limped off, leaving Pro to finally get a close-up of this attractive creature.

"Next," she began as Pro moved closer to the med cart.

"Name please," she asked, looking through her glasses.

Pro noticed her long, naturally beautiful eyelashes and how they complimented her beautiful brown eyes.

"Kadarai Cunningham," he informed her, keeping eye contact.

"Oh, okay," she said in a high-pitched tone as if she recognized the name.

Pro raised an eyebrow, trying to figure her angle out.

"Mr. Cunningham, you have a gunshot wound? Oh goodness." The nurse asked, sounding concerned as she looked at Kadarai's information on her laptop. "How do you feel? Are you okay?" She asked with a sympathetic look in her eyes.

"It's just a scratch, sweetheart," Pro capped, putting on for the nurse.

"Ummm, I guess," she joked, smiling. "Well, here are some dressing changes, and these should last four days. Take these antibiotics for infection," she instructed, pulling some antibiotic packets from the drawer after handing Pro a medicine cup with three pills inside. The nurse also pulled a few packs of gauze and tape from the cart.

"How's your head feeling? Do you have any headaches coming and going?" She asked, reaching to take the bandage from his head.

"It hasn't stopped hurting since the accident," Pro admitted inhaling her perfume as she moved close to him. She appeared to be in her early to mid-twenties and maybe a foot shorter than Pro. She had one of the most hypnotizing smiles Kadarai had ever laid eyes on; she was far from stingy with it.

"Oh, that's nasty," she admitted feeling sorry for Kadarai. Pro's facial muscles jerked from the sharp sting as she pulled gauze from the congealed spot in the wound.

"I'm sorry," she whispered, looking in Pro's eyes as if she hadn't meant to cause him any more pain than he was already in. She took one of the packages of antibiotic cream and opened it. She smeared some on a new gauze with her latex gloves and gently replaced the one she had trashed. After getting Pro squared away, she finally gave him some soda to wash back the pills she had handed him earlier. He threw the contents of the plastic cup behind the pills and washed them away to do what was needed of them in his system, then he let out a sigh.

"Thank you, nurse," Pro said, appreciative of how nice the nurse had seemed, especially with the way people had been making him out to be what the media described as a heartless monster. Pro thought to himself that the nurse must not have known who he was.

"Ms. Woods, do you judge me from what they've made me appear to be?" Pro asked, resenting how his image had been bruised. Ms. Woods pursed her lips to the side shaking her head no.

"Only God can do that, Mr. Cunningham. I'm in no position to," she started, with an almost angelic expression. "Whatever man can do, he is able to undo, and intent is what tips the scales of righteousness and unrighteousness, be blessed, Mr. Cunningham. Good day," she said, almost in tears.

Still unsure if she knew who he was and what he'd been accused of, Pro let her words sink in and left it at that as she turned away to make an exit. Pro watched for a few seconds until she was gone. His high had him stuck holding on to her words and smiling until two loud inmates came in from the rec yard holding a basketball.

"Lame ass nigga go get ya soups and bet some, fuck you talking bout," one inmate said, bouncing the ball hard on the floor with two hands as he spoke.

"Bet nigga, you ain't said shit. Fuck you mean?"

The other snapped back, walking off to get his soup Pro assumed. An elderly guy walked past with a towel on, leaving the shower area. Pro thought of how good the water would feel right about now. Convinced that the timing was appropriate, Pro went to retrieve his washing necessities. He passed Smokey's room then stepped back to peek in, but he was obviously out distributing his merchandise, Pro concluded. Pro got to his room, realizing the new guy was his roommate. Still not in the mood to talk, Pro entered and began collecting the needed items for his shower.

"Oh hey, roommate, I'll be out of your way by the time you get back. I'm just about done," Saduj said, trying to break the ice. Even Saduj hadn't known he'd be sleeping with the enemy.

"Yeah, aight," Pro said dryly, still in motion.

"Saduj's mind started to race along with his heart again, figuring the time might be sooner than later. Puma had given Saduj his word that it would be a cakewalk if he could get rid of the knife before the officers got to him. With the D.A in their pocket, he'd have Saduj out in no less than two weeks tops. Eager to get back to the streets, a variety of plans started formulating in Saduj's mind.

"Yeah, I think I'll get me one of them showers too in a lil bit. Some of the dudes be scared of them gators, know what I'm talking bout?" Saduj laughed, still trying to win Pro over.

Pro just looked at him with a shut the fuck up kind of smirk, nodding his head yeah.

This mafucka, Pro thought to himself. Turning to make his exit, Pro pushed out the door with nothing but a towel on his head and his pants. He threw his shirt onto the bed earlier. Once Pro was out of the door, Saduj rushed to find the shank he'd been handed before coming upstairs by some orderly he never saw coming. The piece glimmered under the fluorescent light above. Saduj took a deep breath nervously as he handled the tool building his heart. After all, he wasn't a killer and had never even faked to be one, but this was a chance to get back to the hoes and money and if it meant killing a killer, then fuck it, he was with it. The time was now, and he needed to catch Pro before he got down the stairs then make it back to the room to flush the piece. Saduj sucked in his bottom lip, pumping himself up, and with one frenzied blink, he was in motion.

Pro slid by Smokey's room in his shower shoes with a towel draped over his head. Adjusting some items in his hand, Pro hadn't even thought to step back by Smokey's room, figuring him to still be out and about. Just after Pro passed the room, Smokey stood up from his bed laughing engaged in a conversation on his phone when he noticed the new dude in the kufi, sheet by his window with a shank cuffed in his right hand. Smokey dropped the phone, scrambling to grab his shank from under his bed, never stopping to put his shoes on, knowing something was wrong with the picture. He rushed out of the door, but it was too late; all he could do was yell, noticing it was Pro who had just received a staggering blow at the back of his neck just below the skull behind his ear. The towel turned red instantly before falling off of Pro's head, exposing the gaping wound in his neck. Pro immediately grabbed the back of his neck, reacting to the sharp pain of the puncture while trying to turn to his offender. Before Pro could get turned around, he was met with two more quick stabs. One caught him in the cheek, denting it in as blood poured from his face while the other landed between the front of his neck and collarbone, sending misting spray of blood up into his face. Pro tumbled back down a few steps trying to catch his balance, then went over the rail. Smokey ran up behind Saduj full speed, cocked back far enough to deliver a fatal blow with his shank but pushed past once he saw Pro's body going over the rail attempting to catch him, but it was too late.

"Aye, what the fuck is going on," the officer yelled. He hit the button on his radio, screaming codes in shock like a stuck pig. Pro hit the floor hard. His head was split badly as blood flowed from beneath him. The inmates looked on in disbelief, trying to figure out how no one saw this coming. There was no argument or tension or any of the typical indicators that shit was about to go down. Saduj made it to the room, slamming the door behind as he broke the piece down to flush it. Smokey looked down at Pro with rage in his eyes as a flame engulfed his heart, it wasn't a far fall, but Pro's body was in no condition for anything of this magnitude. Smokey's eyes grew wide as he almost bit a hole in his bottom lip. Smokey turned his head swiftly, hearing Pro's door slam. Smokey's barefoot carried him to the door of the room as swift as a cheetah on the hunt. Looking in, Saduj was too busy trying to get rid of the evidence to notice, but fortunately for him at the moment, the door was locked. Smokey turned to look at the officer downstairs who had just pissed his pants when Smokey spit wildly two words through clenched teeth, "pop it." Foam sprayed from Smokey's mouth as the officers shaking hands went for the button. Not wanting to become a victim of Smokey's wrath, he popped the door.

Smokey ran in on Saduj like one of the creatures from *I am Legend* hammering away with his shank in Saduj's face, neck, and whatever else he could catch. The main door popped as the tact team ran in, trying to regain control of the unit. The inmates who knew the routine laid face down on their stomachs, hands stretched out. The whole dorm was quiet except the heavy panting and grunting coming from upstairs as Smokey tore open more and more of Saduj's mangled flesh. The officers rushed upstairs to Pro's room to find Smokey making a mess of what was left of Saduj's body. Smokey pounded blow after blow into the squishy tissue until it all just sounded like liquid. The officers grabbed Smokey from the pile of grounded human meat, only knowing it was human by the arms and legs. Smokey screamed from the top of his lungs.

"I want blood for my blood, muthafucker, you hear me? Huh, you hear me? Blood bitch!" Smokey was talking to Sadju like he could respond, but Sadju would never speak again. Regardless of what Puma planned, Saduj's freedom would only come by way of the afterlife.

The officers dragged Smokey down the stairs in cuffs as blood dripped from his hands and chest, all belonging to Saduj. His bare feet followed behind him, leaving a trail like a scene from a Saw movie. Once they made it to the bottom floor, Smokey bucked his body to get a look at Pro, where he lay still like a lifeless animal. The medics rushed over to Pro checking his vitals.

"It doesn't look good," one Medic said to another, shaking his head no.

"Brim, get up blood, get up my nigga, get up my nigga," Smokey cried as the officers pulled him through the main door. "Pro, get up, my nigga, you gotta! Brim strong, homie!" Smokey cried louder as saliva poured from his trembling mouth. The officers let the door slam with Smokey on his way to the hole as the other inmates watched it all from where they lay on the floor. The medics rushed Pro onto the gurney, ready to wheel him out as nurse Woods checked his vitals once more.

Hell on Earth

Riding up I-20, Nassi replied to a text the beautiful Inez Santos had just sent within the exact second he'd received it. The phone was already in his hand as he was just about to text her.

"Let me find out she's a mind reader," Nassi laughed to himself.

"What's up, gorgeous?" He replied swiftly. The smiley face and emoji she sent back brought him to confess against his will and reserve.

"I was just thinking about you," he replied, instantly feeling like he was becoming soft.

Nassi approached the sign for Lee Street overhead, notifying him that his exit was coming up.

"Same here," Inez replied.

Nassi couldn't shake his thoughts of her, she had broken the shell somehow, so when the urge to hear her voice rose, he couldn't resist. "Fuck this shit," he huffed like he was breaking away from some invisible restraint. Nassi began dialing Inez with the urgency of an addict calling for a fix. To his surprise, the phone didn't even get a complete ring before Inez was on the other end, sounding like she'd just won tickets from V-103, the local radio station. With his ego boosted from her apparent enthusiasm, Nassi tried to lay a smooth tone down, trying to cover his excitement.

"Hey, Mami. What are you up to? He asked, overdoing his coolness. Once she'd told him she was still harboring thoughts of last night, his head blew up the size of the Atlanta Aquarium. Even through the churn in his statement, he managed to pull a cool sounding.

"Oh yeah," questioning the calmness of her claim as he exited on Lee Street. The two exchanged a little more small talk during Nassi's commute as she explained what all she'd accomplished in hopes to help him with the case. *She was a natural*, he thought to himself, and her instincts couldn't be taught in any academy. Nassi filled her in on what all he'd been doing thus far today with plans of closing the night out with her and a home-cooked meal. Although he'd kept the plans to himself. In his mind, he'd already put too many of his internal feelings and thoughts on the table during this call, most of which was totally unlike him. Nassi laughed, thinking how he'd actually felt some jealousy before remembering who Terrance was and his preferences. Fortunately, Inez made him feel better when she exposed her hand, questioning the Bloodett he'd met earlier. This episode gave him the opportunity to stroke her ego too. When Nassi turned onto the Johnson's street, his attention was captured by a fight a few houses from the corner. Still holding the phone, Nassi was taken back by what was unfolding in front of him.

"What the hell?" He felt bad rushing off the phone with Inez. He had to gain control of the situation before it got out of hand, which could happen momentarily from the look of it. The last thing Nassi could remember Inez saying was, be safe, and the rest was a blur. Throwing his phone on the passenger's seat, Nassi jumped out of his car almost before it came to a complete stop.

"Aye, what the hell are y'all doing?" Nassi yelled at the kid as three broke in the opposite direction. Four remained, obviously too scared to run, seeing that detective Nassi had his gun drawn. Looking at the badge hanging from his neck, they knew not to test his authority. Even though the detective had his firearm pointed downward, Jamal knew better than trying anything stupid. Nassi only recognized one out of the group, the brother of Fatimah. He was wearing a new earring, a shiner under his left ear. The one now holding his hands up with a revolver enclosed in her palm was apparently coming to aid the Johnson kid. The remaining two who were about to become forgotten names of the losing side almost looked happy that Nassi had arrived. Seemingly had Nassi not come when he did, they'd be laying in the dirt.

Nassi snatched the gun away from the kid with a tug that almost sent the boy to the ground.

"What's wrong with you?" He asked the boy frowning like an angry father. Jamal looked up into Detective Nassi's eyes, mugging as his chest moved up and down from his labored breathing.

"Nothing's wrong with me," the kid answered, tightening his lips after he spoke.

"Yes, there is. You have a gun bigger than you. What do you mean nothing's wrong with you?" Nassi continued to drill the boy. "Where do you live?" Nassi asked, tucking the gun behind his belt and holstering his own. The kid pointed in the direction of his house, almost in tears knowing an ass-whooping would conclude this episode.

"Where do you two stay?" Nassi asked the two larger boys, giving them the same aggression he'd been giving Jamal.

"Two streets over," one explained while the other nodded in agreement.

"If you lay another finger on the kid, you will have to deal with me personally," Nassi began eyeing Hakiel and back to the two boys as he spoke. "I will come looking for you, and when I find you, it won't be pretty. Do I make myself clear?" Nassi snapped.

"Yes sir," the boys said in unison.

"Get out of here," Nassi yelled.

The boys took off running. Nassi looked down at Jamal with a fierce stare. Meanwhile, Hakiel took a look around to see who had them in sight. Primarily concerned if Tara was around. Satisfied, he turned to look back to the detective who was now interrogating his little buddy, now more of a partner in crime.

I hope we don't go to jail, Hakiel thought to himself.

"Do you mind telling me where the gun came from? Or do I need to get your parents involved," Nassi asked, giving the boys hope that it could all end right here without the undeniably deserved beat down.

"I found it," Jamal admitted, with his facial expression a little more civil than before, clearly pleased at the fact that he may not be turned into the proper authorities… his mother….

"Found it where?" Nassi continued. The boys looked at each other and spoke in some silent language of the eyes of how to go about answering. Detective Nassi studied the boys for that silent moment and picked up on a vibe that said these boys were hiding much more than this gun. "Hey, if this is too hard, then we can go talk to your parents," Nassi suggested.

"No, no, I'll tell you," Jamal agreed. "We saw the man that killed my sister," Hakiel broke into the conversation.

"Wait a minute, what did you say?" Nassi asked, looking at Hakiel with his eyebrows touching his hairline. "Who? The gang member?" What did you see?" Nassi asked, grabbing the boy by his arms kneeling down to his height. Just as Jamal started to exchange signs with Hakiel. Nassi's attention was snatched away by the sound of screeching tires coming up the street from the opposite way Nassi had pulled in. Looking up the road, the detective recognized a hit coming as the sight of two men on the back of a pickup holding assault rifles made it obviously clear.

Nassi looked at the two boys, "Run!" he said, pushing them toward the path between the two houses they were in front of. No sooner than the boys took off running, making a few feet away, did a hail of bullets rain down in Nassi's direction. Nassi ran for cover by his car, drawing his weapon still in a crouched position. The gunmen fired recklessly at everything close to Nassi, trying to strike their intended target. Nassi's weapon rang out loudly, throwing smoking shell casings away to the side as he fired back at his attackers. The two men on the flatbed wore ski masks and bulletproof vests. Nassi has to shield himself with his car. The truck, still a safe distance away from Nassi, let the two gunmen off, holding its position two car lengths away in the middle of the street. The shots tore into Nassi's car, knocking chunks away from its frame. Nassi could hear the men communicating.

"Take the other side," one said to the other. Nassi took that opportunity to coordinate his next few moves. Before he could collect his thoughts, he made out the shadow form of one of his attackers closing in on him from the side he'd taken cover behind a car a few feet away. Nassi fired two quick rounds at the attacker as he tried peeking around the vehicle at Nassi. Nassi knew that would only keep him at bay momentarily. The windows above Nassi burst into small shards just as Nassi rolled to the back of the car. To his dismay, the guy on the other side was closing in too. Before long, they would have him pinned down. Nassi had barely finished the thought when a black Tahoe pulled up swiftly behind his car. Three occupants jumped out, guns drawn, killing whatever hope of escape. Nassi had contemplated before he could finish planning. When Nassi took aim at the group directly in front of him, he knew it was over. He was outmanned and outgunned before he could let off his last few shots. To his disbelief, his predicament shockingly changed, giving him sights of a near future. The group who had just jumped out never took aim at Nassi. Strangely, their focus was on his attackers.

The gunmen in the red bandannas over their faces hit a harmony of drum rolls as their machines clapped relentlessly in the direction of Nassi's attackers.

"Pull back," Nassi heard the man yelling from the front of his car somewhere.

The gunman who jumped out of the passenger's seat of the Tahoe sounded more like a gun woman, as the feminine voice yelled over the parade of bullets.

"Brim business bitch, west go mothafucka."

This was no time to reminisce on old songs, but Nassi couldn't help but think of the Tupac song 'Me and My Girlfriend,' when the girl went berserk while busting shots at the same time talking and yelling her piece.

Still a little uneasy, Nassi held his gun up as she ducked low, approaching him as her men continued to bang it out in the middle of the street. Pulling her scarf down, Nassi recognized Hanna Bandanna right away.

"You Ok, dude?" she asked, without a glimpse of uncomfort in her demeanor. Nassi looked into the young girl's eyes, smiling in all.

"Yeah, I'm good. I was just about to handle these cats," Nassi joked. "You ok with all this?" he asked. Still taken back that she was out in the field.

Knowing exactly what the detective was implying, she responded with a wink. "I do this shit." She put her hand on Nassi's shoulder. "Stay down," she instructed before standing up to join her squad.

Nassi watched her move in like an assassin dumping round after round as shells bounced to the ground near Nassi's leg. Nassi, being the only real authority, hard-headedly stood up to his feet after exchanging clips to notice the pickup trying to back up under fire. One man lay in the street crawling as the other took off, running in the opposite direction, talking into a walkie-talkie. The pickup crashed into a car behind it, unable to stir under the heavy fire. The squad wearing the red flag closed in on the other gang man with weapons still aimed. One ran up on the truck's driver as the other stood over the man, crawling and pleading. The guy on the ground had been caught trying to swap clips. Clearly no match for the drums hanging from the heavy equipment that Hanna's crew held. Before Nassi could protest, the guy in the truck caught a disfiguring shot to the side of what used to be his face as everything behind the ski mask fell dripping into his lap.

"Wait, wait, don't do it," Nassi pleaded to the Brim about to finish the man crawling in the street.

The guy who got away jumped into a black sedan at the end of the street, pulling off with his arm hanging by a thread. Sirens were blaring from not too far off, and Detective Nassi realized the position this scene would put him in. He looked over at Hanna, who was hidden behind her red flag again. The two made eye contact, and as if she had read his mind, she took aim at him.

"Put the gun down, mafucka, step back," she yelled at Nassi.

The detective put one hand up as he slowly put his firearm down on the pavement with his other hand, not sure of what this sudden shift meant.

"Let's go, y'all," she yelled at her squad.

The guy who had made an awful mess of the truck driver backed away with his aim on the detective as well.

"What about him?" The other gunman asked, referring to the man crawling in his own blood.

"Leave him," she said firmly.

"Lay yo ass down cop." She demanded, pointing her gun hard at Nassi.

He laid down with no argument as the Tahoe pulled up, allowing them to get in. Before the doors slammed, the truck was already in reverse, returning the way it had come, then it was gone.

Nassi stood up, then picked his pistol up as the neighborhood residents came out of hiding into their yards, chattering amongst themselves.

One old lady yelled to Nassi.

"Baby, you alright?" as she tied her housecoat closed.

"Yes, mam, you guys just stay put until my backup arrives," he requested as he approached the man lying in the street.

"Who sent you?" Nassi asked, kneeling down to where the man lay.

Nassi grabbed the top of the man's ski mask, pulling it up, revealing the man's reddened face. The man looked up at Nassi, frowning hysterically, and let out a sincere, "Fuck you!" The detective shook his head, looking back into the man's eyes. "I figured you'd say that," Nassi said as he turned the man over and placed handcuffs on his wrists.

After reading the man his rights, Nassi walked over to what remained of his car and hit dispatch on the radio inside. After calling in the necessary codes, he placed his radio back on its hook. His phone chimed from where it lay over in the passenger's seat, alerting him of his missed calls and texts. Keeping his eye on the detainee, Nassi stooped into the car and grabbed his phone. He saw a couple of missed calls but

294

figured he'd wait until backup came to look into any of those matters piled into his phone. In less than a minute and a half later, cars began pulling up with red & blue flicking lights against the neighborhood's houses.

"Jesus, what happened here?" An officer asked, looking at the horrific image slumped in the pick-up.

"Just what it looks like, "Nassi began"

"Hell on earth, Nassi's mind swiftly shifted back to the boys as he turned nervously in the direction he'd sent them. Nassi ran over to the path between the houses, searching for the boys who had yet to come out of hiding. The officer who he'd just been talking to looked on at him like he had gone crazy from the sudden movements. Nassi walked all the way into the backyard, looking left and right, but there was no sign of them and luckily no blood trail, which was reassuring. However, Nassi wouldn't feel comfortable until he saw the boys safe and sound for himself. Nassi figured the boys had probably jumped the fences until they had reached the Johnson kid's house. Nassi walked down the path back to the front that was now a live crime scene teeming with more units, yellow tapes, and reporters.

"Detective, what's with this guy?" an officer asked, patting the gunman's head like a dog.

"Take him in," Nassi replied halfway attentively. Walking up the sidewalk and looking between each house, Nassi made his way in the direction of the house he had intended on visiting before this fiasco broke out. Making it to the porch, he met eyes with a distraught feeble looking mother.

"Mrs. Johnson," Nassi spoke, absorbing the pain in her eyes.

She pulled her lips into a scrunch and nodded in reply, too shell-shocked from all the gunplay to speak. It was totally understandable. Hell, a little more than 24 hours ago, she'd lost her baby girl to the same sort of ignorance.

"Mrs. Johnson, I still feel awful for what happened, and if it means anything to you, I will make sure you have justice," Nassi offered.

Mrs. Johnson just nodded.

"I know now might not be a good time but are the boys over here by any chance?" Nassi asked, not wanting to speak too many words.

Mrs. Johnson simply shook her head no as tears began to well up in her eyes accompanied by her heavy breathing. The sight unfolding in front of Nassi's eyes had depth on so many levels that it became unbearable for Nassi to remain in her presence any longer. As Nassi backed away from the porch, it took every ounce of strength he could muster not to become caught in the emotion Mrs. Johnson had stirred in him. Nassi didn't want to alarm her, but he was on edge after hearing the boys hadn't come there. He wanted to stay and comfort her, but she would probably never know the difference. She wasn't really inside of that body standing in front of him. Nassi left the porch headed to the corner. Once he made it around the block, Nassi took off in a full sprint looking between the houses calling for Hakiel.

"Hakiel! Hakiel!" Nassi yelled, becoming more fearful with each passing step.

Nassi recognized the two pedestrians crossing the street the next block over as he ran up to them, desperate for answers.

"Have you seen the boys?" Nassi asked, panting, trying to get his air under control. Tara looked up at Tiva, wide-eyed and confused as Tiva spoke.

"They were outside when we left for the store," She answered in a high pitch like she could sense something was wrong. Tiva nervously exhaled her Newport smoke in no mood for any more mishaps.

"What's going on?" Tiva asked, pulling her cigarette hard through shaking hands.

"Where does his friend stay?" Nassi questioned, still winded looking up the street in both directions. Tara grabbed Nassi's hand, taking a running lead as she began to worry.

"This way," she said, already frightened that the boys were in trouble.

Making it back over to the Johnson's block, opposite end from where Tara lived. The activity on the street instantly made both Tiva and Tara weak, like they were reliving yesterday all over again.

"Jamal! Jamaaal!" A woman yelled, standing in her yard.

Tara pointed out the obvious."

"That's Jamal's mom."

Nassi almost had a panic attack.

"What's going on?" Tiva asked damn near about to cry.

"I'll explain when I get back, Nassi said, taking a few side steps before sprinting off again. Nassi ran back through the middle of the crime scene, looking for a car he could use.

"Detective," McKenzie called out to Nassi.

Nassi looked to where the call had come from and ran up on McKenzie like a wildman on a mission. McKenzie prepared himself for the blow, putting his arms up already pleading.

"Wait, let me explain," McKenzie said.

"What?" Nassi stopped, "Never mind, here's your car?" Nassi asked, appearing hurried. McKenzie pointed, directing Nassi's eye to the Volvo 2 cars down.

"Keys, keys," Nassi rushed him.

McKenzie didn't hesitate to come clean with the keys, not precisely sure what Nassi was doing. He was just positive he didn't want any problems with the deranged-looking detective. Nassi snatched the keys and took off, running toward the Volvo.

"Detective, we need to talk," someone said from the side.

"I can't right now, will explain when I get back," Nassi yelled, never taking a glance over to where the voice came from.

Nassi got to the Volvo and snatched the door open, then jumped inside, jamming the key in the ignition at the same time. Speeding off, Nassi did a quick parameter check trying to locate the boys driving down all the surrounding streets.

"Shit, where the fuck did they go?" Nassi growled, becoming more and more fearful of the worst. Nassi rode around for the better half of an hour, and there was still no sign of the boys. Nassi checked back by the houses periodically, and still nothing. He pulled over and took his phone out. He had been so occupied he'd forgotten to call Inez, and looking through his phone's activity, she hadn't been trying to reach him anymore either. The boys were weighing heavy on his mind, so Inez would have to wait, Nassi decided. Nassi couldn't think straight; he could only train his thoughts in one direction, finding the boys. He wouldn't be able to put out an Amber alert for some hours, and the only other option that made sense was calling Hannah to check if her crew snatched them for some reason. Nassi dialed Hannah's phone as the ring back banged hard through his loudspeaker.

"We gone get it, we gone get it, get it in blood. Nassi thought how appropriate Bloody J's, Get in Blood song was Hannah's ringback tone, especially how she'd performed today.

"Whoooop" Hannah's voice took the place of the song, sounding like she was having a pretty pleasant day.

"Hannah, this is Detective Nassi," Nassi stated, sounding like Hannah owed him an explanation.

"I be knowing," she replied nonchalantly. "West good?" she asked, not allowing Nassi to disturb her apparent calmness.

Detective Nassi, hardly humored by her carefree tone, laughed in disgust.

"What" he started.

"Not a damn thing is good. I got a dead body without a face slumped over in a truck. More than 61 shots fired, a paralyzed asshole with enough cone shell indicators to run a go-cart track without a fucking clue how to explain this shit," Nassi snapped.

"Aye Proof, come get this blunt," Hannah instructed while letting a moist cough escape her lungs. This irritated Detective Nassi even more that after all, he'd just explained none of it seemed to register in her world. Nassi hadn't called for this, he just had a simple question, but Hannah's easiness after today's drama just rubbed him the wrong way.

"Shiiit dats West good foooreal tho, hell that was bout to be yo ass slumped fool," Hannah began.

"So if that's your way of saying thank you, my nigga, don't mention it. Da big homie wouldn't have it any other way."

She had a point. That ass was just about through if she and the Brims hadn't shown up.

"What does Pro have to do with this?" The detective asked, sounding naïve.

Hannah laughed, "What you think we just be pulling up saving pork round this mafucka? The homie says he needs you alive, so that's what it be like," Hannah stated.

"Me personally, I don't give a fuck bout badge-wearing head lice; I'm just following orders, my nig. Hannah stated," making sure Nassi understood her position.

"Look, Hannah, don't get me wrong. I appreciate y'all, I really do, but I can handle this myself," Nassi claimed, sounding dumber now than when he'd started. The detective was no pushover, but the fact was that regardless of what his giant ego would like to believe, he was good as dead today had it not been for Hannah and her crew.

"Yeah, Ok blood, you got that," Hannah said, knowing better.

"So how did you know I was in trouble, or even where to find me, "Nassi asked.

"I'm clairvoyant, my dude," Hannah said, laughing.

The truth was while Detective Nassi walked into the Varsity accompanied by Hannah, who he'd met in the parking lot, Proof bugged his car with a tracker. After that, they pretty much followed from a safe distance, and anytime the car stopped a few minutes later, they'd do a ride by making sure all was well.

301

"Ok, whatever, look, I just need to know. Did your guys snatch up some kids in the midst of the mini-war we had today" Detective Nassi asked, back on track of his call.

"What? Why would we do that, dude?" Hannah asked, sounding offended.

"I don't know, maybe cause you thought they saw too much. I'm just stuck between a rock and a hard place. I was talking to two kids that have information about Pro's case, and now they're missing," Nassi explained with a convicting tone.

"Maybe your big homie ordered that too, I don't know." Detective Nassi insulted.

"Aye, my dude, I really hope the big homie take his blessing off you and let whatever be done to you be done. Fuck you, man," Hannah said calmly before ending the call.

It was the second time today Nassi had heard those exact words, and he was beginning to feel precisely that, "Fucked." The detective went back to the crime scene after checking by the Johnson house for the umpteenth time. By now, the family had begun to worry. Though the detective hadn't explained what had happened yet, his behavior was a dead giveaway. The detective made his verbal report to the higher-ups, took a severe tongue-lashing from Captain Berndant, and watched as a piece of junk, his car, had been reduced to left on a flatbed going to evidence. A few hours had passed when the detective's insurance company replaced his vehicle with a temporary rental. He sat parked in front of the

Johnson's house, waiting to see if the boys would pop up. Tara sat on the porch steps looking as pitiful as she felt while her mother sat on a porch chair, looking seconds away from a breakdown. Tiva had taken off walking through the neighborhood chain-smoking from the packs the detective had purchased for her. Detective Nassi was now ready to talk to Inez, he'd been too caught up to call, but she hadn't either, which was now starting to bother Nassi. The detective called Inez for the second time; still, no answer, and leaving another message would only damage his pride further. Nassi began going through the host of missed texts, totaling 15 in the text log. The last one, or most recent, caught Nassi's attention instantly. 'Nassi, I'm following Officer McKenzie; he says I'm in trouble but didn't feel comfortable speaking at present. I'm scared Nassi, where are you?'

That text snatched a chunk out of Nassi's heart. Nassi checked to see what time that text had come through. It was 2:15 when that text was made, and Nassi had seen McKenzie since then. *Why hadn't he said anything?* Nassi wondered. Realizing that no one knew him and Inez were an item, it made sense that McKenzie wouldn't think to tell him anything. A few more *where are you's* that piled in his inbox took up space before Nassi noticed another message standing out from the repetitive ones prior.

'I'm so pissed!!! Victoria is making me take some days off, and I suspect she doesn't want me to get any further in my research of your crime scene. She's taken all my notes and my lab files, saying someone else will finish it up while I'm off. Some bullshit about too many hours and not enough money to cover the payrolls, which clearly makes no sense.' She texted more, but Nassi's mind started spinning and becoming suspicious of some internal corruption. Nassi scrolled down, looking at several pictures of documents and notes, before starting the engine of the Chevy Malibu. Nassi looked at another text.

'She was on the phone talking to someone when she made me take off Nassi. I don't like this. Something is up. I can feel it.' Nassi threw his phone to the passenger seat and slammed his foot on the pedal.

We're Going To War

"Yeah, this Banger Ru, who you be? Why you got my homie phone?" Banger Ru snapped into the receiver.

"Okay, man, take it easy. I was told to call you if anything ever happens with the Piru Smokey." The man spoke into the phone, explaining his orders.

"Well, what's going on?" Banger Ru snapped again, sounding impatient.

"Right, okay, listen, it was a new guy that just moved in. I think he was one of your brothers, you know?" The man started, really not too sure of Kadarai's affiliation.

"Well, you know he had been hanging with Smokey. That's why we assume," Banger Ru cut the man off as his patience broke into pieces.

"What happened?" Banger Ru yelled.

"Well, okay, okay, a Muslim stabbed the guy Smokey was hanging with a couple times, and he fell from the top tier."

"What do you mean?" Banger Ru cut him off again. The man could tell that Banger Ru wouldn't take the news any better once he'd finished the harsher details.

"Where Smokey at now?" Banger Ru asked, sure he must be in trouble since he hadn't called himself.

"He went to the hole man, it's bad, real bad." The man continued.

"He killed the Muslim that killed y'all brother."

"Hold the fuck on, man," Banger Ru cursed, something that was totally out of his character.

"Man, don't tell me Pro is dead dog, noooo man!" Banger Ru's heart was swollen inside of his chest as his breathing began to escalate.

"Yeah, I think his name was Cunningham. Don't know what yall call um." The man explained.

"Yeah, man, I'm sorry, but he's gone," He finished in a semi-respectful tone. Banger Ru dropped his head, and sadness swept through his skull.

"Aye, if it makes you feel any better, Smokey made it where it's impossible to recognize that Muslim boy who done it." The man informed.

Banger Ru had heard enough. Without another word, a thank you, or anything, he hung up the line. Banger Ru's pulse vibrated like a giant brick engine behind his temples. His cellmate had just walked in, catching the vibe instantly.

"What's good, homie?" Banger Ru stood to his feet then slid them both into a pair of state-issued state boots. Looking in the little homie's eyes, Banger Ru never answered; he just said coldly

"We're going to war."

Mama Mama

"Hakiel, you coming to the store with Tiva and me?" Tara asked, thinking her brother might need a walk.

"Nawl, I'm straight, y'all go ahead," Hakiel answered, still looking like he could use some more rest.

"Well, what do you want then? I got some money." Tara asked, trying whatever she could to get her brother's mind off of their baby sister Fatimah, knowing it was impossible.

"Brang me some Fuego Takis and a red drank," He said, never looking up to make eye contact.

"Brang me some too, Tara," Jamal demanded like she had no choice.

"Boy, please, you better hope my brother shares some with you. I ain't rich." Tara said, rolling her neck.

Just then, Tiva came out of the house, her eyes swollen from the long night of tears with a pocketbook in her hand and a lighter. Hakiel looked up to notice that she wasn't smoking which was a sign she was out. Hakiel hated the smell and was preparing to relocate had she come out puffing one.

"Don't worry, I'm going to get me some rest now," Tiva said, knowing what Hakiel was thinking.

Tiva felt terrible for what they'd been through as a family, and knowing Hakiel could use some affection as well as herself, she pulled him up into a hug.

"I love you, boy, and Tiva gone quit smoking too, okay pooh?"

"Yes, ma'am, I love you too," Hakiel replied.

Tiva put him down before the tears came; she and Tara took off walking for the store.

"You gone let me have some of yo Takis Hakiel?" Jamal asked, dead ass serious about wanting some.

Hakiel just looked at Jamal like he had bumped his damn head.

"Please," Jamal pressed, sounding like the consumption of Takis was equivalent to a bump of coke.

"Shut up, Jamal, you know I'm gone give you some," Hakiel explained with zero tolerance for playing at present.

Hakiel switched the subject to what was occupying his thoughts.

"You think he gone come back today?" Hakiel asked, looking at Jamal with murder in his eyes.

"Hakiel, I don't know, but if he does, we gone burn his ass shawty," Jamal claimed, patting his pocket where the weapon lay quietly.

It was agreed that Jamal would hold the gun. It was too risky for Hakiel to hold it, not wanting to upset his mother if he was caught. Jamal's mom was usually so high from laced blunts and Molly that she would never notice. Tara was under the impression that the boys had followed her instructions leaving the gun stashed in the backyard until she figured out a plan. Little did Tara know the boys were dead ass for real about killing the man who'd had come looking for the gun. The boys waited until Tiva and Tara were halfway up the block before heading towards Jamal's house to look at the images in his mom's phone for the 30th time. Hakiel wanted to zoom in on the man again, trying to get his mind to sponge all he could about the man. It was dark, and there was no clear picture of his face, but the video showed how he walked and some other possible identifiers. Hopefully, Jamal's mom would be passed out again, simplifying the mission at hand. By the time Hakiel and Jamal got to Jamal's house, Tiva and Tara were halfway up the second block on the way to the store. You couldn't miss Tara's loud orange short set. Jamal ran inside the house to see if he could get the phone but quickly noticed that he wouldn't be able to pull it off. The sounds of Jamal's mom getting her back splacked out came loudly from behind her closed door, where he was more than sure the phone was.

Meanwhile, outside, a group of boys around Hakiel's age from another neighborhood were cutting through his block. They made some inappropriate comments about the brown skin girl in the orange shorts they'd just passed. "Damn, she was on go up there shawty," one boy said to one of the others.

"Man, I'd make that my bottom bitch bruh," the taller boy said.

"What's a bottom bitch?" The fat kid asked the taller one as they continued walking and pointing.

"See, I knew you weren't no pimp. My uncle says every pimp gotta have a bottom bitch shawty," The tall skinny boy said.

Hakiel watched, not paying any mind until he realized who they were talking about as they crossed the street coming toward him.

Hakiel stood up, mugging the chauvinists unnoticed by the unsuspecting group. Hakiel came off the porch, ready to fight.

"Fuck you mean, you gone make her a bottom bitch nigga, that's my sister," Hakiel snapped.

The boys all looked in Hakiel's direction simultaneously to find him within arm's reach already.

"What?" The tall skinny kid said, loud like he was looking for a reason to be angry. Clearly agitated how Hakiel had checked him, he snapped harder. "I don't give a damn paanuh, she still a bitch" he continued as he balled his fist up.

"You got me fucked up," Hakiel barked, landing a solid hook into the boys larger than average lips. Blood decorated the kid's shirt almost instantly as the group went to whooping Hakiel's ass. Hakiel was standing his ground until the fat kid caught him from the blindside under his eye. Jamal had just made it back onto the porch to witness that blow as it sent Hakiel stumbling.

"Oh hell nawl," Jamal yelled, pulling out the gun "get off my brudda," Jamal said, taking aim as he walked up on the group catching the fear in their eye.

Jamal made his point, "First mafucka move I'm gone burn yo stupid ass, that's on god, now try me!"

Just then, out of nowhere, a car pulled up. With lightning speed, the man driving jumped out wearing a badge holding a gun of his own. Jamal was the first to see him. When the boys saw Jamal's hands go up, all but two, the heaviest of the group, broke out into sprints, leaving them behind.

"Aye, what the hell are yall doing?" The officer yelled, sounding pretty upset.

The officer snatched the gun from Jamal's hand, almost knocking him down from the strength he instinctively used.

"What's wrong with you?" the officer yelled, frowning.

Hakiel studied the officer's face as he interrogated his friend, remembering him from yesterday. Jamal was mad as hell; Hakiel could tell, but his fear was overriding that at the moment.

"Nothing's wrong with me," Jamal said, acting tough, so his fear wouldn't show.

Hakiel knew him better than anyone, and he could imagine what had Jamal more terrified than the officer yelling at him. There was the chance that his mother could come out at any moment.

"Yes, there is; you have a gun bigger than you," the officer continued. "Where do you live?" the officer asked, putting the gun away in his belt.

Jamal lied and pointed across the street on the next block. Hakiel could tell Jamal was seconds away from crying. The officer asked the other boys who Hakiel had been fighting with where they stayed like he was just as mad at them as Jamal. They lied, too, saying they stayed two streets over. The truth was Hakiel knew every kid his age for a five-block radius. These boys were from another neighborhood. The officer threatened the two boys that if they laid another finger on Hakiel, he'd pay them a visit, and it wouldn't be pretty. Just then, Hakiel caught eye contact with the officer, which felt a little uncomfortable. Hell, Hakiel was the man of his house, and to have another man take up for him felt belittling even at his age, but he stayed silent. The boys agreed then took off running as the officer directed them. Looking back down at Jamal, the officer had a stare hard enough to make a kid tuck its imaginary tail. Hakiel began to think *this isn't going to turn out good* while looking to make sure Tara wasn't on the way back. Luckily, they were good for the moment.

"Damn, I hope we don't go to jail," Hakiel mumbled, thinking of how disappointed and hurt his mother would be. Breaking him from his thoughts, the detective drilled Jamal.

"Do you mind telling me where the gun came from, or do I need to get your parents involved?"

The sound of the officer saying parents could possibly be excluded from this situation made Hakiel hopeful that he wouldn't be disappointing his mother with this. Hakiel was sure Jamal felt better about hearing that too.

"I found it, "Jamal admitted, looking a little more peaceful.

"Found it where?" The officer pressed. Hakiel looked at Jamal, knowing that this would spoil their plans of revenge, but what could they do? They didn't have the gun anymore, and bucking would only make things harder on them.

"Hey, if this is too hard, we can just go talk to your parents," the officer threatened.

"No, no, no, I'll tell you, "Jamal said, not wanting to go that route the officer had just suggested.

Hakiel was done playing, the plan was spoiled, and he figured they might as well tell what they knew.

"We saw the man that killed my sister," Hakiel said, taking the officer's attention from Jamal.

The officer couldn't believe what he had just heard.

"What did you say?" The officer asked, grabbing Hakiel by his arms, shaking him hysterically.

"Who? The gang banging thug we arrested? What? Did you see him do it with your own eyes?" The officer pressed, kneeling down to Hakiel's height.

Hakiel was opening his mouth to tell the officer the gang member hadn't shot his sister when the sound of screeching tires tore through the surrounding silence of the neighborhood. Before Hakiel and Jamal could turn to look, the officer had pushed them away between some houses he'd directed them towards.

"Run" he yelled before drawing his own weapon and going for cover by the car he had pulled up in.

Jamal took off on a sprint with Hakiel close behind. Hakiel didn't want the officer to get hurt, but from the sounds of gunfire behind them, the possibilities were high. Hakiel looked back in the officer's direction to see the car he was ducked behind being riddled with bullets.

"Come on, Hakiel," Jamal yelled, climbing the fence going to the next block behind his house.

Jamal's fence was too high and made of wood to keep nosey onlookers out of his mom's business, leaving them to have to go around to the next block jumping the lower fences. Hakiel made it over the fence shortly after Jamal.

Watching the officer through the chain link fence dumping his piece back in the attacker's direction, Hakiel figured it would be his last time seeing the man. He was young, but he knew the officer's gun was no match for what he could tell was real heavy metal being fired by the attackers.

"Hakiel bring your ass on before you get shot, fool," Jamal yelled back to Hakiel, who was stuck in a trance watching the officer. Hakiel broke away from the hypnotic scene playing out in front of him to get to Jamal, who was now in front of the yard of the houses on the next block. Just as Hakiel reached the front, he and Jamal saw a black Tahoe speed by with a girl pulling a red bandana over her face as they sped by. More and more shots continued to ring out, sounding like one of Hakiel's video games. The boys heard another screech of tires burn into their street, followed by a symphony of even more gunshots, causing them to take off, running toward the other end of the road. As they ran, a dark blue Crown Vic pulled up beside them.

"Aye freeze," the officer said, pulling his badge up so the boys could see it from his window. The boys stopped in their tracks. "Why are you boys running?" The white police officer asked after getting their attention.

"Man, don't you hear all the shots over there?" Hakiel added.

"Shut up, kid," the officer said, getting out of his car with his gun out. "Where's the gun you were just carrying?" the officer said, already aware of everything that had just transpired. He was using it as bait letting the boys know they were in trouble.

"He's going to shoot us if we run, Hakiel," Jamal stated simply, as fear rushed from his heart through to his veins

"Don't move a muscle boys, you're under arrest," Sergeant Hemlock lied, grabbing Jamal while keeping his aim on Hakiel.

Sergeant Hemlock threw Jamal in the back seat then snatched Hakiel from behind, tossing him in as well. Hakiel pounded on the glass after the door slammed in his face.

"Hey, you can't arrest us. We're kids, man," Hakiel yelled, knowing they were in trouble from Jamal's claim.

"Kids don't carry guns," Sergeant Hemlock yelled, just in case someone was watching from a window. It appeared that the block would stay absent of anyone until long after the shots had ceased.

"Were under heavy fire 00 Black," Puma's walkie radio blared. "Shit," Puma cursed, rushing to get in.

Puma hit the gas speeding up to the end of the block then making a hard left, sending the boys into the other door hard from the turn. The Crown Vic slammed on breaks right in front of the retreating attacker with his arm looking like it was about to fall out.

"Mama Mama," Hakiel yelled, beating on the glass, able to see his mother on the porch looking toward the gunfight. She turned to look at the Crown Vic, but the tinted windows hid anything that might be behind them. Puma watched as his man in the pickup caught his end right before he sped off.

It's Him

"Coyote, what the fuck happened out there?" Puma asked as he sped away from the Johnson's street. His comrade had spilled into the passenger's seat after making a narrow escape, nearly becoming a casualty of war. Coyote could barely hear himself explain from the racket the boys in the back seat were making.

"Momma, momma," one of the boys yelled as he bangs on the tinted window behind Puma.

Coyote was in no mood to compete with the whining of some underground brat. Bad enough, he was dealing with the excruciating pain of a pulsing limb agony through his whole body.

"Shut the fuck up," Coyote demanded, looking at the boys through the eyeholes of his ski mask. His plea caused him more pain, and he expressed it with a grizzly sounding roar. "Argggh fuck," he cried.

The boys looked on, unsympathetic to the man's condition wishing that they were big enough to add to his injuries. Coyote rolled the ski mask up to his forehead, allowing the fluff of his full-grown beard to bush out from the sweaty fabric.

"The sons of bitches ambushed us, goddammit," he stopped short in mid-sentence as the tremendous pain throbbed more relentlessly with each shift of the car's movement. At this point, everything irritated Coyote. "Goddamn. Do you have to turn so hard?" Coyote complained as he held his arm in place.

Puma sped down a pretty busy street with the lights of the car's grill forcing traffic to move out of the way. Hakiel's demeanor was scrunched into a hateful frown from seeing the man's face who had attacked the detective. The blood from Coyote's wound found its way through the back seat, streaming its way on the car's floorboard. Jamal looked, noticing it.

"Ugggh man, you leaking all by us, what's wrong with you?" the boy complained, cringing at the sight as he lifted his feet up onto the seat.

"Kid, shut your fucking mouth already," Puma snapped, clearly agitated beyond the boy's grievances.

"Aye, you shut up and don't curse at us, mafucka," Hakiel started. "You were supposed to tell my momma you were taking me to jail. You saw her looking for me, punk ass." Hakeil was in a rage kicking his feet into the cage that was protecting Puma from his assault. "I want a lawyer," Hakeil yelled with a kick, putting emphasis on each word.

319

"Haha, listen at the little smart ass," Puma teased, looking at Hakiel from the rearview. Puma then brought his attention back to the road as he made a turn down into an industrial park. "It's pronounced lawyer, you little shit, but where you're going, you won't need one," Puma threatened with a chilling smirk back into the rearview mirror.

"Why not?" Hakiel asked, still not catching Puma's hint. "My dad got one when he went to jail. The police show always gets lawyers for the people who are going to jail, so don't tell me," Hakiel stated, almost sure of his rights.

Puma pulled into a warehouse as the door behind the car came down hard and fast. The man working the chain to the bay door was a stocky-looking redneck, wearing black cargo pants with a matching shirt. The sleeve of the man's shirt displayed the initials N.A.M. with a skull above it.

"This ain't no jail, Hakiel," Jamal whimpered, not liking the looks of their surroundings.

Hakiel pretty much figured the same. "This ain't no jail. Why are y'all kidnapping us? Help us! Help us, they kidnapping us!" The boys took turns screaming at the top of their lungs as they began to panic.

Puma jumped out of the car without saying another word, which only frightened the boys more. Puma made it around to Coyote's side and helped him out; as he struggled, weak from blood loss, more men came and escorted him out of sight. Puma came back to the car accompanied by two other men. The stocky one who let them in and a more

320

toned, athletic-looking guy who appeared a few years younger than both Puma and the big redneck.

The two men wore the same gear. In fact, all of the men the boys had seen were wearing the same get-up aside from Puma and Coyote. The boys were already aware that something was terribly wrong and looked at each other for some sort of encouragement. Neither of the boys could offer the other any, and fear had replaced the youthful sparkle of their eyes. Jamal's door popped open. The stocky man had worked the handle to gain entry before roughly snatching Jamal away from his seat by the arms and collar.

"Get off me," Jamal screamed as he kicked and bucked his body. The stocky redneck muscled him up onto his shoulders to gain better control of the boy's movements. Hakiel took the opportunity to rush the man from his low position on the other seat. Hakiel slid across the leather until he reached the doors opening and landed a hard kick into the man's groin. The blow caused the stocky man to drop to his knees coughing as Jamal fell hard to the ground. Before Jamal could get up to run, the athletically built man snatched him up. Hakiel never made it out of the car entirely before catching a fierce slap to the side of his sensitive face. Puma snatched Hakiel up after slapping him senselessly.

"Nice try, kid, but that's gonna cost you," Puma promised. Tears filled Hakiel's eye socket, but he didn't make another sound. "Bring your big for nothing ass on Bear," Puma barked in disappointment at the redneck still gagging and coughing on the floor.

321

"Fuck you cock boy," Bear hissed in retaliation to Puma. Bear and Hakiel made eye contact as Bear looked up.

"I'm gon kill you bough," Bear claimed, sounding like a real good old boy. Hakiel turned away, no longer wanting to see the evil smile stretching across Bear's broad face. Hakiel took in his surroundings, noticing at least ten to fifteen men moving about, minus the three who'd helped the injured man Coyote to the back out of sight. The lights were dim, and there were no windows at ground level. They were thrown on the floor near some trash bags that gave off a scent the boys couldn't place, but it was strong? Hakiel continued to protest, but Jamal had become silent, overwhelmed with what was happening.

"You said we were under arrest. This ain't no jail, man. What is y'all doing?" Hakiel continued as he squirmed sideways on the floor. Just as Hakiel ranted his opinion, a door slammed upstairs from the second level. The boys, along with everyone else in earshot, looked upward to the door in unison. The man stood outside of the door he'd just come out of, puffing a cigar as he spoke into his phone. Peering down, the man let out a hearty laugh as the men went back to packaging and moving items throughout the warehouse. The man's laughter was cut short as he snatched the aviator sunglasses from his face.

"I'll call you back," the man said. He could be heard from downstairs as his voice boomed in almost an echo from where he stood. Stomping down the stairs, the man started yelling before he reached the bottom at ground level.

"Why the fuck is there a trail of blood on my goddamn floor?" He yelled, already red in the face. Everyone froze in position, looking and not wanting to be the recipients of whatever repercussions any unwanted response would bring. Puma knew better than to remain quiet.

"It's Coyote's," Puma admitted hesitantly. The boys finally got a good look at the man who seemed to be in charge when Jamal noticed his familiar body language and face.

"Hakiel," Jamal whispered.

"What," Hakiel answered

"It's him," Jamal said.

"Are you sure?" Hakiel asked as the blood began to boil through his little heart.

"I'm positive. I remember his face from the chase," Jamal explained.

"What the hell is his malfunction? Why is his blood trailing through my goddamn warehouse? The sergeant asked, gritting his teeth.

"They were ambushed by the bangers." As he said, I caught the tail end, and from what I saw, there was some pretty big firepower on their end," Puma defended, trying to keep eye contact with the sergeant.

"Get him to receive medical attention for his injuries, in the rest out of here now!" the sergeant barked his orders.

"Sir, yes sir," Puma said, taking off to go get Coyote. Firebird took a power strut around his men, eyeing them all. Meanwhile, the boys watched, taking in all they could of the man Jamal had claimed killed Hakiel's sister, Fatimah. Firebird was wearing a casual button-down shirt, forest green in color, with some khaki-colored slacks. The heel of his cowboy boots clacked against the floor as he walked. He hadn't noticed the boys as of yet, and before he could, Coyote made his entrance through the door of the break room directly under the office Firebird had emerged from. Before Coyote could speak, Firebird was already pitching a bitch. Firebird massaged his temples with the cigar still in hand as smoke drifted into the air.

"Coyote, Coyote," Firebird calmly began. "Seeing how fucked you look, please tell me how worse the other guy is?" Firebird yelled, releasing some kind of built-up rage inside. The warehouse got quiet as all eyes fell on Firebird interrogating Coyote. Coyote could only manage to shake his head in shame. "Coyote, where's the detective?" Firebird asked back in a calm tone like he hadn't just been yelling seconds ago. Puma's phone rang, and he stepped away to take the call but remained in sight with his eyes locked on Firebird.

"We got ambushed by the bangers; they killed Wildcat, and Hawl is either in jail or dead probably, as for the detective," Coyote said in a huff, "We missed."

"You missed?" Firebird repeated, looking over to Puma with a sadistic smile on his face.

324

Puma hung up the phone. Sure that his attention was needed more with what was going on at this side of the receiver.

"Did you hear that, Puma? They missed." Firebird repeated. Puma knew the implications of Firebird's sarcasm and demeanor. Someone's hide would be seriously lashed behind the failure, and Puma desired his to remain unscathed. Firebird looked back to Coyote. His expression turned tranquil and calm with the closing of his eyes. Firebird spoke as if he wasn't bothered anymore by what he'd heard.

"Okay, we missed, no big deal. We'll just regroup, tidy up our losses and give it another go." Firebird stared at Coyote who's pain was evident in his face as he stood there, becoming weaker by the second from the amount of blood he was losing. Coyote still managed to nod his head in agreement with Firebird's strategy.

"Coyote, clean this mess up," Firebird scowled as he spoke. Firebird snatched a shop towel from a nearby table and threw it in Coyote's face. The towel kind of hung from Coyote's beard until he grabbed it into his hand about to speak. Before he could talk, Firebird was already issuing out more orders.

"Get down on the floor and clean this blood up," Firebird said smoothly.

"But sir," Coyote tried to explain something.

Firebird cut him off, "But nothing. And if I have to repeat myself, your N.A.M. membership will become inactive," Firebird said, looking up to the ceiling then back at Coyote with a serious gaze. Coyote dropped to the floor in an unimaginable amount of pain, still bleeding all over the place. As Coyote wiped blood away, more appeared from the large wound in his arm, making the scene resemble a dog chasing its tail.

The boys watched from where they lay on the floor quietly as Firebird continued to degrade Coyote.

"The problem with allowing failure to go unchecked is that your men will become content with underachieving," Firebird began. Taking a look around the room at his men as Coyote wiped at the floor beneath him.

"Bring the girl," Firebird demanded.

Bear, who was finally back in functioning condition, walked past Hakiel towards a cage behind them, kicking Hakiel on the head on the way. Hakiel closed his eyes, growling through his clenched teeth as the painful kick vibrated through to the back of his cranium. Firebird's attention was now on his unnoticed guests.

"Oww, why you do that?" Hakiel hissed, wishing he could snuff the pain of the kick with a hard rub of his hand.

"What the hell do we have here?" Firebird said, looking in the boys' direction. Puma stepped up to whisper who the boys were in Firebird's ear and how he'd grabbed them from the scene.

"Great, we can start a fucking daycare with all the piss ants around here," Firebird shouted, looking back down to Coyote, who was struggling pointlessly.

Bear came back, shoving Inez in her back towards Firebird. The boys hadn't even noticed the lady sitting quietly in the cage until now. Inez's mouth was gagged, and her hands were cuffed in front of her. The sack that had been on her head was in Bear's hands. He continued pushing her closer to Firebird. Inez looked down to the boys as she nearly tripped over them. Their eyes met, wondering each other's fate. From the dried blood and scratches on her face, the boys assumed the worst.

"Ms. Santos, thank you for joining us, sweetheart," Firebird said in sarcastic gratitude. Inez could only mumble through the gag in her mouth, sounding as if she had a lot to say. Firebird walked over and removed the gag from her mouth while asking, "What is it that you so badly want to say, Ms. Santos?" Firebird's look was disturbing and almost haunting Inez's thoughts. However, it wouldn't stop her from expressing the feelings that had been suppressed by her gag.

"Hemlock, you son of a bitch, your ass is gonna pay when the force finds out what you've done, Punto," Inez said before spitting a wad of spit into Hemlock's face. The saliva dripped from his eyelashes to his cheek, causing him to giggle. Hemlock took a finger to clear some of the spit from his eye then rubbed it between his index and thumb. Bringing his fingers close to his mouth, he stuck his tongue out for a quick taste. Inez watched through her widened eyes as the sick bastard displayed his repulsiveness.

"Umm, so you taste like this all along," Hemlock asked, wiping the rest of the saliva off with his backhand. "I see why the detective is chasing the little candy-filled piñata," Hemlock teased, looking at the men who were laughing now.

"That's right bitch, and that's his dick you're tasting," Inez retaliated. "Sweet huh," she snickered, uncaring of the repercussions. The warehouse got quiet until a loud backhanded slap on Inez's cheek broke the silence. Inez fell to the ground from the impact.

Bear snatched her back up immediately. When she was back on her feet, her face met the barrel of Hemlocks 4.5 Desert Eagle that he'd drawn from the back of his waistline. Inez bled from her nose, looking back into Hemlock's eyes, uncaring of her fate. She was undoubtedly her father's child, a real soldier. Her heart and bravery was captivating. The men who watched, especially those who lacked that kind of courage, admired her strength but clearly did not wish to be in her shoes.

"Failure to me are the symptoms of disease," Hemlock stated, looking at Inez intently. "I will not allow disease to fester among us. It will only contaminate the whole," Hemlock said as he chambered a hollow point from the clip into position. The bullet sat ready to be struck by the firing pin. "When I need you to deliver, there is only one option," Hemlock barked.

Coyote looked up from the floor, knowing he was lucky not to be on the other end of the gun pointed at Inez. His failure had been pretty unsettling for Hemlock only a moment ago. Coyote continued aimlessly wiping away. His body had been pushed to its limits. Pale from the loss of blood, he appeared on the verge of collapse.

"There can be only success," Hemlock yelled at the top of his lungs, startling everyone except Inez. Instead, she stared back coldly unmoved by his dramatic ramblings.

"Failure will not be tolerated," Hemlock hissed, inches from Inez's face. Before she could blink twice, Hemlock placed his 4.5 to the back of Coyote's head. Coyote's brain never had a chance to register what happened when it was pushed violently from its place inside of his skull, through the creases of skin that once covered his forehead and onto the floor. Coyote's face fell right on top of the brain matter as the rest oozed into the current of plasma flowing from his mangled forehead. The burnt hair and gunpowder wafted into Hemlock's nostrils, giving him a surge of power from the aroma. For the first time since she'd been held captive, Inez was terrified as her body jerked in reflex from the clapping of Hemlocks cannon.

"I loved this man, Ms. Santo. He's my aunt's second-born," Hemlock admitted, wiping the blood on his gun across her lips. She fought to turn her head, but Bear's strength denied her movement.

"The thing that kills a loving relationship for me, Ms. Santos, is neglect for my feelings," Hemlock explained. He laughed loudly as the boys watched from where they lay, scared to death. "Ms. Santos, you don't look so well," Hemlock teased, smelling her fear. You'll come to understand that I get what I want," Hemlock's voice was just low enough for Inez to hear. You're going to bring the detective to me, and all this will be a mere memory," Hemlock explained.

"I'm not going to help you do anything, you bastard," Inez cried, wanting badly to stop Hemlock from destroying any more lives. "Haven't you done enough," she asked.

Hemlock looked at her as if he was pondering the thought seriously. Sucking his teeth, he answered. "No," his reply was simple, thought out, and firm. Clearly, Hemlock's mission was just beginning. "What do you and the detective think you've got, Ms. Santos? Surely you feel as if I've done some injustice," Hemlock said laughing, looking to his men to join in. All except Bear did; he remained serious, waiting for the command to issue more pain.

"You're a murderer and a crooked cop. You don't deserve a badge," Inez scolded.

Hemlock smiled, "I've been called worse, Ms. Santos, and if you only knew, you'd still be calling me names," Hemlock teased. "I don't give a fuck about any of that. Hell, we place way too much value on human life anyway." Hemlock continued. "Our mission is to set the stage for the future and get out of the way." Hemlock walked over to the boys and looked down at them compassionately. "You're the waist-high maggots who stole my gun, huh?" Hemlock sneered, kicking Jamal in the ribs for attention more than punishment. "Stand them up," Hemlock ordered two of his men, pointing as he spoke.

The boys were lifted to their feet, and Hemlock did a walkabout looking at their posture.

"Answer me, goddammit," Hemlock yelled, standing behind the boys. Hemlock's voice boomed, causing the boys to jump from how close in their eardrums he'd yelled.

The boys were too scared to speak, and Jamal felt he might piss on himself at any moment.

"Do I look familiar to you?" Hemlock asked Jamal.

Jamal shook his head nervously, saying no, then looked away from Hemlock, quickly bringing his eyes to look at the floor.

"Oh no, well, you look pretty familiar to me," Hemlock laughed. "You know it's amazing how early you people start working on your criminal record. Petty thievery, selling drugs and lying to cover it all up," Hemlock stated, with a hand on Jamal's shoulder. Jamal could feel the weight of the gun in Hemlock's hand as he stood terrified under the fist-clenching the 4.5. Hemlock took another pull of his cigar, looking down at the side of Jamal's face. "You know Jamal.

331

I detest a wide number of things. Your rage probably tops my list, but a close second is a failure," Hemlock explained, stretching his hand in Coyote's direction. Hemlock took another pull then blew the smoke against Jamal's face as he stared at Coyote's body through the cloud of smoke Hemlock had blown. "Thirdly, Jamal, I would have to say liars," Hemlock snatched the boy's face to make eye contact as tears began to form from his tear ducts.

"Leave them alone, you stupid son of a bitch," Inez protested.

"Gag that whore someone please," Hemlock ordered.

Bear wasted no time fulfilling Hemlock's wish, nearly being bitten by the feisty Latina.

"That's the second time you called my mother out of her name Ms. Santos. Not that I don't agree, but your voice is such a distraction; I mean, real fucking turn on. Later okay, I promise." Hemlock taunted, grabbing himself, implying there would be some forced sexual activity later.

Hakiel stared at Hemlock like a lion watching its prey, waiting for its opportunity to appease its hunger. Noticing Hakiel, Hemlock smiled, admiring the fury dancing in his glassy eyes.

"Tough lil nigga huh," Hemlock laughed, saying the word awkwardly. Jamal stood stunned that Hemlock knew his name. Hemlock focused back on Jamal.

"So rumor is that the detective has my gun," Hemlock stated, coming down into the boy's face. Jamal tried to avoid

Hemlock's eyes, but Hemlock forced his chin up with his gun. "You're the little boy that was out on the bike that day, weren't you?" Hemlock asked, breathing in the boy's air. Before you answer, remember how I feel about liars," Hemlock threatened, tapping the boy's chin with his gun. Jamal nodded slowly in confirmation as tears rolled down his cheeks.

"That was you huh?" Hemlock repeated. Jamal nodded yes again.

"Yeah, see now that's a good boy, I'm starting to like you, kid," Hemlock claimed, still puffing his cigar. "Do you know who killed the little girl that day?" Hemlock said, eyeing Jamal closely. Hakiel licked his lips, eager to make an outburst, but before he could, he heard his dad's voice.

"Always keep a tight hold on your feelings, son. Your enemies' weakness is only knowing what you allow them to know about you." Hakiel wanted to go into a fit hearing the man who killed Mah Mah mention her. However, his father's voice clicked in like he'd been watching from another dimension protecting his son from saying something that could cost him his life. Hakiel was a brilliant kid, and his father's words were treasures to him. Hakiel assumed the man named Hemlock couldn't have known who he was because he'd pretty much ignored him for the most part. Hakiel thought that it may work to his advantage keeping his mouth shut. After all, this man was clearly a cold-hearted killer. Maybe if Jamal just answered all his questions, they'd be free to go, Hakiel concluded.

"It wasn't the man we locked up, now was it?" Hemlock pressed on.

Hakiel and Jamal tried to look at each other. Only Hakiel's head was allowed movement as Hemlock held Jamal's tightly in his grasp. Hakiel wanted to tell Jamal to say yes so that Hemlock wouldn't harm him. Hakiel knew better that if Jamal told him what he knew, it would cost him. Hakiel did the only thing he could think of to divert Hemlock's attention.

"Yeah, it was the man they locked up, and his ass is going to hell like you for killing your aunt's son," Hakiel's outburst brought a laugh from Hemlock as he squatted, amused at Hakiel's attempt. What Hakiel didn't know was; Jamal's eyes had given him the answer he already knew too well.

"Is that right?" Hemlock asked Jamal, allowing the games to commence. Jamal nodded yes, taking Hakiel's hint.

"Fine," Hemlock yelled, causing both boys to jump in reflex again. Hemlock stood to his feet. "Let's have some fun then," Hemlock suggested, grabbing Jamal roughly by the collar. A sound escaped Jamal's lungs from the snatch as Hemlock pulled him along. "Take the other kid, tie him to the top rail with his arms over the poles. We're going to test his strength," Hemlock ordered the man holding Hakiel. "Ms. Santos, how's about a little show, sweetheart? Would you like that?" Hemlock asked, smiling over at Inez as she tried to overpower the gag. "Ahh, never mind, you like a man that just takes control, no questions asked," Hemlock spat mockingly.

Bear forced Inez into a seat and roped her feet to the legs. "This ought to be interesting," Bear said in Inez's ear as he inhaled her neck, anxious about when the boss would let the men have their way with her. "It will only be a matter of time, Mamacita," Bear said in his heavy southern drawl.

Meanwhile, Hakiel had been tied to the rails on the second level with only his arms free to move as they hung over the poles. Down below, Hemlock had one of the men retrieve a mechanical lift, and he and Jamal accompanied the man as they began to make their ascent with the help of the lift. The mechanical buzz put terror in both boys' hearts, and confusion took over their ability to think. The one thing they could deduce from the way things looked was that neither of them would leave this place alive. Once the lift rose to the second level, Hemlock took another zip tie through the one around Jamal's wrists and made a hoop locking it in on the click. Hakiel's eyes were wide in fear at this point, not too fond of the game Hemlock had suggested. Jamal squirmed, trying to get away.

"Why are you doing this?" he asked, terrified already from the height they'd been lifted to.

"We are going to call this game, 'That's what friends are for,'" Hemlock stated coldly, tightening his grip on Jamal as he muscled him into position. Hemlock lifted Jamal's hands above his head and looped the zip tie into Hakiel's two open hands. "Now, Hakiel, the rest is on you," like they actually had a chance of surviving whatever was happening.

"Please don't do this, sir, please," Hakiel pleaded as tears continued rolling down Jamal's cheeks.

"You guys had your chance, and your attempt to give your friend a hand brought this about," Hemlock explained. "Well, now you can give him both your hands in hopes that their strength will spare him his life," Hemlock gave the lift operator the signal as he braced Jamal's body for the movement.

"Please, sir, I'm sorry," Jamal cried, finally realizing the peril his dishonesty had placed him in.

"Jamal, stop being a girl, for crying out loud. I gave you fair warning," Hemlock said, now a little lower than Jamal's knees, as the lift slowly descended back towards the ground level.

Jamal's cries went from rolling tears to a more audible plea as his eyes took in the floor's distance up under him.

"Don't worry, Jamal, Hakiel has it all under control," Hemlock said coldly.

The lift was now six feet under Jamal and still descending towards the thirty-four more feet it would take to reach the ground level again. Inez watched, horrified at what Hemlock had done. Her heart was pounding, knowing Hakiel wouldn't be able to hold Jamal up for long.

"Jamal, don't look down. Look at me," Hakiel said, already in pain from his friend's weight cutting into his fingertips turned pulsing red nubs. The blood separated from the middle of Hakiel's hands, where he held the tie with all the strength he could find. The band caused the tissue underneath it to turn white as the blood pushed onward towards the creases of Hakiel's fingers.

"Hakiel, don't drop me," Jamal cried, looking up into Hakiel's eyes as they began to tear up for the first time since their abduction.

"I got you, Jamal, just be still and don't look down," Hakiel said, trying to give his friend hope of a better outcome than the inevitable fate before them.

"Boys, I got some business to tend to probably the best news I've heard all day," Hemlock hollered up from the ground level to the boys. Puma just informed him, still holding the phone, that the hit on Kadarai was a success. "Do me a favor, boys, just hang around. I'll be back in a bit," Hemlock smiled like a villain from an evil comic book.

The men scattered about the warehouse, continued packing the items on pallets in individual bags, and then loaded them into utility vans.

"Hurry up, ladies; we've got to meet these deadlines. I want this shit out of here in less than five minutes," Hemlock ordered. The men sped up the pace getting ready for the mass movement. Meanwhile, Hakiel and Jamal's situation was becoming more unnerving by the second as Inez watched the boys struggle.

"I'm scared Hakiel, I don't wanna die," Jamal pleaded in his confession.

"You're not going to die, Jamal. Just try to be still," Hakiel said, knowing he wouldn't be able to hold on much longer. "He will come back in a minute, Jamal, after he's done with that call. I can hold you until he gets back," Hakiel spoke, hopeful that his own words were true.

The weight of Jamal's body pulled fire in Hakiel's hands through the sweat of his palms, and the zip tie began to slide slowly. Hakiel tried cautiously, adjusting his grip. The mistake of that movement brought on more hardship for Hakiel as the zip tie slipped to his fingertips. Putting an enormous amount of pressure on Hakiel's tiny hands. Jamal began to scream as the shift happened, fearful that it was over. Inez's heart stopped for a brief second as it appeared the boy was on the way down. Her muffled cries could still be heard from behind the gag. A warm stream found its way down Jamal's leg trickling to the floor as the beam of light from the window caught it in a glimmer.

Hakiel was sweating hard as big beads of the salty liquid dripped from his neck and forehead.

"I got you, Jamal," Hakiel said, really trying to reassure himself. Hakiel and Jamal had a history for such short years in their lifetime. The boys had been ride or die for each other through all kinds of ups and downs. It was Hakiel who begged his mom to allow Jamal to stay at their house when Jamal's mom's drug addiction had almost cost the woman her life. A near-fatal overdose sent Jamal's mom to the hospital for a few weeks. She almost lost custody of Jamal during that episode. However, Hakiel's love for him wouldn't allow that to happen. Hakiel was more of a brother to Jamal than a friend; he would never turn his back on him, and he knew the feeling was mutual. Hakiel's heart was almost escaping his chest with each beat as the tension from the realization that his best friend and his brother would die if no one came to their rescue soon. Jamal could see the fear in Hakiel's eyes, feeling like a reflection of his own.

"I'm going to die, aren't I, Hakiel?" Jamal asked from quivering lips. He looked down, trying to estimate his chances of survival. The sight of the floor beneath him sent chills up his spine. Jamal began crying harder, feeling himself slide. Hakiel tried to capture Jamal's attention, but Jamal started to panic. Inez could feel her heart in her throat as she tried moving, but her chair was bolted down, and there was nothing she could do.

"I don't want to die," Jamal yelled. "I'm sorry, I'm sorry, I made a mistake," Jamal pleaded. His cries fell upon deaf ears as the men began piling into the vans to pull out. Hemlock had already left as three guards remained, and the rest dispersed.

Inez took a look around with what leeway of movement she was allowed. She saw one guard closing the bay door and the other closing himself in the office upstairs a few feet away from where Hakiel was tied. Inez desperately tried to get the gag out of her mouth, but it was strapped tightly, and there was no hope.

"Look at me, Jamal," Hakiel snapped as the stress began to mount on him.

Jamal looked into Hakiel's distressed face, aware that it was just a matter of time and that no one was going to come to his rescue.

"Hakiel, I'm sorry about Mah Mah," Jamal cried. "I really am."

Hakiel whimpered as tears streamed toward the floor, rolling from his chin. "Shhh." Hakiel mouthed, not wanting to accept Jamal's dying words as if they would prevent the inevitable. The pressure on Hakiel's fingertips felt as if they might explode at any moment as the zip ties cut deeper into his chunky fingers. Hakiel closed his eyes, trying to muster more strength that was failing quickly. Hakiel swallowed hard, trembling, trying with all his might not to let Jamal go. Hakiel opened his eyes to look at Jamal for what he knew would be the last time.

"I love you, bruh," Hakiel said, looking through a blur of tears.

Jamal's tears rolled from both sides of his face down that long distance to the floor.

"I love y'all too," Jamal said, breathing hard. His heartbeat seemed like it would be heard throughout the warehouse. Still, it was only his crying that really made a sound, along with air he tried sucking in through his runny nose.

Hakiel's grip broke, and Jamal's eyes grew wide from shock as he began to yell. Hakiel's eyes closed a split second before already making his mind up that he would not watch his friend die. His sobs tore through the warehouse with the strength of a newborn as Jamal's body slid away from the life that they shared. Jamal's cries were heartbreaking, forcing Inez to turn her head, unable to watch the shattering of the youth's end. The thud of Jamal's body hitting the ground crushed Hakiel's soul. He kept his eyes closed, jumping after it hit. Hakiel cried uncontrollably through his closed eyelids as his mouth salivated and more fluid distorted the sound. Jamal was gone. Hakiel determined he wouldn't look at Jamal that way, just sat there tied to the pole in dark turmoil. Inez cried herself into a silent prayer feeling terrible that the monster had torn so many lives apart in such a short time. Her hatred consumed her like a flame as the tears continued.

Not In The Mood

It was 8:07 pm, and if Detective Nassi was right, he knew exactly where to find Officer McKenzie. Tara looked up, startled as Nassi peeled off. Seconds later, he was gone. After a lengthy commute due to the Atlanta traffic, Detective Nassi pulled into the parking lot of Follies Strip Club off of Buford Highway. Nassi drove through the parking lot until he found Officer McKenzie's Volvo. It wasn't hard to find because the crowd was nowhere near where it would be in the next few hours. By then, Officer McKenzie would be long gone. He wouldn't be caught dead amongst the more outspoken and flamboyant stripper tippers that would be swarming in shortly.

Nassi waited around about an hour and fifteen minutes. During that time, Captain Brendant had called his line relieving him of any more to do with the triple homicide. The captain claimed there was just way too much bullshit stemming from the case with Nassi at the center, so he suggested that Nassi take a break. Nassi put up a hell of a protest and some pretty good points about what he discovered thus far, but the captain was more than fed up. At the end of it all, Nassi was given the ultimatum of stepping down from the case or simply turning in his badge and gun. Needless to say, Nassi would much rather keep his job than not, so he humbled down, bottling up the sour taste it left in his mouth. If this is what Inez had gone through earlier, then Nassi could definitely relate to her being beyond pissed. Officer McKenzie squirmed out of Follies, looking like a kid who'd just stolen a peek at his father's pornos. His body language screamed. He was fresh from rubbing one out in the men's bathroom, unable to handle the excitement of beautiful naked women who under normal circumstances wouldn't even notice him. McKenzie wiped his hand roughly across his shirt as he fixed his glasses with the other. He reached in his pocket, pulling his keys out as a few cars pulled in with bass-thumping from their trunks. McKenzie walked hurriedly to his car, mumbling to himself, never looking up as if he was ashamed to show his face. He hit the remote, and his doors unlocked. Reaching for the handle, Officer McKenzie opened the door to get in. Out of nowhere, a strong black hand pushed his door back closed from over his shoulder.

"Leaving already, McKenzie?" Nassi growled.

McKenzie thought to go for his gun, but the puppy piss pumping in his veins wouldn't allow it.

"What exactly did you want to explain?" Nassi questioned McKenzie as he snatched his body into a turn so he would be face to face.

"Explain what?" McKenzie yelped.

"Don't fuck with me, McKenzie; I'm not in the mood. What did you mean earlier? Let you explain?" Nassi pressed, remembering McKenzie's defensive reaction from earlier.

Key To Salvation

The phone in Hemlock's office rang two times, breaking Wolf, the guard who'd stayed behind from an online game.

"Yeah," Wolf answered, sounding irritated.

"Yeah, my ass, quit jerking off fuck face and answer the phone like you got some sense," Firebird griped.

"Do me a favor, get brat one, and the chic put um away. I'm sure brat two is done hanging out by now," Hemlock continued.

"I got a job for you and Squirrel. The puss in boots just called said he's following the detective right now. Here's his number," Firebird explained, giving Wolf the number.

"Give him a call, get the location, and get it done. Can you handle that?" Firebird asked like Wolf was incapable.

"I'm assuming that's why you picked me, boss," Wolf said in an arrogant sarcasm.

"Actually, smart ass, I just need you to back Squirrel. He's got more balls than you," Firebird laughed, aware of Wolf's talent.

"Okay, I'll let him have the starring role then," Wolf stated, sure Firebird knew who was best suited for the job.

"Listen, jackass, get it done and don't end up like my dear aunt Sally's second-born." Firebird threatened.

"Sure, boss, I'm on it," Wolf replied, not worried about failing Firebird. The phone call ended, and Wolf logged offline to go tend to the commands Firebird had ordered. Coming out of the office, Wolf looked down at the kid tied to the railing. The sniffling and crying were constant as the boy's head rested against the pole. His head was turned in Wolf's direction, and his eyes were closed so tightly it was a wonder how any moisture could escape.

"Kid, knock it off," Wolf said, approaching to take the restraints off of Hakiel.

Wolf was a cold-blooded killer, and he only had compassion for the smaller people of his race. Some years back, he was a father, but his life went downhill after losing his job as an officer. Officer Kevin Reynolds was booted off the force after being convicted after numerous warnings of excessive force. His wife left him after the media embarrassed her vicariously through him. Coming from an upper-class family, she tried to save face with her parents and colleagues by filing for divorce shortly after the incident went public. Kevin' Wolf' Reynolds hadn't been able to see his daughter

346

Jessica since. However, there was a larger margin between his shrub with ruby cheeks and this miniature brown face thing. With the way the world was becoming, he thought he could go without as many as his kind around. Wolf undid Hakiel's restraints and snatched him away from the rail.

"You two little dip shits had to do it the hard way," Wolf pressed. "Guess when it's your turn to come clean, you won't end up like your pal, huh?" Wolf asked, pushing Hakiel to the rail, so he faced his friends' remains below.

Hakiel turned his head and kept to his decision not to see Jamal that way.

"Come on, I got shit to do," Wolf said, dragging Hakiel behind.

They reached the bottom of the steps, and Hakiel began to pull back from Wolf's grasp to keep from going by Jamal's body. Wolf overpowered him and dragged him along anyway. Hakiel closed his eyes, allowing Wolf to pull him along blindly as his sobbing continued. When they got to the mess of all that burst out of Jamal's small frame, Hakiel's foot slipped in the spill, causing his shoe to squeak. Hakiel kept his balance and the footing as a shudder took over him knowing he'd stepped in Jamal's blood. A few seconds later, Wolf and Hakiel were standing in front of an empty tire cage. Once the tire cage was opened, Hakiel was tossed in, and the gate was closed behind him. Wolf called to Squirrel to prepare for their departure while he gathered Inez from where she sat tied to the chair.

Meanwhile, Squirrel went to get the tools for the job and pull the car around to the front. Inez snatched her body wildly, trying to keep Wolf's hands off of her, driven by her emotion and hate for everyone associated with Hemlock. Wolf quickly overpowered her, tossing her in the tire cage with Hakiel. Wolf didn't have any more zip ties for Hakiel's hands, so he grabbed a pair of cuffs, locking Hakiel's hands to the gate. Inez already had cuffs on, so she was cuffed to the other side of the gate then the cage was slammed shut. Inez and Hakiel made eye contact, but his eyes were taking all of his surroundings in like an animal on foreign territory. Inez could see the pain in his eyes as he seemed to look through her. His wild eyes moved on past her stare as his sobbing continued with a mix of guilt and grief.

"Gotta run, guys. Try to behave until we get back", Wolf laughed.

Inez's eyes still fixed on the suffering boy, paid no attention to the words of the jackass speaking. Wolf met Squirrel outside while placing a call to the number Hemlock had provided. The phone rang, and after three rings it was answered.

"Hello?" the voice answered on the other end of Wolf's line.

"Yeah, this is Wolf. Where is he now?" Wolf asked, sure the man would know exactly who he was referring to.

"I'm behind him now, three car lengths. He's traveling eastbound on I-20. We just passed the Candler Road exit," the man confirmed, sounding nervous.

Firebird warned Wolf what a pansy they were dealing with, and his instructions were to off him as well once the job was done.

"Copy that. I'll call back in ten minutes for a checkpoint. I'm pulling out now," Wolf confirmed as he and Squirrel began moving.

Meanwhile, inside the warehouse, Inez had already removed her gag with her free hand. She and Hakiel were probably a good twelve to thirteen feet apart in the large tire cage. Inez wanted to comfort the child in her embrace so bad it nearly caused her physical pain. Hakiel sat on the floor, one arm clamped to the cage above his head, looking at his shoe. Jamal's blood had stained the white sole of his tennis shoes, where his eyes were now glued. The stain on his soul penetrated deeper than what could be cleaned from his shoe. Inez followed his eyes to the sight that had entrapped him. Once she saw the blood on his Nikes, her face contorted into a sympathetic frown. She wanted to bring him from that place he'd drifted to.

"Hakiel?" Inez called to him calmly, a little louder than a whisper.

Hakiel's wide eyes traveled slowly until they found hers. It was as if Hakiel had forgotten that he was occupying the cage with another person. Once they made eye contact, his

349

tear-filled eyes spoke the words his mouth wouldn't. After gaining Hakiel's attention, Inez continued.

"Sweetheart, I know you've been through a lot these past few days," she said, blinking tears back. "Baby, if we're going to survive this, we have to work together, okay?" Inez said as her demeanor revealed the compassion filling her. "Hakiel, can you be strong enough to help get us out of here?" Inez asked, firming her face.

Another tear dropped from Hakiel's brown eyes and off of his cheek as he nodded with his verbal response. "Yeah," his voice cracked dryly, still seeming to be looking through her.

Inez looked back to the bay doors, then what she was able to see of the warehouse scanning for the guard who'd been left behind. Confident that the guard was off busy somewhere, the wheels in her mind began turning. Inez fingered the cross around her neck as her father's words came to mind sounding like he was standing nearby.

"This is the key to salvation Mariposa," he said, calling her his nickname of choice given in her youth. The cross had been a gift for her tenth birthday, and it was something she had never been able to part with from when Colonel Miguel Santos had placed the piece around her neck. He told her to use it in times of need with faithful prayer. Inez had always known it was a sort of key but had never tried to use it on any lock. Now Inez wondered if she could be that lucky and the key might actually fit the cuffs. Doubt consumed her first then her father spoke again.

"Faith Mariposa," Inez said a quick faith-filled prayer. Once she finished, she opened her eyes to find Hakiel looking still awaiting instruction. "Hakiel, watch for the guard. If you see him, let me know fast, okay," Inez instructed, rushing the key from around her neck over her head.

"Okay," Hakiel agreed, quickly taking his post, standing to his feet already on the job. Inez got the key to fit, although Hakiel was paying no attention to her, determined to do his part. She looked wide-eyed in his direction in shock and excitement. Inez turned the key, and the cuff came undone. He looked at Inez in surprise, eager to escape the building and all the horrors it held. Inez took a better viewing of the warehouse from the vantage point, trying to locate the guard. Nothing at first, but then she noticed a trail of smoke floating into the air from behind an area surrounded by panels. As her frayed nerves began pulsing in overdrive, she hustled to the boy's cuffed hand and released the lock. Hakiel had been held against his will by the demons in men's flesh. Their torture had been burned into his memory. The saddened face was still present, but Hakiel was alert and following Inez's lead. The gate had a simple lock, but Hakiel had to take the task from Inez as it was easier for him. He slipped his hand through the small holes to unlatch the bolt as he slid it from the clasp. The cage door was opened, and the two of them quietly moved to try to go undetected as they searched for an exit.

Upholding the Law

Detective Nassi and Officer McKenzie had been in Victory Crossings, an apartment complex off of Glenwood Road. East of Atlanta about an hour already when the phone rang. Nassi had given McKenzie instructions on what to say but stood close by, making sure Officer McKenzie played it as agreed. After giving the man named Wolf the rundown, Detective Nassi and McKenzie prepared for the next phase of Nassi's plan. Detective Nassi had been on a wild goose chase trying to locate two missing boys along with his co-worker and growing love interest Ms. Inez Santos. Nassi had pressured Officer McKenzie to get in contact with the man he had referred to as Firebird. According to McKenzie's testimony, it was Firebird who had been the mastermind behind Inez's abduction. McKenzie claimed that he was unaware of the whereabouts of Hakiel, Fatimah Johnson's older brother, or his neighbor and friend Jamal. McKenzie tried holding out on this information at first, apparently in fear of the consequences of Firebird. However, a few body blows in present time redirected any precautionary measures of avoiding future repercussions. McKenzie explained over an empty stomach that he had never been afforded the opportunity to see Firebird in person, only speaking with him over the phone.

McKenzie went on to explain that he had always used a voice scrambler to disguise his real voice. McKenzie also volunteered more information saying how Firebird knew way too much about his personal life, which was the core of his fear of the man. Firebird knew things about McKenzie's job, his family as well as some of his usual duck-off spots. The latter, by the way, Nassi had tracked him down, was obviously more mainstream than McKenzie had thought.

McKenzie called Firebird as he was instructed, should he be able to get Detective Nassi's whereabouts. However, the detective had been the puppeteer of the call sitting in and listening through the short and discreet dialogue Firebird and McKenzie exchanged. Firebird had wisely sent McKenzie through another channel bringing a man by the name of Wolf into play. Now Detective Nassi and Officer McKenzie sat patiently waiting for the call to come through that Wolf was to make once he was close to the location. Nassi's anxiousness overwhelmed him, waiting for the moment his plan could go into effect. Fortunately, it didn't take long. The phone finally came ringing to life inside Nassi's palm. Nassi hit the talk button and held the phone to McKenzie's ear.

"Yeah, I'm here," McKenzie answered.

"Hey pal, I'm passing the Candler Road exit now. Where do I go from here?" Wolf asked firmly.

"Actually, you could've jumped off right there and made a left. It's ok though, the detective took me on a slight detour to pick up some food," McKenzie lied as he was told. "Listen, ride down 20 on down to 285, then take 285 to the Glenwood exit. That's where I'm tailing him at now." McKenzie informed Wolf according to plan.

"This guy is all over the place, huh?" Wolf questioned, ready to get the detective over and done with.

"Yeah," McKenzie laughed, looking faker to Nassi than he sounded. "I'm guessing this is a fling swing he's got going on. He just came out of the liquor store off the exit here with a bottle of Champagne," McKenzie continued as Nassi swiftly wrote what was to be said in text form on his own phone.

"He already gave up on the Latina?" Wolf asked jokingly.

"Yeah, I guess," McKenzie replied back.

"He might as well, though, because come tomorrow that pussy will be good and torn," Wolf laughed his words out.

Detective Nassi's upper lip curled up towards his nostrils at Wolf's joke. Keeping his emotions in check, Nassi followed through with a timely response.

"Well, it shouldn't matter after tonight. If we can get this guy with his pants down, this will be the last piece of ass he will see," McKenzie replied, reading Nassi's phone screen.

"I'm starting to like you, McKenzie, regardless of what they might say about you," Wolf said smiling.

"What do they say about me?" McKenzie asked, caught in his insecurities.

Nassi popped him hard in the head, causing his head to bob forward.

"Nothing, man, you're a swell guy," Wolf lied, laughing at his inside joke. Wolf described the car he would be in as Nassi took notes listening close. Wolf sounded excited from what McKenzie could make of it, which made him glad to be natural.

McKenzie was unaware Wolf would be sure to kill him as well, along with their plans for Nassi. The men ended the call as Nassi commended McKenzie on how natural he sounded reading from the phone.

"Yeah, I was taking a course that would get into news reporting, so I kind of got good at reading a teleprompter," McKenzie informed Nassi.

"So what happened?" Nassi asked.

"Well, they turned me down channel after channel saying I didn't have *the look*," McKenzie explained like he was looking for Nassi to say that he had *the look*.

"Actually, you don't, man," Nassi said with a face to add to insult. The look on Nassi's face crushed McKenzie's spirit more than his words had. Nassi turned away, uncaring, rolling the tinted window of the old school Malibu down.

"Yall about ready," Nassi spoke to the girl in the passenger seat, backed in next to them.

She blew smoke out of the window up into the air before answering. Cutting her slanted low chunky eyes over to Nassi, she pursed her lips before saying. "Yo blood, how many times I gotta tell you we do this shit, dude?" Hannah Bandana asked in playful disguise.

The two of them had gotten off to a rocky start at the beginning of their interaction due to Nassi's arrogance. After their last conversation, they agreed to bury the past and work towards their common goal. Burying the culprits behind the bullshit going on.

"We waiting on you, homie, everybody in place," Hannah confirmed, looking back over her window to the troops scattered about.

"West the word Bandana?" one of her brothers asked, yelling from a dark spot somewhere by one of the buildings.

"Bee dat, mine ready to pop," Bandana said to Nassi, holding a finger up to say any minute to the eager homie. Hannah looked back at Nassi through the haze of loud smoke with the demeanor that said she would become bored soon if the action took much longer to arrive.

Nassi grinned at Hannah's almost innocent look, wondering how she became so bloodthirsty at a young age. "Give me a sec. I'm bout to find out how close they are," Nassi requested before rolling the window back up. "Aight, let's call Wolf back; he should be close to the exit if not on it yet," Nassi ordered McKenzie.

McKenzie did a drum roll on the steering wheel like he was ready.

"Just find out where he is, and the rest, like I told you earlier," Nassi never did like McKenzie, and all of his extra theatrics reminded him why. Nassi's whole attitude was live at let live, but one thing he's never been too fond of was phony people and pleasing pussies. Although Nassi never expressed this out loud to McKenzie, McKenzie fell right into that bracket. Nassi called the number for what he hoped would be the last time and once more placed it up to McKenzie's ear.

"Hey man," Wolf picked up after half a ring. "I'm on the exit now in traffic. What's your 20?" Wolf asked, speaking enforcement codes for location.

"In the parking lot of an apartment called Victory Crossings," McKenzie began. "If you hurry, we got him sitting pretty right now unaware, he's in the car with some little hot thing, and that mini-skirt she has on should have all his attention," McKenzie claimed. "They just got inside of a yellow old school Malibu; you can't miss it. It's got tinted windows, and it is the brightest thing out here," McKenzie stated.

"Roger that," Wolf said swiftly. "How far from the exit, Wolf asked, sitting up in his seat, already making preparations.

McKenzie gave him the directions and more instructions. "You'll see my car on your right of the road in the parking lot on the other side of the street. My parking lights to the Volvo are on; you'll see me. You'll need to make that left opposite the side I'm parked on, where you'll see him parked over by the dumpster. Look, he may be suspicious from earlier. So drive in, look at the car, so you'll know it's him, then have your ride let you out so you can slip up behind him unnoticed," McKenzie spoke the words given by Nassi. "The complex is quiet, so any movement like pulling up on him may provoke a gunfight. I prefer you be the only one shooting," McKenzie explained, making it clear to Wolf, Nassi would shoot it out if alarmed.

Wolf took the point well and agreed that it made more sense to be the shooter and not be shot at. After the plan for Nassi's murder was in motion, the men ended the call. Hanging the phone up, Nassi looked at McKenzie. "Damn, you're good. I almost got goosebumps hearing you guys plotting on my untimely death," Nassi smiled.

"Ok, let's move," McKenzie, hurrying Nassi, ready to get out of harm's way.

Nassi reached into the bag Hannah had brought him on request with gloved hands. He pulled out a pair of security surplus handcuffs and a walkie-talkie. McKenzie watched, confused at Nassi's nonchalant movements. Nassi grabbed McKenzie's frail hands, cuffing one before running the cuff through the steering wheel to cuff the other, locking them in. The way the wood grain steering wheel was made, McKenzie would have no choice but to stay in place.

McKenzie's eyes popped wide in fear, "What are you doing, detective? You can't do this. You're an officer of the law." McKenzie stated matter of fact. His voice blared at a hysterical tone, sure that Wolf would come shooting first questions later.

"None of that seemed to stop you," Detective Nassi snapped as his smile evaporated. "You've got a good point, though," Nassi said as if he was having second thoughts of leaving McKenzie to die. He looked at the fear-filled eyes behind McKenzie's lenses. "McKenzie, I strongly feel as if justice is about to be served and that I am upholding the law," Nassi's voice was cold and uncaring. With a look in his eyes, McKenzie wouldn't have ever imagined seeing in him. Nassi cranked the Malibu to life then gagged McKenzie before exiting. The loud engine would drown Mckenzie's muffled cries. Before running to his post, Nassi slapped the hood of the classic machine Hannah was riding shotgun in.

"Let's do it, baby girl," Nassi's voice and movement pulled Hanna's attention away from her phone. The driver slammed the 442 in gear, pulling off after Nassi shot past.

Hannah yelled out of the window as they pulled out. "Hey, man, the homies perked up like dogs ears from a dog whistle, alert and ready for attack. Hannah drove towards the entrance, the only way in and out. She pulled into a parking space that allowed her to view everything coming in. Two cars pulled in, neither being the kind Nassi described. Seconds later, the black Pontiac 6-6 entered, coursing slowly through the entrance. Hannah hit the radio as soon as the visual was confirmed.

"Live wire, live wire," her voice blurred over the walkie-talkies.

A deep voice replied back over the airwaves, "Static play, static play," confirming they had spotted the kill.

Wolf and Squirrel cruised in, slowly looking in the parking lots left and right from the paved road they were riding. After a few moments, Wolf noticed a Volvo matching McKenzie's description parked in a dark part of the lot to his right. Just like McKenzie had said, his parking lot lights were on. They could only see a shadowy figure inside, figuring it to be McKenzie.

"There's McKenzie's car, so we need to make this left," Wolf explained as his eyes scanned the lot to the left. "No, no, no, keep straight," Wolf corrected.

Just as the yellow Malibu came into view, Wolf remembered that it would be best to spot the car first then allow Squirrel to let him out unseen. Squirrel kept straight to the next row of apartment buildings to get out of view from the occupants and Malibu. Squirrel quickly hit the lights pulling into a parking space on the backside of the building.

"Let me out right here," Wolf said, sounding more like an order. Wolf's adrenaline kicked in as he readied himself, checking his two handguns. Wolf was pretty surgical with his twin Glock nines, and they gave him the freedom to move swiftly. Most of his comrades enjoyed the heavier machinery. Yet, he had always been most effective with getting things done. As usual, here he was cleaning up the unfinished business of his jarhead colleagues.

"Don't you think I should come with you, Wolf?" Squirrel asked as the clenched of his wide jaw closed his statement.

Wolf knew the kid wanted some action, but it was really unnecessary. This would be quick and simple.

"There will be plenty of opportunities for you to get your guns smoking Squirrel; this will only take a sec," Wolf reasoned. "Leave the car on. We'll be out of here in a blink, kiddo," Wolf smiled, slapping the kid roughly across the chest.

Squirrel signaled Wolf with his head to take off and get it over with. Wolf disappeared seconds later behind the side of the building near the tree line, consumed by the darkness provided. Wolf was pretty confident of his success, knowing McKenzie had already surveyed the layout and that the detective was said to be alone aside from the female

362

companion. Wolf clenched the Glocks tight as the extended clips hung a few inches under his gripping fist, ready to be proven worthy. Wolf peeked from around the building, still cloaked in the darkness, now able to see the yellow Malibu a few feet away running. Several sets of eyes watched as Wolf emerged from the tree line, quickly closing in on the unsuspecting victim inside. Before Wolf could get completely on top of the Malibu, he began hurling rounds through the driver side window, shattering it with the first rounds. The projectiles melted into McKenzie's head and face as chunk after chunk spewed from his melon to other places in the car. Still walking up, Wolf worked his Glocks widely, sending more lead spinning from his barrels and into the body that was becoming more disfigured by the second. In the midst of Wolf's wrath, several homies swiftly ran down on Squirrel with weapons drawn. He never had a chance. Once Squirrel noticed the dark figures on the side of his car, his heart leaped into his throat, pushing the smoke of his cigarette back through his nose. As the smoke escaped the window, it clung in wisps around the barrel pointed in at him.

Where the fuck did they come from, Squirell thought to himself, noticing at least eight fierce-looking bangers. Squirrel couldn't understand how they got up on him so quickly and unnoticed; after all, he was keeping a pretty good watch, or so he thought. Squirrel debated mentally on whether he should reach for his firearm. His rationale kicked in before that thought could finish, saying that surely it would be the last move he'd ever make.

"Get yo ass out the mafucka," S. O. Proof said, showing no signs of understanding, as he pulled the door open.

Squirrel moved slowly with his hands up, placing his butted feet on the ground first. The night air rushed into Squirell's nostrils as the scent of death clouded his nasal passage. The shots from in front of the building could still be heard, then there was silence. Squirrel figured Wolf was done and may be on his way back and able to intervene in the predicament he was faced with. Killing any optimistic thoughts of being saved.

S.O. Proof's radio sounded. "The shooter is inside the Malibu; we're closing in on him."

Wolf heard the voice come over the radio as well, bringing his attention to the walkie-talkie lying in the passenger's seat.

Squirrel's eyes showed panic, and the homies standing around him knew this look all too well.

"Sounds like yo potna bout to get the business over there," S. O. Proof said, laughing looking over to the homie Wildman as he approached.

Meanwhile, back at the car, Wolf studied the mess he had made, holding the walkie-talkie in sight.

"Wolf, pick up the radio," the voice said over the airwaves. Wolf began to grasp what was starting to unfold before his eyes, noticing first the mangled man's body cuffed to the steering wheel. The caucasian hands gave the obvious indication this wasn't the detective's body. Wolf began to fear the worst, knowing this would undoubtedly go marked as a failure. Wolf turned around swiftly, looking around the parking lot while exchanging clips.

"Pick up the radio, or yo little partner in the G-6 catches a bullet," the voice ordered. Sounding impatiently hostile.

Squirrel could hear everything being said over the radio loud and clear. Then within seconds, Wolf responded clear. "I'm here," Wolf said, looking to the destroyed face behind the wheel.

"As you can see, your contact for this little set-up was extremely unfortunate tonight. It's terrible what happened, but I'm not in the least bit sorry for what you've done to him," the voice replied, putting emphasis on whose hand caused the attack. Squirrel's knees wanted to give as he took in the words being said over the radio.

"What the fuck you doing over here, shooting shit up in our zone bra?" Wildman asked, keeping arm with his regard on Squirrels head. Squirrel was stuck, not knowing what to say, contemplating his next move. "I asked you a question, dude?" Wildman stated, becoming irritated.

Meanwhile, back at the car, Wolf was given instructions over the walkie-talkie that he didn't feel too comfortable following, but his options were slim to none. Squirrel listened to the orders and threats issued to Wolf, hoping that he would make the right decision toward keeping life in their lungs.

"I said, put both of your guns in the car and step away," the voice ordered Wolf, repeating himself angrily.

"Why should I believe you'll let me and my partner live?" Wolf pleaded, reluctance steaming from his tone.

A young teen aimed at Squirrel with the Mac-90 he was holding, sending chills up Squirrel's spine as he pictured his life being snatched away in the still of a warm July night. There were already multiple guns aimed at Squirrel, but the teen seemed about ready to let his own out at present.

"What do you want me to say?" Squirrel said, answering Wildman's question with a question.

"Shit, homie, just be quiet," a female said, stepping up behind Squirrel before she thumped a heartless shell through Squirell's skull. The shot sent his body sideways to the pavement allowing Little Hot Head to stand over him, dumping four more shots into his face.

"Fuck y'all be waiting on man?" Little Hot Head questioned her brothers. Little Hot Head frowned at the homies, then stepped over the body, moving towards the path to where Wolf was on the other side of the building.

"Hold up, Little Hot Head," Wildman said. "For what dog, fuck that detective, eat nigga," Little Hot Head barked, with a heart full of scorn. All Hot Head could think of was that these people were connected with what had happened to Pro. She wasn't up for negotiating. When shots rang out,

Wolf's reflexes caused him to take aim and cover. With no clue what to shoot at, Wolf aimed his guns in several directions.

The homies had to grab Little Hot Head off her path before she did anything else outside of the plan. "You tripping Little Hot Head this ain't gone get us who we looking for, now quit that reckless shit dog," S. O. Proof said, holding her arm tight.

A tear dropped in a lonely stream down her light-complexioned face towards her chin. S. O. Proof knew what she felt but couldn't allow her to blow the opportunity of getting the mastermind behind it all. Little Hot Head snatched her arm away but stayed put, listening to S. O. Proof.

"These dudes are the pawns. We need them for the checkmate, now get yo shit together homie and get out yo feelings."

Detective Nassi, disturbed from the shots fired, wondering what happened and why. He spoke back into the radio. "What the hell was that team?"

Hannah Bandana replied, "Aye, what da move?"

"Mishap with da goose," S. O. Proof said, still frowning at Little Hot Head.

Wolf listened closely to every word, knowing that now he had bit off more than he could chew. His survival didn't sound like it was part of the plan, which pushed him to crouch behind the Malibu surveying the surrounding area.

"Once went bad," Hannah responded to Detective Nassi. The detective sat in the Volvo, punching the steering wheel. Things were not going as planned. He could also see Wolf making a move from where he sat watching. "Wolf, don't do that, you're surrounded, and unless you want to end up like that gentleman in the Malibu, I suggest you stay put."

Wolf had made his mind up. He made a run for it, going back to the G-6, thinking he could shoot his way out. Wolf placed one gun into his holster so that he had access to the radio at hand as Nassi continued to order him to stop.

"Be on alert, teams he's moving," Nassi spoke into the device.

Wolf slowed his pace once he made it on the side of the building from where he had come from moments earlier. Wolf could hear the radios blaring from the other side of the building as he turned his down. Things got quiet with the exception of some whistling from not far away as well as in the distance. Wolf heard a ruffle from the trees and brush, causing him to peer into the darkness.

"Wolf, you don't have a chance in hell; give up," Nassi said through the speaker of the radio. The volume was low but still heard. Strangely he didn't hear the other radios like he had seconds ago.

The awkward silence thrust Wolf into a violent mental agitation. Then a barrel followed by the hands gripping the handle attached to it slowly appeared from the corner of the

368

building's side by this end. Clearly, this wasn't Squirrel coming to his aid.

Wolf clashed the firing pin into the bullets being sprung into the chamber from his extended clips. The silence broke into a loud clammer of repetitive shots as Wolf reversed himself back toward where he'd run from near the Malibu, almost tripping over his feet. The machinery behind him erupted violently, tearing patches of dirt away from where it had once laid. Wildman followed closely behind ringing shots of his own from the Rugger in his grasp, missing Wolf by inches as he dodged behind the dumpster near the Malibu.

"Nawl mafucka, don't run now," Wildman said, laughing.

S. O. Proof and Little Hot Head took another route towards the other side of the building, trying to corner Wolf in.

"Wolf, don't make this harder," the detective requested, ready to get out himself and apprehend Wolf. The detective needed Wolf alive, and from the looks of it, the boys in the hood would kill him shortly if he didn't cooperate.

The teen ran in Wolf's direction, dumping from the Mac-90 before he could spot his target. Wolf took advantage of his training and utilized his environment. Wolf stuck his arm around the dumpster and caught the young boy in his chest with two quick shots. The boy's finger clamped down on his trigger as he fell, still sending rounds wildly in the air and bush. Shots from behind Wolf hammered loudly, catching him by surprise as he took off running in another cover spot. Wolf knew that any moment he was dealing with not just a few bangers but a nest defending their neighborhood.

"Aye, there that mafucka go," someone yelled from a pathway one building over.

Wolf clapped his gun sparingly, knowing he didn't have enough shots to take them all.

The radio came to life again as Wolf's heart pounded. "Wolf," before the voice could finish, Wolf slammed the device into the ground until it broke into ragged pieces of plastic and circuits. Wolf's frown dipped into a hard v through the bridge of his nose, knowing his hunters were closing in. Wolf took a move, desperate to escape, sending rounds at the group he'd seen last as he rose from a broken down car he'd ducked beside. Another member of the group fell from the defensive shots Wolf had thrown before a loud clammer knocked Wolf from his balance, "Klow!"

The single shot echoed through the apartment like the shot of an assassin. Wolf fell to the ground holding the knee that had begun to pour. Wolf looked down to take inventory of his damage, noticing the kneecap damn near missing from his leg. Wolf tried to raise his gun to fire on the group again when the high-powered rifle sounded again, "Klow." The bullet sliced through the night air until it met its intended target. The high caliber round pierced its way through

370

Wolf's hand, exiting out of his elbow, bringing a trail of chipped bone and blood behind it. Wolf let out a painful-sounding shrill as he fell back, hitting his head on the concrete, motivated by the bullet's impact. Wolf's gun dropped next to him as his arm fell limp and useless. Before Wolf could gain his bearings, several automatic weapons and rifles were pointed down on him. 1st 48 moved from the second-story apartment window he'd been in, aiming the 223 rifle that had brought Wolf to the ground. Keeping the lights off, 1st 48 stashed the rifle back in its regular hiding place in the crawl space of the attic. The time it took went swiftly as 1st48 finished and made it down to ground level with the homies now poking fun with Wolf's handicapped body.

Hannah hit the radio and barked out some aggressive commands as the detective pulled off in McKenzie's Volvo. "Get the pork to the bleed out," Hannah said. Understanding precisely what Hannah had ordered. The homies pulled Wolf into a dark Bronco that had just pulled up, knocking him unconscious before slamming the back door of the truck closing him in.

Quick & Quiet

Teflon had been on edge watching the head God Body closely since his fit on the phone. It was just no telling when shit was about to pop off. The way things happened in the free world dictated the movement behind the wall and vice versa. It had always been that way, even back in the old days with the big homies before them. In this life, a wise man watched for any signs of tension, especially the unspoken, which time after time proved most lethal. Teflon was the head Brim behind the wall, and his attitude was about as disciplined as a Tibetan monk when it came to his. As he stood in his usual viewing perch, one of his soldiers approached.

"Big bro" Teflon turned to look at the lil homie.

"West good doggy?" Teflon asked the youngin.

"Banger Ru on the line, so I told my girl I'd hit her later; sounds important."

The lil homie slid the phone into Teflon's grasp, so smooth no one noticed, followed by the earpiece to go with it. Teflon slid the phone into his gym short pockets then tucked the earpiece in his ear, hiding it with his skull cap.

"Whoooop," Teflon spoke loudly into the air so the mic would catch.

"West good bro? This Banger Ru. Sounding less than his usual energetic self.

Teflon picked up on the vibe. He knew Banger Ru all too well, and something was definitely wrong.

"What up Ru?" Teflon asked, sounding like he knew Ru had something to explain.

Banger Ru was silent for a few seconds fighting off tears so he could speak the words that were sure to break Teflon's heart into a thousand tiny pieces.

"Ru?" Teflon spoke louder.

Banger Ru took a deep breath then let the words spill from the pit of his churning stomach.

"The Muslim killed Pro in the county homie." Banger Ru explained, biting down in a grimace after he spoke in attempts to keep his tears imprisoned.

"What?" Teflon barked in a pitch his voice would typically find hard to reach.

"YOOOOO B who got killed in the county" Teflon had heard him right, but his mind would take a few more minutes to wrap around what Banger Ru had just said.

Banger Ru didn't re-state what he'd said, avoiding the pain it caused, simply saying, "We bout to go in once I make sure everybody knows west good."

Teflon sat down on the floor in silence like he had been hit with a crippling body blow.

"Tef," Banger Ru said, trying to check the homies mental.

"Aight Ru," Teflon said low, from some trap his emotions had him tangled in.

The lil homie looked at Teflon's bugged-out eyes and knew it couldn't be good. Teflon sat a few more moments, long after the call had been disconnected, as his chest raised up and down, increasing in speed by the second.

"What I need to do, big homie?" The youngin asked Teflon, ready to do whatever Teflon needed. Teflon had named the lil homie Death after he proved to be the tool of Teflon's wrath. Two years back, when Death first arrived at Smith State Prison, he was just known as Lil Mario from Bankhead. Back then, Mario was a civilian with no other affiliations other than being from the city. All that changed when he moved into the room with Teflon. Mario was 18 years old and had just been sentenced to a 30-year bid for killing his mother's boyfriend. Mario had come home one night from the trap to find his mother crying over a toilet full of blood. All the signs of abuse had been present, and they spoke louder than his mother's crying. Needless to say, what happened in detail brought Mario to the residence.

Mario looked up at Teflon and had become the shining protégé of his vicious lineage. He earned his name after Teflon sent him on a near-impossible mission. The scenario was a murder for hire. The target was a pretty notorious player turned rat overnight. His former boss, a kingpin that we won't mention, called the hit in from another camp some 247 miles away. Teflon picked the hit for an undisclosed amount sending Mario to prove his worth, loyalty, and heart. The man was no slouch; in fact, he had been a hitman himself. With the advantage of having years of experience and size, the job would either make or mangle Lil Mario. To top it off, he was told he had to make it inside the man's dorm on a whole other side of the camp and do the hit without being caught. For a scrawny kid of 165 pounds and no former dealings of that kind, the odds were stacked against him. Teflon did at least provide him with the necessary tool and layout to succeed, but he didn't know it would be carried out as perfectly as he'd designed it. When Mario arrived back at the dorm unscathed, he became a celebrated member by the name of Death and a few thousand dollars richer. Word had made it to Teflon before Mario even showed up, as the homies who secretly watched over him spoke of his success with the hit. He stood now noticing the demeanor of his big homie, ready to stain his knife to appease the bloodthirst of Teflon. At any given time, if Teflon received the slightest disappointment in whatever form, Death brought him to his regular self with the shedding of someone's internal fluids. Teflon slowly turned his head to look up at Death like he had said something unheard of. The crazed glare in Teflon's eyes confused Death to the point he thought he'd done something wrong.

"What I do big bro?" Death asked, making sure he hadn't betrayed Teflon's approval in any way.

Teflon stood, breathing hard.

"Put the phones up and bring Quick & Quiet." It was common for the inmates to name their tools of destruction. Teflon had named his twin knives Quick & Quiet. Teflon slid the earpiece and phone back to Death and walked the way of a man on a mission back to his room. Teflon took his Jordan flip-flops off and replaced them with a pair of all-black Jordan fives tying them tight. Teflon threw a sweater on top of his tank top as well as a state-issued jacket. He didn't bother to change his black Jordan shorts, finding an advantage to the dark colors. He warned the people necessary so that they wouldn't lose their belongings should a shakedown occur after whatever was happening. Death showed up in Teflon's room, knives in hand.

"Who are we riding on, big bro? Damn, pardon my tongue," Death caught himself, then corrected his mishap.

"It don't matter, leeh go," he said, handing Teflon his twins and preparing him as well.

"Stand down, homie, just make sho nobody blindsides me," Teflon instructed. Death looked as if Teflon had hurt his feelings.

"Bro I..." Death started before Teflon interrupted.

"You heard what I said," Teflon stated, adamant about his decision as he pushed past Death and out the room. Teflon took a quick but very observant scan of the entire dorm on his exit of the room. Taking a quick headcount that wouldn't have changed his plans, either way, Teflon locked in on his target. The homies in the dorm were in inconspicuous posts watching and waiting for the movement. They were oblivious as to why what was happening was happening but nonetheless, they knew if Teflon was involved, it was happening without a doubt. Teflon moved to the steps swiftly and made it down without drawing any suspicious attention. Death followed more than enough feet and seconds behind to go unnoticed. Teflon's target was standing in front of a friend's door holding a conversation with his hands tucked in his collar thumbs exposed.

"Think y'all gone flatland, my bro, and I ain't coming?" Teflon mumbled to himself, approaching his prey at a stealthy speed.

"I am. Watch!"

It was too late, as some onlooker, obviously catching on to the commotion as it was happening, tried to warn the head Muslim. Teflon hit both sides of his neck with deep plunges to the base of his knives, sending a spray of blood across the walls and door he had been standing in. "Huh, that's what y'all thought," Teflon barked as he continued blow after blow.

"Fuck that!" Teflon spit.

The homies formed a protective barrier around Teflon with knives drawn as more Muslims ran up to aid. The man whose room the Imam had been standing in front of screamed, "Aye man, I ain't got shit to do wit want y'all got going on man," he said, pleading for his safety.

"Shut the fuck up," Death barked, cocking back at the man with his knife.

"Shiiit, say no mo," The man compiled. Before all the Muslims could prepare for battle, police were running up the walk towards the dorm.

"Coming in, coming in, get right," a lookout yells. One of the homies grabbed Teflon, snatching the knives away from him and pulling his jacket from him. Another homie pushed Teflon into a room, locking him behind his door with a complete stranger.

"Everybody down, goddamnit," the officers yelled on entrance. More officers poured in, putting the hands-on treatment on anyone moving slowly.

"You got blood on your face, man," The stranger said to Teflon, looking like he'd been through this a few times.

Teflon looked in the mirror, wiped his face, and then looked back at the old white man with an unmistakable evaluation.

"Hey, I ain't seen nothing, brother. I'm chain gang, know what I mean? Mind your own business or get the business put on your mind" The words of a prison vet escaped the old man's lips. Meanwhile, outside, the noise of the dorm was snatched into silence, except the cries of one Muslim,

"Noooo Aki nooo." The man wailed.

It was no use. The Imam wouldn't be able to survive such a savage attack.

"Shut the hell up!" The sergeant on the floor yelled.

"I'm about to lock this mothafacka down," Sergeant Times scolded.

"I told you sons of bitches you could keep your weed and phones, but this goddamn stabbing had to stop, didn't I?" He continued as the medics rolled the heavy bleeding Imam out of the dorm. It looked like gallons of blood had covered the floor. There was no chance of survival. You could hear the helicopter landing on the field outside coming to airlift the Imam within minutes.

"Bow, who cut this man's jugular vein goddamnit?" The sergeant questioned, sure that the artery had been severed from his military experience. Sergeant Times knew this was a pointless waste of speech on his behalf. Most of the men in the dorm had done a sufficient amount of time and knew the law of the land. Those who didn't know yet were in no rush to find out what happened to those who didn't follow suit.

"Aight goddamnit y'all know what's next if I don't get no answers." The sergeant threatened, sure the reaction would be the same as always. Oddly enough, the homie that had taken the knives stood up, throwing the bloody knives on the floor. The homies looked at him like he was crazy, as Teflon yelled from the window:

"Yooo homie, what the fuck you doing? Teflon said, knowing the homie had gone mad.

"I ain't gone let y'all go down for my shit bra period, fuck AK man, he had that shit coming." The homie said flatly with no remorse.

Teflon shook his head in disappointment but understood the homie's train of thought. He was in for life plus 40, so it was nothing.

"Lock his ass up and give him a free world." The sergeant commanded, implying that new state charges would be pressed.

"He just saved y'all ass, but y'all gone be on lockdown, you can bet that goddamnit," The sergeant confirmed.

"Pop all doors control," the sergeant spoke to his radio.

The doors popped, and the officers stood on post, watching everyone move to their assigned rooms, ready to beat the shit out of the first inmate to breathe wrong. After about 5 minutes, every man was secured behind their respective doors and accounted for, aside from the deceased and the one headed to solitary.

"Bout a month, goddamnit," The sergeant yelled, stipulating the time they'd be behind the doors.

"Come on, sarge, what's that bullshit? The man gave himself up, man?" Someone yelled, apparently displeased with Sergeant Time's decision

"Oh, that's why I ain't shaking down, hell y'all know the drill. This is not a dream, gentlemen." The sergeant yelled over his shoulder, making an exit.

As soon as the doors to the exit closed, a roar of voices quaked the walls. All kinds of arguments ensued. It took the Muslim next in command and Teflon to get things quiet enough for the necessary dialog.

"Teflon, you broke the rules of engagement. Akhi, how did that happen?" Mateen asked, infuriated and saddened.

"Us? Fuck y'all, that's how it happened." One of the homies yelled from a few doors away.

All hell broke loose with laughter, profanities, banging on the doors, and retaliatory comments from the Muslims.

"Yoooo, next homie, speak while I'm speaking; definitely gone get that dip set point-blank, starting with you Red Box."

The homies fell silent, and it took Mateen a few more seconds to calm his men.

"Aye AK y'all took one of mine in the county, my heart dog," Teflon said, too angry to allow any tearing up.

"Really, Akhi, I'm on one right now, and anyone of y'all can get it, flat out," Teflon stated matter of factly.

"Shit, really all y'all can for that matter, Akhi," Teflon yelled, hype on his blood lust.

"Facts," another homie yelled from downstairs, I'll take a dip, big bro, this Lil Nutso, fuck dem niggas," he continued.

The homies began barking and knocking on the doors again with all kinds of objects that would make noise.

"Yooooo, that's it dog. Be the fuck quiet," Teflon said, ready to get everything on the table.

The Muslims were more disciplined for the most part, except a handful of those who couldn't fight the urge to respond. Mateen got them back in line, swiftly raising his voice as his anger began to take more shape.

"I don't know who the brother was that wronged you, Tef, but he will be disciplined severely." Mateen began, "However, what you've done to the Imam is unacceptable. You know he would have shunned the brother who behaved ill towards yours if it was unjust," Mateen said, as tears formed in his eyes for the loving teacher he'd just lost.

"You know he wouldn't condone a Muslim taking a life that way," Mateen yelled, now on the verge of rage.

Teflon remained silent, taking in Mateen's words but unmoved, stuck in his own loss.

"Teflon, I respect you, brother. I'm sorry for your loss, but inshallah, when these doors open, I am going to kill you for what you've done to my Akhi, I swear," Mateen yelled, sounding more like a war cry.

"Shit, you know me, doggy, I ain't through by no means." Teflon snapped back, "I want all y'all kufis in my pocket. So when the doors pop, we make the ground shake; fuck you, man," Teflon snapped, barking his words hard through the door.

"Well, then it's war, brother, for every Muslim's blood is sacred." Mateen solidified the confrontation, and the noise of the dorm broke from its silence in a primal wildness loud enough to be heard in heaven.

...to be continued

About the Author

Tarik Chatman, the man behind the book, was raised in the city of Detroit. Tarik was given an up-close look into life's sometimes chaotic and harsh realities. He has attained various awards and accolades in a variety of genres of expression. However, none of them are important, in his opinion, after finding himself entangled in some of those very similar realities. He began to push his pen from behind the locked door of a cell block, 821 miles away from home. After supplying the need for more relatable reading material to his fellow inmate population in middle Georgia, he decided to take things a step further upon his release. The book in your possession now is the offspring of discipline and determination, coming to the conclusion that his words could bring value and inspiration. Recognizing a very detailed style of writing mingled with a sometimes humorous yet serious flow of entertaining concepts. The author has committed to producing more words, and so without further ado.

www.ingramcontent.com/pod-product-compliance
Lightning Source LLC
Chambersburg PA
CBHW071145100726
47908CB00002B/256